THE CHAMPION'S QUEST

LEGACIES OF TALISIA

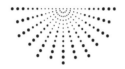

KELSEY BROWNLEE

MOONTREK
PRESS

ATTENTION READERS

The Champion's Quest
Kelsey Brownlee
ISBN: Ebook: 978-1-957243-00-9
Print: 978-1-957243-01-6
On sale: May 10th, 2022
Ages 12 and up

For Gabriel, my husband. To the moon and beyond.

And for Mallory, for believing in me and my story from the first draft.

CHAPTER ONE

*T*he silence was suffocating.

Kailani's vision blurred, sweat gathering on her forehead. She tried to still her shaky hands, swallowing the massive lump creeping up her throat. She could do this. She *had* to do this.

After all, today was her last shot at impressing the gods.

She threw her curly brown hair into a bun on top of her head, looking up from the cauldron she'd been bent over for the past hour. Voices carried through the open window of the classroom she was practicing in as three of her classmates shuffled by. She got up, stretching, and peered over the courtyard. Some students mouthed to themselves, trying to remember every charm and spell they'd learned in the past eight years of schooling. Others swaggered around with their friends. Kailani scowled. For those idiots, it was obviously a front; there wasn't a kid in this school who wasn't nervous for today's showcase.

Every fifteen-year-old mage in the kingdom had to take today's showcase to prove that they were ready for tomorrow's Choosing Ceremony, the sacred ritual to receive their matured magic. Today's test was known for being difficult, requiring complete control over the basics of each legacy of magic. If any of them failed the test, they'd be held back another year to learn better control, alone.

Gnawing on her lip, Kailani took a deep breath and looked at the clock on the wall. She'd gotten to the school at the crack of dawn to secure the best classroom to practice in. Her best friends were supposed to meet up with her, but of course they were late. They didn't need as much practice as her, but she'd hope to spend the morning with them, considering it could be the last practice session they ever had together.

The last session. Ever.

Just the thought made tremors run through her body.

Kailani's hands shook as she flipped the tattered page of the potions book: *Vita for Beginners*. Practice manuals for the other legacies were scattered around her: *Unlocking Brute's Strength*, *How to Think Like a Luminate*, and *Kairo: Mastering Leadership*. She hadn't even gotten to the books for Charm or Strange yet, and there was less than half an hour until the showcase.

It didn't help that she had no idea which legacy she was going to be.

The Choosing Ceremony could be unpredictable, but most students had some sort of idea which magic they'd be chosen for —Patrick would be Vita for sure and Lyla would obviously be Charm. Kailani's shoulders sagged as she surveyed the spread of books before her. Unlike the others, her path was unclear. In the past fifteen years, none of the six legacies of magic had stood out to her more than the others. She was okay at them all, but not great at any. If her friends were chosen for different legacies than her, they'd be off to study in their own schools and make new friends. She'd barely see them anymore.

Her stomach turned at the thought.

The potion in front of her bubbled, a thick white foam forming over the top. She scanned the instructions for the tenth time, grinding together some lilac stems and Queen's moss with her old, trusty marble mortar and pestle. The consistency thickened to a syrup and she dumped in the crushed ingredients. Some of the tension fled her shoulders as the color shifted to the desired shade of lavender.

The classroom door flew open.

Kailani's heart leapt from her chest. She whirled around. It couldn't already be her turn...

Sagging with relief, she let out a long breath. Her best friend, Patrick Mahoney, stood in the doorway with a big grin on his face. Warmth swelled in her smile as he sauntered over, like he had every day since they were six years old.

Kailani rolled her eyes. "You're late."

His messy hair was brushed back to his shoulders and his dad's black hand-me-down robe engulfed his long, lean frame. He was the tallest boy in their class, and a few inches taller than Kailani, but he probably weighed less than most of the shorter boys.

"Why are you so nervous?" Patrick teased, slumping behind the empty teacher's desk in front of the classroom. "It's not like our entire future depends on today."

Kailani groaned. It was impossible to tell whether the gods of magic were actually watching today, but one of them would choose her tomorrow as long as she passed. The rest of her life would be dedicated to that legacy of magic.

Her powers, her occupation, her entire future depended on getting through today.

Patrick took off his oversized black gloves and pulled out his wand. "I don't know why you're worried. *Crescendo Flore!*" A small, pink flower sprouted from the tip of Patrick's wand. He picked it up, flicking it at Kailani, and a ghost of a smile appeared on her lips. Her cheeks burned. "Everyone gets chosen, you'll be fine."

"That's easy for you to say." Kailani sighed, grabbing the flower from the ground and sticking it behind her ear. Bubbles formed on the top of her potion and she stirred. "It's just, I keep having

3

this nightmare. I go through the mountain pass and none of the gods choose me."

Patrick smiled, but it didn't quite reach his eyes. He was worried, too, and that made chills race across Kailani's skin. "You know that's not going to happen."

Kailani shrugged, but her stomach churned. The chance of *none* of the gods Choosing her was slim, though it wasn't like it had never happened before. She'd heard rumors of kids going through the mountain pass, and their magic just didn't run deep enough in them. They were banished. Sent to live beyond the barrier with the magicless, never to see their friends and family again.

Shuddering, Kailani stirred the potion faster and faster. She was getting ahead of herself.

She shook the thoughts out of her head and turned to Patrick.

"Even so, unless we're all chosen for the same magic, we're not going to have the same classes anymore." The pit in her stomach grew, her voice rising with every word. She'd have to leave her best friends. Her only comfort when it came to school. "We'll be training in different buildings. Practicing with kids in our own legacy."

Her heartbeat quickened at the thought. A bit of her potion splattered on the table in front of her, sizzling on top of the wood. "Lyla was supposed to meet me here to study. It might be our last time—"

Patrick reached for Kailani's wrist, but she jerked away. "No, no you can't. I'm fine, I promise."

He raised an eyebrow but slipped his hand back in his glove.

Kailani winced. She hadn't even seen him take it off. Patrick's power of touch was rare, and one touch would take all her worries away. He was the first to offer his power whenever she was in need, but dark smudges lined his eyes. He wasn"t sleeping again. Nightmares, anxiety, or his dad's depression? With him, it could be anything.

4

Turning her frown back to her potion, Kailani bit the inside of her cheek. If they were sent to different schools, who would look out for *him*? Their school wasn't short on bullies, and being two of the very few students from the rundown Saxton district, she and Patrick had watched each other's backs for as long as she could remember. Kailani didn't know what *either* of them would do if they were separated. And it could happen, couldn't it?

The door banged open again.

Kailani squeaked, spinning round with her hand on her heart. Patrick burst out laughing, and Kailani made to throw a bottle of Queen's moss at his head.

Lyla Hollingsworth, the third in their inseparable trio, trotted up to them with eyebrows raised. Her pin straight blonde hair trailed after her, her pearl white nails sparkling in the golden sunlight from the window.

Kailani glared at her, sinking into a chair as her pulse steadied.

Lyla threw her hands up in surrender. "I know, I know."

"We were supposed to practice all morning," Kailani grumbled.

"I'm sorry. There was some crazy stuff on the news and my parents wouldn't let me leave. Rebels in our own town! They were saying they were trying to flee to some place called Mirstone—"

"You pay way too much attention to that news station," Patrick joked. "It's why you're so stressed all the time."

Scowling at him, Lyla turned her nose upwards. "It's important to pay attention to what's going on in the kingdom."

Patrick winked. "Only if it's true."

Kailani snorted, quickly pretending to cough when Lyla shot her a dark look.

As Lyla and Patrick continued to bicker, Kailani tuned them out. Bickering was their friendship language, after all, and she didn't have time to think about conspiracies or rebels.

She pointed her wand at her cauldron. "*Exhauro!*"

The cooled potion spun in a circle and slowly dissipated. A

slow smile crept to Kailani's face. She was fairly confident in Vita magic, and was ready to focus on Charm magic now that Lyla was here.

Her pulse jumped again. When it came to the healing magic of Charm, she needed all the help she could get.

As Patrick opened his mouth to shoot some nonsense back at Lyla, Kailani cleared her throat pointedly.

Patrick simply raised an eyebrow, but at least Lyla looked a little apologetic.

Lyla hopped up onto the teacher's desk, taking out *The Pocket Guide to Healing Charms*, as she had so many times before. After years of watching Lyla study her sacred text, Kailani knew she'd turn to page thirteen and have her start with a simple charm to heal bruises. Just like she knew Patrick would laugh at them while they practiced, playing it off like he wasn't nervous himself. He hated studying before tests, it always threw him off.

Just like that, her heart was pounding again.

She knew everything when it came to these two. She knew Lyla secretly dreamed of adventures to distant places on the maps she studied when her parents weren't looking over her shoulder. She knew Patrick's deepest wish was to discover a life outside of Saxton, working with magical creatures or wandstones. They knew all her darkest secrets too, because they were supposed to be together forever, just the three of them.

But after today, that would change.

They'd almost certainly be chosen for different paths and forced to go their separate ways. Patrick would probably go on to run a magical creatures sanctuary, and Lyla would probably move to Magnolia and become a great healer. They would move on to bigger and brighter things, while Kailani would be stuck in Saxton, without them.

The thought sent waves of paralyzing cold sweeping through her body.

"Where do you want to start?" Lyla asked.

Patrick spun around in the teacher's chair, fidgeting with a loose thread in his robe. "Why bother? You've been practicing every day for months."

"I have to pass," Kailani mumbled, her voice low. She looked at her watch, and her heart fell. They really didn't have much time. She'd be lucky if she could get one or two healing spells in. The Charm portion of the test would surely be focused on healing some type of wound.

"Let's start with something simple." Lyla pointed her wand at Patrick. "*Ferro!*"

Patrick flinched, grabbing his arm as a stream of blue energy collided with it. "Ouch!"

He shrugged off his robe, pulling up his shirt sleeve. A bluish-purple bruise formed on his arm. Patrick glared at Lyla, rubbing the spot. "You enjoy that too much."

Lyla sat up straighter on the desk, hiding a giggle behind her hand. "Okay, Kailani, the spell is simple. Take your time."

Kailani took a deep breath, nodding. She'd performed the spell dozens of times before; she could do it again. She pointed her wand at Patrick's bruise, clearing her mind of everything but her intent to heal. "*Sanaro!*"

Nothing happened.

Patrick and Lyla shared a glance that Kailani pretended not to notice.

"It's okay," Lyla soothed. "Really focus on your intention, picture the bruise healing. Channel all your energy. Try again."

Taking another breath in, Kailani closed her eyes and reached for her magic. In the darkness, it was like a rolling ocean, just beyond her reach. Mentally, she plunged her hand into the depths, but, like water, the magic slipped through her fingers.

Her heart started to race. It was always like this when her nerves were on edge. Patrick struggled sometimes too, and even Lyla occasionally had moments where it was a struggle to harness her power. That didn't make it any easier to control hers. She

7

focused on her wand, on the aquamarine wandstone Mom had given her when she started school. She let the stone's calming energy wash over her and went back for her magic.

In her mind's eye, she waded into the dark depths, focusing on the feel of her magic around her. It was her magic, and it answered to her. It *had* to answer to her, and it would heal Patrick's wound.

Her magic started to stretch towards her. Slowly, at first, like tendrils moving in slow motion. Then faster, like a hurricane, so powerful that it nearly overwhelmed her. She focused on slowing her rapid, panicked breaths, and directed that power towards Patrick's wound. The magic was like a turbulent storm, raging around her. Sparks shot across her palms, but she only had to channel it for a few more moments, long enough to cast the spell—

"*Sanaro!*"

A shriek, a thud, then a muffled groan.

Kailani's eyes flew open, and she gasped, dropping her wand.

The blast had hit Patrick in the arm and sent his chair rolling backwards into the wall.

A strange, tingling feeling crept through her fingertips as her heartbeat pounded in her ears. Her breath caught, and she looked down at her palms. There was nothing there, but she could *feel* it. She balled her hands into fists, trying to get rid of the numbing sensation.

"What was that?" Patrick asked, his eyes wide.

Kailani shook her head desperately. The spell had done something to her. Her magic was off—it was raging beneath the surface, unfocused. "I don't know."

"Look!" Lyla squealed, hopping off the desk and pointing to Patrick's arm. "The bruise is completely gone!"

Kailani gaped at Patrick, rubbing her thumb against her palm to make the numbness subside. She could hardly believe her eyes, but the bruise really was gone. It typically took upwards of thirty minutes for a mage her age to fully heal a bruise, but the color on Patrick's arm had vanished in seconds.

"Great job!" Lyla applauded, grinning. "See, and you were so worried. Maybe you'll be chosen as Charm after all."

Kailani forced herself to smile back, but something churned beneath the surface. It was as if her magic was swirling just below her skin, electrifying, begging to escape. She always felt energized when she used magic. But this—this was different. The energy never lingered after she'd completed a spell, but this time, it was stronger than she'd ever felt before.

A loud voice boomed across the courtyard and Kailani froze.

"All students testing today, please make your way towards the auditorium."

Wiping her sweaty hands on her robe, Kailani looked at her friends. A sense of dread rose in her.

Lyla cleared her throat, suddenly somber. "We should go line up."

But Kailani hesitated, not wanting their private moment to end. This might be the last time they were all in class together. Sure, they would still see each other if they went to different schools. But between their apprenticeship, training, and new classmates, it would be all too easy to drift apart.

With a gulping breath, she strode towards her friends and grabbed their hands, squeezing gently. Lyla smiled. Patrick, for once, looked serious. None of them seemed to want to let go, but there was no escaping the future.

"To the moon and beyond," Kailani whispered.

Patrick and Lyla squeezed her hands, echoing back. "To the moon and beyond."

Squaring her shoulders, Kailani pulled her hands free and turned to pack up her things. She threw her bag over her shoulder and followed Patrick and Lyla out of the door, toward the auditorium. Predictably, they started bickering again. Kailani sank into her own head. Her hands trembled harder with every step.

She took a deep breath, counting to thirteen over and over in her head, thankful for the routine Mom had taught her to calm her nerves. It never fully worked, but the monotonous repetition kept her from passing out, at least.

Lyla and Patrick stopped abruptly. Kailani jolted to a halt, almost flying into them.

Her head shot up to follow Patrick's gaze and her stomach sank. The class bully, Trey, loomed a few yards away. As always, he was surrounded by his crew and laughing at another student whose robes were far too small. Heat filled Kailani's chest. She took a step forwards, but Lyla grabbed her wrist.

"Kailani, no…"

But she couldn't ignore it. Sure, she was nervous about the showcase, but all the nerves slipped away in front of someone as awful as Trey.

"Leave him alone." Her voice was unwavering, carrying through the courtyard.

Her classmates' eyes turned towards her. The malicious chatter died down. Smirking, Trey locked eyes with her and strode over as if he was thrilled she'd challenged him. He probably was.

Kailani's hands curled into fists as he narrowed in on Patrick.

"Nice robes, Mahoney," Trey jeered.

Patrick's eyes were fixed on the floor as his face turned bright red. These were the exact bullies she was worried about leaving Patrick alone with next year. He was one of the nicest people she knew, but that was his downfall—he never stood up for himself.

Lyla craned her neck over the crowd now circling them, surely looking for a teacher.

Turning to Trey, Kailani gritted her teeth. All the stress over the showcase, over being left behind, built in her chest. "Back off."

"It's fine," Patrick whispered.

The burliest of Trey's cronies turned his attention to Kailani. "Yours aren't much better, Saxton scum."

Kailani grabbed for her wand, but as soon as she touched the cool metal, her fingertips sizzled as if on fire. The rush of magic was back, deep within her. She stumbled backwards a step.

Shaking her hands, she tried to make the feeling go away. She looked around for Lyla, but she was gone. She took a deep breath, hoping the bullies didn't notice her hesitation.

Trey's focus had already shifted back to Patrick. "What's wrong, Pat, your dad can't afford new robes?"

Kailani squeezed her hands into fists as a few people in the crowd laughed. Her head pulsed. Magic swirled inside of her. Sweat beaded on her forehead.

Something was definitely wrong.

"Oh wait," one of the other boys chimed in. "He *is* out of the looney bin now, isn't he? Or are you still living in Kailani's shoebox of a home?"

Anger boiled inside her. How *dare* he?

She'd make him pay for that.

Standing up tall, she squared her shoulders, her face burning with the heat now spreading from her fingertips to her arms. "I said *leave*."

"Just ignore them," Patrick mumbled, his eyes still fixed on the ground.

Trey stuck out his bulky arm, knocking Patrick's books and wand into a nearby puddle. Kailani's breath hitched as the dirty water splashed up her robes. She wanted to lunge for Trey, to shoot a spell that'd make boils spread over his skin. But she was on fire. She squeezed her wand tightly. It was just nerves. It had to be nerves.

Patrick scrambled to pick up his books. The crowd's laughter grew louder around them.

"Is that a Jasper stone?" Trey mocked, kicking the wand away. "I'm surprised it can even perform spells."

Kailani snarled. Burning hands or not, she couldn't just watch. She pointed her wand towards Trey—

But an electric shock shot up her arms and through her chest. A rush of energy coursed through her, her magic twisting and turning, slamming against her skull. Gasping, she slammed to a halt. Pulse pounding, with anger but with something else too, Kailani stared at her skin. It looked normal, but electric currents pulsed over her flesh, like magic raged inside of her. Like it wanted to get out.

With another breath, the currents disappeared.

She stumbled backwards, locking eyes with Patrick.

Trey scoffed, but there was something besides contempt on his face. Fear, maybe?

"You both belong in the loony bin."

The words washed over Kailani in a daze, and she knew she was supposed to feel something, *say* something, but her whole body felt cold now. Numb. Trey stalked away, his friends following close behind him. Her fists clenched. Another day, she would've shot a curse at his back, even if her parents would call it dishonorable. Trey deserved to be taken down a notch. But while the electric currents buzzing under her skin were muted, they were still there. She couldn't risk using her magic, not when it was this volatile.

Not when she couldn't begin to understand what was happening.

A professor bustled past, waving his hand. "Move along, move along."

Kailani stood, frozen, as her classmates dispersed with Trey. She wiped the sweat from her forehead. The air was cooler without so many people surrounding her. The professor swept through the last sections of the crowd, breaking them up. Lyla trailed on his heels, biting her lip. Then it clicked: she must've gone to get a teacher before anything serious happened. Kailani breathed a silent sigh of relief. Even if all the other rich Lancaster residents jeered and demeaned those from Saxton, Lyla could always be counted on to stand up for them.

More professors marched through the courtyard, sending students towards the auditorium, but Kailani could only stand in place.

"Line up!"

The courtyard was loud again, students gathering in their cliques. Soon they'd forget about the almost-fight, but Kailani wouldn't be able to dismiss whatever happened with her magic.

"Are you okay?" Patrick asked, his eyebrows crinkled in worry.

She didn't feel okay, but she nodded anyway, crossing her arms over her chest.

"Come on." Lyla tugged at her arm. "We need to line up."

Kailani stumbled after her, tucking her hands under her arms. *One, two, three...*

Everything felt off, like she suddenly had a crack in her magic. She could feel Patrick turning to watch her every few steps, but she kept her eyes locked on the ground.

If *that* happened during the showcase—during the *Ceremony*— if she couldn't control her magic, no god would ever choose her.

Then a loud voice echoed, and her heart dropped.

"Kailani Slate."

Her head jerked up. Patrick and Lyla stared at her with wide eyes. The courtyard fell silent, until all Kailani could hear was her pulse in her ears.

Clutching the strap of her bag, she turned towards the hall and swallowed, twice.

Of course, she was up first.

CHAPTER TWO

One... two... three...

Kailani breathed in and out, forcing her brain to calm. Her magic still buzzed beneath the surface of her skin as if at bay, readying itself for its next attack, but she couldn't let it distract her. As long as it didn't happen during the showcase, she'd be okay.

She squeezed her hands into fists and drifted to the doors of the auditorium, half in a daze. Her classmates' eyes were trained on her. She wanted to turn around, to get one last look of courage from Lyla, a goofy thumbs up from Patrick, but she'd crumble if she looked at their faces right now.

The tall wooden doors seemed to stretch up forever. Soundproof. Spell proof. The auditorium was a safe environment for mages to prove they were ready for their matured magic.

Unless, of course, they weren't.

With wobbly knees, Kailani pushed through the doors.

The air in the auditorium was sticky and hot. Two teachers lounged in front of a large white platform, holding their wands out, papers skewed carelessly in front of them. The bright lights obscured her view of their faces, but she stumbled towards the stage.

"Ms. Slate—"

The warm voice greeting her made Kailani's heartbeat calm. Her potions instructor, Professor Linde, leaned forward and her smiling features came into focus. Kailani sighed in relief, walking more steadily onto the stage. Professor Gorgan, her history teacher, sat next to Professor Linde. She wasn't Gorgan's favorite student by far, but with Linde, maybe this wouldn't be so bad. She took a deep breath.

One... two... three...

She scanned the room and gasped.

Two Protectors towered in the back of the room, their dark maroon robes tailored to their broad bodies. Kailani's heart slammed against her ribs, but she couldn't look away. The color flashed in her vision as if the cloth was dyed with the blood of slain mages that had dared cross them. Protectors were supposed to keep the kingdom safe, but she'd heard rumors of their cruelty and what they could get away with. Why were they *here*?

If she lost control of her magic, would they arrest her?

Shaking herself, she swallowed hard, forcing her eyes back to the only friendly face in the room. Professor Linde gave her a reassuring nod.

She didn't need to think about the Protectors. She couldn't. She had enough to worry about.

"In today's test, you must prove a basic understanding of magic. If you pass, then tomorrow, one of the six gods of magic will choose you to follow in their legacy. You will gain access to your matured magic and be blessed with the abilities of your god. As I'm sure you know, the Choosing will shape what powers you possess, and the jobs you seek in the future."

Kailani nodded. Her hands trembled. She tried to focus on Professor Linde, and Linde only, but she couldn't shake the Protectors' looming presence as they glared at her back.

"Thereafter, you will explore your powers. Devote yourself to your god. Live for your legacy. Today is your final chance to impress the gods. Do you accept this challenge?"

Kailani inhaled deeply, steadying her breaths. She could do this. The flickering beneath her skin had eased. The time was here. And besides, she didn't have a choice.

"I accept."

Professor Gorgan looked bored and uninterested, but Professor Linde smiled warmly. "Then, let's begin. The gods aren't looking for perfection, Kailani. They want to know where your natural abilities lie. Are you ready?"

Kailani's heartbeat quickened, but she nodded.

"Let us begin with Vita magic-"

Her shoulders relaxed. Vita magic was all about nature and grounding. Kailani wanted Vita magic most of all. Mom was a Vita mage, and she'd love to follow in her footsteps.

"The goddess of Creation possesses Vita magic. To prove to her you're worthy of her compassion and creativity, make your best potion with the ingredients at hand."

The table of ingredients materialized directly in front of Kailani. Taking a deep breath, Kailani set her wand down. She wouldn't need it just yet. Her hands steadied. Potions were her speciality. This task, she was prepared for.

Warm gratitude for Professor Linde swept through her. She must have chosen Vita first to ease Kailani in.

Focusing, she scanned river cloves, white caraways, even the rarest of pearl grass from the sea of Regalia itself. A small, black, standard-sized cauldron popped into existence next to the ingredients.

Trying to forget the eyes watching her, Kailani grabbed the ingredients she needed, grinding them together as she chewed the inside of her cheek. Once they were properly combined, she gently tipped them into the cauldron, ignoring the sweat trickling down her back. She knew what she was doing, her head was clear.

She added an equal amount of water to transform it into a mushy, green salve.

She took a deep breath. So far, so good.

She tossed in the river's clove and brought the potion to a low simmer, then she added the golden tea leaf and let the potion cool down. Stepping back, she puffed out her cheeks. A few loose strands of hair on her face, and she shoved them away.

The potion would have to sit for half an hour to be effective in inducing the calming effect Kailani desired, but Professor Linde bent over the cauldron and smiled.

"Great job!"

A small smile flickered on her face. So far the strangeness with her magic had receded. Maybe she'd pass this test after all.

Professor Gorgan sniffed the smoke rising from the cauldron and wrote something on his clipboard. "Pass."

Kailani let out a breath and couldn't help but grin.

The ingredients in front of Kailani disappeared with a whisk of Professor Linde's wand, replaced by an apple.

"To prove yourself worthy of the confident and ambitious god of power, demonstrate Kairo magic by levitating the apple in front of you."

Kailani nodded. With a steadying breath, she held out her wand. Kairo magic had always been more physically taxing on her —and likewise, levitating the apple felt more like trying to heft a concrete block into the air. Kailani forced a straight face to conceal her effort as she lifted the ruby-colored fruit into the air. Professor Linde nodded in approval, and Kailani eased the apple back onto the table.

For Luminate's trial, Kailani gathered ingredients that, when properly brewed, would paralyze the drinker. Then, she was made to create the antidote.

"Great job, Kailani. We've finished the hands-on portion of the test, now we'll move onto a couple simulations."

Kailani took a deep breath. Three down, three to go. Maybe this wouldn't be so bad after all.

Professor Gorgan cleared his throat. "Next up, you will demonstrate your abilities to the goddess of Healing, by using Charm magic. To demonstrate Charm's selfless and proud nature, you will be placed in a simulation. You'll have one minute to heal your patient's wound."

Kailani's pulse jumped. She took a deep breath, suddenly unsteady on her feet. A cool fog creeped along her ankles, sending chills down her arms.

The room materialized into a healer's suite with white walls and a hospital bed. A small boy, no older than five, was seated beside her, crying. He held his arm out to Kailani with a hopeful look in his teary eyes, a small cut open in his flesh.

Kailani flinched, her mouth dry.

She tightened her grip on her wand, frozen for a moment, and then another. Her eyes fixed on the timer above the bed, the numbers dwindling, but it was like her arm was frozen. Squeezing her eyes shut, she pictured Patrick slamming into the wall. Her magic blazing inside her.

"*Sanaro!*"

She flinched at her own voice, small and meek. Nothing happened.

Forty seconds left.

The cries reverberated against the walls and her chest tightened. When Trey was bullying Patrick, her magic had roared to escape, but now it was gone. She could only feel the barest thread of power left. Damn the watching Protectors, she *needed* to pass. Even if it was uncontrollable, she needed *more*.

Thirty seconds left.

She closed her eyes and pictured Lyla's confused face as she examined the healed bruise, trying to summon the power she'd felt, and what it had sparked within her. She knelt next to the child, squeezing his shoulder.

"Shh, it's okay." Kailani steadied her hands, pointing her wand at the wound. "*Sanaro!*"

The child screamed. The cut had only closed halfway.

Fifteen seconds left.

Kailani muttered a curse, a burst of frustration swelling inside her. She stared at her wand. It showed years of use, but her aquamarine wandstone shone like it was brand new, intertwined with the top. It wasn't the strongest stone, but it had never failed her before. She squeezed her eyes shut, letting the aquamarine stone send a surge of calm through her body and jerked her wand forward. "*Sanaro!*"

The child's cries cut off abruptly and Kailani gaped at his arm.

She released a breath. "Good as new."

The healer's room disappeared.

She was back on the stage. She almost stumbled, her legs were shaking so badly, but she squared her shoulders and forced herself to breathe deeply.

Professor Gorgan made a check on his clipboard. "Well done," he said, his voice dry.

"Okay," Professor Linde said, and Kailani swore her voice hitched just a little. Was she nervous?

Kailani gulped. Only two tasks left.

But Professor Linde stepped forward, beaming. "Great job, Kailani. Your fifth task will prove to the god of strength if you're worthy of Brute magic. You'll be placed in another simulation. This time, you'll need to break open a lock on the door to get to your loved ones."

Kailani took a steadying breath as the room materialized into a cool and breezy alley with one abandoned building barely standing in front of her. A splintered oak door loomed in front of her. A shiver ran down Kailani's spine. She breathed once, twice, then tried to open the door—but a large, molded lock blocked her entrance. Must and earth filled her nose. Her hands shook as she tightened the grip on her wand, unsure of what the task was asking. Her brow furrowed.

Gasping, Kailani's eyes snapped open, and she almost collapsed with relief. She pointed her wand at the lock and yelled, "*Apeiro!*"

The lock jingled but didn't open. Kailani frowned, bracing herself to start again.

Somebody banged on the other side of the door.

Eyes widening, Kailani took a step forward but caught herself. It was just a simulation, after all. They were testing her control. She needed to focus, to think. What had she done wrong? Was it her inflection? The movement of her—

Her thoughts shattered at the sounds of her parents' screams.

Before she could think, Kailani was at the door, banging against it with her fists, but their screams only grew louder with every second that passed. Blood pounding in her ears, Kailani wrenched herself away. *Just a simulation. Just a simulation. Need to control...*

But it was impossible to think clearly. They were in agony.

Tears streamed down her cheeks as she pressed her hands over her ears.

The air blowing from the vents above was suddenly too warm. Sweat beaded on her forehead. She was almost done. If she could just...

"Think!" she cried.

Kailani clenched her jaw. She inhaled and exhaled deeply. Every muscle in her body burned with strain. The rest of the world was drowned out by her heart pounding in her chest and her blood rushing through her ears. Exhaustion was quickly over-powering adrenaline. There was no more time to find her inner strength. She had to act *now*.

Kailani's heart dropped to her stomach. The burning sensation covered her fingertips as bolts of electricity flowed through her veins. Goosebumps crawled up her skin.

Gasping, Kailani jerked her wand up. "*Conflio!*"

The wall crumbled before her and Kailani rushed forwards, her heart in her mouth.

Only, there was nobody behind the door.

Pressing her hand to her heart, Kailani willed herself to calm as the auditorium shimmered back into existence.

Eyes wide and heart pounding, she locked gazes with Professor Linde. Professor Linde's eyes narrowed, and Kailani shrunk back. Oh gods... oh gods...

"Let's move on," Professor Linde said quickly. "One final task."

Kailani's stomach lurched as it hit her.

Strange magic. Rare and unpredictable.

It was the most dangerous magic there was. The goddess of darkness didn't bless very many mages with her gifts, and there were only one or two mages chosen as Strange each year throughout the entire Kingdom.

The Queen of Talisia was one of them.

Strange magic was beauty and chaos. She tried to limit her usage. It frightened her, the way its coldness spread through her body, like it wanted to take control.

Gorgan smiled as if he could see the magic bubbling under Kailani's skin, so she wrenched her eyes away from him. One more task. Then she could go home, curl up by a fire and sip Mom's tea.

One more task.

"Lastly, to prove you're worthy of the goddess of Darkness's cunning Strange magic, simply light this candle, and put it out again."

The candle appeared in front of her. Swallowing, she pointed her wand at it. Pulsating beats crept up her arm and she squeezed her eyes shut, trying to ignore them.

"*Ignitis!*"

Nothing happened. Yet, Kailani was forced to suppress a gasp as a surge of magic churned and raged within her. An icy feeling crept up her spine, and her fingertips began to numb. A desperate craving began to form in the back of her mind—a raw scratching like the *scrape scrape scrape* of claws against steel.

The weight of Professor Gorgan and Professor Linde's eyes drilled into her. She swallowed dryly.

Just one candle.

Kailani straightened her arm. *"Ignitis!"*

Then, her heart exploded.

Or, at least, it felt that way.

Magic coursed through her veins, raw and powerful, threatening to swallow her whole. Kailani's vision went spotty. Her whole body tensed up and her arms went numb. A white film crowded her vision, tunneling in front of her.

Electric energy engulfed her. She stumbled backwards, eyes widening. Flames covered the entire table, heat blasted in her face. Smoke rose through her nostrils and she coughed, whipping her head around. Professor Gorgan ran forward, trying to control the flames, but his robe caught on fire and he jumped backwards.

"No!" Kailani cried.

Alarms wailed around her. Water poured from the ceiling, the pressure drenching her robes and leaving them sopping wet.

A hand wrapped around her arm and someone dragged her away. Strands of wet hair stuck to her face as she tried to free herself. The smoke clouded her vision and she swayed on her feet.

"Shh, Kailani, follow me."

Professor Linde burst through the auditorium doors, dragging her along. Kailani's eyes burned. She lifted her hand to block the blinding sun, trying to steady her shaking hands. The ground wobbled beneath her.

"Please, Professor, what's going on?"

"Not yet," Professor Linde murmured.

Whispers filled her ears, but the faces of the other students blurred as Professor Linde hauled her past. Her arm ached under her tight grip, but Kailani stumbled along as best she could. They rounded a corner and Professor Linde unlocked her office door.

The pulses beneath her skin started to ease, and her vision was more clear.

Quills fluttered around the office taking notes. Linde stilled them with a flick of her wand.

Kailani's head pounded. Her throat was dry.

Holy gods.

She'd set the auditorium on fire.

"Professor, please, it was an accident!"

"I believe you, Kailani. Come inside."

Kailani's body ached, but she did as asked.

For a moment she was free as Professor Linde locked the office door. She was about to collapse onto a chair when her Professor grabbed her again. "Tell me what happened."

Fear flickered in Linde's eyes, making bile rise up Kailani's throat. She swallowed.

"I... I don't know," Kailani stuttered. "It was like my magic malfunctioned."

"Has this happened before?" Linde's tone was sharp.

Kailani hesitated.

It *had* happened while she was practicing, but confessing the truth could make everything worse. Then again, if anyone here would be on her side, it was surely Linde. But still, she'd set her freaking Professor on fire. There was no chance they'd let her move on to tomorrow's Ceremony. Her body shook as Professor Linde's patient eyes burned into her, waiting for an answer.

She took a deep breath, bowing her head. "Earlier, while I was practicing. But nothing like that."

Whatever *that* was.

"Who else knows about this?"

Kailani's brow furrowed. "Just Lyla and Patrick. And you... and Professor Gorgan, and probably half the class now..."

Lowering her head to her hands, she groaned.

23

i." The urgency in Professor Linde's voice put Kailani

do not tell anyone about this. Do you understand? I will charm Professor Gorgan and the Protectors to forget what they saw."

Kailani's stomach dropped. It was a crime to charm another's mind. Only very accomplished Kairo mages could even do so. "But Professor, it's illegal-"

"You *mustn't* tell anyone about this," Professor Linde interrupted.

Something cold settled in Kailani's stomach as she stared into her professor's eyes. Why would Linde break the law for her? It was just an accident, wasn't it? But Professor Linde's eyes were wide, her mouth tight, and Kailani's chest tightened.

"Please," Kailani whispered. "What's wrong with me?"

Professor Linde straightened, her gaze darting away. "Wait five minutes, then go straight home. Do not talk to anyone."

"But... Professor..."

Barely thinking, Kailani reached to grab her, her head a mess of tumbling thoughts. But Professor Linde stepped back, not looking at her as she unlocked her office door. Not looking at her as she slipped through it, slamming it behind her.

Kailani couldn't move. Her body was frozen, aching. She could only stare as her eyes burned.

She had just ruined everything.

CHAPTER THREE

*K*ailani's hands shook the entire walk home.

She didn't stop counting in her head until she reached the public portal station at the outskirts of Lancaster. The crackle of magic as the portal's small three-circular beam shot up from the ground typically set her at ease, but today the sound whisked her back to the crackle of the growing fire.

Flinching back, Kailani held her breath until the beams transformed into one giant circle, swirling a vibrant blue color. With a shudder, Kailani stepped through.

She emerged in Saxton's derelict portal station, right down the road from her small cottage home. The decaying rooftops and vine-covered houses didn't offer their usual comfort. Instead, the pressure on her chest grew heavier. A shiver ran down her spine and her head throbbed. Her body felt stiff from the outburst. She squeezed her fingers tight against her palms, trudging down the street slowly.

Slowly, because when she got home, she'd have to tell her parents what happened. Her hands trembled at the thought.

Fresh floral scents filled her nose, drawing her gaze up. Her cottage was a silhouette against the setting sun. Her eyes burned as a desperate urge ran through her. Part of her wanted to stay rooted to the spot, never to understand her outburst during the test or the danger of what might come next. The rest of her wanted to race inside the safety of those walls, curl up and never leave.

Instead, she stood frozen, her hair tossed by a gentle breeze.

Her parents watered plants on the front porch, as they always did in the early evenings. Mom could charm the plants to grow and bloom on their own if she wanted to; she was an accomplished Vita mage, and very good with nature and creation magic. But Mom preferred the old-fashioned way of doing things. She always had.

The plants speak to you, Lani, in a language you'll never learn if you simply put a charm over them. The beauty of some things must be appreciated without magic.

If anyone could make her feel better about the situation, it was Mom. She always knew what to say, even when there was nothing to say at all. Her presence brought peace, comfort. Kailani needed that right now.

Taking a deep breath, Kailani forced herself to move. She checked the mail at the end of her long walkway, a habit she'd formed long ago because her parents forgot so often that the mailman would bang on their door with a bucket of envelopes. She flipped through the post, her heart sinking:

Tommy and Chelsea Slate

LATE NOTICE

The unease was back, full force. She'd tried to forget about the extra money they'd had to fork out for the Ceremony tomorrow, but the message was a painful reminder. Her parents' apothecary shop at the edge of the territory did alright. The residents in the wealthier parts of town, like Lancaster, wouldn't dare step foot in Saxton, but they did send their housekeepers for Mom's famous potions. But it was never enough, not really. Their coin jar was already low last month, and that was before the Ceremony fees.

26

Mom's laugh reverberated through the wind and a sense of calm wrapped around Kailani's heart. Dragging a smile to her face, Kailani fixed her eyes on Mom. A silky scarf was wrapped around her head, and her beautiful coils flowed freely. A wistful smile crossed her face. Her parents were strong. Resilient. And no matter what came next, they'd get through it. Just like they always had.

Dad lifted his head as she neared, a grin spreading across his face. "Lani! How did your test go?"

Kailani's shoulders tensed. She looked anywhere except her parents' faces. "It went alright."

She handed Dad the mail, but he set the envelopes aside without looking at them.

Mom wrapped her in a hug and squeezed tight before letting go. "Did you pass with flying colors?"

Kailani opened her mouth to speak, to tell them everything, but the words caught in her throat. She couldn't tell them about the outburst. She couldn't ruin their happy moods. She couldn't tell them that the only reason she was moving onto the Ceremony was because Professor Linde was committing a crime for her. That if she didn't get chosen tomorrow, it was because she'd failed to handle the one thing every other mage in her grade could do. She wasn't ready for her matured magic.

"I... I didn't do so well on Brute and Strange."

That was an understatement. But she did do okay on the other four branches. That *could* make up for her magical outburst in the gods' eyes.

Her parents shared a look. "Well, that's okay." Dad opened the front door, leading them inside. "As long as you passed. You did pass, right?"

Kailani's chest tightened and she nodded. "Yeah."

Dad blew out a breath of relief. "That's my girl. I knew you would. We'll celebrate tonight, I'll make your favorite stew."

Dad opened the fridge and started pulling out vegetables while

Mom grabbed the teapot. She warmed up on the stove and poured the steaming liquid into a mug.

"Sounds great."

She couldn't look them in the eye. If she did, she wouldn't be able to stop herself from spluttering every last worry racing through her mind.

"Here, baby." Mom handed her a mug of her famous mint lemonade tea and kissed the side of her head. "I am so proud of you."

Kailani forced a smile, taking the mug, but a shudder swept over her as she brushed past Mom. "I'm going out back."

She could feel their eyes burning into her as she rushed outside, dropping onto one of the raggedy white garden chairs and curling into it. Mom's old crystal ball sat in the middle of the table, glistening in the light from the afternoon rays. Kailani cradled her tea, blowing on the steaming liquid as the mug warmed her hands.

A tightness pressed down on her chest, like she couldn't quite get enough air. She set her mug down and crossed her arms. She never lied to her parents. But there wasn't a point in worrying them. Everything was fine. Sure, the outburst had left her body aching and sore, and the headache was getting worse. But everything would be fine.

Kailani felt a soft vibration against her chest and she reached for her talisman necklace, rubbing the cool, teal stone. A moment later, Patrick's voice sounded through the opaque surface.

"Kailani, are you okay? We tried to look for you after the test, but you were gone."

The lump in Kailani's throat grew at the thought of explaining to him what happened. Usually, the talisman was her refuge. Dad had charmed them each a stone years ago, so they could talk whenever they wanted. Moments like this, when one of them was too deep in their own head, they'd always have an outlet. She held the necklace out in front of her, and it lit up again.

This time it was Lyla's voice. "I do hope everything's okay. Kailani, we're worried."

She held the necklace in her hand, even held it up to word vomit the entire incident to them, but she couldn't bring herself to say the words out loud. That would mean admitting what really happened. And she didn't even know what really happened. So she tucked the necklace back under her shirt and tried to ignore their messages coming in every few minutes.

The air was crisp as she stared into the open field behind their home, brilliant hues illuminating the sky as the sun descended towards the distant mountains. She could stare forever, but it'd never be long enough to take in the sight.

Finally, some of the tightness in her chest eased.

Patrick and Lyla's voices came through every few minutes, until it lit up one last time, and Patrick's voice was just a whisper.

"Kailani, whatever happened during the test, it'll be okay. I'll see you tomorrow. Goodnight."

She picked up the necklace again. She knew she should respond, but it was like her throat had squeezed shut. She just wanted tomorrow to be over. Curling her knees into her chest, she sucked in a deep breath and let the necklace fall.

The orange clouds faded, replaced by stars and rays of moonlight that lit the yard beyond. The shimmering barrier lulled and churned in the distance. A wave of nausea hit her hard. The barrier protected the kingdom from the Far Lands, but tonight, the thought of whatever lay beyond the barrier was less intimidating than tomorrow's Choosing Ceremony.

The door creaked. Kailani jumped, her heart leaping into her throat as she whipped around. She placed her hand to her chest, letting out a long breath before laughing softly.

"How long have you been there?"

"Not long." Mom smiled, pulling out a chair and wrapping a blanket around Kailani's shoulders. "Dinner's getting cold. You really should have something to eat. Tomorrow's a big day."

The aroma of Dad's stew wafted from inside, and Kailani's stomach growled. But she didn't think she could keep anything down. She fixed her eyes on the cyan glass orb in the middle of the table, wishing she could look into it and see her future. No matter what, everything would change, but she couldn't shake the dread coiled in her stomach. And she couldn't ignore the way Mom was watching her, the knowing curve to her lips.

Unable to hold back any longer, Kailani blurted, "What if none of the gods choose me tomorrow?"

Mom rubbed her shoulder. "Kailani Slate. You are a talented young mage. That's not something you need to worry yourself about. You'll see, the gods always have a plan."

The crisp air sent a shiver creeping up her spine and Kailani dug her nails into her palms. A plan. Right. After today's failure, the gods might decide the only future she was fit for was working in the deep, dark mines. Or the hydroponics factory downtown. The monarchy might not even trust her with explosive spells. She stifled a groan, but her pulse was pounding, and her stomach churned. She may not even get assigned an apprenticeship, what would happen to her then?

Fear sealed Kailani's throat. She tried to start her counting, but by the time she got to three, terrible visions were flashing through her head. Losing her magic, the gods deeming her not powerful enough. Being shunned from the kingdom. Her friends turning their backs on her.

She squeezed her eyes shut.

Maybe she could run away. Go someplace safe.

Who was she kidding, though? There was no place for her in Talisia without magic, and the Far Lands weren't an option. Stories of horrifying creatures and lost realms lay beyond the barrier, and she didn't want to find out if they were true.

"Professor Linde told me about the showcase."

Kailani's eyes widened, her head snapping to face Mom. Her expression was serious, her smile gone, and Kailani couldn't breathe because she couldn't hide anymore. She wasn't ready for her matured magic; she'd have to repeat the school year. And then it might just happen again, and again, until she gave up trying.

The gods didn't want her.

Her lip trembled. Tears welled in her eyes as she met Mom's soft gaze. "What's wrong with me?"

Something howled in the distance.

Kailani's head snapped up as Mom grabbed her arm. Out in the dark, the faint hue of the barrier turned a deep shade of red. Kailani gasped; red meant highest power, which meant they were looking for runaways. Her stomach wrenched as she clung to Mom, her loose bun falling from its tie.

A raid was coming.

Kailani's fingertips burned and she shot to her feet. Her ears rang. Her heart pounded against her chest as fear swelled in her, suffocating her. Beads of light fluttered in her vision, and she struggled to breathe.

Mom's old crystal ball shattered in pieces. The hair on Kailani's neck raised, as she locked horrified eyes with Mom.

She'd done that. Something was definitely wrong with her.

"I'm sorry!" she cried.

Mom grabbed Kailani's face, rubbing her thumbs over her neck. "It's okay. Just stay calm, and all will be well. Get inside."

Nodding, Kailani forced herself to breathe, allowing Mom to steer her away from the shards of glass. They rushed inside and Kailani placed her wand in the drawer with shaking hands. She took a quick swig of the concoction Mom made to shield them from invasive magic, like she always did, but this time she was more grateful than ever for the protection. If the Protectors read her memories, they'd see what happened at the showcase. She couldn't let that happen.

Dad emerged from the den, looking a bit flushed but calm. He smiled at her and Kailani started counting, taking deep breaths in and out with every number. The Protectors would come and go. Then she could go back to worrying about tomorrow instead.

As Kailani rushed past the entrance to the kitchen with her parents, her breath caught, and she froze.

There was someone standing in the den.

Lurching back a step, Kailani stared, her heart pounding as she squinted into the gloom beyond the doorway. She frowned. There was nobody there. But she'd thought for *sure* there'd been a flash of a purple cloak, of woman's long red hair.

Something glimmered, and Kailani's gaze shifted to the book-case nearest the door. But again, there was nothing there. She blinked rapidly, then squeezed her eyes tight. The elixir had to be messing with her mind. She was seeing things, feeling woozy.

Someone pounded on the front door.

Cursing, Kailani cowered behind her parents, out of direct view.

Dad opened it slowly. Two tall men towered in the doorframe, their wandstones glistening in the moonlight. Hate reflected in their eyes. Breath hitching, Kailani backed up until she was pressed against the wall, putting some distance between her and the men.

She'd heard rumors about what kinds of things could happen during raids. Long nights spent at her parents' apothecary shop let her and Patrick overhear all sorts of mages who had differing opinions on the Queen and her rule. Some of them were surely exaggerated, but if there was even an ounce of truth to their stories, they had to tread carefully.

Her hands trembled as the Protectors stomped down the hall and into the kitchen, their heavy boots slapping against the tiles. They filled the small space, their expressions flat and eyes glinting, and Kailani wished she'd stop shaking. She forced herself to breathe in, then out. They'd all downed the proper amount of the memory blocking elixir. They were safe.

"We're here on official orders, looking for runaways," the first

Protector said. His deep voice rumbled down Kailani's spine. "Dangerous rebels, believed to be practicing dark magic."

Kailani's mouth fell open, but she quickly regained her composure. Her family was safe. They weren't associated with any dark magic.

The second Protector held out a black, rectangular device, floating it in front of them. Kailani's heart raced. They weren't Protectors from Farrow, not with a Jemison Controller. Those were reserved for monarchy Protectors, and they *never* came to Farrow.

Kailani rubbed her thumb on her stone necklace, seeking comfort in the smooth surface. Their scans would come out clean and the Protectors would leave. They wouldn't be able to find out what happened at the showcase.

The Protector waved his wand over the device. It projected a male and female, turning slowly in a clockwise rotation. Despite her nerves, Kailani leaned forward, squinting at the figures from across the room. Everyone in Talisia had to be registered so the monarchy knew exactly who every person was and what they looked like. It was meant to be a census, but it felt more like an advanced mugshot. These projections looked a few years old, but she was too far away to catch any details.

"We have strict orders to scan everyone in the house. Any information you don't share with us before the scan can and will be grounds for Atonement," the second Protector said.

Kailani's head snapped up, her eyes darting to her parents. They could send them to prison? But she drank the elixir... she was safe. Even so, an accidental outburst wouldn't send her to prison, would it?

"We haven't seen them." Mom's voice was shaky, but her gaze didn't break from the Protectors.

"You're sure?" The Protector's eyes narrowed. "Look closely now."

Kailani clenched her jaw, trying to keep her teeth from chattering. They didn't know anything about dark magic or runaway rebels. Why wouldn't he just leave already? A low heat brushed over her fingertips but she paid it no attention.

Dad shook his head. "You're welcome to scan us, but we don't know those two from anywhere that I can remember. Take a look around if you need to, there's no one hiding here."

The two Protectors exchanged glances and let out mocking laughs.

"We're not staying in this wasteland longer than we have to."

Kailani's cheeks flushed warm, the heat in her fingertips building to a buzz, and she gasped. A Protector shot her a dark look. She smothered the gasp with a cough, and he turned back to Dad.

"Luckily, we don't have to rely on your word. Place your hands out, palms up."

Mom and Dad placed their palms up, but Kailani stood frozen in place. Her hands trembled behind her back. Shocks ran down her arms. Desperately, she tried to catch Mom's eye, willed Dad to look at her. She didn't know what to do, but she couldn't lose control, not here. Not now. Not *again*.

Why was this happening to her?

The Jemison controller sent out a signal, scanning Mom and then Dad's memories as a red laser hovered over their palms. Kailani held her breath, but the light turned green, and she sagged with relief. Their readings were clean.

With a snarl, one of the Protectors ripped a scroll from his pocket. Kailani jumped, the bolts of electricity now crackling up her spine as she struggled to focus. She let out a short breath, thankful the Protectors hadn't honed in on her just yet. But guilt twisted in her stomach as he shoved the scroll beneath Mom's nose.

"This was found outside of your residence. Do you know what it is?"

Mom scanned the paper and shrugged, as if she wasn't worried at all. "It looks like a blank scroll."

"A blank scroll?" The Protector raised his eyebrow. "Or a scroll charmed to hide its content?"

Dad shook his head. "We wouldn't know."

The Protector stepped closer to Dad, looming over him. Before she could stop herself, Kailani winced. Their eyes jerked towards her and she froze, trembling, her hands curled into fists.

"Kailani." Dad's voice wavered. "It's okay."

But one of the Protectors was already stepping towards her, lips curving into a smirk, his frame towering over her.

"Well, aren't you a pretty one. I've never seen you in the Pits, have I?"

Kailani swallowed, her mouth dry. The Protector laughed, making a show of looking around the small cottage. He bent down so his face was next to hers, his hot breath brushing her cheek. Her stomach turned.

"It looks like you could use the coins, girl."

"Just perform the scan, it'll come out clean," Dad pleaded, his voice barely concealing his anger now. "She's only fifteen and hasn't done anything to warrant your scrutiny. Do what you came to do and leave our daughter alone."

The Protector's eyes narrowed but he didn't leave her face. The lump in Kailani's throat caught as he reached his long, cold finger out, stroking her cheek. She jerked her head back.

"Keep your hands off of her," Dad hissed.

The Protector's smirk stretched. "Hands up."

Panic pulsed through Kailani's veins. She couldn't show him her hands. They were on fire.

But the Protector leaned closer. "I'm not going to ask you again."

She heard footsteps, then the other Protector growled, "*Prohibio!*"

A red light flashed beside her and her parents struggled, Brute magic rooting them to the spot. Dad, maybe Mom, must've been trying to get to her. If Kailani didn't act, if the Protectors didn't get what they wanted, then her parents would be the ones to pay.

Taking a deep breath, Kailani held out her shaking hands. Sneering, the Protector grabbed them. Blood pulsed in her ears as his focus shifted to the Jemison Controller. Sweat gathered on her forehead. She was going to pass out, or be sick, or—

The light flashed green, and Kailani's shoulders slumped with relief. Clean. She just needed to keep herself together a little longer, like her parents. She had to ignore the stench of alcohol and stale tobacco stinging her nose as she breathed in shallow breaths, even if it made her want to vomit. It'd be over soon.

The Protector swooped close to whisper in her ear, "Lucky this time." His hand moved from her cheek to her chin, and she flinched. But he didn't release her. Not until he tipped her chin and winked.

Mom and Dad fought against the Brute magic, but they were rooted to their spots. Kailani locked eyes with Mom, her heart racing. She had to stay calm. She just had to stay calm.

The Protector released her, and for a moment Kailani thought they'd made it. But then he moved towards Mom, and spat, "Saxton scum."

Something stirred in Kailani's stomach.

Dad's face flushed. Mom's jaw tightened.

The Protector shoved Dad back, pinning him against the wall. He thrust his wand in Dad's face. "Our sources say you were the last people the rebels talked to. Who's lying? You or them?"

Kailani barely heard his words. All she knew was that Dad was hurting, that Dad was in danger.

"We know nothing of the rebels," Dads chin lifted higher in the air, but the Protector's wand pressed into his skin. "I swear."

The wand dug deeper into Dad's throat. Kailani's palms burned as a band of fear wrapped around her. But Mom wasn't looking at Dad. Her wide eyes were fixed on Kailani as she mouthed, *It's okay. Stay calm.*

"*Inpulsa!*"

Red streams of light hit Dad directly in the chest. He jerked, his body falling to the floor and convulsing. His mouth wrenched open in a soundless scream.

"Dad!" Kailani screamed, darting forwards, but the second Protector flung his wand toward her face and she staggered to a halt.

Dad's body seized, the force of the curse growing stronger with every moment. And then the second Protector grabbed Mom, pinning her against the wall and digging his wand into her neck. As if they were going to do the same to her, as if this wasn't going to stop.

His mouth was next to her ear. "Where are the rebels?"

"Leave them alone!" Kailani screamed. And in that moment, she didn't care about their wands, or who they worked for. She ran towards them, knowing only that they had to *stop*.

An invisible force slammed into her and she gasped, flying backwards as if she weighed nothing. She slammed against the wall.

Head spinning, body aching, she shot up quickly and her chest tightened. Mom was on the ground thrashing, the Protector standing over her with a smirk on his face. Kailani stared in horror, her vision spotty and her lungs burning. Her body tingled and her hands felt hot, like they were over open flames.

An echoing bang ripped through the house.

Darkness flooded her vision until she could see nothing.

For a moment, all Kailani knew was her heartbeat. It pulsed in her ears, then surged through her body. Every inch of her skin tingled, as if something cold had been draped over her. Then her vision returned.

She blinked. Then she blinked again. She was lying on the kitchen floor. Why was she lying on the kitchen floor? Frowning,

Kailani tried to lift her head but colors and light spun and swirled. Flopping back, her stomach lurching, she forced herself to breathe through the nausea. Blinking and blinking until the colors settled, and she was able to sit up.

Kailani was jolted back into the moment.

Dad was writhing on the floor, but now the Protectors were sprawled next to him.

They jumped to their feet, eyes wild as they swung to her. The bigger of the two stumbled over, and Kailani tried to scramble away but her body was too slow. He yanked her to her feet, shoving her against the nearby kitchen table. She winced at the sharp pain in her back, still shaking her head to clear it.

"I should arrest you right now for treasonous use of magic," he roared, spit flying in her face.

Kailani could only gape up at him, her thoughts tumbling over one another. Her body shook violently. The Protector didn't just look angry, he looked…scared. Just as Trey had looked in the courtyard.

What had just happened? Did *she* do that?

"It was an accident," Mom pleaded, kneeling next to Dad with an arm wrapped around him. "She's being chosen tomorrow; her emotions are high." Her voice came in a rush, her composure lost. "You know how that can affect powers during the final stage of development. She's a good kid and would never use magic maliciously. She didn't even have a wand in her hand!"

Kailani's heart all but stopped at the confirmation. She'd lost control again.

The Protector's face contorted with a rage Kailani couldn't comprehend. "That's a fifty-thousand coin fine for not cooperating with a mandatory memory scan. Accidental use of magic notwithstanding."

Her jaw dropped open, soul-crushing fear gripping her heart. She gripped the edge of the counter, trying, *failing*, to stay upright.

Fifty thousand coins? No one in Saxton could afford even that.

"We'll be back to collect in two weeks," the Protector promised. He bent towards Kailani and she leaned back, but she had nowhere to go. "And if you can't pay—" he grabbed her wrist and yanked her closer to him— "you can fight your debt off in the Pits."

He shoved her away as he released her, and Kailani slammed back against the counter with a cry. She clung to the edge, her chest heaving with every breath. Finally, *finally* the Protectors were leaving. Her parents rushed to her side, wrapping their arms around her.

The Protectors slammed the door behind them, and Kailani burst into tears.

CHAPTER FOUR

Kailani's alarm blared.

Groaning, she fumbled for her wand, pointing it lazily at her singing alarm clock. *"Silentium."*

Silence. Smiling into her pillow, Kailani turned back over and burrowed into her bed, ready to sleep for hours yet. She tuned her ears to the sounds of the ocean—she'd been so sad when they moved to Saxton, so Dad had charmed her walls to look and sound like her favorite old beach—and matched her breathing to the waves. Yawning, she let her mind drift—

Her parents' screams of agony echoed in her head.

She gasped, her eyes flying open. Heart racing, she stared at her palms, but there was no sign of the chaotic magic she couldn't understand.

Unlike what happened last night.

It all came flooding back and her stomach turned. She stared at her wand lying on the floor, her chest immediately tightening. She didn't know what was causing the outbursts, but if she didn't touch her wand—if she avoided doing any magic—maybe they wouldn't happen. Glass shattered in her memory, the Protector's cold finger ran down her cheek as his rancid breath twisted up her nose. She'd do anything to avoid seeing that Protector again.

Squeezing her eyes shut, she pulled her knees into her chest and focused again on the shushing of the waves against the charmed shore. She dragged her thoughts back to her favorite spot, the place she'd felt most safe. Her childhood memories were hazy, but she'd always remember it. With each whispered wave, her thundering pulse eased.

The Protectors were gone. She was safe.

But today was the Choosing Ceremony, and that was something she couldn't avoid.

A light knock on her bedroom door made her raise her eyes and her throat constricted. Mom walked in with a box in her hand, smiling like usual, as if Kailani hadn't ruined their entire lives last night. Wrenching her gaze away, Kailani stared at her knuckles.

There was no way they could afford the fine, and the Protectors weren't likely to be generous with them.

"Lani, you need to get ready. We have to leave soon."

Kailani gnawed at her lip, wishing she could sink into her bed and disappear. But Mom closed the door and moved closer, and Kailani knew silence wouldn't work. Taking a long breath, she mumbled, "Do we have to go?"

"Yes. But don't worry. It goes by quickly, and everyone's too busy focusing on themselves to focus on you up there."

Unless she had another outburst.

Kailani winced. "Doubt it."

The bed squeaked as Mom sat down, rubbing her back. "It's not just about the Ceremony. Remember all the games and vendors that will be there. It's supposed to be fun."

Sighing, Kailani leaned into her hand. The Ceremony had always been her favorite day of the year. Carnival games, food charmed to allow endless consumption, magic at its best and brightest. She used to think getting her full powers would be the best day of her life. Everything she'd worked towards would come to fruition. She'd daydreamed endlessly of the Queen placing the Vita pendant around her neck, then being able to manipulate the water and air around her, to see into the unknown. She wanted to get a placement that allowed her to travel throughout the Kingdom. But now, the looming Ceremony just made her chest heavy.

"Don't stress," Mom said, pulling her from her thoughts. "This is a big day, but you should be celebrating."

Kailani grabbed her oversized quilt and threw it over her shoulders.

Mom laughed. "I have a surprise for you. I've been waiting for today to give it to you."

Kailani peeked out from the mountain of her quilt to see Mom holding out a flimsy parcel wrapped with a glowing string. She couldn't help her lips turning upwards. She reached for her wand to open the gift, but as her hand lingered above it, she pictured the box combusting in her tiny room and untied the string herself.

With a gasp of delight, Kailani pulled out a beautiful robe, its gorgeous teal color shimmering in the morning sunlight coming through the open window. She slipped out from under her quilt, holding the robe against her body. The Vita symbol was embroidered on the right chest.

Her heart sank as her grip on the robe tightened. Only mages who had a lot of coins could afford such colorful embroidery, and something like this would have easily cost years' worth of the wages her parents made in the shop. There was no way they could afford it, especially not with the withstanding fine. Her excitement dwindled.

Mom set aside the box, her smile widening. "It was your grandmother's."

Kailani's mouth fell open. "Really? But I've never seen you wear it."

"Because I knew she'd want you to have it. She'd be so proud of you."

Biting her lip, Kailani ran her fingers over the robe. She didn't know much about her maternal grandparents. Her grandmother had been an accomplished Vita mage, her grandfather Luminate, mirroring her parents. They'd all lived together when Kailani was a baby, but they died fighting in the War of the Magicless. Her parents fought, too, but escaped to Saxton before things got too bad. Mom didn't talk about them much after the move. She never liked to talk about the war.

"It's beautiful," Kailani whispered, gazing at the robe, her heart fluttering. "But I can't accept it."

Mom frowned, but Kailani looked away from her. She didn't want to hurt her feelings, but this was ridiculous. "Mom, we could sell this at the Ceremony. I mean, look at it! We could get some money for the fine. I know it won't cover the whole thing. But we—"

Shaking her head sharply, Mom reached for the robe and set it aside, pulling Kailani in for a hug. "This is non-negotiable. Your grandmother wanted you to have this for your Ceremony. The gods would send her straight back down from the Wonder Grounds if she found out we sold it."

As her chest tightened, Kailani stared at the robe over her mom's shoulder. It really was beautiful and would fetch a high price. But she knew her mom, and her mind was made up. With a soft smile, Kailani pulled back from the hug to grab the robe again. Maybe having a piece of her grandmother with her during the Ceremony would give her strength. She'd need it, after all.

"Get dressed and I'll do your hair."

Rolling out of bed reluctantly, she shuffled towards her closet, rifling through the unkempt drawers. Everything was wrinkled, which felt about right seeing as her gut was coiled with dread. She glanced back at her wand, remembering the spell Mom had taught her to steam her clothes, but left it lying on the floor. She couldn't risk another outburst.

She put her new robe over her usual ensemble of jeans and a

black t-shirt. She was still dreading the Ceremony, still dreading what could happen with her magic, but—like always—just having Mom close calmed her.

Kailani sat down at her vanity and winced at the dark circles under her eyes. Maybe Mom would have an elixir somewhere for that. She'd given up a long time ago on trying to borrow any of Mom's cosmetics—Mom's skin was a rich brown, and her own skin was somewhere between that and Dad's pale skin. The result was that none of Mom's cosmetics worked for her, so she was left to turn to magical solutions.

Mom picked up a brush, then set it aside and raised her wand. Kailani bit back a sigh. She had the same issue with her hair as she did with cosmetics. While Mom's hair was fierce and free, and Dad's effortlessly shaggy and wild, Kailani's hair was hard to manage and often Mom's best charms couldn't tame the frizz, let alone a brush.

Wand in hand, Mom smoothed the frizz out of her hair as best she could, and soon her curls were perfectly in place.

Eyeing herself in the mirror, Kailani couldn't help but stare. Usually, she'd say that she was ordinary at best, while her parents' features were bold and brilliant.

Today was different, though. The shimmering robe was magnificent, and despite everything else going on, she couldn't wait for Lyla and Patrick to see it.

Grabbing her talisman necklace from her nightstand, she put it on, rubbing the stone.

"Ready?" she whispered into the stone, which lit up as she talked.

Not long after, the stone vibrated softly against Kailani's chest. She held it to her ear.

"Leaving," Patrick's voice whispered.

His voice was another balm to her fears and, for the hundredth time, she silently thanked Dad for charming the necklaces for them all those years ago. Squeezing her talisman, Kailani took a deep breath. Maybe she could get through today after all.

KAILANI STOOD at the front door, tapping her foot and staring at the clock.

Mom and Dad were running around the kitchen looking for Mom's lucky scarf, and Kailani was half a breath away from screaming. The last thing she needed was to miss the portal.

Huffing, Kailani pulled herself away from the door, stepping out into the fresh air. She breathed in Mom's lavender plants, willing herself to calm down. With every minute the Ceremony drew closer, her pulse pounded faster. Mom had calmed her earlier, but Mom wouldn't be there when she lined up to meet the Queen. As Kailani's hand reached up to curl around her talisman she heard footsteps, and her head jerked up.

A smile blossomed on her lips. Patrick was shuffling down the street with his father in tow, turning onto her driveway. His eyes were trained on the dirt path, his hands stuffed into his pockets.

Kailani stepped towards him eagerly.

Patrick must've heard, because he lifted his head, and his jaw hung open.

Grinning, Kailani strolled up to him, waving at Mr. Mahoney who stood a few paces back. As always, his glassy eyes stared at the overgrown weeds sticking out from the dirt and his shoulders stooped as if the weight of the world was on them. Fighting to keep a frown off her face, Kailani turned to Patrick. His face was red, as if he knew exactly what she was thinking, so she held out her arms to distract him with her new robe. His wide eyes blinked rapidly, then he laughed.

"Look at you breaking out your colors to impress me," Patrick taunted, throwing an arm around her shoulders.

Kailani relaxed into his embrace, already feeling better now he was here. "It was my grandmother's. Weird, right?"

His eyes lit up. "It looks like it was made for you." His face suddenly turned serious and he nudged her. "Hey, are you alright? You didn't answer any of my messages last night or this morning. What happened at the test?"

She held his stare for just a moment, her cheeks warming beneath the morning sun. This was Patrick, her best friend. She could tell him anything. She *did* tell him everything. Steeling her nerves, she opened her mouth to do just that, but then the roar of a portal swirling to life snapped her back to reality. Stomach lurching, she stared down the road at the waiting portal, then glanced back at the house. Her parents *still* weren't outside yet.

She closed her mouth, gnawing the inside of her cheek. A frown tugged at Patrick's lips, but then he glanced at a few of their neighbors jumping through the portal and his expression softened with understanding.

"We can talk about it later."

Kailani nodded, grateful for the reprieve. Only, now she was thinking about it again—the shattering glass, the Protector's touch. Despite the warm weather, she shivered.

Sensing she needed a distraction, Patrick nudged her again, his frown twisting into a smirk. "I bet Lyla is wearing that frilly pink robe she got last week."

Kailani looked to the portal, her anxiety increasing, but chuckled despite herself. "You know she will."

The moment was broken by clattering footsteps and a burst of laughter. Kailani didn't look at Patrick as her parents locked up and joined them, so vibrant and vital compared to his father. She knew he noticed too.

"Ah, Seneca," Dad said to Patrick's father. "How have you been?"

"Alright." Seneca's voice was barely audible. He didn't look at any of them as he spoke.

Mom gave him a hug. She didn't understand personal boundaries very well, but Seneca was like family. "How did you like the Sunny Disposition Potion I sent over? Did you notice a difference?"

Patrick's face turned red. Kailani locked her arm through his, and dragged him towards the portal. He'd practically grown up at Kailani's, and they were always there for each other. After his mother died, his dad had to pick up extra hours to afford their home, sometimes dragging on late into the night. Her parents had kind of adopted Patrick, and helped Seneca as much as they could. Their bond was unbreakable.

The vibrant blue of the portal started to dim.

"Oh no," Kailani whined, hitching her robe and picking up her pace. "Come on!"

Patrick scoffed. "You're just mad because you're always behind schedule."

"Five minutes does not make me late!"

He laughed and took off running. "Whatever you say."

Glaring at his back, she sprinted through the crackling gate of light. Her body was compacted and colors and shapes morphed together like a kaleidoscope.

Lyla was lucky. Her family had their own private portal. No fines, no regulations, and definitely no cut-off time of three minutes. Kailani snorted as she came out on the other side. No one in Saxton would ever have that kind of luxury.

Saxton scum, the Protector's voice whispered, and Kailani shuddered.

She pushed the thought aside as she drank in the sight before her.

The Choosing Ceremony was the biggest event of the year. Nearly everyone in the Kingdom came out for the event, and, as Kailani emerged onto the cobblestone paths of Magnolia, a sea of people were crowded into the Kingdom's most serene territory.

The air felt cleaner here, more refreshing, and a sense of calm washed over Kailani at the sight.

Mount Vita crackled with the energy of the gods of magic. The Strange mages always charmed the territory with an expansion charm, so there was plenty of room, and plenty to do.

Back in the day, the descendants of the gods would have a parade, put on a show. But now, Queen Stasorin and her uncle were the only descendants left, and the festival was hosted by the committee for The Advancement of Magical Society.

Mom's hand rested on her shoulder, and Kailani jumped.

"We're going to our seats. Good luck, Lani. You'll do great."

Kailani's hands shook. She looked around at the thickening crowd, her heart rate soaring. "Do you have to go now?"

"The Ceremony will start soon." Mom pulled her in for a hug and whispered, "No matter what happens today, we are *so* proud of you. After the Ceremony, we're going to go somewhere wonderful. You'll be able to see the water again."

Kailani pulled away, eyes wide. "What? Really?"

How could they afford a vacation with everything else going on?

"We've got it all worked out," Dad said, taking his hug now. "You'll do great, Lani. We love you so much."

Dad kissed her forehead, walking towards the mountain pass with Mom and Patrick's dad. Kailani rocked forwards onto her toes, ready to run after them, to beg them to come back. But she caught herself, squaring her shoulders as she watched them disappear into the crowd. If they weren't worried, then she shouldn't worry. Maybe it would all work out.

Maybe she would get to see the water again.

With that thought soothing her, she turned to find Patrick's eyebrow raised. Shaking her head, she grabbed his arm again.

"Let's go," she said, with as much cheer as she could muster.

Together, they walked towards the central square. Music and laughter filled Kailani's ears. Kailani's eyes darted every which way, but she'd never take in the entirety of the territory. The beauty of Magnolia was unreal. Tall, bushy trees lined the cobbled streets. Even though Magnolia still experienced seasons like the rest of the kingdom, the plants were charmed to withstand the cold, so they were always green and vibrant. Everywhere she looked, there were half-moon bridges curving over tiny streams, which flowed through the entire town. Each building looked like a palace compared to the considerably less funded Saxton territory, where Kailani was sure every building was designed by the same person who designed the kingdom's prison, Atonement.

Kailani led Patrick into the center square. She spun around, her cheeks aching from smiling so wide, and her stress seemed to melt away. The town square was much bigger than the one in Farrow. Shops lined the streets in every direction, striped awnings shading the storefronts. Colorful displays with everything from candy to robes filled the windows. Vendors of potion shots, delis, and pastries lined the streets and people bustled around, stopping to talk to people they knew.

Large projections danced in the sky, the same continuous loop that played every year plastered across different areas of the district. Kailani's eyes were drawn to them today. Talisia's emblem came first, followed by each legacy, then their symbols, most renowned qualities, and the abilities they would soon be given to master.

Kailani's stomach turned, and she dragged her eyes away. She should think about the vendors, about the promise of the sea, but her hands trembled as they walked the streets. Though she was no longer watching them, the symbols played on a continuous loop in her head, making her mind fixate on her botched showcase. Professor Linde may have charmed the others, but the gods still witnessed everything that happened in the showcase.

She pressed her palms against her forehead, groaning.

"Are you okay?" Patrick asked.

One. Two. Three.

She looked up, startled, as Patrick's hand gently curled around her left wrist.

"No." Kailani jerked her arm away, putting space between them as her stomach hollowed. She *wouldn't* let him use his powers. Her fears were her burdens to bear, and the last thing he needed was to add all her stress on top of his own.

Patrick frowned, slipping his gloves back over his hands. "I don't mind."

Smiling, Kailani stepped close again. "I know. I appreciate the offer, but I'm not doing that to you."

And anyway, him taking her worries away wouldn't stop the looming Ceremony.

Patrick leaned over and stuck his pinky out. "No matter what happens, we'll always have each other."

She wrapped her own pinky around his and smiled. "Forever."

As they continued to walk down the street, they spotted Lyla. Kailani stifled a shared laugh as she spotted Lyla's expected long, pale pink robe.

She stood a few booths over with her parents, and Kailani smothered a scowl. Blair Hollingsworth was badgering the shopkeeper about the quality of wandstones being displayed, and he shrunk away from her tirade. Kailani wasn't sure how such horrid people had managed to raise Lyla into a decent human being, because the Hollingsworths were awful.

The wands were displayed on the most elaborate suspended platform Kailani had ever seen. Stepping foot on the floating showroom would probably require mages to show proof they could afford to be there. She couldn't help but notice how the Hollingsworth family fit right in with the upper-class mages in Magnolia. It was more than their money, though they clearly had that. It was a sense of superiority that came with belonging.

But Kailani was used to the Hollingsworths by now. Dragging a smile to her face, she waved and shouted, "Lyla!"

Her friend spun, her eyes widening as she danced over. "Kailani, your robe!"

"It was my grandmother's." Kailani smirked, watching Mrs. Hollingsworth's jaw drop from the corner of her eye. Lyla's mother recovered quickly, her lips curling into her typical disdainful scowl. Kailani was experienced at ignoring it. "My parents were saving it for today."

"It's breathtaking." Lyla ran her hands over the embroidery, then grabbed a fistful of her own pink robe. "I got a new one, too, but it doesn't have a cool history."

Mrs. Hollingsworth put a hand on Lyla's shoulder and her smile vanished. "You'll wrinkle it before you even get to the mountain pass. Enough."

Lyla tensed, her eyes darting to the floor. Kailani's jaw clenched. As she was fighting not to say something *very* blunt, a bell rang overhead.

The crowd fell silent, and the absence of sound was a weight on Kailani's chest. The Hollingsworths and their snobbery was forgotten. She locked eyes with Patrick, and then Lyla, both looking as terrified as she felt.

It was time.

"Let's go find our seats. We'll meet you afterwards." Mrs. Hollingsworth paused to adjust Lyla's already perfect hair before grabbing the bags from her hand. "Good luck, dear. Remember to smile so that everyone can see you."

CHAPTER FIVE

*K*ailani took a deep breath.

Now the moment had come, she felt strangely calm. Relieved, even. At least it would be over and done with soon.

Lyla stared after her parents before turning and walking the opposite way, towards the mountain. "They've been unbearable."

Frowning, Kailani crossed her arms and followed Lyla. She wanted to point out that Lyla's parents were always unbearable, but she held her tongue. At least she didn't have to live with them.

A gentle breeze tossed Kailani's hair and laughter floated to her ears. She looked around the festival at kids crunching leaves, people laughing and playing carnival games. It was hard to believe that just last year, that was her, Patrick, and Lyla, completely unworried about the start of the Choosing. Their biggest concern had been how much food they could eat before the day was over. But now, the festival just seemed to mock her.

Did everyone feel this way before they were chosen?

Three girls who looked a few years older than Kailani walked past with blue Charm symbols embroidered on their white robes. Healers.

Lyla stared after them too, with longing in her eyes. "I just need to be chosen as Charm so they can get off my back."

Kailani sighed, thinking back to the Hollingsworths. "At least you have an idea who will choose you."

"But that's the exciting part, isn't it? Your possibilities are endless." Lyla dropped her head in her hands and groaned, rubbing her temples before finally looking back up. "My story has been written since I was born. My parents practically messaged the gods themselves guaranteeing me Charm magic."

Lyla tapped each finger to her thumb, a tell tale sign her anxiety was creeping up. Kailani looked down at her shoes as they walked in silence. She just wanted to get the Ceremony over with, so she could enjoy the rest of the festival with her friends. Lyla and Patrick probably felt the same way, but it was completely different for them. Lyla's path may have been carved for her, but a life as a healer was a comfortable one. And with Patrick's power of touch and empath abilities, he was pretty much guaranteed Vita magic.

Her Choosing was as unpredictable as her magic.

Kailani breathed in and out slowly, focusing on the mountain up ahead, letting Lyla and Patrick's voices fade away. As she strode a few paces ahead of them, she crested the next rise and her breath hitched.

The pink Magnolia trees the territory was named for released their intoxicating smell into the air as Kailani took in the breath-taking view that greeted her. Mount Vita towered above them, pebbles and pine needles lining a long, winding path up to the mouth of the pass. Six tall, narrow towers sat along the mountain-side connected by vast walls of sandstone. One shrine for each god of magic. The engraved symbols represented the six children the gods had sent long ago to establish Talisia. They'd built the shrines to honor the gods, and to allow them to visit where the veil of the otherworldly was just thin enough for the gods to choose mages to follow their paths.

Awed, Kailani only forced her gaze away when she heard a surge of other voices. They'd arrived at the line, and she eyed all the other fifteen-year-olds in front of them, not only from Farrow but from the other territories as well. Many were giddy, huddling together with their friends. Some sported golden ties across their robes, indicating they were children of the Magi Elite, the wealthiest families in Talisia. Most stood silent, their eyes locked on the mountain pass up ahead.

Kailani wanted to talk to them, to find out what life was like in Prestil, the Kingdom's military territory, or Regalia, the Kingdom's capital. How different they must be from Farrow. She'd never seen such intricate robes and wands in her life. Her classmates from Lancaster had some gorgeous wandstones, but when she looked around, she spotted kids with milky moonstones, deep green aventurines, even beautiful red ruby wandstones that sparkled from feet away. Her chest burned with longing. What she would give to test out such powerful stones. Perhaps it would amplify her magic.

Or maybe they would enhance the outbursts.

A shiver ran down her spine.

Her eyes were drawn to the projections up above, depicting the stage and large crowd on the other side of the mountain pass. Her eyes trailed the crowd, looking for her parents, but there was a sea of people waiting for their own family member to step out from the pass onto the stage. Kailani's hands started to clam up and she rubbed them on her jeans, not wanting to get her new robe dirty. Thinking about going through the magical pass inside Mount Vita, being face to face with all the territory leaders, Queen Stasorin herself on the opposite side of the quarter mile path—it was almost too much for her to handle.

A horn sounded and everyone fell silent, looking at the projection of the stage.

The crowd rose, and an anthem played as fog rolled around the bottom of the stage and Queen Stasorin stepped out. Her hair was pulled back in a tight bun at the base of her neck, her lavish emerald robe fluttering at her feet. The crowd cheered and clapped. Cameras floated around them, capturing every angle. The Queen waved to the crowd, motioning for them to sit before turning her wand into a microphone.

A hum of anticipation spread across the crowd on the projections, but behind the mountain pass, Kailani went deathly still. The other students seemed to do the same.

"Welcome, Talisia, to the 5071st National Choosing Ceremony. I hope everyone has been enjoying themselves thus far."

Kailani looked to Parick, but he offered her no comfort. His eyes were glued to the ground, his gloved hands shoved deep in his pockets. She dragged her eyes to Lyla, slowly counting in her head. Lyla mumbled to herself under her breath and stared up at the projections, nodding as if she was giving herself a pep talk.

If *she* was this nervous, what hope did the rest of them have?

A weight formed on Kailani's chest and energy swept through her body. Her magic flickered beneath her skin. Beads of sweat gathered on her forehead and she stared at her fingertips, silently begging them not to lose control.

"Today is a big day for our young mages. At fifteen years old, a mage's magic matures. The moment each of you step into the pass with your wands, your entire being will be evaluated. The gods and goddesses' past have determined the fate of each mage by way of this Choosing Ceremony to determine what legacy of magical practice is the best fit for each individual. Before today, students have had the ability to practice magic in each category, but never at full capacity. Some of you have attempted to train or study your way into a particular legacy. We will discover today if those efforts remain true to your destiny. As each of you know, the determination at the end of this ritual will be engraved directly into your wands and cannot be overturned. All rulings are final."

Behind Queen Stasorin, the emblem of the legacies appeared and the crowd cooed in amazement. The bright purple of Vita stood out above the rest and Kailani sent a silent prayer to the goddess of creation that she would choose her.

"You will spend the next three years of schooling perfecting your magic, training to become a vital part of this kingdom. Petitions for transfers to other territories will be considered only after your schooling is up and will be based upon skill and availability."

Kailani looked at Lyla and Patrick and her heart twisted. She could picture Lyla being transferred to this very territory, she'd fit right in at Magnolia Medical. And Patrick could surely score an apprenticeship doing something with magical creatures, traveling throughout the kingdom. She rubbed the back of her neck, an empty feeling in the pit of her stomach. If only she had an idea where she'd end up.

A golden roll of paper floated from the Queen's podium and she cleared her throat, smiling at the crowd. "The first of our graduates today, Cora Addington."

A girl with long black hair and a maroon robe stepped forward, staring up the rocky steps that led to the mountain pass. Cameras floated around her, broadcasting her face to projections in the sky. Cora's chin trembled. She looked about as nervous as Kailani felt. Taking a step forward, she held her head high and walked towards the pass, looking back at the cameras and smiling. Then she stepped in, disappearing into the mouth of the mountain.

Kailani couldn't help thinking about what the mountain pass would show her when it was her turn. If she was chosen as Vita, she'd probably see the endless hours she'd spent in her parents' shop, mixing and experimenting with any potion she could come up with. Maybe she'd see memories from when she was a kid, at the beach, or even her grandparents again. Warmth swelled through her at the thought. The earliest memories could shape the gods' decision, and she wouldn't mind reliving a few of them.

Minutes later, Cora emerged on the other side of the pass. She no longer looked timid and afraid, but she held her wand up in the air with a look of triumph on her face. Kailani squinted up at the projections as the crowds cheered, their voices echoing from the floating speakers surrounding them and from the other side of the mountain.

"Cora Addington of Viden, Bromerwald. Daughter of Shane Addington, teacher at Bromerwald Academy and Rupert Addington, Wandstone researcher at Testing Bureau of the Enrichment of Wandstones. You have been chosen as a Luminate mage." Queen Stasorin placed a pendant around Cora's neck, and the cameras zoomed in on a golden Luminate symbol engraved upon the pendant's stone. "Congratulations. Your apprenticeship, while you learn to control your matured magic, will be at Testing Grounds for Advanced Magical Genetics."

Cora stepped off stage and Queen Stasorin called the next mage to go through the mountain. One by one, the line of students dwindled down.

Kailani squeezed her eyes shut, taking deep breaths, counting in her head. Warmth buzzed over her skin. If she could just control her emotions, maybe she could control her outbursts.

When she opened her eyes, Lyla's face was deathly pale. Kailani willed herself to ask if she was alright, but her voice was gone. The words got stuck behind the expanding lump in her throat.

One of her classmates was granted Luminate magic, and a mage from Prestil was granted Kairo magic. She closed her eyes and let herself imagine what they were seeing as they walked through the pass. Leaders, scientists, healers, teachers—there were so many options for her future. But none of them spoke to her. Not like Charm spoke to Lyla or Vita spoke to Patrick. Lyla would probably see hours and hours of flipping through books, healing Kailani and Patrick's cuts and scrapes when they were growing up. She might see the sweet moments when she slid potion ingredients in Patrick's backpack, when she knew Seneca couldn't afford the school's assignments. Maybe she'd even see the day she broke it off with Lena, her one and only crush, when she realized Lena wouldn't hang out in Saxton.

Beside Lyla, Patrick's hands trembled. He'd probably see the hours spent reading about every magical creature in Talisia and beyond. He was obsessed with creatures; he could read their emotions and somehow formed a bond with any animal he came in contact with. Maybe he'd see the endless nights at Kailani's house, reading tarot cards and learning to see the future from Mom, or the hours experimenting with recipes with Dad and Seneca. He'd also see the countless emotions he took from people —his dad, when he was too drained to get out of bed. Lyla, when she was on the verge of a breakdown from the constant pressure her parents put on her. Patrick would even offer his services to mages in her parents' apothecary shop when he could sense they needed to unload, until her parents found out and put a stop to it. Patrick was such a good son, such a good friend.

She clenched her jaw, wrenching her gaze away from them. What she wouldn't give for another night of normalcy. Her, Patrick, and Lyla tucked away in her bedroom, each completely indulged in their own book of choice. Stopping every few minutes to snack and tell each other about what they were reading—no matter what was happening, no matter their differences, reading was their common ground.

She had no idea what would happen in the mountain pass, but with everything that had happened in the past twenty-four hours, the one thing she knew for sure was that everything would change. There would be no more peaceful nights spent reading with the two of them, curled up in her room or the shop. And if she couldn't keep her magic at bay, if these magical outbursts affected the outcome of her Ceremony, she'd have to tell Patrick and Lyla about them. She'd have to face them head on, and then what would they think of her?

"Lyla Hollingsworth," the Queen called.

The blood drained from Lyla's face as she locked eyes with Kailani, then Patrick. Reaching forward, Kailani wrapped her arms tight around Lyla and squeezed. She didn't let go until a camera hovered above them, inches from their faces, bobbing up and down as if telling Lyla to move along.

Kailani pulled away, grabbing Lyla's hand while Patrick grabbed the other.

"To the moon and beyond."

"To the moon and beyond," Lyla echoed, stumbling forward. Her palms steadied and she turned back to smile at them before entering the pass.

Kailani held her breath, her eyes glued to the projections. Lyla was smart. Brilliant, really. But until she got out from under her parents' thumbs, her nerves would always stand in her way. There were so many times when Kailani wanted to ask Lyla if she even *wanted* to be Charm. But every time the conversation got brought up, Lyla's anxiety would skyrocket. Kailani's heart hurt for her, and whatever it was that she was seeing in the pass, she hoped it would make her happy.

A mixture of sweat and body odor filled the air and Kailani shifted on her feet, staring at the projections in the air. Blair and Paul Hollingsworth were on one screen, a band playing on another. Patrick stared at the projection next to her, biting his lip. She opened her mouth to tell him to ease up before it started bleeding, but her words were drowned out by the crowd cheering loudly.

Lyla emerged from the mountain pass and Kailani's shoulders relaxed. Lyla looked relieved as she stood up straight and presented her wand to the Queen.

Stasorin spoke solemnly. "Lyla Hollingsworth of Lancaster, Farrow. Daughter of Paul and Blair Hollingsworth, both teachers at Farrow Elementary Magical Academy. You've been chosen as a Charm mage." Queen Stasorin placed a glowing blue necklace of the Charm symbol around Lyla's neck. "Congratulations."

"Thank you!" Lyla's eyes shone bright and Kailani smiled.

"Your apprenticeship will be with the medical administrator at the Williamson of Magical Wellness in Lancaster."

Lyla's face fell. Kailani's heart skipped a beat, and she blinked a few times, staring in shock at the podium for confirmation that she'd heard it wrong. She *must* have heard it wrong. Lyla would be perfect for the prestigious apprenticeship she'd hoped for at Magnolia's hospital, and no one else deserved it more than her. But Lyla's face was still pale and defeated. Desperately, Kailani's eyes shot to the projection of Lyla's parents, and for once in her life she actually wanted to see Mrs. Hollingsworth's smug smirk and her husband's superior, haughty look. She'd deal with their snobby attitudes if it meant she'd heard wrong, and Lyla had actually got the placement she wanted.

Their faces made her stomach sink through the floor.

Her mother's jaw hung open and her father's brows furrowed, but they were quick to recover with the cameras floating in front of their faces. Both Hollingsworths quickly smiled through clenched teeth.

Lyla stood in front of the podium in silence.

One moment passed. Then two. Kailani could only stare in horror. It just wasn't fair. Lyla had worked so hard for a placement that would help her on the road to Magnolia Medical, only to have it dismantled with an admin apprenticeship that would keep her healing skills at bay.

Kailani locked eyes with Patrick, who reached out instinctively to take away her pain before squeezing his hand into a fist. "She needs to say something."

"Anything," Kailani breathed.

Queen Stasorin cleared her throat, snapping Lyla out of her trance.

"Th—thank you, Queen," Lyla stammered, her face growing red. She stumbled off the stage and her parents rushed to pull her aside, dragging her out of the crowd as Queen Stasorin called another student forward.

"They'll petition for sure," Patrick whispered.

Kailani nodded, but she didn't think Lyla's parents held the proper status to get her placement changed, even if they sucked up to the monarchy. Her heart ached for Lyla, but maybe, just maybe, the three of them would still be together when this was over. Out of the three of them, Lyla was the one who was most likely to be given a great placement. So what did that mean for her and Patrick?

A student from Bromerwald, Talisia's technical advancement territory, came out of the mountain pass with Kairo magic. He was given an apprenticeship in Regalia with the council. Kailani's shoulders slumped. Being from Farrow—being from *Saxton*, Farrow's poorest district—they were destined to fail. The monarchy always reserved their best apprenticeships for the students who lived in territories that the monarchy benefited from.

"Patrick Mahoney," the Queen called.

Patrick's lip trembled as his desperate gaze shot to Kailani. "I can't do this."

Kailani grabbed his hand and squeezed. "You've got this." She nudged him forward. "Good luck."

Patrick quickly walked to the mountain, tripping on his over-sized robe. Snickers from the students echoed as he caught himself from falling. Kailani cracked her knuckles, her muscles quivering. Nothing ever went in his favor.

He hesitated in front of the tunnel for a moment, and Kailani held her breath.

Then he stepped inside.

Lyla may have been chosen as Charm, but if she and Patrick were both chosen as Vita, at least she'd still have him to go to classes and study with. Crossing her fingers, Kailani fixed her eyes on the projection of the exit from the tunnel. Her pulse jumped, her foot tapping, as she gnawed on her lip.

Come on, she thought.

Come on, come on, come on.

There—Patrick. He stepped out of the mountain and Kailani leaned forwards, squinting through the sunlight until a weight lifted off her chest. He was smiling, which could only mean one thing. Kailani let out a sigh of relief.

"Patrick Mahoney of Saxton, son of Seneca Mahoney, factory worker, and the late Mya Mahoney, you've been chosen as Vita."

Patrick's face brightened further as Queen Stasorin placed the Vita pendant around his neck.

"Your apprenticeship will be with a crystal miner at Lancaster's Stone Shop."

Kailani gasped, letting out a shaky laugh. Patrick would be going to Lancaster. Lancaster!

Patrick's mouth dropped and tears welled up in Kailani's eyes. "Thank you, Majesty," Patrick said, shaking the Queen's hand a little too enthusiastically. "Thank you."

Patrick ran off to find his father, beaming, and Kailani beamed too. Seeing such genuine excitement on their faces put her nerves at ease. If anyone deserved a break it was them. Patrick had grown up constantly wondering if his father would be able to make payments on their home, or at the very least, if he'd have enough to pay for food on their table. With an apprenticeship in Lancaster, it was possible for Patrick to get a job there after graduation. He was fascinated by the power each wandstone held, so he'd be a great fit. In Lancaster, he could probably make more than her parents made together. But more importantly, he'd finally be able to help his dad, and get the wand of his dreams.

Another classmate was called to the pass, jolting her back to the moment. Kailani looked around, but there weren't many of them left. The lump in her throat crawled back. Without Patrick and Lyla standing next to her, the mountain suddenly seemed bigger.

"Kailani Slate."

Kailani froze.

Her chest tingled. Heat rose to her face as she looked up, but she didn't move. Not for one second, then two. She could only stare at the mountain, which seemed impossibly far away.

One of her classmates jabbed an elbow into her back and she stumbled forward. Sucking in a long breath, and all too aware of the cameras broadcasting her face to the entire kingdom, Kailani forced herself to keep walking.

Her hands were still burning, still sparking. Her stomach was flip flopping all over the place. But she had no choice. At least it would be over soon.

Holding her head high, she stepped into the pass.

A swirl of colors filled the air. A cold breeze brushed against her skin as sparks ignited in the dark tunnel. Her brow furrowed. The colors seemed to be at war, vibrant blues, greens, purples, and reds twirling together, then lashing out. A streak of orange shot towards the top, and a flash of gold pulled it back down. Sand dunes appeared on the ceiling, the edge of a castle in the far distance. She'd never seen that castle before, what could that mean? Her stomach lurched. Was she going to be chosen as Kairo? She wouldn't be a good leader...

Kailani shuddered. Her heart pounded, and she tilted her head to the side. There was so much happening. Too much to see, to understand, and it was all changing so fast. She twisted around. A book appeared. She squinted, trying to get a closer look at the title, but a streak of gold slashed the scene and blue and purple swirled together.

Pressing her fingers to her pounding temples, Kailani groaned.

A purple light sparked and dimmed. An old couple smiled down over a woven bassinet. A familiar book was in the man's hand, *Spirit and Song*, a spell book her grandparents passed down to her. The man reached down and kissed a baby on the forehead. Her grandparents? Her great grandparents?

Heart aching, she tried to run, to get a better look, but the scene was gone, replaced now by trees. They stretched as far and wide as she could see. She was in the middle of a clearing and a cabin appeared behind her in the vast forest. She started towards the cabin, but faltered, the warring colors obscuring the scene.

The image switched and breathtaking salt flats covered the entire pass. There was a throne in the distance. A blonde girl sat there. Queen Stasorin? No, it wasn't her. But she resembled Stasorin. The same hazel eyes. The same petite nose. The beautiful girl smiled at her. It was a warm and welcoming smile that made her insides heat up, then drop as the girl's face transformed into a black hole and green flashes cut the scene. Stunned, reeling, Kailani stumbled back.

A long, metal staff floated in the air, a brilliant bloodstone encircled by sharpened points. She frowned. The staff got closer and closer until it was right in front of her face, then she shot backwards as the bloodstone exploded. All six colors swirled together in unison, spiraling out and forming a multicolored unity symbol—the symbol from the middle of the emblem.

Kailani's head whipped around. Her name echoed in various tones. Whispers grew louder, but she couldn't make out what they were saying. No one had ever mentioned voices before…

Then a single, deafening voice filled the pass.

"Kailani Slate."

Hands flying to her ears, Kailani whipped around, and her jaw dropped.

An ethereal woman floated in front of her, her long blonde hair seemingly glowing as her body floated inches above the ground. Her black crown shone bright in the mountain pass and her eyes sparkled. The woman opened her mouth to speak, and her voice boomed all around Kailani.

"Do you know who I am, Kailani Slate?"

Kailani could do nothing but stare, as a blast of cold air chilled the sweat covering her face. No one had ever mentioned having a *conversation* in the mountain pass. Just one more thing that was wrong with her. One more thing that wasn't normal.

"I see my descendants have failed to preserve my memory. How shameful." The woman looked over her shoulder, her long hair swishing around her, and her features abruptly became serious. "We don't have much time. You may know me as Fia—"

"Azarro," Kailani breathed, her voice rushing out of her as chills climbed her spine. The second she'd said Fia, the blonde hair and black crown had clicked in her memory. "You're the goddess of Darkness."

Fia dipped her head.

Kailani's mouth hung open. Strange magic... was she really being chosen as *Strange*? How could this be? Did the goddess interpret her outburst as malice? Kailani leaned backwards, putting distance between her and the goddess. A deep cold crept into her bones and she went numb. Would this be her life now? Tapping into the coldest, darkest, most terrifying parts of her magic?

She breathed slowly. This was happening, whether she liked it or not. At least she was being chosen. She could deal with the stigma later. Maybe Strange didn't have to be so scary...

"On the next blood moon, a strange evil will bring your kingdom to ruins. Only by wielding my staff can you stop the ritual from taking place. Embrace your power. Control your power. Before darkness succeeds."

Kailani blinked rapidly, making sure she wasn't dreaming, but Fia was still floating in front of her. Still talking, but faster now, more urgent.

"Save us, Kailani Slate. Save your people. Be our champion—"

Fia's eyes widened as she disappeared, then the pass went dark.

Kailani was at the end.

She turned around, there was nothing besides an empty walkway. The Ceremony was complete.

A sense of dread rose from her chest. Her heart pounded. She couldn't move.

Then she looked down at her wand.

Her stomach lurched and she whimpered. None of the six symbols were branded into the core. Instead, the unity symbol was carved into the metal.

This couldn't be real. If Fia wanted her to use her gift, shouldn't she be Strange? Shouldn't she at least have *one* of the symbols?

Her mind raced, searching for answers, but none came to mind. Trembling, she stumbled out of the tunnel. Kailani took one look at Queen Stasorin and cringed. She must look as disoriented as she felt, because the Queen's eyes narrowed at her.

Squinting, Kailani reached her hand up to block the bright sun. Her hand shook. The crowd seemed larger now that she was in front of them. She searched for her parents, but their faces were lost among the many. A terrible pounding throbbed behind her eyes. Sucking a deep breath in, she focused on putting one foot in front of the other to walk towards the Queen. Blood pulsed in her ears. Her eyes shot towards the exit behind the Queen's podium. If only she could run...

"Your wand, dear." The Queen was staring down at her.

Kailani lifted her wand. Her skin tingled.

Queen Stasorin's eyes widened, and she gasped. Kailani's mouth went dry. Her fingers tightened, her breathing stuck, and—

The heavy silence of the Ceremony shattered.

Kailani stumbled. A deafening boom echoed from the valley. Her head whipped up as a blast of debris swept over the assembled crowd. Gasps and screams filled the air.

Kailani dropped to the ground. Another blast went off somewhere behind her.

Everything seemed to be moving in slow motion. The crowd surged away from the mountain and the stage.

Sparks of light shot from all directions as Protectors attempted to gain control of the crowd, but people were panicking. *Kailani* was panicking. Her gaze swung wildly as she crawled to the lip of the stage, desperately seeking her parents.

There. Mom.

Their eyes locked and Kailani's stomach dropped. Mom looked afraid. But Mom was never afraid. The crowds of people were pushing back and forth but Mom struggled forward, trying to get closer to the stage. To her.

Kailani's fingers trembled, and she nearly lost her grip on her wand as she teetered on the edge. She debated staying put or jumping off the stage, but her feet were lead, and they were too heavy to move.

A scream tore through the air. A woman knelt over a still form, wailing and tearing at her hair, but she was lost behind more bodies falling. People were running. Screaming. Kailani's head spun. This couldn't be happening.

Mom was at the security gates, waving frantically for her to get off the stage.

A hand gripped her shoulder, pulling her to her feet. She whipped around and found herself face to face with Queen Stasorin once more.

"Come with me."

Kailani glanced at Mom. Dad was at her side now, trying furiously to break through the gate. Protectors ushered them away from the chaos.

A third explosion rocked the stage. Kailani screamed, darting towards the exit, but the crowd swelled. This time, when she looked for her parents, they were gone.

A Protector's meaty hand closed around Kailani's arm. She whirled around, eyes flying wide open, as a second Protector gripped her other arm. Her fingers dug into Kailani's skin.

"Come with us."

Kailani's heart raced. The noxious scent of smoke filled her nose. "Wait," she cried, but the Protector's grip tightened, and she stumbled forward. She tried to break free of their iron grips. "Mom!"

It was useless. Her arms pulsed under their grasp.

She staggered, almost losing her footing. Ringing filled her ears. Her vision blurred.

A blast sounded and Kailani was flung backwards, her head slamming against something hard.

Her eyes fluttered shut, and everything went dark.

CHAPTER SIX

*L*ights sparkled in and out of focus.

Kailani blinked rapidly, her head pounding against her skull. Blurred ceiling tiles came into view. She squeezed her eyes tight, the blinding light making the ache in her head pulsate.

Groaning, she tried to roll onto her side, but her body felt heavy. It would be easier to sleep, to keep her eyes closed and stop thinking.

A door creaked. Footsteps clattered.

Tensing, Kailani took a deep breath and opened her eyes to slits. She was just able to make out a man in a long white cloak, a blue charm symbol visible on his robe.

Oh *gods*. She was in a healer's room.

Chills raced across her skin as it all came crashing back to her: her time in the mountain, Fia, then the explosions. She'd been thrown back against the stage. The crowd was running wild. Kailani's pulse pounded, the room spinning. Were her parents harmed? Her friends?

"What's going on?" she rasped, struggling to sit up, but a burning sensation shot up her arms and her eyes flew wide.

She was secured to a bed.

Her breath hitched. She looked around wildly as the pain traveled from her wrist to her shoulder to her chest. In her panic, her head cleared and now she saw everything clearly. Thin, glowing ropes bound her wrists and ankles to a hospital bed. Tables lined the room with herbs, mortar and pestles, and gemstones. A sweet aroma filled Kailani's nose and she tried to place the scent. Shelves of potions and salves lined a wooden shelf and the healer pulled small glass vials, creating some sort of concoction on the table.

Heart racing, she tugged—but fire shot through her nerves, and a cry tore from her lips. The ropes tightened, the heat growing more intense. Surely they hadn't used death binders on her. She was only fifteen, and these were reserved for dangerous criminals.

But the ropes continued to sting.

Her eyes sought the healer, but his back was turned towards her as he leaned over a table.

"Help me," she cried, heart in her mouth.

If he heard her, he made no sign.

Kailani's fingers twitched towards the rope on her other wrist. If only she could loosen it, so it wasn't so painfully tight—but with every tug, the burn intensified, until tears poured down her cheeks and a scream lodged in her throat.

"Gods," she cried, "please!"

The healer finally turned, a mixture of confusion and sympathy on his face. "Please keep calm. The pain will only get worse if you struggle."

Kailani froze. Chest heaving, she stared through blurred vision at the healer. Horror and desperation raged like a storm inside of her. *Deathbinders.* Yes, the healer was right. As she fell still, the ropes cooled, and she was able to think. They'd learned about these ropes in school, about how they'd been charmed.

Now scared to move, Kailani laid still as her lip trembled. "Please, I…"

But the healer was turning away, moving back towards the door.

"No!" Kailani jerked forward, then slumped back as the ropes burned again. Cursing, she cried, "Please, wait, I…"

The door shut. The healer was gone.

Kailani's chest tightened, the pressure so intense she couldn't breathe. Her magic was a tempest brewing beneath her skin. Beads of sweat lined her forehead, and then a thought struck so hard bile rose in her throat. She'd destroyed the simulated door during the showcase, set fire to a table, shattered the glass at home —gods, she had done this. She had caused the explosions.

That's why they tied her up.

It was an accident. If she'd done it, it was an accident.

Squeezing back her tears, she tried to remember exactly what happened when she came out of the mountain pass. She was meeting the Queen, and then, she was ducking. Mom was running towards her. Then she was with Dad at the security gate. And she'd—

The door slammed open.

Kailani jumped, then cried out as the ropes tightened and seared her skin. She opened her mouth to beg, to plead, but the words died on her tongue.

Her eyes widened as two Protectors walked into the small room, followed by the Queen herself. She looked disheveled, shaken. Her hair fell in loose strands around her face and her emerald robe was full of soot. She met the Queen's eyes, but her thoughts were hidden behind a cold, steely mask.

Queen Stasorin walked slowly towards her, her boots clacking through the silence. Kailani could only stare as the Queen reached out a finger to curl under her chin. It was cold as ice. Kailani shivered, her thoughts racing back to the Protectors the night before.

"Hello, dear."

Kailani swallowed, once, and then twice. Her eyes were locked onto the Queen's icy gaze as she tried to speak, but her voice was hoarse.

"Please," she managed. "Where are my parents? Why am I here?"

Queen Stasorin pointed her wand and Kailani flinched, squeezing her eyes shut and digging her head into the pillow.

No, please! It was an accident!

She wanted to blurt out, to scream, but the Queen and the Protectors' presence filled the room with a thickening aura and Kailani couldn't get the words out. She braced herself for a spell, for pain—

But no pain came. The Queen recited a spell Kailani didn't recognize and a soothing sensation washed over her ankles and wrists as the ropes fell to her side.

Breathing shallowly, Kailani instinctively reached for her raw wrists.

Queen Stasorin grabbed the salve the healer had been working on, handing the liquid to Kailani. "I told them not to use those on you. Here, this will help the pain."

Kailani reached a trembling hand towards the mortar, recognizing the aroma now from her parents' shop. She spread the salve on her skin and the pain was immediately alleviated.

"Tell me about them," urged the Queen, her voice soft, "Your parents."

Kailani shook her head, trying to clear the pounding in her skull. This had to be some big misunderstanding. If she could just answer the Queen's questions, she'd be out of this whole mess soon.

She took a deep breath. "Their names are Tommy and Chelsea Slate, we're from Saxton—please, where are they?"

"They'll be here shortly. We're just clearing a few things up about the bombing."

Kailani's mouth dropped open. "The *bombing*?"

A pressure lifted from her chest. So it wasn't her magic after all. But did she say... why would anyone—?

"Kailani, we have reason to believe the rebel group calling themselves The Underground tried to stop the Ceremony from happening today. Have you heard about them?"

Rebels? Kailani placed her palm over her heart, tension unexpectedly releasing from her body. Tears welled up behind her eyes. So it really wasn't her magic.

But—oh *gods.*

Her stomach lurched.

Her parents... Lyla and Patrick...

She looked up, and the Queen was smiling down at her. "Your parents are safe. They will be here shortly. But we must know if they're in danger. Have your parents ever mentioned The Underground, Kailani?"

She tried to piece together her words. "I—no, I mean only from the news."

Queen Stasorin nodded. She was silent for a long time, her eyes fixed on Kailani. "Do they have any close friends? Family? Your parents, I mean."

"No." Kailani shook her head. Now that she'd started talking, it was easier. "Their family all died in the war, and their only friends are Patrick's dad and Professor Linde... but what does this have to do with the bombing?"

Her eyes flicked to the Protectors, looming in the shadows. Her skin crawled, and she returned her attention to the Queen's smiling face.

"We're just trying to figure out if anyone would have a motive to hurt them."

"Hurt them?" Kailani echoed, blinking rapidly.

"Since the bombs went off while you were on stage, we think you and your family may have been targets. Are they involved in anything dangerous?"

The words swam in Kailani's mind, and a chilled pit dropped

into her stomach. The rebels wouldn't target her family. They didn't have anything valuable, and Mom and Dad didn't have any enemies beyond the occasional disgruntled customer. They certainly weren't involved in anything dangerous.

"No, of course not. They run an apothecary."

"Of course, of course," said the Queen, nodding as she perched on the edge of the bed. "Do they go on a lot of trips, see a lot of people?"

"No. We…" Kailani's cheeks flushed, and she looked down at her shoes. "We don't really have a lot of money."

"Ah. I see." The Queen's brow furrowed, and she leaned closer to Kailani. "I know that can sometimes drive people, good people, to do things they wouldn't normally do. Do they ever take on extra jobs? Dabble in some… unsanctioned activities?"

Kailani recoiled. "No, never—"

"Are they in possession of anything that might attract unwanted attention?"

Kailani's mouth went dry. Her parents might have a few spell books that were banned, things they said the Queen could never know about. But that was harmless stuff, which had nothing to do with rebels and bombings.

"I'm not concerned about the law right now, dear. We're just trying to figure out if there's any reason you might be targeted."

The room closed in on Kailani, spinning in circles as her heartbeat thrashed in her ears. Who would target her family? They were nobodies. Just a simple family from Saxton. Unless the symbol on her wand…

The doors burst open.

Kailani shrunk back, her eyes wide with horror. Kiran Azarro, the Queen's famously awful uncle, stode in. His face contorted into a rageful smirk, and Kailani shuddered as the rumors about his thirst for power and cruel reputation circled in her mind. Unspeakable horrors, countless slaughters, carnage and destruction… Some of it had to be exaggerated, but the facts were cemented in history classes: he'd been passed over for power on the royal council many times, first for his brother and then for the Queen herself, back when she was only nineteen. After that, he'd become even more ruthless and cruel. Now, eleven years after the royal council was slaughtered, he'd become the most powerful man in the kingdom, second only to the Queen.

And to hear it from the rumors, she didn't exactly keep him on a tight leash.

Kailani trembled, magic pounding against her skin as her heart raced faster, and faster, until her power was roaring to be released. She squeezed her eyes shut, willing her magic to stay inside, where it couldn't do any more damage.

"The rebels have been apprehended." Kailani's eyes snapped open at Azarro's deep voice, and his eyes traveled from Queen Stasorin to Kailani. He looked feral, unhinged. "Has she spoken yet?"

Kailani's stomach dropped.

Queen Stasorin glared at him. "I am handling things, Uncle."

But she'd told her everything she knew, her parents didn't have anything to do with this—

Azarro was in front of her before she could think, let alone speak, rushing forward to slam his hands on either side of her chair. His face was inches from hers, and Kailani shoved herself back. "Your parents will rot in Atonement for what they did today. I suggest you tell us everything you know."

Kailani's eyes darted to the Queen as her heart pounded. She thought her family were the targets, but he was acting like they were the criminals. But the Queen simply stood there, watching as if mildly curious, and Kailani's eyes burned.

Azarro slammed a fist against the chair. Kailani screamed.

"Don't look at her, girl, look at me."

Shaking, Kailani did. The rage burning in his eyes made her wish she could sink into nothingness. "I... I don't..."

Queen Stasorin cleared her throat. She didn't say a word, but she didn't have to.

Azarro pulled back immediately, though the look he shot at his niece wasn't much nicer than the one he'd pinned on Kailani. Still, he didn't move far from the chair, and Kailani stared at her feet, trying to remember how to breathe.

"Kailani." Queen Stasorin's voice was cold. "I know it's hard to hear, but we have reason to believe your parents were involved in the bombing today. If you know anything, it is imperative you tell us now. It could save their lives."

Kailani's vision blurred. This couldn't be happening. This was a mistake. Pressure built behind her eyes and she shook her head wildly. "No, you're wrong!"

With a growl, Azarro stepped in front of the Queen. "Stop treating her like a child and start interrogating."

He leaned closer again, stopping just inches from Kailani, his breath hot on her cheek. The Protectors from last night flashed in her mind and bile rose in her throat. Recoiling, she squeezed her eyes shut. She'd thought that had been the worst night possible, but apparently, she was wrong.

It had to be a dream. A horrible dream caused by the stress of the Ceremony.

Wake up! Wake up!

"Tell me everything you know," Azarro hissed in her ear, "and I might let your parents live."

It didn't feel like a dream.

Kailani's breath was raspy. Her hands flew to her face as she sank further into the chair. She didn't know anything, and there was no way her parents were involved. She tried to tell him, but her throat constricted, robbing her of speech. He was too close, and his breath reeked of rot, and—

The looming closeness of Azarro withdrew and a breath escaped Kailani's lips.

Then something stabbed at her throat and her eyes flew open.

Her heart pounded in terror—his wand pressed into her skin. "Who are they working for?"

She could only shake her head. "No one," she rasped, desperately.

Apparently, this wasn't the answer Azarro had been hoping for. He dug his wand deeper into the flesh of her throat. "Why do you people insist on lying to me?" he snarled. "Do you really care so little for your parents? This is your last chance. Tell me the truth."

Kailani shook her head. She could hardly breathe—let alone speak—and her eyes burned from the overwhelming reek of Azarro's pine cologne. "I'm not lying—"

"Fine." Azarro withdrew the tip of his wand from her neck and stepped back. Kailani yelped, but the relief was short-lived. Her eyes widened as Azarro aimed his wand at her forehead.

"Have it your way." Azarro's grip tensed. The whites of his eyes began to fill with a gruesome black liquid. Then, he whipped his wand forward, voice booming: *"Conlida!"*

Electricity shot through Kailani's body. Her back arched, jaw ripping open in a silent scream. Pain coursed through her, hot and biting and oppressive; thousands of blades tearing her skin into ribbons, thousands of hammers breaking her bones.

Then it stopped. Kailani fell to the floor, wheezing to catch her breath. When she looked up, she realized with terror that the world had gone dark.

Am I dead?

Kailani staggered to her feet. It felt as if her limbs were fighting through honey, but she forced them to move. She shivered as the air around her dropped rapidly.

"Kailani, help!"

Dad?

Kailani turned around. "Dad!" she gasped.

Dad lay on the ground before her, sunken waist-deep into the darkness. "Kailani, what's going on? What is this place?" Dad's nostrils flared, betraying his anger, but his body was rigid. The shadows were like quicksand, swallowing him inch by painstaking inch.

"I'm coming, hold on!"

Kailani broke out into a run and began to race towards Dad. Yet, the floor stretched impossibly beneath her, and her feeble attempts to get to him were only punished by a widening gap between them.

"Kailani, why aren't you doing anything?" Kailani's head spun around. The shadows were swallowing Mom too. Mom reached for her as she sunk further into the darkness, her voice cracking and sounding so far away. "Help me! Please!"

"Kailani!"

Kailani whipped around. Behind her, Patrick and Lyla suffered the same fate—but the shadows had eaten them up to their necks. The voices grew as their bodies sunk deeper and deeper, bouncing off the walls in a horrendous cacophony of tortured echoes.

"Kailani!"

"Help! It hurts!"

"Don't you love us?"

Kailani could do nothing. She felt tears spring to her eyes—misery, frustration, and shame, all taking the same liquid form as she fell to her knees and slammed her fists against the ground. She nearly wailed in frustration when the impact caused her no pain. She needed something to ground herself with. Anything.

"Stop!" she screamed. "Please, I can't…"

They were all calling her name. But who was coming to help her?

Kailani called on her magic, but the thread beneath her skin was far away. She begged her powers to come through so she could save herself from this nightmare. But there was no reprieve. She sunk further into the shadows, her mind a cacophony of screams and jeers. Louder. Louder. Until she could hear nothing else.

"*Uncle.*"

Kailani blinked. She was back in the room with Azarro and Queen Stasorin. She took tender, shaky breaths as her head drooped to her chest in defeat.

"That's enough," Stasorin warned.

"Enough?" Azarro scoffed. "She was hardly under my spell for ten seconds."

Kailani blinked rapidly, her chest tingling. There was no way that was only ten seconds, it felt like hours.

Queen Stasorin's voice was hushed. "I said enough. If this gets out, if the public finds out you tortured a child—" She sucked in a harsh breath, but Kailani didn't have the energy to lift her head. "This is *not* an interrogation. We will question her when she is of sound mind."

The pain of the spell vanished. Kailani's shoulders sagged, and she gasped for breath as tears fell from her closed eyes. It wasn't real. She was back in the room with Azarro and Stasorin. It was just a spell.

She fought to keep still as her chest burned with sobs.

"That's a mistake, Nina." Azarro spat the Queen's name like she was a child being scolded. Kailani lifted her eyes. "We have a chance of gaining valuable information while she's in—" He smirked. "This state of mind."

An ache formed in the back of Kailani's throat. That spell had to be Strange's illusion magic. He must've used it to try and break her mind, to try and get her to slip up and give him information about her parents.

Well, he failed. They were innocent.

"We're done," Queen Stasorin snapped, stepping in front of Kailani.

Azarro's eye twitched, and for a moment the black liquid that filled the whites of his eyes was back. Kailani's teeth chattered as he growled, a look of pure derangement spreading over his face.

Then he straightened, with a mocking salute to the Queen.

"Yes, Your Majesty." Azarro walked towards the door, but paused in the doorway. "Soon, you will have no choice but to follow my will."

Then, he left.

Kailani let out a breath. The pain was gone, but her heart was lead in her chest. Queen Stasorin's eyes were narrowed at the door as it slowly clicked shut, blocking them off from Azarro.

For now.

The fear was back, sealing her throat. If he was willing to torture her with Strange magic, what else was he capable of doing to break her? He was horrible, evil, and she never wanted to see him again—

Kailani's eyes widened.

Evil. *Strange* evil.

The goddess's words came back to her, floating around in indistinct phrases. *A strange evil. Before darkness succeeds.*

Could the goddess of darkness have been talking about Azarro?

"Baylock," Queen Stasorin called, crossing the room and picking up Kailani's wand. The General of Farrow territory appeared in the doorway, locking eyes with Kailani.

Kailani hunched over. Drained.

The Queen held her chin higher. "Take the kid. And don't forget our conversation."

General Baylock grabbed Kailani's arm and pulled her to her feet. She swayed as her her knees threatened to buckle. The world swam before her eyes. Kailani tried to jerk away, to run. To where, she didn't know. She didn't care. But General Baylock squeezed her arm tightly. Unsteady, Kailani looked back once, locking eyes with Queen Stasorin, as General Baylock pulled her out of the room.

CHAPTER SEVEN

*B*ile rose in Kailani's throat and she leaned forward to throw up, but then her body slammed into the ground. Stunned, she looked up through swollen eyes.

A cold draft floated from the ceiling, surrounding dreary gray stone walls that illuminated in the flickering light. For a long moment, Kailani wondered how the hospital grounds had changed so dramatically in one breath. Long metal bars now stretched before her, and she could see others beyond, in the shadows. A horribly damp smell crept up Kailani's nose and a jolt of fear shot through her body.

Protectors.

There were Protectors everywhere, guarding, watching, staring. Pressing her shaking hands to her mouth, Kailani looked up at the General, whose eyes were full of sorrow.

She'd teleported her to the dungeons.

The hair stood up on Kailani's arms. She didn't know which territory they were in, but it didn't matter. They thought her parents were the rebels, so they were locking her up. Her ears burned. Her heart raced. She couldn't stay here; she hadn't done anything wrong.

Her knees shook as General Baylock escorted her down the row of cells. People were curled in the deep, dark corners. Sniffling and moaning escaped from the cells. Kailani's eyes widened. Frantically, she searched for her parents, but General Baylock pulled her along to an empty cell in the back. A Protector pointed his wand forward and the iron bars slid open with a click.

"I don't understand." Kailani's voice cracked. As she looked around, her heart dropped into her stomach.

This couldn't be happening, she couldn't prove her parents innocence from *here*.

General Baylock pulled Kailani into the cell. In one corner, a thin mattress with disheveled sheets was shoved against the wall. In the other stood a small, dingy sink, with a single toothbrush and toothpaste. Paint chips peeled from the damp walls, symbols and words sprawled along every inch. A mixture of must and bleach filled her nose. Kailani collapsed on the saggy mattress, springs squeaking under her. Her body throbbed, but she didn't care. She didn't care if the entire place blew up, because what difference would it make?

"You'll stay here until things are sorted out."

"But please," Kailani whimpered, wiping her eyes. Sweat and soot blurred her vision. "I didn't do anything—I—"

General Baylock locked eyes with Kailani and a lump formed in her throat. "Do what you're told, and all will be well."

She pulled the cell door shut with a bone-shaking clang.

EVERY BONE in Kailani's body ached.

She cracked her eyes open, wincing as light blared through and pain split her head. Groaning, she forced her head up, blinking back the pain as she tried to absorb her surroundings. Her heart lurched into her throat.

A cell. Prison.

Kailani's eyes burned. Resting her head against the cold stone wall, Kailani waited for her eyes to adjust to the wavering light. The blankets were scratchy on her skin, and her neck ached from the lumpy pillow. She didn't know how long she'd been locked up. Worse, she still had no idea what had happened to her parents or her friends.

From outside her cell, someone coughed and footsteps crept in the distance. Kailani instinctively reached for her wand, but her pockets were empty.

Without her wand, she didn't have any hope.

A sob escaped her lips. The Queen would know of the symbol, surely. If she had her wand, could she use it to hear Fia's quest? Know who the quest was about? And, if it was about Azarro, what did that mean for her? She was here, locked up, with no means of getting out. And she had no idea what ritual she was supposed to stop, or how.

Kailani gasped as a thought struck her. She reached under her robe to grip her talisman necklace, and a surge of energy pulsed up her arm. Her necklace. Her friends.

Kailani squinted into the shadows beyond her cell. No doubt there were Protectors close, but she couldn't see any. Heart pounding, she licked her lips and squeezed the talisman tight.

She took a deep breath, hope blossoming in her chest.

"Is anyone there?" she whispered.

Slowing her breathing, she counted in her head to thirteen. It didn't work to calm her nerves, but she tried again, desperate to keep any semblance of her old life intact. Her parents would be proven innocent, and she'd be out of here in no time. The monarchy would realize this was all a mistake and everything would go back to normal.

Her stomach twisted. Even if that were true, life would never go back to normal. Ever since the showcase, her magic churned beneath the surface of her skin as if it was no longer under her command. It came and went, soothed and surged. And then there was the unity symbol on her wand. How could something like this happen to *her*, of all people?

But Fia Azarro had stood in front of her. Called her by name and given her a quest.

Shaking her head, Kailani laughed bitterly. Just yesterday—or days ago, depending on how long she'd been stuck here—her greatest worry had been the fine. She'd thought the raid was the worst thing that—

Kailani's eyes widened.

The *raid*. Dad had come out of the living room, and hadn't she seen a flash of somebody else? Heart pounding, Kailani gripped her talisman tight. The Protectors had been so aggressive. Maybe…

No, they couldn't possibly be involved with the runaway rebels. It was a ridiculous notion, and she hadn't seen anybody.

Wrapping her arms around herself, she breathed in deeply. The warm, musty smell wasn't helping her churning stomach. Nor were the muffled groans and cries of the prisoners she couldn't see.

Her parents were *not* rebels. Sure, they had some spell books that were deemed illegal, but none of them were dangerous. Just some old books passed down from their ancestors, back before the monarchy put so many restrictions on learning. They would never hurt anyone…

Kailani jumped as the talisman vibrated against her chest. Gasping, she grabbed the stone and pressed it to her ear.

"Kailani."

The weight on her chest eased and her eyes fluttered shut. *Patrick.*

Standing, she peeked out from the iron bars. No one was there. She held the stone to her lips and whispered as low as she could.

"Are you okay? How's Lyla?"

"We're okay, Kailani, where are they holding you?" Lyla's voice shook through the stone, and despite the fear in her friend's voice, Kailani let out a breath of relief. She was alive.

"I'm—" Kailani's voice cracked. A prisoner yelled down the hall and Kailani's throat sealed. So much had happened. So much had changed. But if there was any chance of salvaging any of this, she needed information. "What happened at the Ceremony?"

"It was chaos," Patrick said. "Bombs went off and the crowd went wild. It looked like they came from the mountain. Everyone was so confused. But Kailani… what they're saying on the news…"

"It wasn't them." Her voice came out loud—too loud. She clapped her hand over her mouth and muffled the talisman, not catching whatever Patrick said next.

One moment went by. Then two. No Protectors.

She lifted the talisman back to her ear as Patrick's voice came through. "I went by your house, but the Protectors ransacked it. I'm going back tonight to make sure they didn't take anything."

"No, Patrick!" Kailani's heart raced, and she fought to keep her voice down. "You can't go there."

"They can't keep you! You didn't do anything wrong!"

"Yeah!" Lyla chimed in. "What they're saying about your parents is insane."

"Listen to me." Kailani shot another look beyond the bars of her cell. "Don't go to the house. If the Protectors question you, just—" She trailed off, floundering. How could she give advice? She didn't know what to suggest, what they could possibly do. All she knew was that Lyla and Patrick couldn't get wrapped up in whatever *this* was. They'd been chosen by the gods. Their futures were bright. Swallowing a lump in her throat, Kailani forced her voice to steady. "Just distance yourself from me as much as possible. For your own safety."

"No," Lyla said sharply. "No, you're our best friend, Kai, and you haven't done anything wrong—"

"We were with your parents when the bombs went off,"

Patrick said. "They came from the mountain. Kailani, they'll be proven innocent."

A creaking noise came from down the hall and Kailani froze. "Quiet!"

She squeezed the talisman stone tight in her hand, holding her breath as she stood, straining her ears to hear whoever was about to walk down the hall of cells. But no one came. Kailani waited, blood pounding in her ears, but as the seconds stretched, she relaxed. It must have been another prisoner. Sinking to the ground, she dragged her thoughts back to what Patrick had been saying. If the bombs had come from near the mountain, then her parents would have been nowhere near them. They were innocent.

"I know," she whispered into the stone. "This is all just... a misunderstanding."

For a moment, there was a heavy pause and Patrick and Lyla whispered something Kailani couldn't quite make out. Her heart ached. They were still together. Without her.

Then Lyla spoke, her voice soft and hesitant. "There *have* been some strange reports though. Is it true that you have the unity symbol on your wand?"

Kailani was silent. A chill trickled down her spine. She could picture Lyla's rigid parents huddled around their news reporting station talking about how they 'always knew' Kailani was trouble. She could only imagine the things they were saying about her parents. About her.

"Yeah." Kailani swallowed. "It's true."

"That is so cool!" Patrick's voice crackled so loudly that Kailani winced, shoving the stone beneath her robe. She really needed to put the stone away, but talking to Patrick and Lyla was the best thing that had happened in—days? Hours? It was impossible to tell how much time had passed.

Patrick's voice jolted her out of her thoughts. "But what does that mean? Did the gods give you a quest?"

Groaning, Kailani dropped her head onto her knees. "I guess, but it has to be a mistake."

Lyla's voice was suddenly proper, like they were back in school listening to one of her lectures on misunderstanding the homework assignment. Despite everything, Kailani smiled. It was a little slice of normal in all the chaos.

"According to legends, the unity symbol signifies a blessing from all the gods. Typically, the chosen champion will be given a quest that only they can complete. It's only been reported twice in the Kingdom's history—"

"Both times when the kingdom was on the brink of destruction," Patrick chimed in. "Once they do, they're rewarded with riches and fame."

"And of course, the kingdom doesn't crumble," Kailani muttered, her heart sinking. Now that they mentioned it, she vaguely remembered a conversation they'd had while reading one night, years ago, when Patrick found the legend in an old book. "But this isn't a legend, it's real life. And I'm not a champion. It *has* to be a mistake." Another creaking sound came from down the hall, and her breath hitched. "I have to go," she whispered urgently into the stone. "I'm serious, keep your distance—"

"Kailani—"

She shuddered as her stomach turned to ice. Flashes seared her mind, of burning rope wrapped around Patrick and Lyla's wrists, Azarro inflicting his interrogation methods upon them. She could picture it clearly, and suddenly Kailani was trembling again. How could she feel any hope when she'd *met* Azarro? She'd felt the agony of his torture as his magic put her in a state of despair.

Wincing, she tried to block the images forming in her mind, but she could hear screaming. And she couldn't tell if it was her imagination or her friends screaming from the other end of the necklace. Biting her lip, she shook herself, the moss-slick walls fading back into focus. There was no sound except the leak of the faucet, the shuffling of other prisoners.

"Look, until this is all figured out, just *please* do this for me."

"Okay." Lyla's voice was soft, shaky. "We love you. Everything will work out."

Footsteps clanged against the flat stones in the hallway, and voices echoed in the cavern. Breathing rapidly, Kailani shuffled the stone under her robe. She kept a death grip around it, praying that neither of them spoke and drew the Protectors' attention. The voices grew louder and louder, and every muscle in her body tensed as she stared through the bars with wide eyes, her heart hammering.

Then the voices and footsteps faded away.

She didn't dare move, but when she'd gone through her counting four times and the only sound was still the haunting drip of a leaky pipe, she edged an inch closer to the bars.

The coast was clear.

It took a few seconds of staring at the dark, endless stone hallway before her eyes caught up with her mind and she finally allowed her fingers to unclench from around the stone. With a deep, ragged gasp of air, she wiped the sweat from her forehead.

Moisture stung her eyes, and she bit the inside of her lip to keep the tears from falling.

She wanted to cry to Patrick and Lyla, to go over every last detail until it all made sense. But she couldn't risk the Protectors overhearing and going for their families. It was bad enough that she'd talked to them at all. Slumping against the moist cement walls, she slid down to the floor, bringing her knees to her chest and choking back another sob.

Between the unity symbol, Fia Azarro's quest, and her parents, this was all too much. She was no champion, she couldn't even control her magic. The quest was make-believe. A legend that made people feel better about a kingdom's dark history. But she couldn't stop replaying Fia Azarro's words in her head.

On the next blood moon, a strange evil will bring your kingdom to ruins. Only by wielding my staff can you stop the ritual. Embrace your power. Control your power. Before darkness succeeds.

Even though she was sure this wasn't real, that she couldn't be a champion, Kailani couldn't help wondering.

What would happen the night of the blood moon?

CHAPTER EIGHT

*W*hen a door slammed open, startling Kailani awake, she knew they were coming for her this time.

Footsteps pounded down the dark hallway. Kailani's hair lifted from the nape of her neck, and paralyzing fear shot down her spine. She backed into the dark corner of the cell, trying to make herself invisible, but it didn't work. Three Protectors appeared before her, pointing their wands while the tallest of the three unlocked her cell. Kailani lifted her hands in front of her face and yelped, the burns from the deathbinders flashing in her mind.

"*Amarra!*"

Ropes flew from the tip of the Protector's wand and the splintery rope dug tight into her raw skin. She pressed her body against the cold stone wall, desperate to get away as they rushed forward.

Her body tensed. "Please," she cried, unable to stop herself whimpering, "I don't know anything."

"*Minuo!*" another Protector shouted, and Kailani's magic slipped away under his Brute spell. "Come on," the Protector grumbled, pulling her to her feet and dragging her through the door.

She sagged between them, her body going limp, like all the blood rushed out of her at once. Chills raced up her skin. Her body tensed, and fear took over. One second her magic was empty, the next, it was a swell inside her ready to burst.

Only, she was too terrified to fight, and her chaotic Brute magic was no match for the Protectors trained fury. Her voice rattled as she tried again, whispering, "Where are you taking me?"

The Protectors were silent, hauling her along the narrow hallway. The musty air was thick with a dampness that clung to Kailani's skin; the sickening scent of blood filled the air. She fell over herself on the uneven ground beneath her, and the *drip, drip, drip,* of a distant pipe was the only thing she could focus on as she tried to keep her mind from wandering back to the hospital room with Azarro. Groans and whimpers came from the adjoining prison cells. Her eyes darted left and right. She dreaded seeing her parents, hoped to see her parents.

As Kailani's heart rattled in her chest, she locked eyes with an older woman pressed up against the bars of a cell. It was such a shock to see somebody else that Kailani dragged her feet, tried to linger. Her robes were tattered and falling off her shoulders and she was thin, feeble. Her skin was sallow and her eyes were dark with exhaustion. She didn't look like a criminal, but she must have done something to end up here.

Maybe she was a rebel.

Or maybe she, too, was being held without proper trial.

The woman smiled, and the Protectors yanked Kailani away.

Wincing at the Protector's grip on her arms, Kailani swung her gaze to the door ahead, trying to ignore the sticky feeling in her gut. The knowledge that it could lead anywhere made a pit yawn wide in her stomach. Freedom. Another cell. An interrogation room. Bars rattled in the distance and a shriek made Kailani's bones go cold. She closed her eyes, hoping to escape—

Fresh air washed over Kailani as the Protector flung the door open. The relief was so great her knees gave out, and she would have fallen if the Protectors didn't catch her. Leaning on them, she tipped her head back, sucking in long breath after long breath.

The hydroponics factory loomed far in the distance. Stormy clouds floated ominously around the peak of the tower. Blinking rapidly, Kailani shifted her gaze to a building sign.

Lancaster Court House

Kailani's breath caught. They were in Farrow.

Maybe they really *were* setting her free.

The Protectors led her behind the building to a small patch of grass with a few picnic tables. A sour taste filled her mouth as her relief turned to dread. General Baylock and Queen Stasorin sat together. The other two tables were empty. Queen Stasorin turned towards her, smiling, but the smile quickly disappeared as her eyes landed on Kailani.

"No need for restraints." The Queen glared at the Protectors. "She's a child."

Kailani's heart fluttered. The Protector pointed his wand at her wrists and recited a spell. The ropes fell to the floor. Kailani wiped her sweaty hands on her jeans as her mouth went dry.

The Protectors retreated, eyeing each other, but they lingered from the corner of her eye. She tried to ignore them, and how her entire body shook. She tried to focus on the cool air, and the pockets of sunshine that created shafts through the gray sky—how good it felt to be outside despite the dewy mist in the air.

Queen Stasorin reached out as if in slow motion and placed a hand on her shoulder. Her blonde hair flowed freely as her violet robe fluttered in the breeze.

"Sit." Her voice was calm but commanding.

The pressure in Kailani's chest built as Queen Stasorin settled next to General Baylock like they were old friends. Baylock's face could've been carved from stone. Her eyes never left Stasorin as the Queen leaned back and patted the spot next to her.

Kailani staggered, lowering herself stiffly in the seat.

Queen Stasorin stared at her like she was waiting for Kailani to speak, but Kailani had no idea what she could say. Insisting she was innocent hadn't worked so well so far. As the silence stretched, the Queen smiled, and Kailani wanted so badly to take comfort from that smile. Only, it didn't reach the Queen's eyes, which were cold and unblinking.

Kailani shivered.

Queen Stasorin tilted her head. "Let's get down to business, shall we?"

Kailani's shoulders hunched inward, as she looked from Baylock back to the Queen. "Alright…"

"I wanted to personally come check on you, Kailani. I know it can be hard to accept when your parents break the law—"

"My parents didn't break the law. They're innocent." The words came out like vomit. Kailani squeezed her palms together, wincing at the Queen's annoyed expression.

Queen Stasorin was quick to recover, though, plastering her smile back on. "It's normal to feel that way. But some very trust-worthy people came forward to testify—"

Kailani shook her head, gripping the edges of the bench. Her chest pulsed, like something was trying to rip out of her. Her breath hitched and goosebumps raced along her skin. If someone testified, then her parents would be tried and possibly even executed. There couldn't be proof they'd set off the bombs…

"Who testified?" Kailani stammered.

"The *who* is not important, what is important is the *why*. If you can help us understand, Kailani, we may be able to help keep your parents alive."

Her words were like a punch to the stomach. The Queen went in and out of focus as she processed the words. Mom, who spent her days talking to flowers and saving animals, and Dad, whose heart was bigger than any fine the monarchy could throw their way. They *wouldn't* do something like this. They were peaceful.

As tears filled her eyes, Kailani tried to piece together her fuzzy thoughts. Her hands shot to her head.Her body shook violently. She tried to speak, but words wouldn't come out. She had no control…

"Kailani, it's okay, dear. Let's take it back a notch. Let's focus on you. Do you have any family outside of your parents?"

Kailani stumbled over her words, struggling to breathe. "Um, no, not living."

Queen Stasorin nodded. "And have you ever lived anywhere outside of Farrow?"

A breath. "We moved from Magnolia." This was easier. "When I was a little kid."

Queen Stasorin nodded again, seemingly pondering Kailani's words. "And your wand."

"My—my wand?"

Queen Stasorin nodded towards Baylock. Kailani gasped as the General pulled her wand out and handed it to the Queen. Watching it with hungry eyes, Kailani yearned to hold it again, fearful of what the Queen might do. Her eyes flicked to Baylock, whose lips were pursed, and Kailani's anxiety skyrocketed. She was shaking so hard the bench trembled, and she didn't know if it was from her broken magic, or her fear.

"The symbol of unity," Queen Stasorin said breathlessly.

She didn't look angry; she didn't even look smug. She looked just as confused as Kailani.

Sparks ignited in her chest. She thought back to her conversation with Patrick and Lyla, trying to remember anything else she may have learned about the symbol in school. No one had paid it much attention; they were too concerned with what branch they'd get. But the unity symbol connected them all.

Without unity, there'd be no peace.

But why had the gods given *her* the symbol?

"There is quite the legend surrounding the unity symbol, but to my knowledge, it's just that. A legend," Queen Stasorin said. "Curious, isn't it, General? Have you seen anything like this before?"

"No, Your Majesty."

Kailani shot Baylock a look, but the woman's unreadable eyes stared straight ahead, giving away no emotion.

Queen Stasorin looked coolly back at Kailani. "What branch of magic did you hope to get?"

"Vita," Kailani said, fighting a swell of emotion. "I wanted Vita, like my mom."

"Hmm." Queen Stasorin seemed to think about this for a moment. "What did you see in the ritual? Vita's purple did not present itself at the end?"

Kailani bit her lip. She didn't want to tell anyone what she saw in the Ceremony. It was supposed to be hers and hers alone. And she didn't want to admit she was confused by what she saw, or the lack of what she saw. But there was a chance the Queen could help her. She had no idea where Fia's staff could be, if it even existed. But the Queen was a Strange mage, after all, and it was the Queen's patron goddess who had spoken to her.

Still, Kailani hesitated. The Ceremony pass was the one thing that was hers. The one thing that was sacred. She didn't fully understand what Fia's quest meant, but if it had anything to do with the destruction of Strange magic, the Queen might be the *worst* person to tell.

As Kailani struggled, Queen Stasorin's eyes bore into her. She wasn't getting out of this without giving up some information.

Taking a deep breath, Kailani lifted her shoulders. "No, it was a mix of all the colors."

Queen Stasorin only stared, and with every second that passed, Kailani's pulse pounded harder.

Licking her dry lips, she quickly added, "I just saw my parent's apothecary shop, mainly. And potions."

It was a lie, and she didn't even know if it was a believable one. She didn't know what other people saw in their mountain pass. A destiny, or a dream, or whatever they wished they could be. But she *was* certain that telling the Queen about Fia Azarro presenting herself, saying Kailani was their last hope, wasn't even close to normal.

Finally, Queen Stasorin nodded. "Well, what I think happened, Miss Slate, is that the bombs interrupted your Ceremony. Once things are—" she paused, as if searching for the right words "—settled, we'll have you go through the pass again to determine your magic."

Kailani's head shot up, and her eyes widened. "So, you think there's a chance of me still being chosen for one legacy?"

A chance to be normal.

Queen Stasorin smiled. "I do."

She made it sound so simple. So attainable. Just another stroll through the mountain pass and everything would be back to normal. And Kailani wanted it. She wanted it so badly that tears leaked from her eyes and her bottom lip wobbled.

Queen Stasorin cleared her throat. "Thank you for your time, Miss Slate. While the fate of your parents is decided, you will stay with the Hollingsworths. I've already worked everything out with them."

Her relief deflated, leaving her cold. Even if she was chosen, her parents were still imprisoned. Wrapping her arms around herself to ward off a sudden chill, Kailani repeated, "The Hollingsworths?"

The Hollingsworths hadn't so much as let Kailani study in their home after school, let alone stay there while her parents were on trial for an assassination attempt.

"Can't I stay in Saxton? With my friend Patrick?"

"I'm afraid not, dear." Stasorin stood, brushing the wrinkles off her robe. "General Baylock will teleport you home to get your things. Then she'll bring you straight to their house. Our people are very close with them, so we'll be able to stay in constant communication with you."

Kailani swallowed hard and nodded. The Hollingsworths had to be getting something out of it, but at least she'd be with Lyla.

And maybe when she was out of the dungeons, she could look for information about the staff, or at the very least, evidence to clear her parents' names. The pressure on her chest lifted, and she breathed a little easier. She'd get to see her home. With that thought, Kailani's racing pulse settled.

"We'll be in touch," the Queen murmured to Baylock.

"An honor, as always," Baylock said, bowing before her.

Two Protectors rushed forward to escort the Queen away, and General Baylock stood in silence watching after them. Kailani sighed, mentally preparing herself to see Blair's gods-awful smirk. But anything would be better than the dungeons.

She turned towards the General, but her eyes were glued to the fleeing Queen and Protectors. Then, suddenly, she whipped towards Kailani and pulled her in the opposite direction.

She moved her feet fast, trying to keep up as Baylock pulled her down the hills opposite of the courtyard. The sun was creeping behind the mountains in the distance and the air was starting to feel chilly. Kailani tried to pull back, confused, but Baylock gripped her harder, and her pulse spiked.

"We must hurry," Baylock urged, looking around them.

Kailani followed suit and her heart dropped at a sudden rustling of the leaves, but it was only an animal scurrying away from their quickened steps.

Baylock paused. Panting shallowly, Kailani scanned the area, but there was no one in sight. Then Baylock gripped Kailani's arm and before she could think, they were twirling, thrashing through the air.

CHAPTER NINE

_K_ ailani's head spun as she landed with a thud in a
forest of overgrown shrubs and plants.

Everywhere ached, and her stomach twisted as if she'd been
through a tornado. She would not soon get used to the feeling of
teleportation. Rubbing her head, her eyes adjusted to the dusk light,
and she steeled herself to come face to face with Blair
Hollingsworth. A low hum buzzed overhead, giving off a vibrational
heat, and she looked up to see the barrier in the near distance.

Blinking rapidly, she slowly managed to clear the dark spots
crowding into her vision. The dirt covered roads beneath her led
through a patchy acre of trees towards a small cabin shop. Kailani
gasped. She was on the outskirts of Saxton. That was her parents'
apothecary shop. She looked to Baylock, who was wrestling a
small pack out of her bag.

"I don't understand…"

Baylock shoved Kailani's wand, pack, and a heavy book in her
hands. Her eyebrows furrowed. _In Spirit and Song_, her family's
book of spells. All her family's potions, charms, and lullabies were
tucked away in the book's mess of pages. But it didn't make sense.

Her parents had this hidden away at home. Only Patrick, Lyla, and Seneca knew the location.

She narrowed her eyes at Baylock. "How did you get this?"

"Look." Baylock's eyes darted around the patchy trees and Kailani squeezed her arms to her chest, a lump heavy in her throat. "I need you to hide out here. I'm sorry I can't take you further, but I'll contact Alesia at Mirstone. She'll be here to collect you shortly."

Kailani's heart stopped.

Mirstone?

She opened her mouth to speak, but a rustle sounded from the bushes and Baylock yanked Kailani to the cold earth. She held her breath, trying to blend in with the tall shrubs. Trying to remember where she heard the name *Mirstone* before.

Leaves tangled in the grass. A gust of wind brushed Kailani's hair in her face. Baylock's fingers were steady around her wrist, her eyes searching through the fading dusk light.

No one appeared.

Baylock slowly pulled Kailani to her feet and Kailani's body trembled. "I can't go anywhere! My parents are innocent, if I can just go through the mountain pass again—"

"The Queen fed you a nice little story, but she has devious plans." Baylock pulled her along towards the shop. Kailani tried to stop, but Baylock's grip was tight, her voice urgent. "You must listen to me. I work with your parents. Get to Mirstone, and they'll know what to do."

Kailani opened her mouth to speak, to ask more questions, but she slammed to a halt.

Her throat constricted.

Mirstone.

Lyla mentioned the name the morning of the showcase—she'd heard it on the news.

The rebel territory. So, did that mean…

99

Baylock pulled her towards the shop, yanking her out of the horrifying train of thought.

When her eyes landed on the shop, her heart was fit to burst. The store was cast in shadow, but the sight of the bowed roof and the field outside brought tears to her eyes. The door was split in half, hanging from the frame. Somebody had kicked it in. Her heart thundered. Baylock pulled her against the wood frame, peering around the corner to see if anyone was inside.

"We don't have much time. The Queen thinks I'm bringing you home to gather your things before taking you to the Hollingsworths. But when we don't show up, they're going to come here."

Clenching her fists, Kailani sucked in a deep breath of cool air. She stared at the damage, unblinking, unable to move…

She rubbed at her eyebrow, her mouth hanging open. "So… so my parents—"

She paced back and forth on the weathered porch, unable to let the words out. The fresh air seemed to make her dizzy as beads of water misted her face.

"Your parents didn't set off any bombs, Kailani." Baylock seemed to read her mind. "But there are things you don't know. Things you will learn."

Kailani stared at *In Spirit and Song*. The book was heavy in her hands. Drawing in a ragged breath, she dragged her eyes up to Baylock. "Why are you helping me?"

Baylock stiffened. "Because, if it weren't for your parents, many people would be dead."

Kailani's legs trembled. Desperately, she scanned the porch for the lawn chairs, but they were flipped over and torn apart. Stuffing bulged out of the ripped cushions. As her weak knees threatened to drop her to the splintering floorboards, she stumbled back and pressed herself against the wooden walls, clutching the window sill for support. Mom's vibrant flowers, usually blooming on the sill, were a charred mess in a cracked clay pot.

One more casualty of the Protectors storming into her life, one more casualty of her parents being...

She couldn't bear to finish the thought.

"I know it's a lot, but I have to go. I'll report that you had a weapon hiding in your home, that you used it against me and got away."

All of Kailani's thoughts froze. "Wait, what, I—"

"Wait here. Alesia will be here soon with the rebels, and they'll explain."

Baylock poofed away, leaving behind a thick fog of black smoke that dissipated in the wind. Kailani stood in shock, unable to process what just happened.

Mist turned into drizzle and the sky darkened, the rolling clouds circling overhead.

Clenching her jaw, Kailani raced inside the smashed doorway.

Her fists tightened as she entered the shop and processed the mess inside. Potion bottles and art were thrown all over the floor. Broken glass crunched under her boots. Bending down, she picked up a smashed frame. Tears filled her eyes as she looked at Mom, wearing a long, flowing white dress by the sea. She was pregnant with her. Mom threw her head back, laughing, then stared at the camera in the five second clip. Kailani slumped to the ground, shoving *In Spirit and Song* into her pack and clutching the photo to her chest.

When she could finally muster the strength to get up, she went to the back office and pushed the door open, flinching at the destruction. The couch was flipped over, the bookshelf thrown to the floor. A salt lamp was scattered on the ground in jagged pieces.

She'd spent more time back here than in her own bedroom, every summer reading up on new magical spells, brewing potions for the shop, reading tarots, and making affirmation cards with Dad on the slow days.

But now, it was barely recognizable.

A glimmer caught her eye and she darted to the ground, grabbing at a tear-shaped blue stone. Shakily, she stuck her thumb on the stone's flat top. Her breath caught as she waited for the coordinates to calculate. She ran her hands through her hair. The number of times her parents had used these devices to check in on her while they were at the shop was endless. They'd never not been able to locate each other. Once charmed, the user's thumbprint would activate the location of whoever had the other piece of the stone.

But this time, where her parents' location normally hovered above the stone, a single line of red text appeared: 'UNDETERMINED LOCATION'.

Her heart sank as she looked around. Books were strewn across the ground, ripped covers hanging from the spines. She grabbed her pack and pulled out the heirloom spell book, frowning. Why had Baylock had it? Why had she given her the book, of all things, and brought her back here?

Turning it over, she brushed it off, pausing to run her fingers over the worn cover. She traced the title with a finger. Flipping it open, her eye caught on the familiar note on the first page:

To Kailani, my dear great granddaughter, know that you are very special, and I hope you will always be able to find your light. You have the power of generations behind you, and your family will always be with you, in spirit and song.

Kailani's shoulders slumped. If only her grandparents were still alive, she could go live with them. Her great grandfather wrote her all the lullabies in the book and promised to always watch over her. When she was a little girl, Mom had told her the most amazing stories of their adventures, but over the years, Mom just stopped talking about them. She was too emotional to bring them up.

As tears welled up, Kailani sank to the floor, holding the book on her lap. Distantly, she knew she shouldn't linger out in the open. She knew she should hide until someone came, if anyone really was coming for her. But something pressed on her chest, so hard that she couldn't breathe. She needed a moment, just a moment.

Dragging in a ragged breath, Kailani hummed the first song in the book. Her throat tightened, the sound catching, but she kept humming until slowly, slowly, the pressure on her chest eased. With tears on her cheeks, she sang aloud, breathing slowly.

Goodnight sweet angel, close your eyes
Sleep tight and wait for the sun to rise
I know you have questions to ask of me
Oh, curious child, how bright you'll be

Kailani's hands jerked as the book warmed in her hand. A burst of raw energy encompassed her entire body and a soft golden glow emanated from a tear in the cover. Her brow furrowed. The song stuck in her throat, but before she could examine the tear, the glow disappeared. The book still pulsed, though, as if a living heartbeat was calling to her. Speaking to her. Shaking, she sang again.

I will do all I can to keep you safe and sound
But you should know, there is magic abound
The place that you hold close and truly dear
It holds more magic than it may appear

The glow reappeared. Her eyes widened as she stared at the golden light. Her entire body tingled. She carried the book into the main lobby of the shop and stared at the shattered picture of her parents. There was so much she didn't understand. So many secrets.

The light faded on the book. Pulse thrumming in her ears, Kailani flipped through the pages with trembling hands. School had warned her of the dangers of magic that she couldn't understand, but this couldn't be dangerous. Her parents had sung this lullaby to her hundreds of times, and nothing like this had ever happened before. And it connected her to them, to her family. She kept going.

There might come a day when I feel far away
But worry not little one, I leave behind things that will stay
You need only to recite the spell
Most Royal Kailani, I now bid you farewell

The book glowed again, and her heart pounded. This time it was stronger, a pulsing golden light seeping through the worn pages before slowly fading away. She narrowed her eyes, running a finger along the page, then sang the lullaby once more.

She stroked her hand over the book's inside cover and it shone beneath her fingertips. This glow was slightly different though, following under her fingers as if at her demand. As her heart thundered, she sang the last stanza of the song. Words appeared in glowing, golden script.

Royal by birth, Royal by right. Allow me inside on this dangerous night. I vow to enter alone. Only a Royal may enter this stone.

Kailani gaped at the book, opening and closing her mouth as an oval cutout appeared on the cover. She'd seen that same shape before, but where? The riddle mentioned a stone, so maybe she needed a...

Her necklace!

Kailani's pulse raced as she grabbed the talisman from around her neck. Dad had told her to always keep it close, that it would come in handy one day, but surely he hadn't meant this...

Her knees went weak. The shape was a perfect match.

Kailani pressed the talisman into the cutout, and the book dissolved before her eyes.

What the...

Kailani shot to her feet. Where the book had fallen, a flat tri-fold paper lay on the floor. She snatched it, dazed.

Her jaw dropped. She was looking at a map of Talisia, all the territories and districts painstakingly outlined and labeled. As she skimmed over it, her eyes caught on something out of place, and she did a double take. Just outside the boundary of Talisia, on the edge of the Far Lands, a small territory had been drawn.

She would have written it off as one of the smaller territories abandoned during the war, but someone had very carefully named it.

Mirstone.

Her eyes almost popped out of her skull. Mirstone *did* exist. Her parents knew about it this entire time. Baylock wasn't lying, so was her contact really coming for her?

There were other places on the map, too. Places she'd never heard of. Halfway between Farrow and Mirstone was a large asterisk labeled 'safehouse', with a note.

You'll find the answers here.

Right next to the barrier, someone had written '*Scindo to get through*' in scribbled, messy handwriting.. The ink was smudged as if the map had been closed before it dried. Kailani's jaw hung open. She ran her fingers over the path when a horrible thought struck her. Her parents must've been beyond the barrier. If they had this map, if Mirstone existed and her parents wanted her to go there, if her parents were rebels, what else didn't she know?

A floorboard creaked at the front of the shop.

Kailani jumped, her heart racing, as she inched away from the door leading into the lobby. She folded the paper shut and it materialized back into a book, the same book she'd grown up with. Pressing it against her chest, Kailani grabbed her wand and backed into the corner of the office. Her mind raced through spells she'd learned at school. None of them seemed like they'd help her fight.

Kailani clenched her jaw. She wasn't sure if they would, but she'd sure as hell try.

The door to the back office creaked open and she leapt from the shadows, jabbing her wand forward.

In Spirit and Song tumbled to the ground as her hand shot to her chest. She released the breath she'd been holding.

Lyla stood in the doorway to the lobby, her face full of shock and adrenaline. The world seemed to slow around her, and her gaze shifted to Patrick. His eyebrows crinkled together and his lips parted. They were here, actually *here*. They ran towards her, their arms wrapping her into a tight hug. She let herself fall into them and she squeezed hard, not wanting to let go. As long as she could stay right here, in this moment, she would be okay.

But she couldn't. If Baylock was telling the truth, the rebels would be here any moment, and Patrick and Lyla couldn't be here when they arrived.

As her heart sank, she pulled herself away from them.

Kailani flinched as Patrick looked around, his eyes focusing on an overturned desk he'd sat at so many times before. They'd never sit here again, doing their homework, experimenting on potions with Dad, mixing ingredients with Mom. He stepped around shattered potion bottles and picked up *The Handbook of Dryads* from the ground, attempting to put the pieces back together.

Lyla's voice wrenched Kailani's eyes away. "What happened?"

Kailani shrugged. Her hands shook as she tried to remain nonchalant, as if her entire world was not a complete and utter lie. "The Protectors." Kailani gestured helplessly at the carnage before turning back to them. "How'd you know I was here?"

"Lyla," Patrick said, grasping the talisman necklace and holding it up.

Kailani grasped her own necklace, now, with a new appreciation for Dad charming the stones.

Lyla's face turned bright red. "I overheard my mom and dad talking to the Protectors…" Locking eyes with Patrick, Lyla brushed her hair behind her ears and darted her gaze towards the ground.

Kailani already knew she was supposed to be staying with them. Maybe the Hollingsworths changed their minds, it didn't make much difference now. But Lyla's chin trembled and she squeezed her eyes shut. There was something more, something Lyla couldn't spit out. A heavy fog seemed to sift in the air and Lyla looked up, her eyes sparkling with tears.

"Lyla?" Kailani's breath hitched.

She pulled her hands up, covering her face. "They testified against your parents."

The world stopped, spinning out of control. Patrick and Lyla circled her vision. Her feet were moving but she wasn't moving them. She staggered back until she was flat against the wall. The Protector's haughty laughter echoed in her ears, their blood red cloaks flashing in her vision. Lyla's face swam back to focus. She searched her friend's eyes for any hint that she'd heard wrong, but Lyla's face was contorted with sorrow.

"I'm so sorry," Lyla cried. "They were trying to make a deal. I overheard everything! The monarchy was going to send us to Magnolia in exchange for their testimony. It's all so messed up! I couldn't—"

"Wait." Kailani's thoughts whirled. "But how'd you know I'd be here?"

"General Baylock sent me a mind message. It was really crazy, actually, I didn't know what was happening. It was pretty cool magic. I—" Patrick cleared his throat and Lyla shook herself. "Sorry. She was there when my parents spoke with the Protectors. She saw me listening. She must have known I was going to do something crazy—because I was! I swear, I was ready to call the news station myself and spill everything. I mean, they're lying! Straight up lying, I couldn't believe it—"

"Baylock told Lyla they were framing your parents," Patrick interrupted. "And not to do anything crazy because she said she was getting you to Mirstone. That they had a plan. But we couldn't let you go alone."

A weight sank to the bottom of Kailani's stomach, and she shook her head. Here they were, her best friends, out past curfew and with a breakout prisoner. If they were caught here, they'd be locked up, just like her.

Closing her eyes, she whimpered, "You guys shouldn't be here. We have to get you out."

"No way." Lyla's head bobbed as she spoke with a confidence Kailani hadn't noticed before. "We came to go with you. We're not just going to leave now."

Kailani's heart all but stopped. Patrick and Lyla stared at her in the dim light, and while Lyla's face was etched with determination, Patrick's eyes crinkled. Judging by the dark look in his eyes, he wasn't going to back down. For a moment, she allowed herself to imagine it, and hope swelled in her chest. She wouldn't be alone. She'd be with her best friends.

But the cold rush of dread followed fast, and she tore her eyes away from them. They had futures, and as long as they steered clear of her, they were safe. She couldn't drag them down.

"You don't understand," Kailani groaned, peeking around the corner into the main lobby of the shop. "You can't—"

"We're coming," Lyla and Patrick said together.

Lyla crossed her arms. "We're going with you, Kai. Someone has to stop you from getting yourself killed."

There it was again, the hope warring with her fear. Kailani swallowed a swell of emotion.

"Friends don't let friends go on world-changing adventures alone." Patrick reached out and squeezed Kailani's hand. "There has to be an ancient rule written about that somewhere, right?"

The broken front door fluttered on its hinges.

Kailani dropped to the floor instantly, panic choking her. Lyla and Patrick ducked down beside her and crawled behind a shelf of potions. Patrick's shaky breaths rattled in Kailani's ears as she listened for footsteps. Maybe it was just an animal, or maybe it was the rebels, ready to explain everything and bring them to safety.

Or maybe it was the Protectors, here to lock up her and her friends.

She couldn't go back to that cell. She wouldn't let her friends go down with her. They needed a plan.

Kailani swallowed, pressing her hand over her mouth in an

effort to muffle her staggered breaths. The rising moon outside illuminated Patrick's pale face. Kailani winced. What were they thinking, coming here? She had told them to stay away. Whether it was the Protectors or rebels or a wild animal seeking shelter, they were not safe here. She'd gotten herself in this mess—or, rather, her parents did. But somehow, she'd have to find a way out. For all their sakes.

Voices echoed from the front of the shop. Heart in her mouth, Kailani held onto her friends, fighting down panic. She stepped slowly, one silent foot after the other, and peeked out the door to the front room. Her body went cold.

Protectors.

They stomped around the disarrayed lobby, kicking around the broken pieces of Kailani's life. Sweat trickled down her neck, and she fought hard not to cry out. They couldn't run. Not without being seen. They couldn't wait for the rebels without being found. And the voices were growing louder. Kailani wracked her brain for a solution. Her eyes fell to the back door of the shop. It was a horrible plan, but what other choice did they have?

She nudged Patrick and Lyla, jerking her head towards the back door. Lyla nodded, peeking around the shelf and gulping. All the blood drained from Patrick's face. Kailani held her breath. The Protectors rummaged through the carnage, opening the register behind the table. If they could just creep out...

She pulled her friends forward. The room seemed to close in on Kailani and her vision tunneled on the door, seemingly growing further and further away. Just four more steps... three... two...

She pulled the door open, and a horrifyingly loud creak filled the room.

"Over there!" a deep voice called.

She sprinted with Lyla and Patrick on her heels, heading for the forest. Her home was too far, and offered no protection. Even if they made it to the portals, she had no coins on her and nowhere to go. Nowhere to hide.

The barrier crackled in the distance and a shudder racked her body. Beyond the barrier were the Far Lands, and the map showed Mirstone out there. Her parents had written the spell on the map. They must've intended for her to use it. Their chances of survival outside of Talisia were low, but it wasn't like she had a lot of options.

Gasping for air, she sprinted towards the barrier. Her voice rasped painfully against her throat as she called for Patrick and Lyla to follow her.

If she could just get through the barrier, maybe she'd have a shot of meeting up with Alesia and the rebels. Maybe they'd get out of this.

Kailani peeked over her shoulder, pumping her legs as hard as she could. They had a decent head start, but there was no way they were faster than the Brute mages.

"*Atro Dora!*"

Kailani jumped behind a tree, barely missing the stunning curse the Protector shot at her. She pointed towards the barrier.

"How are we supposed to get through?" Lyla cried, ducking as the Protectors shot another spell their way.

They were close.

"The barriers are just small energy fields!" A curse cracked the wood of the tree Patrick cowered behind and he flinched, glancing at Kailani. "We could try a division charm, that might put a hole in it—"

"*Scindo* is the spell!" Kailani's voice cracked. She ducked as a shower of sparks rained down around her. "Lyla, your wandstone is the strongest, you have to do it!"

"I can't!" Lyla shrieked. The crunching of leaves grew louder as the Protectors closed in. Lyla shook her head, crying. "I'm not strong enough!"

"You can do it," Patrick said, his voice eerily calm. "Lyla, now!"

Lyla held out her wand, but a curse landed directly in front of her. She leapt back, screaming.

"Hurry!" Kailani cried.

The Protectors were yards away. They were out of hope. Patrick and Lyla would be tortured, sent to the Pits, all because of her. Kailani's panicked gaze swung from her friends to the rushing Protectors. They were out of time, but she couldn't simply stand there and watch as her friends were taken.

Like at the showcase, like at the Ceremony, her skin crackled and burned.

But this time, Kailani welcomed it. She urged it on, flexing her fingers, letting it flow.

Snatching Lyla's wand, Kailani pointed it at the barrier. Electricity filled her body. *"Scindo!"*

A tumultuous tearing sliced the barrier apart, the blues and whites clashing together. Kailani staggered back. She pleaded with her feet to move, to jump through, but she was frozen. Her parents' plan, Fia's quest, they were both mysteries. But the Far Lands held another type of mystery, one that included monsters and magicless and unknown.

Kailani glanced back and her chest twisted. The Protectors, frozen in shock, locked eyes with her. One bared his teeth. Kailani closed her eyes, reached deep inside her. She pulled at her fear, clung to it, wrapped her magic around it. Opening her eyes, she stuck Lyla's wand out towards the Protectors and mimicked their own spell.

"Atro Dora!"

The blast was effective and swift. The Protectors flew backwards, sprawled out along the ground. All of Kailani's senses were on overload. Suddenly, everything around her was extremely clear. The barrier crackled, the opening ablaze with static energy. She stared at it. Willed herself to go through.

But her body was stuck.

Patrick's hand wrapped around hers. He squared his shoulders, pulling her and Lyla through. Her entire body was on fire. Then, as they fell on the other side, a coldness hit her so hard that she collapsed to the ground. Disoriented. Euphoric. She pointed Lyla's wand at the barrier, but couldn't bring herself to mumble the spell. Her arm hung in the air as if it was made from steel.

Patrick and Lyla screamed beside her, their mouths opening and closing, but she couldn't hear anything except the barrier crackling in front of her. She swallowed, hard, and raised Lyla's wand.

"Scindo!"

The tear sewed shut, slowly, like the wound closing during her showcase. Then, it was silent.

They were in the Far Lands.

CHAPTER TEN

*W*ind whipped Kailani's face.

As her teeth chattered, she pulled her robe tight around her. The moon was full and had provided plenty of light while they were in the outskirts of Saxton, but now, as they sprinted deep past the barrier, its light faded away leaving pockets glimmering from the treetops.

The forest in front of them was limitless, radiant, and blooming. But they didn't stop running. They couldn't stop running.

Curling branches stretched from every tree. A mismatch of flowers clung to any space she could find, brightening up the matted undergrowth. A disharmony of wild sounds, belonging mostly to fleeing animals, echoed in the air, broken up by the low squeaking of bats swooping overhead.

Kailani clutched her wand tightly in her fist, Lyla and Patrick trailing behind her as she led them deeper into the forest. The Protectors weren't following them. Yet. But it was only a matter of time until they woke up and realized what she'd done. Her body ached from the magic. She still couldn't comprehend what had happened, or how she'd used the spell. She'd just known she *had* to get Patrick and Lyla out of there, and she *still* had to do that. There was no going back to her normal life, not now.

Kailani held her breath, willing the leaves below her feet to be silent. She glanced back to check on her friends and staggered to a halt. A few yards back, Lyla hunched over, trying to catch her breath. Whirling around, Kailani sprinted back to them.

Patrick patted Lyla's back. "Are you okay?"

Lyla huffed through deep breaths. "Yeah, I just need a minute."

Guilt twisted Kailani's stomach at the fear on their faces. They were beyond the barrier. The barrier that had kept them safe all these years. Kailani shuddered, stories about what lay beyond her memory. Magical beasts, traps, magicless…

Lyla straightened her spine, her eyes widening towards Kailani. "What was that?"

Kailani tensed. Her eyes darted through the trees and her grip on her wand tightened. Breathing shallowly, she steeled herself for a sudden attack—.

But Lyla shook her head. "No." Her breath still heavy, she pointed back in the direction they came from. "*That.* How did you do that kind of magic?"

Kailani stuttered, trying to explain, but nothing seemed right. "I told you guys not to come with me! There's so much you don't know, you don't understand."

She found herself mimicking Baylock's words and cursed under her breath, crumbling under Patrick's expectant eyes. She was terrified they'd be angry with her, that they'd regret coming. But she owed them the truth.

Sucking in a deep breath, she tried to explain. "These outbursts, they've been happening since the showcase. I—my magic, it's like it's a bomb going off inside me. It happened during the showcase, and again when the Protectors were searching for the rebels the other night. But that was the first time I was able to control it."

Lyla raised an eyebrow. "What exactly happens?"

Bats fluttered overhead and Kailani shivered, wrapping her arms around herself. "It's hard to explain. I can feel my magic, beneath the surface. Different from how it's always been at school. It's like it wants to break free all the time and maybe sometimes I'm able to stop it, but I'm so afraid of it just spilling out of me. When it happened before, I had no control over where it went or what it did. It was…" she swallowed a lump in her throat, "terrifying."

"And it's random?" Patrick asked.

"It seems to happen when I'm really stressed, or afraid, or even angry. It's like a pulse before it happens, like it's spreading through me."

Patrick rested his pack on the ground and pulled out three waters, handing her and Lyla each one. Kailani took the bottle and sucked the liquid down, thanking the gods again that she wasn't alone.

"Do you think it has anything to do with the unity symbol?"

Kailani shrugged. "Maybe." The truth was, she hadn't given much thought to the symbol on her wand. Or Fia Azarro's quest. She'd been a little more than preoccupied. She wanted to tell them what she'd seen in the mountain pass, in case they knew what it meant, but she didn't think standing around in the middle of the Far Lands was the best idea.

Lyla seemed to share the same sentiment, because her eyes bolted back and forth from the shadows, and her hands shook. Silence lingered between them, the trees whooshing back and forth in the wind.

"What are we supposed to do now?" Lyla asked.

Kailani sighed, pulling out her family's spell book. Lyla looked confused as she pulled off her talisman necklace, whispered the lullaby as quietly and quickly as she could, and placed the stone in the oval shaped cutout. As the book transformed into the map, Lyla's jaw hung open and a huge grin spread across Patrick's face.

"What the…"

The map lit up between them. A faint glow emanated from the paper, which was probably enchanted to stay visible in the dim light.

"Baylock gave me this when she broke me out of the prison. She said she was working with my parents." Kailani pointed to Mirstone, then to the safehouse. "I don't think the rebels are going to find us out here, but if we can make it to the safehouse, I think we can get help there."

Patrick ran a hand through his hair and squinted into the darkness. "But how are we supposed to make it there?"

Gnawing on her lip, Kailani tilted the map sideways and squinted. Of course, that didn't help her understand what she was looking at. She'd never read a map before in her life, and certainly not while on the run from Protectors, but she had to put on a brave face. They just needed to make it to the safehouse.

She attempted a smile, pointing through the trees. "Looks like we need to go east."

Lyla looked as if she was going to vomit. "Let me see." She snatched the map. Her breathing steadied and her finger trailed over different pathways, as she'd done so many times before with the maps she loved to study. Kailani hovered over her shoulder. Patrick stood just behind her. Lyla hummed to herself, then nodded. "I think I can get us there, but we have to move qui—"

The bushes behind them rustled.

Kailani froze as Lyla grabbed her elbow. Slowly, the three of them turned to squint through the darkness, and Kailani gripped her wand tight. Protectors, magicless, something worse? It didn't matter—*something* was coming.

Her pulse pounding in her ears, Kailani pointed her wand at the bushes, trying to ignore how her arm trembled. She didn't know quite how to control her power yet, but she knew she could channel *something*, at the very least. The barrier had proven that. She pulled deep inside of herself, felt the heat of Brute magic, the adrenaline of Vita, even the emptiness of Strange. She wrapped herself around the magic, readying herself—

Something leapt from the bushes, and the three of them fell back, screaming.

Only, they weren't attacked or cursed. When Kailani blinked, she just caught the bobbing tail of a rabbit before it sprinted away.

Kailani pressed a hand to her chest, spinning to face her friends. For a moment, the three of them simply stared at each other through the dim light, their eyes wide and chests heaving.

Then, all at once, they burst out laughing.

And it felt good to laugh, despite everything. Kailani bent in half, digging her hand into her side. She laughed until she cried, until her lungs burned, until her friends' faces turned somber. And then the weight of the forest, the darkness, hung heavy on her shoulders once more. Wiping her eyes, Kailani gripped her wand and straightened. It had felt good to laugh, but maybe next time it wouldn't be a bunny hiding in the bushes.

She took a deep breath, giving a silent thanks to the gods that she wasn't alone. She'd be so screwed. "We should get going."

So, they did.

With every step, Kailani's chest tightened and her legs wavered. The pit in the bottom of her stomach grew by the minute, dread and anxiety mixing in a noxious mass, but she forced herself to focus on the chirping crickets and hooting owls drifting along in the wind. She didn't wander into the forest much in Saxton; it was too close to the barrier for her parents' liking. But being in the Far Lands was like being in a new world. Small flowers and mushrooms lit up around their feet, glowing brighter as they passed as if calling out to them. She wanted to stop and examine every inch of the new land, but any time she tried, Lyla rushed her along, shoving the map and compass in her face.

The longer they walked, the less she heard the animals, and a chill ran down her spine. Her adrenaline had fully worn off, and every limb on her body throbbed. Every noise brought up an intense visual of the horror stories she'd heard growing up. Her eyes darted from shadow to shadow as a rotting stench oozed between the trees. She didn't mention it, hoped the others didn't notice, but they all slowed as they picked their way over fallen branches and piles of leaves, guided only by the glowing light of the map. The little light that crept through the trees had faded away completely, leaving them in a foggy mist that sent shivers across Kailani's skin. The further they walked the more the trees seemed to be broken apart. Entire trunks had collapsed to the earth, and the trees that remained standing stretched spindly branches to the skies as if screaming for mercy.

As they walked, Kailani told them what happened after she was dragged off stage. How the Strange magic felt when used against her, and how Azarro so horribly lived up to his reputation. She told them about the prisons full of people she wasn't sure deserved to be there, and how confused she was about the Queen's fake kindness.

"There's still something I don't understand," Patrick said, lifting a low branch for Kailani and Lyla to duck under. "The Queen didn't think anything of the unity symbol?"

"She seemed to think it was a fluke. That if I went through the mountain pass again, a real symbol would appear and everything would go back to normal. But… " Kailani hesitated, biting her lip. "There is one thing I didn't tell her."

"What?" Patrick leaned closer, anticipation shining in his eyes.

Kailani opened her mouth to speak, but her body went rigid. Hushed murmurs filled the air. She squinted into the darkness, gesturing with her hand for Patrick and Lyla to stay still, but nothing happened.

A few silent moments went by before Lyla whispered, "What is it?"

"I thought I heard something." Kailani twisted her head slowly, but she couldn't hear anything but the rustling of trees above. "It must have been the wind."

Patrick continued walking, and Kailani followed, wrapping her robe tighter around herself.

"Fia Azarro appeared in the mountain pass. She spoke to me." Lyla gasped.

Patrick's jaw dropped. "So, it's true. A real-life quest." He kicked at a pile of leaves on the ground, shaking his head with a shocked expression. "I can't believe it."

"Fia told me I had to find her lost staff and use it to stop a blood moon ritual. You guys, I think it has to do with the monarchy."

Lyla flinched, pulling a spider's web from her hair. Her lips formed a tight line. "Well, that would make sense. They're trying to make you seem unstable. When I was listening, they said something about you being a danger, following in your parents' footsteps."

Kailani ground her teeth together. They had it all wrong. She wasn't a danger to society, she just—well, her outbursts did happen at random. And people had gotten hurt... even if it was just those disgusting Protectors and Professor Gorgan. But that was just because her magic was close to maturing. Mom said it would all make sense after the Ceremony.

As quick as the thought came, Kailani's stomach flipped.

Here she was, after the Ceremony, with even more questions and no solutions.

Lyla looked at Kailani, her face serious. "If the monarchy is involved in something sinister, they're definitely trying to push it off on your parents. They're afraid."

"And I know your parents, Kailani," Patrick reassured her. "They wouldn't hurt a fly. If they're really involved in all this rebellion stuff, they *had* to have a good reason for doing so."

A voice drifted through the trees. Kailani slammed to a halt, wincing as her boot cracked a branch. Someone was moving towards them, their steps heavy, making no effort to silence their footsteps. Whoever they were, they didn't feel the need to hide.

"You check over there," a deep voice yelled, suddenly close. "I'll look over here."

Kailani sucked in a sharp breath.

The Protectors were here.

Floundering, Kailani looked to Lyla and the map, but the glimmering light revealed panic gleaming in Lyla's eyes. If they strayed too far west, they might never find their way back. But the Protectors catching them wasn't an option.

Lyla must have had the same thought, for she closed the map, letting it materialize back into Kailani's family spell book, and shoved it in her pack.

"Come on," Lyla whispered. Her brow furrowed as she stepped off the path and towards the thickest of branches.

Nodding, forcing herself to calm, Kailani turned to follow her, only to walk into her back. She staggered back a step, looking up, and her heart stopped.

Her body screamed for her to run, but her feet were stuck like cement, her arms trembling at her side.

They were face to face with four burly Protectors, whose lips turned upward in smirks.

Without hesitation, one Protector pointed his wand at them. "*Amarra!*"

The red light flew towards them as if in slow motion. Kailani grabbed Patrick and Lyla's hands and dragged them down. The beam of light soared over their heads.

"Run!" Kailani screamed.

She didn't think, she barely breathed. She had to hope the other two followed as she crashed through the trees. The press of rotting trunks and twisting branches exploded and splintered beneath curses meant for her, and she might have been glad for their protection. Only, more footsteps echoed through the trees, more voices. The noise was attracting more Protectors and Kailani didn't know which way to run. She just moved her feet, praying to the gods her luck would hold. She wracked her brain for some way to defend herself, but it was empty. Blank.

A jolt of energy shot up her arm, and a memory flourished in her brain. Gasping, she spun and shot off the first spell that came to mind, one she'd only read about in her Brute magic training class, one that was supposed to stun another person's wand from working.

"*Apro Veita!*"

Red light bounced off a tree trunk, disintegrating in the air. She'd missed, but heat spread through her body, the release of magic churning a vortex within her. Adrenaline pounded through her veins, and she sprinted faster, branches and twigs scratching her face and catching her robe. She glanced left and right to see flashes of Lyla and Patrick still with her, dodging spell after spell.

Her eyes darted back to see how close the Protectors were—

A current collided with her back.

She arched, her foot smacking against an overgrown root. With a muffled cry, she tumbled to the ground. The breath gusted out of her, but still she pushed on, lifting her head to see her friends rushing towards her.

"*Run!*" she cried, tears filling her eyes.

But as the current passed through her entire body, flickering across her skin as if on fire, they didn't run. They fell to the dirt beside her, covering her head with their arms. The three ducked together, and though Kailani wished so badly for Lyla and Patrick to be safe, she was so grateful that she wasn't going to die alone.

It was over. They were caught.

But then, the pain stopped.

The pain *stopped*.

For a moment, all Kailani could hear was the rushed breathing of her friends. Agony continued to sear her twisted ankle, but the current had passed, and no Protector had grabbed them yet. Heart thumping in her chest, Kailani peeked up.

The Protectors were still there, mere paces away, but their eyes were focused on something behind them.

A different sort of rushed breathing filled the air, and Kailani's stomach sank like a stone. Heavy, fierce snorting filled the air. She squinted past the Protectors. Glowing red eyes surrounded them. She could barely make out the figures in the fog before they were right in front of them.

"Gods," Lyla breathed.

The creatures were on all fours, creeping ever closer, and the stench of rot in the air intensified. Now, Kailani could see their sharp teeth and pointed ears. Their skeletal bodies, and their near translucent flesh. She didn't dare move; she wasn't sure she could if she tried. Horror and revulsion held her trapped, along with Lyla and Patrick.

One of the creatures growled.

Before she could blink, the creature pounced on the Protector, tearing into his flesh with its sharp teeth. Kailani's throat burned with bile as more creatures launched themselves at the Protectors. The Protectors fought back, but there were too many.

And they were getting closer.

"This way," Lyla cried.

Patrick dragged her arms, yanking her up as her ankle burned in agony. Jolted back to herself, Kailani struggled to move. Hot pain shot up her leg with each step, but she pushed through, stumbling into Patrick just as a creature pounced where they'd cowered moments before. A streak of light hit the creature in the chest and it fell, shaking, to the dirt.

Kailani gasped for breath. They had to take advantage of the chaos, but her body was so heavy. She dragged her good leg forward, but she had no idea which way to turn. More screams pierced her ears.

Then, her heart all but stopped.

A small, rustic cabin was now visible, with thick logs jutting out the ends and leaves scattered across the roof.

That was *definitely* not there before.

She stumbled towards it, wincing every time her foot struck the ground. Patrick was instantly beside her, his expression lit up. Heavy breaths fluttered towards her as Lyla caught up with them, her cheeks smudged with dirt and blood, then she and Patrick looped their arms under Kailani's and dragged her forward. Even with them half-carrying her, her ankle still throbbed. She clamped her lips shut, forcing herself to keep going.

The Protectors' screams were distant now. Lightheadedness and nausea took over. Any moment now, she'd surely pass out. Her body begged her to stop, to find relief, but her legs kept moving. Ten seconds passed, then twenty, thirty. The pain never subsided. But they couldn't stop, because no matter who'd won the fight, Protectors or monsters would soon follow.

Exhausted and unable to focus, Kailani winced as a burst of tearing pain pulsed through her skull. Her head was heavy. Half-panicked, half-determined, Kailani limped towards the door of the cabin. Maybe it wouldn't be any safer than the forest, but it was a risk they had to take.

A growl. Two growls. Footsteps pounding behind them.

Holding her breath, Kailani turned her head.

Three beasts sprinted, gaining on them. Patrick and Lyla grabbed Kailani's arms and pulled her forward. Icy, sharp pains shot up and down her leg.

She wasn't going to make it.

"Go!" she screamed, and using her last burst of energy, she turned to face the beasts. She summoned her magic, praying to the gods to give her strength.

Kailani held her wand up high and took a deep breath, but the beasts crumbled to the ground before her. Flashes of gold and orange light pierced the night air. Screams and growls echoed throughout the clearing, until it was silent, the remaining creatures annihilated in a few slashes of a wand.

Kailani's mouth hung open as she turned, slowly, to find an old mage towering behind them. His beard was long and tangled, and his robe looked centuries old.

"Welcome," he said, smiling, "to my safehouse."

CHAPTER ELEVEN

*S*moke lingered in the air. Energy from the spells
dissipated in the breeze and lit up the air around them.
Scorched tree trunks sizzled, branches falling to the ground
where the bodies of the creatures lay sprawled out, stunned.

Kailani's breath steadied.

The elderly mage stepped towards them. Kailani flinched,
scrambling back. Patrick's knuckles were white as he took a step
forward, shifting in front of Lyla, who trembled, her face drained
of color.

"Who are you?" Kailani's breath was shaky.

But the old mage walked swiftly past them, lifting his wand,
and chanted an incantation she couldn't quite hear. A shimmering
hue lifted from the ground and encircled the cabin like a dome.
All noise of battle, of the woods, was cut off and the only thing she
could hear was her own raspy breaths.

She sighed, her body going limp with relief.

They were safe. From the Protectors and monsters, at least.

"Well, come on in." The mage walked through the cabin door,
leaving it open for them to follow. "It's rather cold out here."

Kailani shot a worried glance at Patrick and Lyla, but really, what other option did they have? Leaning on Patrick, she ambled up the stone steps, hovering in the doorway.

"What if it's a trap?" Lyla whispered, clutching her wand and shooting anxious glances at the open door.

Kailani chewed on her lip. Lyla had a point. If this safe house was the one on the map, it *should* be okay. Her parents wouldn't lead her into a trap. But really, who was this man?

Her heart pounded again, and she took a deep breath. There was something about the old mage. A vague familiarity. She couldn't quite put her finger on it, but she didn't think he was there to harm them. A strange pull called to her, like this was where she was meant to be.

Kailani winced, taking a step closer to peek inside the open door. "We can't run. How far am I really going to get with this ankle?"

"Lyla can heal you." Patrick nudged Lyla, and her eyes widened. "What, you're a Charm mage now."

"I haven't trained…"

"You've been training your entire life!"

"Shh." Kailani waved a hand. Leaning against the doorframe to take the weight off her ankle, she peered into the safe house.

Her breath hitched at the sight, and a lump formed in her throat. The room that opened before her was like something pulled from her wildest dreams. Her parents would have loved this place. Greenery and colorful shrubs spilled from pots and hung from the ceilings. The walls were a deep blue which magnified the green hues even more brilliantly. Shelves were lined with dozens of herbs that, when combined, would form countless medicines. She blinked back tears.

A place like this simply couldn't be bad.

"Guys," she said, stepping over the threshold. "I think we're okay."

She heard them slip inside behind her and Kailani glanced back, smiling widely. She couldn't explain why, but it warmed her heart to see Lyla's breath of relief, Patrick's eyes widening and his lips parting in wonder. After the night they'd had, they were finally—truly—safe.

The aroma of lemongrass and coconut hung in the air. A burnt orange couch sat, almost hidden by plants, against the wall. Kailani wanted to remain wary of this strange place, but the cabin reminded her so much of home that she felt herself relaxing, as though her body had decided on her behalf.

Still, pain shot through her ankle, and as her heart rate slowed, she became aware of her other injuries. Cuts and scrapes from running through the trees, bruises from where she'd fallen. She drew in a long breath to steady herself, but as the adrenaline faded, she swayed. A hand appeared on her shoulder and her gaze flicked to Patrick. Concern was etched on his face. She allowed him to lead her to the couch just inside the door. After her night in the dungeons, the squishy cushions felt like a dream and she sank back against them with a sigh.

"Are you okay?" He squeezed her shoulder gently.

She'd need proper medical care soon, but for the moment, she nodded. It felt too good to sit.

"Excuse me?" Lyla called. Kailani looked up as Lyla peered from the open living room into the hallway. She had her arms crossed, and was rubbing her hands along her forearms. "A little help, maybe?"

Kailani bit back a laugh, distracting herself from the pain by examining more of the room. The only thing that outnumbered the plants were books. They were everywhere, and the musty odor of ancient and withered pages filled her nose, mixing with the smell of growing herbs. Kailani smiled as warmth swelled inside her. She tried to focus on the few in front of her, piled on a coffee table. *500 Uses for Herbs, Potions: A Master's Guide, Defense Spells Against Brute Magic.* From the look of things, there was probably a book on every subject she could imagine. If her ankle hadn't been so sore, she'd already have started browsing, picking out the ones she most wanted to read. She'd never seen so many books in her life.

"General Baylock contacted me when the rebels got to the shop and you weren't there."

Kailani jumped. The old mage appeared from the doorway on the other side of the room with three vials of liquid in his hands.

"They searched the Far Lands with no luck. We were just about to send out a larger search party when the alarm bells went off and I lowered the enchantments. I must say, you three made it here much faster than I anticipated."

Kailani's shoulders relaxed, and she gave Lyla a thankful smile. If it wasn't for her, they never would have found this place.

"You may call me Grayson," the mage continued. "It's lovely to finally meet you, Kailani."

His eyes misted and Kailani shifted on the couch. Baylock must have told him her name, but the way he was looking at her, it was like he knew her. Then it hit her, and she jolted forward, her eyes widening.

"You know my parents. They left me a map with this safehouse on it."

Grayson's wide smile crinkled his eyes. "I do. The Underground is a rebel organization against the monarchy. We've been gaining interest for a long time now. Many mages are afraid of Azarro's reign, and for good reason. Your parents were head of the Saxton division and helped many mages and magicless escape to Mirstone."

The wind was knocked out of her.

Kailani hadn't expected that it would hit her so strongly. Baylock had practically confirmed it outside the shop.

But still, Grayson's words hit her like a fist to the gut and her breath hitched. Rebels. Her parents were rebels. Not just rebels, but rebel *leaders*. The type of people that she'd spent her whole life being warned about at school: ruthless radicals, grave threats, dangers to all of society...

Her parents. Her kind, dorky parents.

Rebels.

Patrick's warm hand settled on her shoulder and she loosed a ragged breath, dragging her eyes up to Grayson.

With a sad smile, he handed her a bubbling yellow liquid in a thin glass container. "Drink. This should help you feel better."

Kailani didn't take it. She felt Patrick tense beside her, and even Lyla was staring at the potion with a wary look in her eyes. There was no telling what it was. It could be poison. Her parents knew him, but did she even know her parents?

It was guilt, more than anything, that made her snatch the vial. Of course she knew her parents. No matter what secrets they'd kept from her, she trusted them—trusted that the last fifteen years weren't a lie, that they loved her and would always do what they thought was best for her. If they thought it was safe for her to come here, it had to be safe to trust this mage.

Her muscles groaned in agony, and as she held the glass to her face, she recognized the strong scent of lake blossoms present in most healing potions. Swishing the translucent liquid in the vial, she pressed the glass to her lips. The liquid was sticky in her mouth. She grimaced. It wasn't sweet like Mom's potions. She held back a chuckle—Grayson was definitely not Charm or Vita. But warmth spread through her limbs as the potion soothed her aching muscles. For the first time since before her very first outburst, she felt her body relax, like a stream flowing through her.

So when Grayson handed her another vial full of a pink liquid this time, she gulped it down and savored the soothing effects. He handed two more vials to Patrick and Lyla and while Patrick slurped his down, Lyla held hers at a distance, a slight tremble to her hand.

"What is this stuff?" she asked.

"A special formula," Grayson whispered. "It'll help with the aches."

Kailani's breath hitched. Next to her, Patrick leaned forward and it was Lyla's turn to swish the potion, surely trying to figure out the exact recipe the mage used. She brought it to her nose, and whatever she smelled must have won her over, because she sipped the potion. She grimaced at the taste, but swallowed hard. She visibly relaxed as the potion worked its magic.

"We'll have to wait until we're at Mirstone for the good stuff," Grayson continued.

Kailani froze, every muscle in her body going rigid. Desperately, her eyes shot to Lyla—if anyone had answers, it would be her. But Lyla just gaped at Grayson, her eyes wide and unblinking, as her jaw moved without sound. Kailani tried to speak what was on both their minds, but no words came out.

It was Patrick who shattered the spell, in a voice scarcely louder than a whisper. "So, it's real?"

"Of course it's real." Grayson mixed together a salve with a mortar and pestle and leaned closer. "May I?"

In a daze, Kailani nodded. He spread the salve along her scrapes, and they quickly began to seal. "I still don't understand. So—so my parents are rebels? They've been lying this entire time?"

For a moment, Grayson's lined face was creased with what seemed to be centuries of pain and grief. The twinkle in his eyes flickered out, and the hurt in his gaze made a cold, hollow feeling seep through Kailani's chest.

"It was never a lie, Kailani," Grayson said, his quiet voice thick with emotion. "They love you. Everything they've done, they did for you, so you could have a brighter future."

That made her feel about two inches tall, and she slumped into the plush cushions of the couch, hugging her arms to her chest. She didn't want that to be true, because that would mean that they were in prison because of her. But it was the only thing that made sense. She couldn't think of any other reason her parents would get wrapped up in a rebellion—as long as she could remember, their only goals in life were to help others and protect her.

Her throat tightened.

Grayson sighed, conjuring a floating tray from the other room, on top of it four cups. With a wave of his hand, the cups floated off the tray to hover in front of each of them. Lyla offered a ghost of a strained smile, undoubtedly amazed at the magic, as they each grabbed a cup. Kailani sniffed the concoction and her face froze.

"Lavender moon tea," Grayson explained. "My favorite."

Her face flushed; her hand trembled. Pressure built behind her eyes. It was Mom's famous drink. For the past ten years she'd enjoyed the sweet warm tea before bed. It was a secret family recipe, or so she'd thought.

It must've clicked for Patrick too, because he lowered the tea, his gaze darting from Grayson to Kailani. "Wait, lavender moon tea... Kai, isn't this your mom's drink?"

Yes, she wanted to say, *it is*, but it was impossible to speak through the lump in her throat. She turned to Grayson, shaking, and silently begged him for an answer. Something simple. Perhaps he'd tried it one time, and Mom had given him her recipe... but Mom didn't give out the recipe to anyone. Even Patrick, who had wheedled and pleaded with her for the recipe, hadn't been able to pry it out of her.

A cold chill swept through Kailani's body.

Grayson took a sip, then set his mug down. Kailani's heart was pounding—his eyes glistened as they met hers. "I'm afraid I have some shocking news for you today. This wasn't the way I was hoping to tell you, in fact, we had our own Ceremony planned..." Grayson rummaged in his pocket for something. "We were waiting until after the Choosing Ceremony... well, I'm rambling now. Best to just show you."

He pulled out a small, white marble, placing it on top of the table and waving his hand. *"Retego Mistiere!"*

"My baby Lani..."

Mom? She turned sharply, gripping the edge of the couch tight, but her heart sank. A projection materialized from the small marble and Mom floated above the table. Kailani gasped, leaning close, tears springing to her eyes. Mom looked worried. Her breathing was ragged and quick, and her eyes darted back and forth to the door. Kailani reached for her, but her hands went through the translucent body and her stomach clenched.

Then Mom spoke. "If you're hearing this, then I'm gone, but there are things you need to know…"

Tears welled in Mom's eyes and Kailani's hand flew over her mouth. Mom had never cried in front of her before. She was always the strong one. Always the happy one. Trembling, Kailani leaned closer to the projection.

Her heart wrenched as Mom hesitated, picking at a fraying thread on her sleeve.

Then her world turned upside down once more.

"You're a descendant, Kailani."

Stunned, reeling, hardly able to breathe, Kailani jolted back. The words rang in her ears, growing louder, louder, until she had to clap her hands to her ears to shut them out. Beside her, Lyla gasped. Or was it Patrick? She couldn't tell. Patrick brushed against her arm, leaning closer to the hologram. But Kailani could only remain frozen against the cushions, staring through wide eyes at the small projection of Mom. Her shaking hands slipped uselessly to her sides, as the words continued to echo: *descendant. Descendant.*

Her, a descendant of the gods?

She didn't know whether to cry or scream.

Mom collected herself and continued. "My mother and grandfather, Kai Neptuna and Grayson Mistrahl, sent us into hiding when you were a little girl. We faked an explosion, erasing our existence from the world. We had to start over, it was the only way to keep you safe. Ever since, the rebellion has been waiting for your powers to fully mature. Gods, I don't even know where to start. There's so much I have to tell you."

Kailani's eyes, wide as the moon, darted to Grayson. Her mind spun, and suddenly it was all too easy to imagine this frail old mage with a scraggly gray beard as a regal man twenty years younger, with colorful purple robes and a gleaming golden crown on his head. Grayson leaned back in his chair, his amber eyes squinting. Amber eyes. *Her* amber eyes.

She wrenched her attention back to the recording. Mom had straightened up, wearing a familiar look of determination on her face.

"Take the map. The monarchy will know about our identities soon, and they'll come after you. Find your great-grandfather, Lani. Go to the safehouse. He'll give you the answers you need." A noise sounded from the video and Mom's eyes darted towards the door again, then back to the video. "Hopefully nothing happens, and I can destroy this recording tonight. But just in case... your father and I love you. Don't be afraid, Lani. We will always be with you, in spirit and song."

Mom looked at the door once more, then her projection flickered, and Kailani's gut wrenched. Her voice cut out. The projection vanished. Without thinking, Kailani launched forwards, but she stumbled as her head started spinning. Patrick reached for her, but she shrugged him off, staring at her trembling palms pressed against the wooden table. Her chin quivered, and her shoulders shook as her vision swirled with tears. She was a descendant? Mom was a descendant? This couldn't be happening. If that was true...

She turned to Grayson, who blinked rapidly to clear his misty eyes.

Kailani stared at him for a long moment. "I don't understand..." The pressure in her chest built. "So, you're..."

He managed a wavering smile, then nodded. "I'm Grayson Mistrahl. Descendant of the goddess of knowledge, Gaia Mistrahl.

The rightful king of Talisia. And, best of all, I'm your great grandfather."

"There's no way…" Patrick's eyebrows were almost touching, and he was looking at her like she'd lost her mind.

Kailani's head pounded as she shook herself from her thoughts. Patrick was right. This couldn't be true… yet a lot of impossible things had been happening. She stood, pacing back and forth across the room.

Lyla's eyes were wide, her face pale as a ghost.

Kailani rubbed her eyes. This was some sick joke. She was an average mage, nothing special about her. She couldn't be descended from the gods…

"You're lying. This is insane…"

"Please, sit."

"No!" Kailani cried. "You're crazy! This is crazy!"

She slumped in the corner, Mom's voice echoing in her ears. *You're a descendant, Kailani.*

Burying her head in her knees, Kailani held back a sob. How was it possible that this could be true, and her parents hadn't told her any of it? Was this the reason the symbol was on her wand?

An arm curled around her shoulders and her head snapped up.

Lyla's smile was soft, and she squeezed Kailani gently. "It makes sense, Kai," she whispered. "Your mom is the most talented Vita mage I've ever met. And you, you've always been special. I think he's telling the truth."

Grayson stared at her with a pained expression on his face. "I'm so sorry, Kailani. We never meant for you to find out like this, but with everything that happened at the Ceremony, things got quite urgent."

Lyla faced Grayson, her eyes squinting as she moved her hand back and forth. "Wait, wait, wait. But we saw the projection of the attack on the council. You…"

"Died," Patrick said.

It was true. Just last year in history class, they'd astral projected and witnessed the gruesome event themselves. They'd watched, horrifed, as magicless burst into the royal council room and murdered Grayson Mistrahl, along with every royal descendant on the council.

Kailani tried to think back to everything she'd learned about the old king. His daughter and sister had been on the royal council too. It was the last time Talisia had a representative from each legacy on the council. The war that followed the murders was brutal, and most royal descendants died, including Grayson's granddaughter and her family.

Mom. Dad. Me.

"Ah, yes," Grayson said, as if having a simple conversation over tea. "The problem with history is that it is written by the victors, and they tend to leave out the facts."

Kailani's shoulders trembled. This was all too much. "But, we saw it happen, we went to the memories of that day."

"And memories can be manipulated."

Kailani just gaped at him. Then, blinking, she glanced at Patrick, who was giving him a flatly disbelieving look—probably because what he'd just said went against every history text he'd ever studied. Finding no answers there, Kailani turned to Lyla. Her eyes were narrowed in suspicion, but she was nodding distantly.

"I know it's a lot to process," Grayson said, rising to his feet. "I'll have one of my Kairo specialists at Mirstone show you everything once you've got a chance to rest."

"In Mirstone?" Patrick's voice was shrill. "A territory that no one says exists but you, a king who is supposed to be dead? How do we know this isn't a lie?"

Grayson turned to Kailani, arching an eyebrow. She was struck once again by his eyes, *her* eyes, which held a sincerity that seemed too genuine to fake.

"We can trust him," she said, wincing as she pushed herself to her feet. "My parents do."

Patrick didn't look like he was entirely convinced, but Lyla nodded. "If you trust him, so do I."

With a small smile, Grayson rose from his chair, his billowing robes flowing around him. "Then let's go to Mirstone, shall we?"

CHAPTER TWELVE

*K*ailani had been through portals before, but this time was an entirely different experience.

Her body twisted violently, like she was in a very compact and violent tornado. Her stomach lurched and her vision swirled until she landed with a thud. She stumbled to her feet, gripping her wand and shaking her head to clear the disorientation.

Blinking slowly, Kailani drank in the sight before her. She opened her mouth to speak, but she couldn't find any words.

She was standing on top of a cliffside. Below her, waves crashed against a sandy shore. Greenery occupied every inch of her vision. The air was dewy as if it had just rained, and a rainbow flowed into the depths of a shimmering ocean. The sun peeked over the water, thin rays glistening from one gentle wave to the next. A sense of tranquility overcame Kailani, as if the sea's nurturing sway had possessed her, freeing her of all worries. It was like her bedroom, like the paintings she loved to create in the garden, only this time the water whispering comfort was real. The waves washed against rocks sprouting along the vast cliff, their foam forming laces against the everchanging blue.

Closing her eyes, Kailani drew in a full breath of warm air. Her magic called to her, but instead of the chaotic buzz she'd felt since the Choosing Ceremony, warmth radiated and a sense of stillness made her calm. She felt clear. Exhilarated. Like the ebbing flow of nature soaked into her skin, recharging her.

Like she was home.

Home. That was enough to break her out of her trance, to remind her of her friends, and she glanced back. A sigh brushed her lips at the sight of them behind her.

They were mesmerized by the sea's spell, too. Patrick stared, wide eyed. His mouth hung slightly ajar. Even Lyla, whose parents could afford vacations to Magnolia's seafront each year, had an awed smile on her face. Swallowing a sudden lump in her throat, Kailani stepped back to stand between them. The sun continued to set, and she never wanted to look away.

The air shifted, and Grayson materialized ahead of them. Kailani stiffened as he closed the portal. Reluctantly, Kailani turned to him. She still wasn't sure how she was supposed to feel about this strange man that was supposedly a king, and allegedly her great grandfather. But his eyes twinkled under the rays of the sun, reflecting the depths of the water. He, too, seemed mesmerized by the sea's spell, and a bud of warmth took root in Kailani's chest.

"The view gets me every time," he said, turning those warm eyes to meet hers. "Welcome to Mirstone."

Kailani's lips parted. She'd been so bowled over by the view that she'd forgotten exactly where Grayson had taken them. Now, it came rushing back. Tearing her eyes from the horizon, she whirled on the spot and gasped.

Mirstone.

A sea of shops sprawled before her and up ahead, people were wandering around a little town. She wanted to run towards them, to explore every inch of this place. It was as if it had been torn from her dreams.

Grayson smiled at her.

Kailani's chest tightened. But, as her gaze shifted back to the water, all the pressing issues clamoring in her mind slipped away in the beauty of the scene. A lighthouse towered in the distance. Down on the beach, families were sprawled out with picnic baskets full of colorful fruits. Back in Saxton, Mom and Dad loved preparing picnics.

Her memory screeched to a halt as Mom's face appeared in her mind, her worried eyes darting from the projection to the door. Her head pounded. Everything she knew before was a lie. If Mom and Dad knew this place had existed all this time, they could have moved.

There were so many things that could have been done differently, but now it was too late.

A stifled giggle jolted her back to the moment, and Patrick's voice carried through the wind. Tears still stung Kailani's eyes, but the pressure in her chest eased. Kailani took a deep breath and turned to face him.

The circles under Patrick's eyes were darker than usual as he pointed out a bush of orange flowers to Lyla. Lyla looked worse. Her tangled hair hung about her face, her clothes were ripped and torn, completely at odds with the prim and proper way she usually presented herself. But she was grinning as she bent down to smell the flowers. Patrick grabbed one and stuck it in Lyla's hair. Her laughter sang along with the ocean.

Despite her confusion and her grief, Kailani smiled. Because if she had grown up here, she'd never have met her best friends.

"What about their parents?" Kailani kept her eyes trained on Lyla and Patrick. "Can they come here?"

"I will have someone reach out to them," Grayson said, softly. "In the meantime, I'll show you three to your cabin. You really should get some rest, as tomorrow you'll start training your powers."

Kailani's heart raced. She knew she had to train on her powers, but she hadn't expected to start so soon. She didn't know what she did expect, even.

Kailani's heart juddered as her gaze snapped to meet Grayson's. She knew she had to train at some point, but she hadn't expected to start so soon. Stuffing her hands into the pockets of her robe, Kailani cast another look out to sea, a part of her yearning to run down to the beach and not look back. It was a dream come true to be here, and yet she was terrified.

But Grayson waited patiently beside her and Kailani didn't run. Squaring her shoulders, she nodded for him to lead the way. She could feel Patrick and Lyla's eyes on her as they fell into step, but Kailani kept her own on her feet. They seemed happy enough; she didn't want her worries to drag them down.

As they walked through the cliffside trail, Kailani wrestled her anxiety. Her entire life she'd been mundane with her magic, never thinking she'd amount to anything great. But here she was, a descendant with all six powers of the gods. She felt the crushing weight of the quest on her shoulders. She had no idea what she was supposed to do, and the blood moon was only a few weeks away. What training could she possibly follow to be ready?

Her eyelids drooped, and her muscles grew sorer with every step, but it was impossible to feel miserable as they arrived at what Grayson called Mirstone proper. A raindrop pelted her cheek, and she looked up at the rolling clouds. As if in a dome, rain splattered along a clear ceiling. She looked at Grayson, a question on her lips.

He answered before she spoke. "There's a charm over the town so the rain doesn't get through." A smile crept on his lips. "But sometimes it falters."

Kailani wiped the raindrop from her cheek. Shops lined the streets in every direction, with striped awnings shading the store-fronts. Colorful displays with everything from candy to robes filled the windows. Vendors of potion shots, delis, and pastries hawked their wares and people bustled around, stopping to talk to people they apparently knew. She watched the people closely, some wore mages robes and some dressed in street clothes. Some branded their wands and some had them safely tucked away. She'd never seen such colorful and decorated robes in her life, not even in Magnolia, and she couldn't help but smile.

Mountains loomed in the distance and little cabin homes jutted out from behind the hills. Grayson led them down a back street and Kailani watched a little girl picking out apples from a suspended fruit stand. She had her wand pointed at the apples, shifting them around midair. It seemed like she was looking for the best one.

"Hurry along now," an older gentleman called to the girl, and she giggled, finally picking an apple and biting into the fruit.

"We have people from all legacies of magic here," Grayson explained, leading them through the colorful streets, "but we all do our part to help out. I imagine we'll find something each of you love to do in time, but you'll need to train your matured magic first."

"You mean we get to choose what we want to do?" Lyla asked.

"Well, of course," Grayson said.

Kailani smiled as Lyla's eyes sparkled.

A group of children ran past them, giggling as they chased each other. Their smiles warmed Kailani's heart. Saxton was too cold, too dreary to see many kids out and about. The three of them had never spent much time outside in Saxton; they were always at either Kailani's house or the shop.

"How long has this place been here?" Kailani asked, unable to pry her eyes away from the bustling streets.

"After the attack on the council members, I slipped away to the Far Lands. I thought it'd be better for me to stay hidden, to assess the damage."

"And that's when my parents went to Saxton?"

Grayson nodded. "They didn't want to be on the run. You were so young. But we knew Azarro would come looking for them, so we staged the explosion."

Patrick scratched his head, stepping over a large rock on the ground. "So, Chelsea and Tommy, those names are fake?"

Kailani's eyes fixed on Grayson, and his silence was confirmation. Her knees trembled as they walked. "And my name? That's fake too?"

Grayson's eyes crinkled as he sighed, watching his feet. "Your parents had given you the beautiful name of Lani. When they moved, they added on Kai, after your grandmother."

Kailani turned the name over in her head, Mom's voice ringing in her ears. *Lani.* They'd kept her name, and added a tribute to her grandmother. That made Kailani feel a little bit better, at least, although she couldn't help feel a flicker of anger towards her parents at all the secrets.

"It took quite a long time to establish Mirstone," Grayson went on. "I started with the safehouse, but eventually I was able to secure enough time to gather some reinforcements. It took awhile, but we were able to put up enough enchantments to stay hidden."

As her eyes swept over the wide road ahead of them, Kailani could only shake her head in wonder. She didn't even want to think about how much magic it took to hide an entire territory.

"They weren't looking for us, remember. Azarro believed us to be dead. Nina Stasorin took the throne and declared war on the magicless. They fled to the Far Lands to get away, but there was no way to survive out there. Not without magic. We set up more safehouses and looked out for those on the run. It was hard, though. Even though I knew many of people, I couldn't tell them all I was alive. But over the years, the word spread, and the Underground was formed. The safehouses grew, and so did Mirstone."

A cool breeze blew Kailani's hair in her face and she threw it into a low bun with a scrunchie. An older man nodded and waved as Grayson strolled past. Kailani scanned the crowd. It was impossible to tell who had powers and who didn't, but she hadn't been around many people without magic. After the war, few had remained in Talisia. A lot of news reports claimed that maicless attacked those with powers. Hunters, the news called them. The monarchy put up the barrier soon after the war, and a line was clearly drawn.

Kailani glanced at Grayson, but if he noticed her staring, he made no sign. His shoulders were pressed back and his head was held high, just like the photographs in her history book. Gorgan hadn't talked about Grayson much, but those who remembered his reign said he was known for bringing the branches together, for celebrating magic, and ending the violent stigma the magicless had. Magic was much more free under his reign, and that's how she thought of Mirstone. Mom and Dad would always tell stories of the shenanigans they got into when they were young. Still, in spite of how wonderful the stories were, Kailani couldn't help but feel disconnected from them. That wasn't the world she'd grown up in.

She tried to picture Mom growing up with Grayson, roaming the castle and being a part of the royal news frenzy. She didn't know when Mom moved to Magnolia, what her life was like as a royal, or why she didn't want to be a part of politics. She didn't even know if the story of how she met Dad was true, or if it was all a part of the lie.

A wash of heat and a climbing crackle jolted Kailani back to the moment. Up ahead, a portal swirled to life at the most elaborate portal station she'd ever seen. Kailani paused as shadows flashed within the vortex and formed seven figures. With a pop, they stepped out onto the cobbled roads, dusting themselves off and laughing with one another.

Kailani's lips parted in awe as she lifted her chin.

They all wore tight black uniforms with symbols printed across their chests—three red Kairo symbols, one orange Brute, one blue Charm, one purple Vita, and one green Strange. Kailani squirmed. Standing beside them, in their aura of power, was more intimidating than slinking through the halls of Lancaster Academy on her first day there. This group was unlike any of the upperclassmen at Lancaster Academy, though. They all held a confidence about them that made her uneasy, but she wanted to be around them at the same time.

"Sir." A broad young man with the Brute symbol on his chest nodded to Grayson, then bowed.

"Please." Grayson waved him up, clearly exasperated. "How did the mission go?"

Kailani looked from Grayson back to the rebel, eager to hear about the mission Grayson was talking about.

"Aside from having to babysit this one—" Another girl, this one with the red Kairo symbol, nodded towards the young man as she punched a code into the portal. The swirling stopped. A metal frame closed over the entrance they'd stepped out of. As the girl turned, she narrowed her eyes at the man she'd gestured to. "Everything went surprisingly smooth."

Kailani glanced at Patrick and Lyla, who looked just as intrigued as she did. She stepped closer, hoping they didn't notice her and hoping they did. She wanted to know what kind of missions they went on. She wanted to know *everything*.

"What's the fun in espionage if you can't mess around a little bit?" The young man laughed, then his eyes landed on Kailani and his smile stretched wide. "Well, if it isn't Kailani Slate, in flesh and blood."

Frowning, Kailani shot Grayson a look. The group's eyes burned into her and heat rose to her cheeks. "How do you know who I am?"

"Everyone knows who you are. The descendant. The daughter of the great Rose and Leo—well, I suppose you would've known them as Chelsea and Tommy Slate." He winked. "You're the champion."

Kailani's ears burned, and she looked at her feet. Was that why everyone had been staring? Did they *all* know who she was? Did they all think she was some great champion on a cool magical quest?

Lyla and Patrick were staring at her, too, and that just made it worse. Patrick was the one with the special ability to touch people and take their worries away. Lyla was the best spell caster she'd ever met. Kailani's shoulders slumped. She wasn't special. She never had been.

"Hi, I'm Josie." Kailani looked up and the young woman stepped forward, nudging the young man aside. She swept her thick black hair behind her shoulder and pointed to the Brute mage. "This is Briggs. Leonard, Arun, Roca, Nyia, and Tilly." She went down the line of her fellow Kairo mages, then the girls who were Charm, Vita, and Strange, respectively. "It's lovely to meet you."

"You too," Kailani mumbled, looking towards her friends.

Lyla took a step forward, brushing her hair behind her ear. "I'm Lyla Hollingsworth."

Her cheeks flushed as she grinned at Roca, and Kailani bit her lip to keep from laughing.

Their eyes trailed to Patrick and he shoved his hands in his pocket, not meeting anyone's gaze. "I'm Patrick."

Briggs nodded at them, then Grayson. "I imagine we'll meet you three properly in training tomorrow."

Kailani froze as the realization hit her. She'd be training with real rebels, real soldiers who went on real missions in the Far Lands and the kingdom. She felt like a fraud just standing next to them.

"I'm second in command of the Underground militia," Briggs went on. "These guys are part of the team."

Kailani bit the inside of her cheek, her head spinning. She was tired, overwhelmed. She wanted to impress these people, but she knew she wouldn't. And tomorrow they'd all realize that she was no champion. The thought made her stomach turn.

All of this was happening so fast. A few days ago she was just some girl from Saxton. Her biggest hope was to be chosen as Vita, to help her mom in the shop, to be normal. But here she was, in a rebel territory, meeting rebellion leaders who not only knew her parents, but knew her. It was all too much.

"Well, we'd best get going." Grayson waved, and Kailani lurched towards him, grateful for an excuse to get away. "We will see your team in the morning."

Grayson led them up a hill and towards a row of cabins. Kids played in the street, laughing and shooting bursts of light at each other in a game of tag. Kailani wanted to let herself fully immerse in the magic of Mirstone, but she dragged her feet, unable to fully push aside the worries clawing at her mind. Lyla and Patrick talked with Grayson up ahead, but she didn't bother trying to figure out what they were saying. She was still hoping to wake up, hoping to find out this was all a dream. Only, she knew better than that. Patrick and Lyla weren't oblivious to her mood, as she caught them shooting her looks every now and then, but she pretended not to see the worried glances they exchanged as they walked through the cobblestone streets.

She was just glad that didn't say anything; the last thing she wanted was for Grayson to notice. She just needed some time to think.

When they finally walked up to a small cabin, Kailani felt some of the tightness in her chest ease.

"I'll see what I can do about reaching out to your parents," Grayson assured Patrick and Lyla, before turning to Kailani as she caught up.

She wanted to look away, fearing what he'd read in her eyes, but forced herself to hold his gaze.

He smiled. "I know you have a lot of questions, and I promise I will answer every one. Only now you must rest. Your life has changed greatly, but I can assure you we are working endlessly to find your parents." Then Grayson's eyes misted, and Kailani's gaze flickered away. "I am glad to have finally met you again, Lani."

His voice thick with emotion, he strode off, leaving Kailani standing in the doorway of their cabin with a pulsing headache and a storm of emotions she barely understood.

"Shall we?" Patrick broke her out of her trance.

Kailani nodded, pulling open the cabin doors.

"This is *incredible!*" Lyla rushed in the cabin, spinning in a circle as she took in the view.

In a daze, Kailani drifted after Lyla and Patrick and – despite her pounding head – she smiled.

A seating area with a fireplace sat on one side of the living area, across the room from a little kitchen. Stairs led upwards towards an open loft. Two bunks were stacked on top of each other in one corner, and a lone cot was set up on the other. Massive windows the size of half the room spanned the living area, one side overlooking the deep blue water and the other facing the mountains.

Even though Kailani was about to drop dead of exhaustion, she couldn't help but admire the view. This place really *was* amazing.

As if the room knew who its tenants would be, the beds were made just like their ones at home. Dangling plants hung from a desk with a salt rock, crystals, and incense burning a lovely lavender aroma. A cauldron waited at the foot of the lone cot, and a gleaming crystal ball held up a leaning pile of spell books on a bedside table. The light from the windows danced over the rustic log walls, and rugs were scattered across the floor.

Patrick dropped his pack on the lone bunk, falling into the pillow. His voice was muffled as he said, "This is nice."

Kailani sank onto the bottom bunk, Lyla having already clambered up top. With a sigh, Kailani flopped back, savoring the relief of her aching muscles. Their first official training session would be tomorrow, and they hadn't slept properly in days. Kailani doubted she'd sleep all that well even now. How could she, with the literal weight of the kingdom on her shoulders? She had no idea what they'd cover in her training session tomorrow, or what powers she even had. But, still, if she was going to have a restless night, she was glad the bed was comfortable.

Lyla – unable to stay still – roamed the loft, opening drawers and examining every inch of the space. She moved to the table at the end of Patrick's bed and rubbed a hand over the crystal ball.

"Come look at this!" Lyla gasped, as mist danced on the opaque surface. "How cool!"

Patrick groaned. "I can't move."

"Come on, this practically has your name written all over it! Kai, doesn't your mom have one just like this?"

Kailani rubbed her temples, going back to the night of the raids when her magic shattered Mom's crystal ball. What she wouldn't give to go back to that night, when the Protector's fine was her biggest problem. Her head pulsed and all she wanted was silence. But Lyla moved at lightning speed, jabbering away. She was just so *loud*.

There was a clatter of another drawer, then, "You've gotta see this too! Look! This is the same deck we got last summer, isn't it?"

Kailani rolled over to face the wall, staring at the chipped blue paint, just like in her own room. She squeezed her eyes shut, trying to drown out Patrick and Lyla's voices.

"Kailani, look!"

Her jaw clenched and a part of her knew she should just explain, tell her how she was feeling, but then they'd ask questions. Or, worse, they'd tell her everything was going to be okay. So, she ignored them, pretending to be asleep, only Patrick was up and about now. She could hear his heavier footsteps pounding around the cabin. Each step rattled her skull. Grinding her teeth, Kailani grabbed the pillow and pressed it over her head. But their voices grew louder and louder until–

"Please," Kailani snapped, jerking upright. "Stop! I just need a minute."

Lyla and Patrick froze, staring at Kailani with wide eyes. Breathing heavy, Kailani felt heat flush her entire body. She didn't mean to be angry, they'd given up everything for her, but this wasn't a fun little vacation they could leave whenever they wanted. Things from here on out would only get worse, and Kailani just needed some quiet. Some space to think.

Unable to bear the looks on her friends' faces, Kailani slumped back onto the bed, curling her body towards the wall once more.

In the sudden silence, all she could hear was the thump of her heart in her chest. For one awful moment, she thought they weren't going to move, that they might ask her if she was okay. And she so desperately didn't want that, because she knew she'd break.

"Sorry, we're sorry," Lyla's voice was soft, her footsteps light as she walked over and sat on the edge of Kailani's bed. "There's more important things going on, of course."

Kailani's chin quivered. They were allowed to be excited. Allowed to not be miserable. They'd given up everything—

"No, I'm sorry. It's just… a lot. And I'm tired."

"Of course," Lyla repeated. "We should all get some sleep, anyway. We'll be training tomorrow."

Some of the tension left Kailani's shoulders. Her body craved sleep, but she turned to face Lyla and smiled. "Yeah, you'll need the energy, especially if you're training with that Charm soldier Roca."

Even in the low light Lyla's cheeks flushed red. She snatched a pillow and playfully shoved it at Kailani. "So funny."

Patrick dragged his feet across the room, holding out his pinkies. Kailani took one while Lyla took the other, and silence filled the cabin.

"To the moon and beyond," Kailani whispered.

"To the moon and beyond."

Kailani turned back to face the wall, and to her relief, she heard Patrick shuffling quietly across the room, then the creak of Lyla climbing to her bunk.

Loosing a long breath, Kailani tried to relax. But she twisted and turned on the cot, unable to get comfortable. Her thoughts churned. How could her parents have kept her in the dark for all these years? Now she was stuck here trying to figure this all out without them. A spark of anger rushed through her, and then tears of guilt and frustration filled her eyes. How could she be angry at her parents when they were in so much danger? But she *was* angry. Why hadn't they told her anything? What did Grayson expect from her? She was only fifteen. She'd never even trained in her matured magic, but now she was supposed to complete a quest?

Flopping onto her back, Kailani stared at the base of Lyla's bunk. She knew she should be happy to be here. She'd escaped Azarro, found her great grandfather, found *Mirstone*. But that just made it worse. How could she be a descendant or a champion when her body felt like it was rejecting her gift? And what gifts did she even have, when, according to legends, the symbol engraved on her wand hadn't appeared in thousands of years?

She closed her eyes again, praying to the gods, asking for any sort of guidance on what she was supposed to do. How she was supposed to feel. But they were silent. The blood moon was in seven days and she still didn't know what ritual she was supposed to stop, or how she was supposed to prevent this supposed destruction. She was powerless, and she was no closer to saving her parents. Grayson seemed to think training could help, but how much could she really learn in seven days? Would her parents even be alive by then?

He believed in the gods. So, shouldn't she?

Kailani's eyes burned, but she kept them firmly shut. Because the blood moon was fast approaching, and if the Kingdom did fall to darkness, it would all be on her.

CHAPTER THIRTEEN

*E*arly morning light grazed Kailani's skin as she stepped out of the shadows and onto the flat ground of the training arena. Butterflies fluttered in her stomach. She didn't know what to expect of her training, didn't know what was expected of her.

"This place is massive!" Lyla spun in a slow circle, her eyes devouring the grand structure.

Long, jagged fissures ran up the stone bleachers like petrified lightning bolts, and a large chunk of the barrier in the far back had been demolished and re-fortified with haphazard wooden splints. The floor of the arena was covered in sand for traction, though there was polished limestone peeking out from beneath.

Grayson gestured to the outer rim of the arena, where three of the girls from yesterday stood: Roca, with the blue Charm symbol that Lyla was already staring at. Along with the Vita mage—Nyia, that was her name—and... Kailani racked her brain, but the last girl's name eluded her. She was the Kairo. Her name was...

A blank.

Kailani gave it up as the trio strolled over, chatting amicably. Her heart started beating faster the closer they got.

"You remember Roca and Nyia." Grayson clapped his hands together. "They'll be training Lyla and Patrick today. Kailani, you'll be with me and Josie."

Kailani's stomach fluttered as she repeated the name *Josie* over and over in her mind, trying to make it stick. She couldn't help feeling excited about the possibilities of so much new magic, even with the weight of the quest on her shoulders.

Roca, a young woman composed of sharp angles and strong features, turned her head. "Lyla." Her eyes twinkled. "It's lovely to see you again."

Lyla blushed. "It's nice to see you as well."

Kailani held back a grin. Lyla couldn't help herself when it came to pretty Charm girls.

Patrick turned to Nyia, who flashed a radiant smile. "I guess I'm with you?"

"I suppose you are. Come on, then." Nyia waved Patrick over.

Dust kicked up from their feet as they made their way to the back of the training arena with their new mentors. She couldn't help wishing that she'd been chosen for one legacy, like them, off to study potions or healing—or even Strange magic, if it meant that she'd know what was expected of her.

Their chatter faded, but judging by their gestures and Lyla's irritated expression, they'd already started to banter.

Slowly, Kailani turned to face Josie.

"We're actually going to be in my office for the morning," Grayson said. "Josie will be using astral projection to help us figure out the quest, but give us a private moment, Josie, will you?"

Kailani's heart sank. Josie smiled at Kailani, then nodded at Grayson. Kailani turned to the other side of the arena. Patrick and Lyla were all smiles, talking about something she couldn't hear as they got set up at their assigned tables.

Grayson was probably worried her outbursts would make an appearance, which had to be why he didn't trust her in an enclosed space. Her heart wrenched and she sighed, wishing she could go with them. But instead she turned, and followed Grayson out of the arena.

Pulling her robe tighter around herself, Kailani shivered as a chill ran up her spine. Early morning fog covered the mountains in the distance. She scanned the slopes for the cabins, but they were too far away now. When they'd met Grayson this morning, they'd taken a portal to the west side of Mirstone where the training facility was built, bordering the Far Lands. Here, open acres of fields were surrounded by a vast sea of trees covering the grounds. This part of Mirstone reminded her more of Saxton, surrounded by woods and stiff stone buildings, completely opposite of the oceanic cliff sides she saw yesterday.

Grayson led Kailani to a small building not far from the stadium. "This is my office," he explained, taking her through a set of double doors. The room looked like a smaller version of the safehouse. Papers were scattered across a large desk and four cozy blue chairs sat around a circular table.

Grayson moved his wand around the room, and a shimmering gold hue encircled them. "So we're not overheard."

He sank into one of the chairs, leaning back into the soft cushions.

Kailani's chest tightened as she rubbed the back of her neck. She took a deep breath, her body light at the prospect of figuring out the meaning of her quest, but her chest tightened at the thought of finding out what she must do.

"I know you're eager to train with your full powers. But I thought we'd start by trying to piece together this quest. What exactly did you see in the mountain pass?"

Tipping her head back, Kailani closed her eyes and tried to remember exactly what she saw. "The colors were fighting, they never presented as just one. And the images... I was confused. There were flashes of scenes. I saw you, I think, with *In Spirit and Song*. And I saw a castle. Then I saw the safehouse. I wasn't really sure what it all meant. It was like the gods couldn't choose one thing to show me, like they were fighting for space just like the colors were. They showed me a metal staff with a bloodstone in the middle. Then..." Kailani bit her lip, cracking her eyes open. Grayson simply waited, patiently, a gentle smile on his face. She took a deep breath. "Then the goddess of darkness spoke to me."

Grayson's face didn't give way to any emotion. "And what did she say?"

Kailani thought back. It was easy enough—the words were engraved in her memory. "She said a strange magic will bring the kingdom to ruins. And I have to find her lost staff and stop the ritual on the blood moon." Kailani groaned. "But how am I supposed to know what ritual she's talking about, or how to stop it? And how am I supposed to find her staff? It's a legend... and it's lost. And I don't even know how to use Strange magic..."

"This is all making sense," Grayson stoked his beard, not even seeming worried.

Kailani rubbed the base of her neck. At least one of them seemed to have confidence in the quest. "What is?"

Grayson paused for a long moment, like he was debating what to say. Kailani shifted in her seat. She was getting used to his backwards way of explaining things, but she really wanted answers.

"Your friend Lyla mentioned you and your classmates astral projected back to the day of the council murders in school. Did you notice anything off about that projection? Anything that looked out of the ordinary?"

Kailani shook her head. She'd been fourteen, it had *all* looked out of the ordinary to her. First, the richness of the council, and then the bloodshed. She was about to say as much, but Grayson's gaze upon her was steady, almost challenging. And so, she frowned, casting her mind back to a memory she'd happily buried.

The council members, one descendant from each legacy, had

sat around their plain table as they welcomed Nina Stasorin on board. She could remember Stasorin mentioning her uncle—Azarro. Kailani shuddered as his face flashed into her mind. She rubbed her wrists where the rope had burned. She remembered Stasorin stating that Azarro wanted revenge for what the magicless had done to their family—murdered them in cold blood.

But that was all common knowledge. It was what they'd learned.

Nina Stasorin's father had left a legacy of hate, and her uncle Azarro had a savage reputation, so the council had chosen her to represent the Strange mages. To distance herself from her family's notorious brutality, she'd taken her mother's name instead of her ancestor's, the goddess Fia Azarro.

And it had all been going well, until the doors had burst open and a rabid horde of magicless swarmed the room with weapons.

But nothing out of the ordinary came to mind, and Kailani shrugged.

"During an astral projection, you are at the will of the memory of whoever is projecting," Grayson said. "You see events as they did. But memories can be tampered with. It's subtle. Most wouldn't ever see it, but if you see a glint of silver over a memory, it's been altered."

Kailani's eyes widened. Now that he mentioned it…

"There *was* a streak of silver. I thought it was weird at the time. It was like the projection flickered right before you were… well," she mumbled awkwardly. "Killed."

Grayson nodded, clearly unmoved by casual conversations about his apparent death. "You're a wise mage."

Kailani couldn't help it—she felt a burst of pride. It was almost like she was back in Professor Linde's class, before her world had been turned upside down. She ducked her face to hide her smile.

"I told you we were going to be working with Josie today."

Kailani looked up eagerly as Grayson lowered the enchantments on the room. "As a Kairo mage in the militia, she has many roles. There must always be one Kairo present during missions for every other soldier, to teleport out when needed. But another role the Kairos have is astral projecting, piecing together information from memories. Josie is going to project you to my memory of the event. I think you may see things a little differently, this time around."

As Josie came into the building, Kailani's excitement faded and her stomach started churning. She wasn't particularly keen on the idea of returning to the visceral scene. Professor Gorgan had claimed it was important for them to see the murders, first hand, for them to fully understand what happened before the war. Why the war, the barriers, the restrictions were necessary. Mom almost hadn't signed the permission slip, but after some convincing from Dad, Kailani was forced to watch the scene with the warning that this was only one person's memory of events.

Kailani bit her lip. The warning made sense, now.

"I know it's not an easy scene to revisit. But it's important. If at any time you feel like you cannot handle it, simply close your eyes and say 'Reditus' and you will be transported out of the memory."

Josie pulled out her wand. "Are you ready?"

Kailani nodded.

"*Projectura!*"

Grayson and Josie vanished. A white fog crept into the room, slowly at first before growing thicker and thicker, covering her feet completely. A dull static started tingling at the arches of her feet. Kailani's pulse pounded in her ears. The fog enveloped her entire body, swallowing it whole, the static swelling as it shot just under the skin until all her limbs were numb. She felt as if she was floating through the air when the fog finally began to clear, but was still seated.

She closed her eyes, taking a deep breath in before opening them and preparing herself for the projection. The office was completely gone. Just like when she projected in school, Grayson —*King Mistrahl*, back then—sat at the head of a long rectangular table. The projection was only ten years previous, but Grayson looked much younger in the projection, as if the past decade had aged him far beyond the years. Around him sat the other elected council members, one royal descendant from each god of magic. Kailani's lips parted in awe as her eyes trailed over Indra Mistrahl, Grayson's sister and the Luminate representative. She had no memories of the woman or if she'd ever even met her. Next to her sat Everest Therris, then Serena Heilari, then Ivan Stark. Kailani's heart jumped as her eyes fell on Kai Neptuna. Grayson's daughter, and her grandmother.

She was beautiful. Looking back now, really focusing on her, she could see the resemblance to Mom. Pressure built in her chest. In her mind's eye, Kai Neptuna fell to the ground with a brutal slash of a sword, her robes staining crimson as the flashback seared into her mind. Her heart ached. She couldn't do this, she couldn't watch, knowing now that her family was about to be slaughtered. And for a moment she wanted to say *reditus*, to project out of the memory and never revisit it again. But Grayson thought it was important enough to show her. So she bit her tongue and counted slowly in her head.

Kailani was hovering above the ground, like she had so many times in various astral projections at school, but this time felt different. The projection was clearer, for one. Unlike the ones in school that seemed like she was watching a film, this projection felt like she was standing right in front of the royal council. A weight was heavy on her chest. The previous memory must've been charmed with an aura manipulation spell, because she hadn't felt so crushed and helpless then. Or maybe this feeling was because of what she knew now.

Her eyes darted to the door. Just like last time, a young, frightened-looking girl stumbled into the room. Her eyes were red and puffy, and her pale skin looked clammy. Her fingernails were bitten down, her fingers trembling slightly. She looked no older than eighteen, and Kailani couldn't help note the major differences between the girl she was looking at now and the Queen she'd met just a few days ago.

Just a few days before this meeting, her parents and younger sister Ember had been brutally murdered by a group of Hunters. And her father's seat on the royal council needed to be filled.

"Ah, Regalis Nina, welcome."

Before, Kailani hadn't paid much attention to Grayson Mistrahl. Now that she studied him, his voice sounded the same, but he had less wrinkles. His salt and pepper hair was slicked back and a crown sat atop his head.

Kailani's hands curled to fists as Stasorin walked slowly across the room and sat at the table.

Grayson eyed the girl, his eyes filling with sorrow. "We deeply regret the vicious attack on your family, Nina. Please know we are doing everything in our power to find the magicless responsible."

Shaking her head, Stasorin glanced towards the door. "My— my uncle," she stuttered. "He wants war. He wants revenge."

Stasorin's hands trembled. Kailani couldn't have fallen if she'd tried, but she suddenly felt like the world was sliding out from under her. Was Stasorin—was she *afraid*?

"Well, dear, that is why you were voted onto the council over your uncle," Kai Neptuna said. "Only a small faction of magicless rebelled. If we waged war against them, it would likely mean their extinction. Many magical lives would be lost as well."

Pressure built behind Kailani's eyes as she watched her grandmother. A burst of pride filled her chest. She didn't want war. She was *good*. She wanted to reach out to her, to hug her, but it wouldn't make a difference. She stood still, her body trembling, her throat constricting.

"We do not want war," Grayson stated resolutely. "We need to work towards peace with the non-magical community."

Stasorin's eyes shifted back and forth from the assembled

regents to the doors, where in just a few moments, the magicless would burst in and slaughter everyone except her. Last time, Kailani had barely noticed Stasorin's nervous glances. But this time, she tracked each glance at the door, and by the fourth one, a vague sense of discomfort had taken root in the back of her mind.

"Are you expecting someone, Regalis?" Grayson asked, apparently noting her divided attention. But he didn't look concerned.

"No—no, King Mistrahl."

Her stammering voice wavered. Kailani's eyes narrowed as she followed the Queen's gaze to the door once again. Flashes of magicless carrying long silver swords, dripping with her grandmother's blood, darted through her mind.

Shuddering, Kailani forced herself to look away from the door. To focus on her relatives, while she still had a few moments to memorize their features. Indra's shiny black hair and sharp features, Grayson's regal posture and kind eyes, Kai's warm and welcoming smile. Still talking, still moving, still *living*. Just for a few more moments.

"As I was saying," Grayson went on. "Tensions between mages and magicless are at an all-time high. Hunters are growing by the day. That's why we brought you in, Regalis Nina. A fresh face for the Azarro bloodline. Your uncle is a great wizard, but there is a severe lack of trust in the descendants of darkness."

Stasorin nodded. "I understand."

"We thought you might see our way of thinking. And of course, taking your mother's maiden name will help ease the tension the mages of Talisia have grown to associate with your bloodline."

Stasorin nodded again.

"Welcome to the Grand Supreme, Nina Stasorin."

The doors flew open. Masked magicless brandished their swords.

Kailani's hands flew to her head as she lunged forward.

"No!" she screamed, but no one in the projection could hear her.

Stasorin jumped up at their entrance, her movements rewarding her with a stab to the leg. She fell to the ground as the council members reached for their wands in a daze. The rest was a bloodbath. A Protector stormed in and grabbed Stasorin, who was closest to the door, then pushed her out of harm's way. But the Protectors were too late. The magicless' weapons slashed through the remaining council members.

Her grandmother raised her wand and yelled something Kailani didn't recognize. One of the magicless fell down in front of Kailani's feet. She gasped before remembering they couldn't touch her, then the past collided with the present and she remembered what happened next. She screamed so loud her throat went raw, and lunged towards her grandmother. Her hands traveled through her translucent body just as a non-magical came up behind her, reaching around her and slitting her throat. The bile was back and she squeezed her eyes shut. *Breathe. Breathe. Breathe.* She kept her eyes shut until the last moment, when she opened them to see a pile of dead bodies: the royal council, Protectors, and a few magicless.

The pile of bodies lay in front of her. Just like in the original projection. But this time, the projection didn't shift to another scene.

Little specks of translucent particles floated above the bodies. Kailani fought the urge to get closer, to examine the particles. The soul fragments. The stench of blood filled her nose and she gagged. Three magicless survivors stood, looking at the chaos as Kiran Azarro rushed in.

Kailani's throat closed. Her entire body went cold.

Her hands flew over her head and she instinctively ducked, squeezing her eyes shut. Flashes of paralyzing fear crept through her. But no pain came.

He can't hurt me here.

She forced herself to keep watching as Stasorin limped in beside him. The magicless didn't attack. Instead, they looked at one another as Stasorin bent over to clutch her bloodied leg. Tears swam in her eyes and Azarro laughed.

Chills raced along Kailani's skin as his haunting laugh reverberated in her ears.

"Had to make it look real."

Kailani was frozen to the spot, her jaw on the floor. *This...* this was not the version of history she was taught in school. This had to be why they cut the projection off when they did. Her teachers couldn't know they were projecting a lie, that their memories had been modified.

Stasorin's eyes were cold as she scanned the room full of corpses. Kailani's heart dropped into her stomach. Her grandfather had moved just a fraction of an inch, but Stasorin's gaze, razor-sharp, shot to him.

Kailani didn't breathe, didn't think she could even if she dared to try. Grayson cracked his eyes open. His fingers, covered in blood, scrabbled at the floor beside him. *Two inches left,* Kailani nearly shouted. His wand was only two inches to the left, so close... but as his fingers closed around it, a freezing chill cut to Kailani's core. His wand was snapped in half, smoke still rising from the severed metal.

There was nothing he could do.

He tilted his head to the side, and Kailani followed his gaze to Kai Neptuna. She was sprawled on the floor in a pool of blood, her face frozen in shock. Quickly, Kailani averted her gaze. Grayson must've seen her body, because a tear streaked down his cheek, cutting through the spatter of blood clinging to his skin.

All along, though it couldn't have lasted longer than a few seconds, Stasorin watched.

Grayson closed his eyes.

Stasorin looked from him to her uncle, and her lips parted.

Then she turned back to Grayson, now unmoving, and closed her mouth.

Neither Azarro nor the magicless had noticed.

One of the magicless men moved forward, his sword aimed at Azarro. "We require payment, sir."

Azarro took out his wand and in a swift motion, killed the remaining attackers. Stasorin winced, ducking as the men fell to the floor.

Kailani jumped back, muffling a scream. He was a monster, then and now. And Stasorin looked so young... so terrified, standing next to him.

"We couldn't leave any witnesses," Azarro explained coldly.

Stasorin's eyes darted to where Grayson Mistrahl lay motionless, but she didn't say a word. Kailani thought back to the day she was interrogated, how Stasorin seemed to loathe her uncle. How she stopped him from torturing her. Here, she was just a girl. A girl who had just brutally lost her family. Azarro gripped the back of Stasorin's neck and she whimpered, her face straining to hide the pain.

"Go collect their life forces, child."

"I—" Stasorin cried, her face pale. "I can't."

Azarro rushed her, pinning her against the wall. Stasorin cried out, trying to duck out of his grip. "There's enough Azarro blood on your hands to last a lifetime. Do as you're told."

Kailani's jaw hung open. This girl was *not* the Queen who ran Talisia today. Stasorin was just a few years older than herself here and... she was petrified.

Kailani shook her head. She had to focus. The astral projection hadn't ended, which meant there was still something she had to see.

Stasorin got up and limped to the bodies. Kailani forced herself to watch, swallowing bile as it burned her throat. She took a deep breath, but the smell of blood made her woozy. Steadying herself, she thought again about retreating, screaming *Reditus* and telling Grayson she couldn't witness any more. It was too much. Far too much.

But from the corner of her eye, her grandfather hitched a breath and she knew she had to stay, had to see what happened.

Stasorin pulled out small glass vials from her pocket, her hands trembling, and used her wand to preserve the particles of light floating above them. Kailani's entire body filled with dread. If this was the life force Azarro was talking about, what did he plan to do with them? Azarro took out a knife and bent next to Stark. Cutting a wound into his flesh, he collected goblets of blood. Kailani swallowed hard. Black specks floated in her vision. She swayed on her feet.

Stasorin's face turned green as red, sticky liquid pooled on the floor around them. Kailani shielded her face, unable to watch the gruesome details.

"Hurry up!" Azarro screamed.

Kailani peeked through her fingers. Stasorin stumbled as she lined the vials up at Azarro's feet, and he conjured a small cauldron.

"Are you sure this will work?" Stasorin's voice was shaky.

Azarro spit on the floor. "This is old magic, Nina, and your father and I have been working on this for decades."

An evil glint flickered in his eye. Kailani held her stomach and bent over, trying not to mumble the safety words to get her out of this.

"The royals don't think Strange mages can run this kingdom, but we don't need them. And we don't need the gods. Soon, I will possess *all* the gods' power."

This man was insane. How did he think he could get the gods powers from *this*?

"And then—" Azarro carefully dumped the life forces into the cauldron, followed by the blood and other ingredients he had stashed in his pack. "No one will ever be able to lay a finger on our family again. I will be untouchable, forever more."

A bright light, like a burst of lightning, flashed throughout the room. Azarro and Stasorin were thrown backwards. Kailani gasped, bracing herself for the blow, but it never came. The projection kept her safe. Azarro and Stasorin lay motionless, and Kailani's head shot to Grayson. His eyes were wide, his mouth slightly open. He moved, slightly, but groaned in agony.

Stasorin moaned and Grayson shot back to the floor, lying motionless. Stasorin looked over at Azarro, who glowed a brilliant golden hue, then her eyes widened. Her entire body trembled. Azarro was still unconscious, but his skin lit up like sparkles of sunshine.

Kailani edged closer, her jaw hanging open. What was going on?

Pale-faced, Stasorin stumbled to her feet. Her breathing was ragged as she stared at the corpses piled around her. She lingered over Grayson, but he didn't move, then her eyes fell on a sword near her feet. Slowly, as tears ran down her cheeks, she picked up her sword and turned to face her uncle.

And despite knowing this was the past, despite knowing Azarro was alive and evil as ever, hope burst in Kailani's chest. *Yes,* she wanted to scream. *Do it.* Her heart thumped in her throat, as Stasorin lifted the sword.

Then she turned it on herself.

"No!" Kailani cried, lurching forward without thinking. Stasorin dropped the sword with a start, and for a moment—as it clattered against stone—Kailani thought the Queen had heard her. Then Grayson shifted, locking eyes with Stasorin.

Neither moved a muscle.

Stasorin dropped the sword. It clanked to the ground.

Azarro groaned, and Kailani's stomach sank. Why hadn't Grayson killed him then and there? The moment had passed, his chance was gone, even though it had really passed many years ago. Grayson was motionless once more as Stasorin rushed to her uncle's side, the sword forgotten.

"Are you okay?" she asked.

Azarro shoved her back and stood up, admiring the shimmering hue coming off his skin. "It worked. The ritual worked." His eyes grew black and Kailani's skin crawled. "Dear child, now I have the power of the gods."

CHAPTER FOURTEEN

og crept back into the room, the tingling flowing through Kailani's body in one brief wave. She didn't fight it. She didn't want to look at those people anymore, didn't want to see the bodies and the blood. As Grayson's office came back into focus, Kailani's head pounded against her skull. All she wanted to do was crawl back into bed, back home, in Saxton. Drink some lavender moon tea and listen to Mom and Dad's crazy stories.

Blood magic... Never in a million years did she think something like that could be real.

"Thank you, Josie, for showing her the truth."

Josie nodded, standing and bowing to Grayson before walking towards the exit. "Good luck, Kailani," she said, closing the doors behind her.

Kailani couldn't speak. She couldn't think. She was in over her head. This type of magic wasn't supposed to exist...

"Kailani, it's okay." Grayson reached out for her, but she pulled away.

His voice was soothing, just like Mom's, but it brought her no comfort. Still, she didn't look at him. She didn't want to see the look on his face.

Burying her head in her hands, she let her racing heart slow. "So, Azarro…"

A shiver shot down her spine just mentioning his name. Her grandmother's sunken body flashed through her mind. Azarro's knife, his black eyes. Words wouldn't form.

Grayson let out a breath. "The day of the council murders, Azarro performed blood magic to lock the gods in the mountain pass. He hired the magicless to murder the royals, because he knew we would not go to war over the murder of his brother."

Kailani lifted her head up, but she kept her eyes trained on the grain of the wooden table. She couldn't meet Grayson's eyes. Shivering, she wrapped her robe tightly around herself. "But why did he want war?"

"Other than revenge against the magicless? The Azarros wanted power, a lot of it. They believed the Strange mages deserved the throne because they're the most powerful."

Kailani scoffed. "Looks like they got their wish."

Grayson sighed. "Yes, but things didn't go exactly as planned for them. The Azarros planned the murder of the royal council long before it happened. They wanted a reason to abolish the magicless. A reason to take the throne. The Azarros had gained a following. People who believed in their power, in their hate. In their fear. They created an army, and they made lots of promises. They planned to take over the Kingdom, but there was always something in their way. The rest of the council."

A shiver raced along Kailan's spine. In her mind's eye, the royals sat around the table, oblivious to what was about to happen to them.

"When the Hunters killed Stasorin's family, Azarro knew he must act quickly or risk losing his momentum for good. He murdered the royal council, then used old blood magic to lock the gods in the mountain pass and siphon their power for himself."

Kailani froze as a rush of cold swept through her, raising the hair on her arms and sending shivers shooting across her skin. Azarro hadn't just stolen the gods' powers, he'd actually locked them away. That shouldn't have even been possible. But, of course, he'd found a way. Blood magic. *Gods.*

That had to be why the goddess of darkness presented herself in the pass. Fear sealed Kailani's throat. She swallowed rapidly, gripping her wand for strength. If the gods were already locked away, what ritual was she supposed to stop? What was she supposed to do with the staff? And Azarro...

Her body tensed as his voice rang in her mind. She could almost feel the death binders around her wrists. Feel the eternal cold that spread over her while under his spell.

"But why?" Kailani asked, looking up. "What does he want?"

Grayson was squinting into a burning candle's flame.

"Magic is full of gifts, and one must be gracious with their blessings from the gods. The Azarros wanted power at the expense of the other deities. The gods have been locked away for some time now, and each year, the kingdom dives further into darkness. Azarro's selfishness is corrupting the kingdom. The powers given by the gods at the Choosing are growing weaker. They're running out of magic to give."

"Growing weaker?" Kailani narrowed her eyes. It was impossible for the gods to run out of magic. They were the gods, after all. But she had heard the notion before, in not so many words. Older customers in Mom and Dad's shop, grumbling about how the younger generations were getting weaker by the year. Apprenticeships complaining that the newer students didn't seem to have the same grit as the previous years. "So does that mean those of us chosen since Azarro's first ritual have weaker powers?"

Grayson nodded, solemnly, and Kailani's head pounded. The gods running out of magic—that could mean the future generations wouldn't receive legacies. They'd go through the mountain pass and come out with nothing.

"The gods are angry," Grayson went on. "I'm afraid that time has done more damage than the Strange mages ever could. Azarro has rooted a deep fear of the magicless into Talisia's citizens, and the magicless are terrified of those of us with power. The war was gruesome. The toll on nature and humanity was irreparable." Grayson trailed off with a mournful look on his lined, drawn face. He stared into space, as if replaying the horrors of the war in his head. Kailani shifted in her seat and Grayson's eyes flickered back to her, his lips going flat. "When you went through the pass, something broke free. The gods weren't able to fully be released, but Fia was able to speak with you. I believe that the magic the gods used to try to escape was what triggered the explosions."

A wave of relief flooded through Kailani. "So my parents really had nothing to do with it? There were no bombs?"

Grayson shook his head. "No, but your parents are in danger. Blood magic can only be performed on a blood moon. If the goddess of darkness said a strange evil was set to destroy the kingdom, my guess is that Azarro's curse is running out. The veil is growing thin—"

Kailani's head was spinning in so many directions she could hardly make sense of what he was saying, but she managed to find her voice. "His curse is running out? What do you mean?"

Grayson folded his arms, clasping his hands in the billowing sleeves of his robe. "The magic Azarro performed is temporary at best. Azarro thought the ritual would make him immortal, like the gods. But his mortal body couldn't handle their magic. He can keep the gods trapped away, yes, but their magic will slowly drain from him. He'll start to lose his own magic as well. In fact, it's probably started already."

"I don't understand."

Grayson pulled out his wand, drawing a silvery line in the air between them. A faint green thread, the color of Strange, coiled together with it. "It's like a tether. Azarro probably didn't realize the enormity of what would happen when he performed that ritual, but his magic was joined to the gods'. Think of it as a game of tug-of-war." He twitched his wand, and the wispy silver line pulled taut, then jerked back and forth as if invisible hands were pulling at it. "The gods are trying to pull their powers back, and inevitably, they'll succeed. Azarro is only mortal, after all. The gods won't be able to break out of the mountain unless someone breaks the tether, but they can drain Azarro's magic from him—theirs and his—and the only way for him to stop it is to set them back again, by performing another ritual. Otherwise, he'll lose everything."

The thread he'd conjured suddenly went flying to the left, rising through the air until it vanished in a puff of smoke.

"Another ritual," Kailani echoed, as Fia's words came back to her.

"Yes. I believe that he plans on performing another ritual on the blood moon, using your mother, to lock the gods away once more. The gods chose you to free them."

Something cold sank to the pit of Kailani's stomach and she shivered. An image of Mom slumped over, Azarro collecting her blood, her life force. It was too much. Grayson reached across the table for Kailani's hand, but she pushed to her feet, unable to sit still.

Air. She needed air.

Bursting through the double doors, she let the fresh breeze wash over her. Took a deep breath. The double doors opened behind her but she didn't turn around. She could feel Grayson watching her, and frustration built in her chest. None of this made any sense, and it certainly didn't make her feel better about the quest.

The gods had chosen wrong.

"But why me?" Kailani turned to face Grayson. A sudden gust of wind blew her hair in her face and she squeezed her eyes shut. "I never wanted any of this! Can't they choose someone else?"

"The gods don't make mistakes."

"Well, it feels like they did." Kailani's voice cracked, tears burning behind her eyes. Slowly, she sank to the ground and hugged her knees to her chest. Her head was spinning. Her skin hummed, like her magic was restless. "I've never been anyone special. How in the gods am I supposed to stop him?"

Grayson knelt down beside Kailani, then took a deep breath. "Have you ever heard of the Realm of Chaos?"

She lifted her head, still not meeting Grayson's eyes, and shook her head.

"A long time ago, long before I became King, a Strange mage named Nerezza stole Fia's sacred Staff of Darkness. Nerezza believed that she was better than her magical counterparts, and believed she should decide who was worthy of magic and who was not."

Kailani's stomach lurched. She vaguely recalled Gorgan mentioning the history of the lost staff—it was one of the six wonders of the gods. All she could remember was that a Strange mage had destroyed it.

"Though many believed Nerezza was driven mad by the staff's power, destroying herself and the staff in the process, others believe the energy of the staff created the Realm of Chaos."

Kailani grabbed a fistful of grass, her throat tightening. She almost didn't want to know, but her need for answers outweighed her fear of what the answer was. "What is that?"

Grayson swallowed hard, the silence between them deafening. The only noise was the stream flowing from the base of the Far Lands down to the portal station. Kailani watched the water, felt its current inside her, until Grayson finally sighed.

"While it's true Nerezza was driven mad by her own corruption, she didn't simply vanish. Her corrupted magic created a darkness so vile that the energy around her collapsed on itself, forming the Realm. It's said the staff is still in the middle of the Realm, waiting for someone powerful, worthy, to wield it."

A shiver ran down Kailani's spine and she locked eyes with Grayson.

"You're not saying the staff is our key to stopping the ritual? Who's to say that the staff is actually in the Realm? No one has seen or heard of it for centuries!"

"It's there."

Kailani stared at him incrediously. "So the staff... it's real?"

Grayson nodded. "The other gods' wonders are out in the open for anyone to see. But the goddess of darkness was always more reserved. She was afraid of magic, of what it could do. She worried her magic would corrupt her creations. She wanted a way to ensure order. So she was said to have created the staff for instances where a mage has lost control of their power. Strange magic is fickle, you see. It can drive a person mad if they let it. I think Azarro has already crossed that line."

Kailani leaned forward, her heart racing. The staff was said to drain a mage of all their power. If she could find the staff, she could use it on Azarro, and stop the ritual. "So how do we get to it?" Her voice was breathless with energy.

"It won't be easy. In fact, it will be close to impossible. The realm will feature Strange magic at its most evil, most dangerous. The illusions will try to destroy you. Stronger mages than you have gone insane trying to find the staff, trapping them for eternity in their own illusions and shadows. You will need to train, Kailani, train your powers. They'll need to be precise if you wish to wield the staff."

Kailani's head jerked back. "Wait, you want *me* to go to the realm? Can't it be someone else?"

"If I could take your place, I would. But I'm afraid I can't. You were chosen by the gods, which means you alone are worthy."

Kailani's heart thundered. Little beads of rain fell from the sky and Kailani looked up at the charmed dome. The stream rippled from the water for a few moments until the rain stopped, and Kailani ran her hands over the wet grass.

"And Kailani–"

Kailani tore her gaze away from the stream and back to Grayson. He tapped his thigh with one hand, twisting his beard with the other. A sinking feeling fell over her. "You must train on your powers. Because if the staff deems you unworthy, it will drain your magic, for good."

CHAPTER FIFTEEN

*N*o *pressure.*

Really, *those* were the parting words Grayson chose as he dropped her back off at the arena, promising her that the Underground militia would have no problem teaching Kailani what she needed to know before they set off to find Fia's staff.

No pressure. But if she failed, her parents were doomed. The kingdom was doomed. The gods of magic were doomed. But, no pressure.

"Don't look so anxious."

Kailani turned to find Briggs walking out of the arena doors towards her. He had on the same smirk he wore yesterday, when he was joking around with his team. Kailani shifted her weight from one foot to the other. Briggs knew her name, knew her parents. But she knew nothing about him aside from his rank, second in command to the militia, and what legacy he was gifted with—the orange symbol plastered across his chest told her he was a Brute mage.

"Our goal isn't to master all of your magic today—it's just to make progress," Briggs continued. "You can try that, can't you?"

"As long as I don't blow up the entire arena," Kailani mumbled.

Briggs quirked an eyebrow, his lip twitching upwards. "We'll try to reign in the damage as much as possible."

He led Kailani into the middle of the arena, and she tried to peek at what Lyla and Patrick were up to, but he discreetly positioned her body so her back was towards the others. Kailani gulped. He was probably making sure the blast radius was directed away from them.

"So, what will we be working on today?" Kailani asked, trying to ignore her twisting stomach.

"Well, that's the thing, isn't it? As a champion, we aren't sure exactly what your abilities are just yet."

Kailani bit her cheek, shuffling her shoe in the sand. Since she'd gotten to Mirstone, her magic had felt much clearer than it had since her very first outburst. But she hadn't been using her powers. What was to say that the moment she cast a spell, the entire arena wouldn't blow?

"So, what does that mean, I just shout out spells and see what I can do? Hope I don't have an outburst?"

Briggs laughed. "Quite the opposite. Today we're going to work on control. Let's start with something fun: element manipulation." Briggs pulled out his wand. A brilliant obsidian stone sparkled from the tip of the cool metal. "From what I've gathered, you've got a lot of raw power—but you need to learn to control it. Such control comes in the form of physical and mental discipline, which I'm sure you've covered in school—but it also comes in the form of emotional regulation."

"I control my emotions just fine." Kailani picked at the hem of her robe. "I'm sure that's not the problem."

"You *repress* your emotions just fine, so I've heard," Briggs corrected. "That's not the same as control. Trust me."

"What's the difference?"

"Well, say you've got a pot in danger of boiling over. Putting a lid on it would be repression—whereas lowering the flame beneath it would be control. Throwing a lid on the problem can hide it, but eventually, the pot is going to..." Briggs made the motion of an explosion with his hands. "Resulting in your... *outbursts.*"

Kailani's eyes flickered downward. Maybe Briggs had a point.

"In any case, once you learn to control your magic, you'll be able to manipulate it to basically do whatever you want, within your physical bounds. For example... *industria!*" Briggs lifted his wand towards one of the toppled arena walls. With a twitch of his wrist, he summoned one of the boulders to him.

Then, with a second flick, the center of the boulder began to move and swirl until a perfectly round circle had been carved into the stone.

"As a Brute, I'm able to manipulate most solid forms of matter. Vitas can manipulate water and air, while Stranges can manipulate fire and earth. With your... situation, I'm not sure what form of element control you'll be capable of—rather, if there are any you *won't* be capable of—but it shouldn't matter. The fundamentals of element manipulation stay the same." Briggs used his magic to repair the hole in the boulder before continuing. "Elemental magic is all about focusing your energy—physically, mentally, and emotionally. It can be quite draining if not performed correctly, so make sure you check in with yourself as you're working with it. I wouldn't want you to pass out in the middle of our lesson."

Kailani took a deep breath. "I can do that."

"Good. Then, I'd like you to manipulate this stone by putting a crack in it—no larger than my hand, and no smaller than yours. Do you think you can do that?"

Kailani gripped her wand at her side. Briggs' requirements didn't give her much leeway. Still, she couldn't give up without trying. Her parents were depending on her. The *kingdom* was depending on her.

And besides, it couldn't be that hard to put one measly crack into a boulder.

She took a deep breath and nodded.

"Remember, elemental magic requires only one spell. Industria. Your energy will tell your magic what to do. Harness your wandstone, feel the power flowing through you."

Kailani threw her hand forward, feeling a warm flow of energy rushing along her arm, through her fingertips, and out of her wand. *"Industria!"*

BOOM!

The boulder exploded, shards of rock flying everywhere across the arena. Briggs barely managed to stop one of the rocks from nailing Kailani head-on.

"Is everything alright over there?" Roca called from the other end of the arena.

"Everything's just fine!" Briggs shouted back.

Kailani could've died right on the spot. She groaned, thumping her forehead with her palm, and stared at the mound of rubble through the gaps between her fingers. She braced herself for a harsh telling off—something she'd grown rather accustomed to in her many years of being a Grade-A disruption in class—but it never came.

Instead, Briggs moved his wand, bringing the pieces of boulder back together, forming them into a single stone once more.

Kailani squirmed where she stood. "I'm sorry."

Briggs didn't acknowledge her apology. "You've got a lot of power, that's for sure." His brow furrowed, as if he was just beginning to understand what he'd gotten himself into by agreeing to train her. "But we're focusing on *control*, remember?"

"Yeah, I know." Kailani rubbed her arms.

Briggs looked like he wanted to comment further, but apparently thought against it. Kailani was glad for his restraint.

"Let's try again, okay? Now, focus. Remember, controlled magic should always be intentional."

Taking a deep breath, Kailani faced the boulder again. She lifted her wand, attempting to do so with *intention*. Whatever that meant. Aiming it at the boulder, she imagined her magic driving a small crack into the hard surface. Only, this time her magic didn't surge at all. Screwing her face up in concentration, she tightened her grip on her wand and glared at the boulder. Still, nothing. Her head pulsed behind her eyes and Kailani let her arm drop to her side with a frustrated huff.

She didn't want to look at Briggs, but she could feel him watching her intently.

"Is something wrong?"

She almost laughed. "I blew that boulder to bits just minutes ago, and now I can't even put a single dent in it." Kailani groaned. "I don't know what's wrong with me."

She cast a longing glance at Lyla and Patrick. For Lyla, Roca had set up a small station stocked with healing crystals, salves, potions, and a small cast iron pot for brewing. Not far from them, Patrick and Nyia were gazing into a crystal ball with a dire intensity—as if it held the answers to the universe within it.

Why can't I be like them? Why can't I just have one legacy? Everything would be so easy if that was the case...

Her ability to harness every kind of magic should have been a gift. Instead, it was feeling more like a curse—the abundance of power within her was so overwhelming that she was unable to limit and control her magic.

A small poof of sulfuric yellow smoke began to rise from Lyla's iron pot. Roca patted her protégé on the back.

Kailani's eyes burned and she tore her gaze away. "It looks so easy for them."

"Sit down."

Blinking, Kailani shot Briggs a confused look. "What?"

"Let's take a break."

"I *can't* take a break. If I don't learn to control my magic soon, then Azarro will—"

"Kailani." Briggs cut in, sternly. "Sit down."

Relenting, Kailani dropped to the gritty sand of the arena floor. For a moment, Briggs didn't speak. Kailani listened to the garbled sound of Lyla and Patrick's faraway chatter.

Finally, Briggs sat next to her. "People haven't been very patient with you in the past, have they?"

Kailani could only shrug. Other than Linde, her teachers *hadn't* been patient with her—but could she blame them? She'd be a hypocrite if she detested others for not having patience with her —after all, she was beginning to wear her *own*patience thin.

"Magic is an art," Briggs said. He pointed to her wand briefly. "And while we have tools to manipulate this art, it must be treated with respect to get a desirable outcome. Even though the gods bless us with their gifts, what we can do with those gifts depends on the person."

"What do you mean?"

"For example, I'm a Brute mage. My spells are best when I have complete control over my physical strength. Different types of magic work with different abilities. Anyone can do a spell that unlocks a door. Yet, a Brute spell might burst the door to pieces; whereas a Luminate's spell works within the lock, acting as the key itself."

"That doesn't help me at all," Kailani muttered. "I have access to all the magic."

"That's why it's going to be so much harder for you to control. You have to be many things at once," Briggs explained. "Magic is fickle and not everyone can command a wandstone to their favor."

"Is this supposed to make me feel better?" Kailani asked.

"No. It's supposed to help you forgive yourself. You've been challenged with a very difficult task, Kailani, and you must give yourself the room and the space to fail." He paused, before adding, "It's clear that the rock isn't working. Let's try something new, okay?"

Kailani didn't want to try something new. She wanted to bury herself in the sand of the arena and tell the gods to pick a new champion—because clearly, she wasn't the right one. But Briggs seemed to believe in her, and she didn't want to disappoint him. So, reluctantly, she rose to her feet and followed him out of the arena.

The afternoon sun beat down on her as it rose higher in the sky. She followed Briggs down a rolling hill towards a small flowing creek.

Kailani knelt down, swaying her hand in the water, letting the cold liquid energize her. "How is this going to help me with my magic?"

"Water might be easier for you to control than stone."

"What makes you say that?"

Briggs stared at the water with intensity, the warmth of the sun reflecting in his deep brown eyes. "It's much more volatile." He gave her a wry grin. "Elemental magic all comes from the same inner source—and each mage, even in the same legacies, will be able to do different things with their abilities. I was thinking it might be advantageous to seek out the magic that suits you, rather than forcing you to suit a certain type of magic."

"So, what should I do?" Kailani asked.

Briggs stepped on a dry spot of land next to the creek. "Use your magic to splash me," he said simply.

She raised an eyebrow. "You're sure you want me to do that? I might send a typhoon your way."

"I'll trust that you won't." Briggs laughed.

Kailani bit her lower lip, raising her wand. She aimed it at a spot in the stream between her and Briggs and focused on driving the water upwards. "*Industria!*" The familiar rush of magic built inside her and she tried to restrain it as it began to flow into her wand.

Unfortunately, her restraint must have been too much— because instead of her magic splashing Briggs, it backfired and doused her instead. Kailani coughed as water went down her throat. She grit her teeth and took a deep breath. The cold water dripped from her sopping hair. A wave of soreness ebbed into her arm—the muscles had to be overworked with magical tension.

"Don't give up! Let's try just one more time, okay? Remember that unlike stone, water moves!" Briggs shouted.

How is that supposed to help? was what Kailani wanted to say, but she swallowed the words with a sigh and raised her wand against the will of her exhausted body. She began to summon her magic.

Then, it clicked.

Instead of trying to force the creek, Kailani imagined guiding the water—carving out a new path for it to flow through without breaking its current inertia. She absorbed the energy of the flowing creek, allowing herself to become vulnerable to its will. *Water is not like stone.* It felt like wrangling a wild horse as Kailani directed her magic to lead the water up and towards Briggs.

"*Industria!*"

She felt the familiar twitch in her arm—the urge to push her power to the maximum and send a huge wave hurtling —but managed to direct it into finer control of the water she'd already begun to manipulate.

As her heart pounded, Kailani coaxed the water with as much gentleness as possible, until it hit Briggs in comical slow-motion.

Kailani gasped, releasing the spell. The water splashed down. Spots of black loomed around the edges of her vision as her chest heaved.

"That was excellent, Kailani!" Briggs exclaimed, racing towards her to pat her back.

Pressure seemed to uncoil from Kailani's heart, and she felt light as air as she wrung out her soaking robe. She'd done it. She'd actually done it. As she struggled to climb the damp, slippery bank, Briggs gripped her forearm to help, and his smile was as wide as hers. Thankfully, he didn't talk much as they made their way back to the arena, allowing Kailani to catch her breath and recover from her magic use. It was strange—the huge explosions she'd created by accident with her magic had never drained her quite as much as the elemental manipulation did.

As they reentered the arena, Lyla and Patrick were packing up and crossing the arena.

"What happened to you?" Patrick laughed, looking her up and down. The robe had taken most of the splash but her jeans and shirt were still damp.

Kailani's cheeks burned and she looked at her shoes, but Briggs nudged her, plastering a smile on his face. "She controlled a wave."

Kailani glanced up as Patrick's eyes traveled from Briggs then back to her.

Lyla's mouth opened and she gasped. "That's amazing!"

"But we're not done yet." Briggs crossed his arms. "What do you say we give the rock another try?"

"Definitely." Kailani grinned. Finally, she'd actually learned some control.

Lyla pushed her hair behind her ears, brushing sand off from her clothes. Her eyes traveled from the arena towards the portal station, then back again. "We don't mind waiting. We can cheer you on."

Kailani's lips turned upwards and she almost said yes, but the stench of sulfur filled her nose. Lyla's robes were stained with potions. The odious scent of the ingredients clung to the air around them. Next to her, Patrick's hair was damp with sweat, his eyes drooping.

"No need to wait," Kailani assured them. "I'll meet you back at the cabin."

Patrick frowned, meeting her eyes, and Kailani nudged him. "I'm serious, I'll be fine. Go get yourselves cleaned up."

Patrick chuckled, giving a shrug. "If you say so."

Turning away, he and Lyla walked along the river path towards the portal. A spark of jealousy ignited in Kailani's chest as

Lyla punched in coordinates and the portal swirled to life, sending a breeze all the way up to the arena. She wished she could go with them, wished she could enjoy Mirstone and her new powers without the crushing weight, but she turned to Briggs instead.

"Ready?" he asked.

Kailani stood next to the large boulder and positioned her wand.

"Now, I know it might not seem like it, but this boulder moves much like the water—just on a much smaller scale. To make this work, you'll need to tune into the movement of the boulder. But instead of channeling the warmth of Vita, try finding the force of Brute. Do you think you can do that?"

Kailani nodded, reaching deep inside herself. She felt the chaos of Brute igniting inside her, felt anger and fear, and almost let it get to her. But instead, she commanded it, grabbing the thread and pulling it towards the surface. For the first time since receiving her matured magic, she felt control. She took a deep breath and tried to feel the boulder's movement. She closed her eyes, hoping to sense the vibrations within the rock, nearly breaking concentration to cheer when she found them. It was quiet, almost like a whisper—but it was there.

Breathing deeply, Kailani imagined the vibrations at the front of the boulder and pictured her magic slowly pushing the pieces of rock apart. Her head began to pound, but she pushed through the pain.

"*Industria!*"

A small crack rang out.

Kailani eased her eyes open, then gasped. A perfectly straight fissure had opened in the boulder. She pressed her trembling palm next to it, and a laugh bubbled in her throat. The fissure was just a bit smaller than her own hand.

"Great job!" Briggs clapped her on the back. "See, it's in you."

Kailani's chest swelled. She had *controlled* magic. She'd done something without blowing something else up in the process.

Sure, she might not be able to use that against Azarro. And sure, her body was practically screaming at her now—her muscles sore and angry, her head thumping like a drum—but it didn't matter. She'd *done* it.

"Think you have any more left in you?" Briggs asked.

Kailani shook her head. She didn't want to push her luck and ruin her good mood.

"Then, class dismissed. Go get something for lunch and we'll meet up again tonight." Briggs tucked his wand in his robe pocket. "Great job today. Seriously. And don't be so hard on yourself. Mastering matured magic is a feat on its own, let alone mastering all six legacies. Your outbursts are just an example of the raw power within you. Learn to harness that power, and you will be more than capable."

Kailani grinned, letting his compliments sink in. She was exhilarated, could feel the different legacies of magic buzzing below her skin like never before. "Do you think I can?"

"I think you can do that and so much more," Briggs said, without a moment's hesitation. "But it will take time. That's all."

Kailani nodded, staring down at her wand. It was only her first practice session, but maybe, just maybe, there was a chance she could complete the quest.

She had to, because her family depended on it.

CHAPTER SIXTEEN

S ea oats blew in the wind and Kailani danced in the sandy field overlooking the ocean. The water was the only place she felt at ease. Teal and turquoise swirls stretched as far as she could see. Warm sand welcomed her bare feet and salty air caressed her face as she walked, closer and closer to the sea. Dad ran along the coastline, splashing in and out of the water while he chased the seagulls resting on sand dunes up ahead. This was peace. This was tranquility. Mom's voice sang beautifully with the songbirds, peals of sweet laughter reverberating with crashing waves.

It was her favorite place on earth.

But storm clouds swirled beyond the water, until the beach was overcast and a low darkness fell over Kailani. Her heart raced as the scene in front of her changed. Fallen bodies and broken debris took the place of shrubs and plants. The sun-kissed sky brushing the water's edge was crimson. Footsteps echoed behind her, quickening their pace.

Kailani whipped around. No one was there.

Dark blue waters crashed against the shore, majestic against the rolling gray clouds swirling above. Her hair tangled as the sea breeze pelted her with salty dew.

"Kailani."

Her heart raced. She turned again, hearing the whisper of a young woman's voice.

"Kailani Slate."

"Who's there?" Kailani's voice shook.

Streaky lightning emblazoned the sky, followed by a thunderbolt like an explosion. The waves were colossal. Far out, a boat rocked back and forth. Taking on water, threatening to sink.

"Kailani!"

Mom's screams pierced her ears. She squinted out to the sea. Mom and Dad were thrown overboard, and the water pulled them under.

She ran as fast as her legs could carry her.

But the sandy beach stretched on and on.

The ravaged sea overtook the boat. Mom and Dad's screams echoed inside of her. She screamed too, but the water was out of reach.

She turned, and Queen Stasorin appeared on the sand.

Her face was blank. She watched the sea as if she'd seen the destruction before.

Rage overtook Kailani and she swerved towards Stasorin. She lunged forward, but as she reached for the Queen, her hands brushed through nothing. Stumbling, off balance, she landed hard on the ground. Gasping, she looked back up with wide eyes. Stasorin was here, but she wasn't, and now she looked transfixed, staring out to where the boat was taken under. A final, haunting scream ripped through the air and Stasorin's face crumpled.

"Ember..." she whispered.

Kailani's eyes narrowed as she pushed herself up. Ember? Mom and Dad were dying, and Stasorin was thinking about her dead sister? Why was she here? How dare she just stand by and watch them drown?

187

"What do you want from me?" Kailani screamed.

Stasorin looked at her as if seeing her for the first time, then her eyes widened. "You come here too. This same beach..."

Chills raced down Kailani's spine. Stasorin shook her head, and her expression settled into a blank mask. "You can't save them. Whoever you see is gone. Believe me, I've tried..."

Heat burned Kailani's ears. "This is all *your* fault."

Stasorin laughed. Not a menacing laugh, but a humorless, bitter chuckle. "You are the cause of all this destruction, can't you see?"

"No." Kailani shook her head wildly. "No. I didn't start a war. That was you. And the kingdom's been in chaos ever since!"

"Stupid girl," Stasorin cooed. "Reunited with your great grandfather for a day and you think you know everything, do you?"

Her grief turned to rage, and her skin burned. "I know that it was you who lied to the kingdom for years about what really happened to him. But you made a grave mistake that day."

"And what was that?"

"You didn't kill him. And you didn't kill me."

Stasorin smirked. "Trust me, if my uncle knew your mother survived, she wouldn't be alive now. In fact..." Stasorin's eyes narrowed. "You are the only one who may be able to keep her that way."

Kailani's heart lurched. "And how's that?"

"Give yourself up."

The hair on Kailani's arms stood up as the breeze blew salt water in her face. She lifted her chin, trying to appear more confident than she felt.

"What do you want with me?"

Stasorin's eyes went wide. "You don't know, do you?"

Kailani snarled. "I know you trapped the gods! But you won't get away with it. I *am* the champion, and you won't complete the ritual again."

Stasorin laughed, without mirth. "We already have everything we need to complete the ritual. Resistance is futile. The only question is, will you try to save your parents, or hide like your cowardly grandfather?"

Kailani's breath hitched. Mom and Dad were alive now, but how long would they stay that way? If she failed her quest, Azarro would complete the ritual using Mom's blood. The gods would stay locked away, *and* she'd lose her parents.

As if reading Kailani's mind, Stasorin went on. "There's only one thing that will set your parents free."

"Yeah?" Kailani asked, trying to keep her shaky voice confident. "What's that?"

Stasorin grabbed Kailani's arm before she could react. She touched the tip of her wand to her forearm and Kailani screamed, trying to jerk her arm out of Stasorin's grip. But Stasorin was stronger. A burning sensation pulsed through Kailani. When Stasorin released her, a bloody scar was seared into her arm. Kailani stumbled backwards. The unity symbol was carved into her. The same symbol on her wand.

"Your blood for theirs."

Kailani stared up at her through wide eyes, clutching her burned arm as her pulse hammered in her ears.

"You have no idea what you've done. What the gods created. They marked you for certain death. Give yourself up, take their place in the ritual, and your parents won't die for you."

Kailani's heart sank. Azarro wanted to use her in the ritual…

"The only way this will end is in death." Stasorin pointed ahead.

Kailani turned and gasped.

An army of rebel soldiers battled against a sea of Protectors. The wounded spread across the beach, littered with destruction, cloaks, and crimson. The air, once light with salt and sun, was now covered in thick smoke and embers from curses gone awry. The haunted faces of survivors flashed in Kailani's mind, faces she wouldn't soon forget.

With a cry, she spun back to Stasorin.

But she was gone.

Kailani glanced around, biting her lip, her body heat rising. She rubbed her temples.

This was a dream. It had to be a dream. A horrible, terrible...

"Kailani."

As her heart sank to her stomach, Kailani's head shot up.

Dad.

She whipped around, barely making out two figures in the mist. Mom and Dad were on land now. Hovering by the water, reaching out to her. Calling for her. She ran for them, but the closer she got, the further they seemed. Heartbeat thudding in her chest, lungs on fire, Kailani panted for air. Her legs couldn't move any faster. But still she sprinted.

"Help us!" Mom screamed.

Then, they disintegrated into thin air.

"No!" Kailani cried.

She sat bolt upright in her bed, her body throbbing with the force of her beating heart. Someone was shaking her shoulders.

"Kailani! Kailani!"

Gasping for breath, Kailani scanned the room from dark corner to dark corner, and her throat seized with panic until she remembered where she was. Lyla and Patrick's faces came into focus, leaning over her.

"Kailani, are you okay?"

One. Two. Three.

The cabin. Mirstone. Still, that wasn't enough for her to relax, to shrug it off as a horrible nightmare, because her forearm pulsed.

Swearing, she wrapped her hand around the spot Stasorin had touched and squeezed tight. It throbbed, but it was too dark to see if the scar was still there. Her eyes shot towards her wand on the table, the lamp across the room. But Patrick and Lyla's gazes were trained on her, and the last thing she wanted to do was rehash what happened in the dream.

"Just a nightmare." She tried to focus on steading her breaths as she waited for the pain to pass. Sweat rolled down her forehead. Her chest heaved. She wanted so badly for it to have been a nightmare, but dread coiled at the base of her spine. Strange mages were known to visit people in dreams, and Queen Stasorin was one of the most powerful Strange mages there was.

"Are you sure?" Patrick's eyebrows drew together.

The moon lit up his features and he shared a concerned look with Lyla.

Gods, she was sick of that.

She nodded, pulling the covers up to her chin. Scenes of the destruction flashed in her mind, of her parents, of the Queen's warning.

Grayson's words came back to her.

The toll on nature and humanity was irreparable.

"Do you want to talk about it?" Lyla asked.

"No." She didn't mean to sound so forceful, but they wouldn't understand. "I'm fine, really, just a nightmare. Go back to bed."

Another shared glance. Lyla's eyelids drooped and Patrick yawned. They had to be just as exhausted as her, but they weren't just going to drop it. Kailani slowed her breathing, letting her blanket fall to her lap. She reached for her mug on the bedside table and took a sip of water.

"Really." She managed a stiff smile. "I'm fine."

Patrick frowned, tilting his head. Kailani's hands shook. If she said one more word she was going to word vomit, and she was trying too hard to suppress the gruesome images flashing through her mind. Trying too hard to ignore the searing pain wrapping around her wrist. But Patrick crawled into bed, pulling her into his arms, and tears brimmed her eyes.

"I have them too," He spoke into her hair. Kailani looked up at him and he stroked his hand over her shoulder. "About dad. Every night since we got here."

Lyla sat on the bed, wrapping the blanket in her hand and twisting it tightly. Her head hung low. "Me too." Patrick pulled her close. Her voice was low. "I know it's not the same. I shouldn't even care after what my parents did. Sometimes I have nightmares about losing them. But mostly I have them about if I would have stayed."

Kailani reached a hand over and grabbed Lyla's arm, and they huddled together in the dark, as silent tears streamed their cheeks. As her heart raced, Kailani stared at the ceiling through wide eyes while Patrick and Lyla curled up on her bed. Sleep was no longer an option. She waited until she heard Lyla's shallow breaths, Patrick's deep snore, before grabbing her robe and tiptoeing across the cabin. As quietly as she could, she slipped outside and turned to face the ocean.

She sucked in a lungful of night air, stealing a glance at her forearm. Her heart dropped. The unity symbol was there, just as it had been in her dream.

The Queen *had* visited her. Which meant it was real.

She could save her parents. But that meant…

She'd have to sacrifice herself. Sacrifice the kingdom.

She lowered her head to her knees. There wasn't a good option. Dread coiled inside her. If only she could talk to her parents, they would know what to do. How to fix this. If she turned herself in, there was a chance they'd be safe.

But there was a chance Stasorin was messing with her, and she'd use them all to complete the ritual.

Her powers were growing stronger. Stasorin underestimated her. The gods chose her for a reason. She could do this.

Fixing her eyes to the stars in the sky, she counted in her head to thirteen, a small comfort of her normal life.

She would train, every free moment if she had to, to save her parents before the blood moon.

CHAPTER SEVENTEEN

*K*ailani didn't want to get out of bed.

She'd twisted and turned all night, ending up going to Lyla's empty bunk to finally fall asleep. Patrick and Lyla were like stones slumped on her mattress and no matter how hard she tried, she couldn't get comfortable.

Couldn't get the images of her parents' sinking boat out of her mind.

But she dragged herself out of bed and fixed herself some mint lemonade tea. She had her first training session with illusion magic today, and she'd promised Lyla and Patrick they'd go into town to do some exploring before her afternoon session with Grayson. And while she wasn't particularly keen to delve into illusion magic after Azarro's episode at the hospital, and her dream last night, it was her only shot at securing the staff in the Realm of Chaos.

The scarring on her forearm was completely gone, but the mark still burned as if Stasorin had caused an invisible brand. She only used the pain as a reminder of what she had to lose.

Kailani squinted into the morning sun as she stepped outside, letting the fresh air wake her up. Lavender aromas filled her nose and she smiled at the hanging plants outside her doors, reminding her of home. Patrick and Lyla were already outside, spread out on a blanket each with books in their hands. Lyla closed hers when she saw Kailani, then nudged Patrick.

"Ready?" Patrick asked, folding the blanket and throwing it on the floor of their cabin.

Kailani nodded, taking one more sniff of the lavender before heading for town.

She was used to being an outsider, with no one paying much attention to her, aside from occasional sneers from Trey and his cronies. But as she walked with Patrick and Lyla down the cobbled streets towards Mirstone proper, all eyes were drawn to her. Whispers seemed to follow wherever she went, which made Kailani's ears burn.

'The champion has arrived in Mirstone.'

'How many days until the blood moon?'

'We trust in the gods.'

As she strolled down the road hosting an array of colorful cabins, kids played in their front yards, waving as Kailani passed. Her heart lurched at one young mother watering her garden outside her front door, her son playing by himself in the grass. The mother noticed Kailani staring and smiled. Tears welled in Kailani's eyes as she forced a smile back.

When they left the neighborhood and walked into Mirstone proper, some of the tension released from Kailani's shoulders. Shops of all sizes and colors lined the streets, some long and narrow with doors that you had to walk through sideways to fit, and some short and bulky, in odd shapes with unique features. Kailani walked past a bookstore called *The Night Owl*, where the building was built and painted like a book stack shoved together. A vendor was set up outside a shop called *The Teapot*. Patrick grabbed a free sample of a purple smokey drink called Dragon's Breath. Lyla stuck up her nose after Patrick's entire body turned purple.

"That was amazing!" Patrick laughed and grabbed one more, before continuing down the road.

They passed shops called *Enchantments, Lionhead Quills,* and *Fantastic Fashions* before coming up on the stone-walled edge of the cliffs. Artists lined the cliffs edge, painting the sea slamming against the rocks below while shore birds flocked around them. A gust of wind knocked a paint can over and Kailani gasped, but before it could spill all over the street, the can caught itself and tipped it upright.

Lyla giggled. "This place is a dream."

Kailani laughed, soaking in the view. It really was. The only place she could compare Mirstone to was Magnolia during the Choosing Ceremony each year, but even Magnolia's street fairs didn't compare to the magic being used at Mirstone.

"Do you think the rest of the kingdom is like this? Outside of Farrow?"

"Hard to say," Patrick said, wandering up to another vendor passing out samples of scones and berries.

Kids sat in front of a stage up ahead, where two Strange mages performed illusion magic, creating an entire circus show of imaginary animals. They gained an audience quickly. People came out of shops to watch and the kids laughed, screaming out animal requests. Lyla chuckled when one of the mages created a mouse riding on top of an elephant, but her face turned serious when she looked back and caught a glimpse of Kailani's face.

"How do you feel about starting your work with illusions?" She asked.

Kailani bit her lip, forcing her eyes away from the stage. Her stomach was uneasy. She didn't know a lot about illusions, but her experience so far wasn't creating much confidence. "Not great."

They stepped up in line and Patrick ordered three stones, turning around and handing one to each of them. "Just think of it as one step closer to conquering your magic."

Kailani took a bite of the scone. White chocolate and raspberry burst in her mouth. It was almost as good as Dad's.

"That's easy for you to say," she muttered. "You don't have to fight them."

Patrick shared a look with Lyla and looked away. Kailani sat on the rock wall overlooking the cliffside, a few feet away from a group of kids around their age. One of the girls locked eyes with Kailani and her eyes flew wide. She mouthed something to her friends and jumped down from the wall, skipping over.

"Oh my gosh, it's you, it's really you!"

After days of getting that reaction, she still had no idea what to say, so Kailani just gave her an awkward smile. The girl was jumping up and down, gawking at her. She had dark skin and curly brown hair, with eyes that made the hair on the back of Kailani's neck stand on end. Wicked scarring ran across half the girl's face, over her right eye. One eye was deep brown, while the eye underneath the scar was opaque and white.

"I'm Nori." She reached out and grabbed Kailani's hand.

"Hi. I'm Kailani."

"I know." The girl laughed, her eyes trailing to the right. "And you're Lyla, and you're Patrick. Your faces are all over the news."

Kailani's breath hitched. She glanced over at her friends—Lyla's face had paled, and Patrick looked confused, crumbles of his scone dropping to the ground.

Lyla stumbled with her words. "What do you mean 'all over the news?'"

Shorebirds pecked at the crumbs of Patrick's scone. Nori shooed them away as a broom floated over and swept up the dessert.

"The Queen is saying you're, like, dark mages and stuff, you know, because they're all mad they didn't catch you. You're the youngest person to have ever run beyond the barrier!"

Kailani clenched her jaw as Lyla let out a loud gasp.

"And don't get me started on the champion rumors. People are really thinking you could end the Dark Queen's reign." Nori grinned, then whirled around. Waving to her friends, she called, "Hey, I'll catch up with you."

They waved goodbye and turned the other direction.

"The Dark Queen?" Kailani frowned.

"Yeah, you know, Queen Stasorin. The rebels call her the dark Queen." Nori smirked. "So does half the kingdom, probably, just in secret."

Kailani's head thundered against her skull. Saxton residents didn't love the sanctions placed on them, making it harder to find work, harder to learn, harder to thrive. But most Lancaster residents loved the Queen. She'd always assumed that was how the rest of the kingdom felt, too.

Apparently not.

"I think it's cool," Nori continued. "It's about time we get some excitement around here. You know, for a rebel territory, these people are so boring. I was just about to get some lunch. Are you guys hungry?"

Kailani looked at her friends. Patrick shrugged. He was always ready to eat. Lyla was clicking her thumbs on her fingers and probably running the worst news headlines over and over in her head. Surly she was thinking of her parents, and what they must think. A distraction could be good for all of them. They still hadn't learned much about the missions or inner workings of Mirstone, and Nori seemed like she had been there awhile. Maybe she could learn a thing or two before her training session.

"Sure." Kailani shrugged.

"Great! The food here is wonderful. This is where people usually hang out. There's so many shops here, and new ones pop up every week. Magic is really explored here, unlike back in the kingdom. Everyone says the Dark Queen really limited what was taught in schools. They didn't want anyone becoming too powerful, you know?"

Mom and Dad always talked about how different school was

for them growing up. It could be the sanctions, they didn't do anyone any favors. But it could also be the fact that since Azarro's first ritual, the magic gifted to mages grew weaker year by year, without anyone even understanding.

They continued down the path of shops along the jagged cliffside. Patrick's eyes widened as he pressed his hands up to a tall, thin shop window that was named *Hera's Wands and Wonders*. He peeked inside.

"Wow," he breathed, in a voice full of wonder.

Kailani couldn't see through the window, but the awe in his voice made her throat swell painfully. He'd be working in one of these shops right now, if it wasn't for her.

"Come on!" Nori said, opening the door and leading them in.

An old woman with a small gray bun greeted them. The nameplate on her green desk read Hera. Star and moon shaped gems dangled off the pointy hat perched on top of her head. Faded posters of wandstones and their properties hung around a small square room, where shelves of wandstones were displayed.

Patrick ran his hand over the platforms. "They're so beautiful."

Lyla gravitated towards the Charm stones, naturally, and she eyed a large, shiny amethyst. She looked it over before dropping it back down on the shelf, and her eyes lit up as they roved over the quartz, amber, and pearl stones that were also associated with Charm magic. She waved a hand over them, closing her eyes, before stopping over a plain milky quartz stone. She picked it up, closing her fingers over the stone, and smiled.

Kailani couldn't help but smile, too.

"This is nothing." Nori raised her eyebrows up and down, a grin spreading across her face. "Look what's back here." She led them to the register and motioned towards a windy set of stairs behind the desk. "May I give them the tour?"

"Go ahead." Hera smiled and pushed her glasses up on her face.

As they climbed the stairs, it was like they were in another shop entirely. Kailani shivered. The temperature was much cooler than the bottom of the shop. Hundreds of wandstones were scattered along long rectangular tables, most still covered in earth. Jewelers in long black robes with gold and purple emblems chipped away dirt, while others polished stones that looked like opals, rubies, aquamarines, and some she didn't even recognize. Another table was full of sheets of metal where a mage melted metal and crafted the liquid into beautiful wands.

"Wandstone jewelers," Nori said.

Patrick's eyes were fixated on the jewelers. "How did you get all these stones?"

"Some of the mages go out and mine for them. Grayson was able to find unoccupied land in the Far Lands when he was King. He blocked some off as unincorporated territory before the war began. He figured we'd need stones someday. Good thing he did. They send our miners there all the time. They even go to the islands and other kingdoms. They've found stones no one else in Talisia has."

"Wow." Patrick's eyes were as wide as the moon. "So, you make all your own wands here?"

There was a fire behind Patrick's eyes as he watched the miners work. Kailani bit the inside of her cheek. If it wasn't for her, Patrick would be training to be a wandstone miner as they spoke. He'd be learning how the different stones worked for each branch of magic, maybe even going on an excursion later in the year. But instead, he was in hiding, on the run, away from his dad, the only family he had left. If he could join these miners, he might even like that more. Undocumented territories, no monarchy stepping on his back. No one taking the best stones for the Magi Elite.

"Yeah, pretty cool, huh?" Nori pulled out her wand. "I used to have a moonstone wand, but I had to leave it behind when I came here. So, they made me a new wand with a Lapis Lazuli stone. A fresh start, you know? My magic has never been stronger!"

The blue stone was gorgeous. Specks of white and gray made it unique, just like Nori.

"I'm sure they wouldn't mind making you guys new ones, if you wanted."

Kailani gripped her old wand in her pocket. The aquamarine stone always blended so well with her Vita magic, and Mom had given it to her when she started school. She couldn't imagine parting with it. A new wandstone might help her master her new powers faster, but she couldn't give up one of the only things she had left from her family.

Patrick hovered his hand over every single Vita stone and Kailani bit her lip, holding back a smile. He was in his element, and she made a mental note to ask Grayson if he could pick one out for himself, and maybe even work with the miners once training was over.

If the jewelers noticed them, they didn't show it. They were in their own world as they polished and examined the stones before placing them in baskets and moving onto the next. Kailani followed Nori and her friends back down the steps. A few people were browsing the shelves and a swell of warmth filled Kailani. She could get used to living in Mirstone.

"Thanks, Hera," Nori called, as they left the shop and headed towards the trail leading to the water.

"Check this out!"

Kailani locked eyes with Lyla and shrugged as Nori walked to an empty vendor cart.

"Four watermelon slushes," Nori said to the cart.

The cart creaked and spit out four large cups full of red slushy liquid. She handed them each a drink. "Pretty cool, huh? You just say whatever you want and it pops right out. This stuff is addicting."

Kailani reached for hers, the cold sweet drink sending shivers down her skin as she slurped it down. She walked down the winding path until the cobblestone turned to sand, and the waves rushed the shore in front of them. She couldn't help feeling like she had missed out on so much not growing up here. Lancaster Academy taught them that magic was strict, only for the purpose of bettering society. But in Mirstone, magic seemed fun.

Lyla danced in circles in the sand, her arms stretched wide, and their laughs reverberated as Kailani closed her eyes, all her worries over the past couple of days slipping away, if only for a moment.

"What kind of things do you do around here?" Patrick asked.

"Well, I like to work in the lab with the scientists. They create the tech for missions. I even have my own lab and work on designs of my own sometimes."

"That's amazing!" Lyla said.

Kailani leaned forward. They'd never be allowed to work on tech of their own in Farrow. Even with an apprenticeship, they were closely monitored. "What have you been working on?"

"I'm working on a vest right now that will absorb the energy of a spell cast at you and send it back to the spell caster. Then I won't have to worry so much about my brother going out on missions."

"Your brother is a soldier?" Kailani asked.

"Yeah, he's the second in command of the militia."

Kailani's jaw dropped. "*Briggs* is your brother?"

"Yeah." Nori laughed. "Don't worry, I'm much cooler than him."

As Kailani looked closer, she could see Briggs' sharp features in Nori's smaller face. Briggs was different from Nori, though. He was tough, calculated, whereas Nori seemed like the bubbliest person in the world.

Kailani leaned back too, letting her feet float in the water. "What kind of stuff does the rebellion do?"

"Lots of cool stuff. Briggs is working on evacuating the Pits, actually."

Kailani's heart leapt. She'd almost been sent to the bloody arena, where the Magi Elites pitted mages against wild creatures for battle. Pitted legacies against other legacies in duels. It was always hanging in the air in Saxton, where her neighbors were always worried that if they couldn't pay their bills, the Protectors would drag them off there. If the rebellion could evacuate the Pits, that would be a miracle in itself.

"That's amazing."

Nori nodded. "Yeah, he's pretty cool." She turned her head aside so her eyes were cast in shadow. "It's disgusting what the monarchy finds fun. They're horrible, all of them. You know they do experiments? On *people*? Magicless and prisoners. Dr. Might is…" she shuddered, and her voice got really low. "Horrible."

Kailani's eyes widened. "What type of experiments?"

Nori opened her mouth to speak, then caught herself. For a moment, she stared into the water, tugging on her sleeve. Then she forced a brittle laugh and shrugged. "Who knows, but they've been doing it for years. They all just want more power, like what they have isn't enough."

Kailani had the distinct impression Nori knew a lot more about these experiments than she was letting on, but she didn't pry. Instead, she changed the subject.

"Did you guys grow up here?"

"No, we've only been here a few years."

"What about your parents?" Lyla asked.

Nori fell silent and looked out to sea. Kailani's stomach churned. The energy around them shifted. Suddenly Nori looked much younger, and the scars along her eyes stood out in the bright sunlight.

"No, it's just me and Briggs," she said quietly.

Making eye contact with Lyla, Kailani decided she probably shouldn't pry any more. Instead, she dug her toes into the sand, looking up to the sky and letting her skin bask in the sun. The waves were her energy, caressing the shore and retreating back to the safety of the open water. She wanted to dive in, to escape in its wondrous depths.

Patrick slurped the rest of his slush. "I'll never get tired of the food around this place."

As Kailani lifted her glass to her lips, the portal station near the rocky edge swirled to life, and she just about choked on her drink.

Liquid splashed up on her, and she jumped, spinning to look at Patrick. He'd dropped his cup, and his jaw hung open as he gaped at the portal. Now that her own shock had passed, Kailani's heart swelled.

Grayson had come through on his promise.

Mr. Mahoney stood twenty feet away and a moment later, Patrick launched forward to wrap his arms around his dad.

Grinning, Kailani followed him, with Lyla and Nori close behind.

"How did you get here?" Patrick asked, his face flushed and his eyes shining.

Another figure shot out of the portal and Kailani's jaw dropped.

"General Baylock?"

Scratches covered Baylock's face and arms and she had a bulging black eye. She caught sight of Nori and smiled. "Ah, Nori, making new friends, I see?"

Nori beamed. "Always am!"

Kailani stiffened, scanning Baylock's injuries. One of the cuts above her eye was still bleeding. "I don't understand, what's going on?"

"Grayson asked me to retrieve your friends' families, per your request. Unfortunately, things didn't go quite as planned."

Baylock's eyes flickered to Lyla for a fraction of a second and frowned, before turning back to Kailani.

A sudden motion on her left drew her attention. She turned as Patrick reached for her, his eyes soft and glowing, and wrapped his arms around her. "Thank you, thank you so much."

Kailani's ears burned. Patrick had left his entire life behind on

203

a whim that this place was real. The least she could do was bring his father to him. She grabbed his hand and squeezed tightly. "No, thank you. For everything."

"There's an empty cabin a few down from where you three are staying. You can show him the place, if you'd like," Baylock told Patrick.

Patrick nodded enthusiastically. "Yes, of course, thank you, thank you so so much!"

Patrick led his father up the stone steps leading to Mirstone proper. Seneca already looked different here, like a little more magic might do him some good. But her heart sank as she spotted the expectant look on Lyla's face.

Licking her lips, Kailani turned back to Baylock. "What about the Hollingsworths?"

She tried to ignore how Lyla's eyes lit up, especially when Baylock's expression hardened.

"I'm afraid they didn't want to hear us out."

"What do you mean?" Lyla's voice was low.

Kailani braced herself, anticipating what was coming.

"We tried to tell them you were safe, and that we would bring them to you. To freedom. But they didn't want any part of it. We couldn't give away too much information. They called the Protectors on us." Baylock frowned. "They've grown close to the Magi Elite since you've disappeared. Have made all kinds of deals."

Lyla shrugged as if she didn't care, but her eyes misted up. "I'm not surprised. They just don't get it." She turned, wrapping her robe tight around herself, and drifted back towards the water. Nori bowed to Baylock in a mock curtsy, before following Lyla.

Kailani's chest was heavy. She'd had a feeling the Hollingsworths would react to their daughter joining the rebellion exactly the way they had, but that didn't stop her heart from breaking for Lyla. Guilt twisted her gut. She was lucky. Her parents may not have told her everything about her past, but only to protect her. All Lyla's parents cared about was control.

Kailani shifted her eyes back to Baylock, wincing at the purple bruise forming on her cheek. "Thank you for bringing them here. Do you have to go back now?"

Baylock squinted into the sun. "I'm afraid I can't go back to Farrow. The Hollingsworths know I'm a part of the Underground now. It'll be all over the news by morning."

Kailani stole a quick glance towards Lyla and then back to Baylock.

"They wouldn't even hear us out. The Protectors were there in minutes. I barely made it to Seneca's house before the Protectors showed up. We had to break through the barrier, just as you did, and find the safe house."

Kailani watched Seneca and Patrick talking as they moved their way up the cliffside. Seneca had braved the Far Lands to get Patrick back. He believed in Patrick enough to go with a complete stranger, no matter the danger. If something would have happened to him out there, it would have been all Kailani's fault.

"What happens now? For Farrow?"

Baylock looked down. "They will appoint someone new, probably someone who they can influence."

Kailani winced. Her parents and Baylock had helped so many people escape to the Underground, but now they were all gone from Farrow. And from the sounds of it, things were getting worse back in the kingdom. It would only get worse from there on out.

"And Kailani—they testified."

Kailani's heart stopped, her head jerking to Baylock.

"The execution date has been set for the day of the blood moon."

Kailani's heart twisted. Her body went rigid. They were going to murder her parents and cover it up as an execution. Her stomach churned, she was going to vomit.

"I must go get cleaned up and find Grayson. I'm very glad you made it here safely. I'm sorry I couldn't do more for you."

Kailani nodded, half in a daze, as Baylock headed up the cliff. Kailani couldn't move, she could barely think. She looked back down towards the beach. Lyla was hunched over on a beach towel that Nori had spread out, drawing circles in the sand with her finger. Nori was comforting her, but Kailani was too far away to hear what she was saying.

She wanted to walk back to her, comfort her, but her feet were cemented in place. She needed to see Grayson. To start training. She had to do *something*. Things had been so twisted since the day of the Choosing Ceremony. So different. She wanted to see what the news was saying about her parents, about her and her friends, but it wouldn't change a thing. She didn't know how many people in the kingdom believed her to be a monster—believed her parents to be monsters—but there was only one way to prove them wrong. Only one way to save her parents.

The Realm.

CHAPTER EIGHTEEN

Grayson's laboratory was enormous.

The double doors clicked shut behind Kailani, casting the room in deep shadow except for the sparkles of light streaming in from the windows, lighting up the bookshelves lining the walls.

Standing four stories high, each level of the lab was dedicated to different types of experiments. The first floor held shelves of potions, ingredients, and a vast assortment of ancient books, most covered in dust. Kailani imagined curling up on the couch and going through every one of them. The second floor was dark, lamps lighting up small areas of the floor where scrolls and quills were spread out. The third floor was full of telescopes looking up to the sky with large windows where the walls should be. And the fourth floor was labeled off limits.

Goosebumps spread over Kailani's skin as Nori's words about the monarchy's experiments came back to her, but she shrugged the thought off immediately. No way was Grayson involved in any experiment Dr. Might was working on. He'd formed an entire rebellion against people like Might and Azarro, after all.

"Ah, Kailani, welcome."

Turning towards the voice, Kailani smiled as Grayson appeared from the shadows. Her eyebrows pinched together when she realized Grayson wasn't alone. A tall girl in a skintight black shirt and black skinny jeans stood next to him. Kailani recognized her from the day she arrived at Mirstone, but without her uniform on, she couldn't remember which legacy she was. Her eyes were dark and held an air of mischief that made Kailani wary. She leaned against Grayson's desk, one black combat boot resting against the wood, the other planted on the ground.

When Kailani stopped a few paces away, she pushed herself forward to close the distance between them. The green Strange emblem was stitched on her dark gray jean jacket and Kailani gulped. The girl pulled her thick, curly hair into a ponytail at the base of her neck and smiled.

"Oh look, the champion's here. This ought to be fun."

Kailani shifted from one foot to the other, rubbing her arm. "Hey."

Her ears burned. As much as she hated it, standing in front of this woman made her feel small and meek.

"Kailani, you remember Tilly. She's part of Brigg's team. She's going to be helping us with illusion magic today."

Tilly crossed her arms, one side of her lip twitching upwards. "Ever dealt with Strange magic before?"

Kailani's chest twisted, and she looked down at her shoes. Flashes of Professor Gorgan's robes going up in flames popped into her mind, followed by Azarro's mind tricks. A paralyzing cold swept through her body. She bit her lip, nausea rolling in her gut.

"Just for the practicum."

She could feel Tilly's eyes on her, watching her, so she tore her gaze to Grayson. She thought she was ready to start training in illusions, but electric pulses fluttered up her arms and her palms were starting to sweat. "Will you be training with us?"

She was finally starting to learn what legacies she was capable of, and understand how they felt when she reached for them. But she was still only working with surface level magic. The thought of practicing such powerful magic made Kailani's skin crawl, her previous outbursts playing through her mind. But if Grayson was there to help ground her, it might not be so bad.

"I will be here."

Kailani swallowed hard. Pressure built in the back of her head. She'd let the fun of training, the magical intrigue of Mirstone, fog her mind on how close the blood moon was. She was getting better at her magic, sure, but she was nothing in the face of Azarro and his army.

"What about my parents?" Kailani asked, trying to stall. "Have you figured out where they are? What if we were able to get to them? Then Azarro wouldn't even be able to complete the ritual."

Tilly sighed, looking at her fingernails. Kailani shifted. It might not have been the best suggestion, but the thought of reaching for Strange magic, the waves of cold and darkness that seeped deep into her bones when she tried to wield it, made her shudder. She didn't want to try it. She didn't want to think about it.

"Without the staff, Azarro will find another means to his end. We must strip Azarro of his powers, break the tether, to stop him once and for all."

Kailani sighed. It didn't matter if he tried again, as long as her parents were safe. They'd help her figure it out. They'd know what to do. But she didn't have a choice, right now, so she took a deep breath and nodded. "Okay."

Grayson waved a hand towards the empty chairs in front of his desk, his long golden robe swooping with his movement. "Have a seat, then."

Kailani followed his instructions, and Tilly took the chair next to her while Grayson strode behind his desk. To try and distract herself from what was coming, Kailani scanned every inch of her grandfather's laboratory.

Grayson was messy. Like, really messy. He sat behind a large oak desk with papers lying everywhere. A tall organizer was in one corner, almost as tall as Kailani. With a flick of his hand, the papers fluttered in the air into different bins.

Kailani's lips parted in awe. Very few people were capable of doing magic without a wand.

Emboldened by his display of magic, Kailani leaned forward, eager to learn despite her nerves. She wanted to know everything about the Realm of Chaos, about the magic it would take to get there, to secure the staff. Even if it meant wielding Strange magic.

It wasn't that she believed the rumors that all Strange mages were dangerous. It was just that she didn't know any in real life, aside from the Queen and her uncle, who'd tortured her and locked her up. That didn't exactly earn them a lot of trust. Then again, she'd felt a strange sort of peace when she was in the presence of Fia Azarro. That could have been because she was a goddess, but surely Strange magic wasn't supposed to be dangerous. And she'd have to harness it if she wanted to save her parents.

So she'd have to listen to Tilly, even if she was intimidated by her powers.

Tilly leaned back in her chair, pulling out a beautiful golden wand with skull and floral filigree. A large Labradorite stone was encircled at the top by metal thorns. Kailani stared at the wand-stone with wide eyes. She'd only ever seen this particular type passing by shops, but never planted in a wand before. Thinking back to *Charmstones for Beginners*, she tried to remember what the Labradorite stone represented. They were finicky stones, very powerful to be able to handle the intense emotion Strange magic required. Labradorite represented transformation. Amplification. Guidance. A beautiful stone. A powerful stone.

"Today we're going to be focusing on illusion magic." Tilly twirled the wand in her hand. "The realm of Chaos will test you. You will have to be strong enough to determine what is an illusion and what is not. It will try to keep you away from the staff."

Kailani's chest tightened and she shifted in her chair.

As if reading her mind, Tilly gave her a wry smile. "Strange magic may have a bad rep, but there's really no reason to be afraid. Strange magic is loyal to its user. You just have to be confident in yourself."

Kailani nodded, but her palms were already starting to sweat. Confidence wasn't exactly her virtue. She'd been okay at a lot of things, never great at anything specific. Her elemental magic had been improving, sure, but she'd have to be near perfect in Strange magic before she could retrieve the staff.

"Go ahead then," Grayson told Tilly.

And before she knew what was happening, before she could even think, Kailani was drowning.

She sucked in a breath but water filled her lungs. Thrashing, she looked around for someone to save her. Anyone. Floating specks of shattered light peeked through the water, surrounding her, the pressure on her chest was insurmountable.

Squeezing her eyes shut, she focused on her breaths.

It's not real.

It's not real.

But she plunged deeper into the water until everything was dark. The pressure on her chest was so strong she was sure she would snap. She *couldn't* breathe. It *was* real.

And she was dying.

This was it. It was over before she started.

Red pulses of light flashed at the edge of her vision. Her chest exploded as if fingers wrapped around her heart and twisted, pulled, shattered.

She saw Lyla and Patrick, watched them mourn her, move on without her. She watched Azarro complete the ritual, Mom and Dad slumped over as his body glowed a golden, sparkling hue.

Then the screams started.

Mom and Dad. Their voices cut like blades on her skin, gargled through the sea's depths, but present as ever.

Kailani, help me!

Kailani, over here!

Numb. Vacant. Hollow.

Desperately, she inhaled.

Salt. Her throat raw, chest on fire—

Slowly, the pressure lifted and she gasped for air. Grayson's lab flittered back into focus. Dark blue spindles raced across Tilly's skin like a spiderweb, and her black eyes were trained on Kailani.

Kailani fell forward off the chair, crashing to her hands and knees, gasping. She shivered, curling herself into a ball.

"You're holding yourself back."

Kailani's head snapped up. The whites of Tilly's still dark eyes were back. Her skin was mostly normal now, but still pale, sickly.

Clenching her jaw, Kailani sucked in a deep breath. Her entire body trembled as she lifted herself up and flung herself back in the chair.

Tilly didn't understand. How would she like it if she heard her parents cry for help, but couldn't do a thing about it? The illusions might have been fake, but the situation was real, and as the panic subsided, something else bubbled in Kailani's veins.

Anger.

"You gave me no warning," Kailani snapped. "What the hell was that?"

Her blood pounded through her body and Brute magic whispered in her ear, her palm throbbing as if the magic was begging to escape. To release her fury.

Tilly just smirked. "You think you'll have warning in the Realm?"

Kailani could only gape. Tilly was insane. This was her first lesson with illusions, what did she expect?

"Now, now—"

Kailani's eyes cut to Grayson. He sat behind his desk, fingers pressed together, watching them as if they were a science experiment. Brute magic raged in Kailani's veins. Mom was his granddaughter, for gods' sake. How would he like it to trade places, hear the screams, watch them go time and time again?

He cleared his throat. "I know it's hard, believe me."

She leaned forward, ready to leave. Then Grayson's hollow eyes misted up, his throat bobbing, and Kailani slumped back. All traces of the roaring Brute magic fled her body, leaving her cold and empty as she choked down a breath.

He didn't need to trade places with her. He'd lived it. Watched his sister and his daughter ripped from this world, their life forces snatched from them before they could move on to the Wonder Grounds. Her grandmother's smiling face popped into Kailani's mind, then the scene ripped apart as if claws scratched through a photo.

Grayson didn't need to be tortured with illusions. He'd seen the whole thing.

"But it's the only way to fight them," Grayson continued quietly, his voice still choked with emotion. "And if they don't have power over your mind, they don't have power over you at all."

Kailani sniffled. He glanced at her, but before she had more than half a second to register that there were tears in his eyes, he'd already raised his billowing sleeve to wipe at his face. He looked at her—but whatever he saw must've reminded him of whatever he was trying not to think about, because he cleared his throat and stood abruptly.

"Excuse me," he muttered gruffly, brushing past them towards the door. "I'll return in a moment."

Frowning, Kailani looked over her shoulder, then froze. A regal painting in a golden frame smiled down on her, of a woman in a teal robe with curly dark hair and amber eyes. Below the painting, a golden plaque read *Kai Neptuna-Mistrahl*.

Her eyes darted to Grayson, but the door had already shut behind him.

Kailani sucked in a breath, then let it out slowly. With one last look at her grandmother's portrait, Kailani squeezed her palms together and turned to Tilly. The sunlight creeping in through the windows cast her in a shadow. Kailani couldn't gauge the expression on her face.

"I don't want to hear my parents screaming. I can do anything else."

"That's not how Strange magic works," Tilly snapped, her narrowed eyes coming into focus as she leaned out of the shadow. "I don't always choose the illusions. I hack your brain, and your subconscious does the rest. That's what the Realm of Chaos will do to you. It takes your deepest fears, your darkest secrets, and uses them against you."

"Then I can't do it!" Kailani's voice cracked. "I'm not strong enough for this!"

"Afraid?" Tilly asked. "Good. Use it."

"Being emotional hasn't really helped my magic in the past," Kailani snapped, as her fingers tightened around her wand.

"Being emotional is the only thing that *will* help Strange magic," Tilly countered, arching her eyebrows. "I know you're going through a lot right now, and it seems like the only way you can cope with it all is to shove everything down. But with Strange magic, those emotions will eat you alive. Your magic will overtake you. You have to bring your feelings to the surface, deal with them head on."

The memory of her parents' screams echoed in her ears and a knot blocked her throat. It didn't matter if it was only an illusion. She didn't want to think of that. She didn't want to feel that. Every time she did, a crushing sense of helplessness seized her, because there was nothing she could do—

"Look," Tilly said, softening her posture, "I get that it's scary. But everything in life has repercussions. Magic included. Some take a more emotional toll, like Vita, Charm, and Strange. Some take a more physical toll, like Brute, Kairo, and Luminate."

Kailani nodded, picking at her fingernail as she tried to ease her rolling stomach. She'd learned all this in school. She knew Strange magic took a certain kind of power, a kind of power she didn't have.

"Strange and Vita magic are the most powerful. The magic of creation and darkness—you can't have one without the other. Take your friend Patrick, for instance. The perfect embodiment of a Vita. His emotions are a part of him. He wears them on his sleeve and his creation magic flows through him freely, constantly warming him. Well, Strange magic's emotion is deeper. People think we're cold, but we're more of a burst of light, a spark of energy. You have to dig deep inside yourself to find that spark. That's when you'll be able to fully harness Strange magic."

Kailani licked her lips, her eyes flicking up to Tilly and away again. The webs were gone from her skin but burned into Kailani's mind. Strange magic took, drained, debilitated.

"It's driven people insane..."

"Only when people can't control it properly. Strange magic is the most fickle, and it changes with your emotions. If you lock down your emotions, you lock down your magic. If you lose control of your emotions, you lose control of your magic. It's that simple."

Kailani folded her arms. "That's hardly simple."

"Well, if you're determined to be negative," Tilly scoffed, shaking her head. "Let's try a different route. Try picturing somewhere you feel at peace."

"I don't—"

"Try it," Tilly said firmly.

Kailani grit her teeth but closed her eyes and let her mind drift to the kitchen of her family's little cottage, where Mom and Dad were laughing and passing plates around. That only made her eyes sting, as did other memories of her parents, home, and her life before all this. So, she pushed those memories away and let her mind wander to the afternoon she'd spent with Lyla and Nori by the water. She remembered how it had felt as the water lapped around her and Nori chattered away with the birds chirping above them. Slowly, her jaw unclenched as the memory of the sun's glow warmed her skin.

"Now I want you to think of what's stressing you out. Try and let the good memory outweigh the bad, change it in your head."

Kailani cracked her eyes open, resisting the urge to laugh. Like only *one* thing was stressing her out.

Tilly leaned forward, resting her elbows on her knees. "Eyes closed."

Kailani did as she was told, taking a moment to find the peace of the sun on her skin again. As the memory washed over her, she frowned. What *wasn't* stressing her out?

For a moment her thoughts raced, and all memory of that moment on the beach vanished beneath the crush. Her power, the blood moon, her past. But then, one thing loomed largest. Her greatest worry. That was her parents, and their safety.

Leaning back in her chair, Kailani took a deep breath. She imagined her parents in their garden back home, laughing and singing and—

Kailani's heart dropped to her stomach. She was sinking again, thrust into an illusion, but this time, it wasn't water.

It was quicksand, and it was up to her waist in a breath. Breathing fast, she clawed and scraped at the sands but that only caused her to sink further. Her head snapped up, her mouth opening on a scream for help, but her eyes caught on the boat from her dream rocking back and forth ahead of her.

Azarro stood over her parents, fire crackling at the end of his wand as someone—Mom or Dad—cried out.

Kailani's heart raced. Suddenly, she was in the Realm of Chaos. The staff floated in front of her. She reached for it, the only thing that could save her from this mess. But when she grabbed it, the metal froze her skin, little trickles of ice spreading up her arm and over her entire body. She was hollow. Her magic gone.

Kailani took a deep breath, remembering Fia Azarro floating in the mountain pass, her hair flowing behind her.

'Save us, Kailani Slate. Save your people. Be our champion—'

Those words echoed in Kailani's ears, thrummed through her heart. The goddess had chosen her that day. Now, Kailani thought of the true astral projection Grayson had shown her. How the Queen had been lying to her people this entire time. How Azarro siphoned the gods' power, selfishly, at the expense of the people of Talisia. How they repressed the kingdom's magic all this time.

Her fists clenched. She was meant for this. She had to be.

The gods don't make mistakes.

A coldness deep inside her spread through her chest and her limbs. Her palms were numb, but instead of flinching, she harnessed the feeling, wrapping it into a ball in her hands.

And there, she felt a flicker.

The flicker was deep inside of her and she reached for it, pulled at it. Her body felt light as air, like she was floating, and the fog cleared from her brain. She pictured the sun from the beach, heard Patrick and Lyla's laughs, Mom's singing, tasted the lavender moon tea, and smelled Dad's raspberry scones. The blackness faded. She slashed through the illusion and it disappeared, replaced by the staff of darkness.

Every bone in her body felt light as air. She reached for the staff once more, but all her worries crept back in her mind and suddenly she was sinking again, further, further, her shoulders going under.

Hurry, Kailani, we're running out of time.

Chills raced along her skin and the coldness that overtook her leveled her mind.

Fia still floated in front of her.

Gasping for air, Kailani held her chin high to keep from going under completely, struggling to move her arms through the sand. They were like cement, but she pushed anyway, screaming with the effort until her arms burst through the top of the sand in an explosion. A blue light flickered from her palms and the sand moved as she commanded.

Then she was on solid ground and the blue ball of energy turned orange. Azarro was back, still standing over her parents. She hurled the ball of energy at him, but his appearance twisted, growing larger, stronger. Kailani was weightless. Something cracked inside her head and she jerked, grabbing her entire swell of magic and slamming it in his direction.

He disintegrated. Tiny specks of gray floated through the air.

Her heart all but stopped in her chest. As she slammed back into reality, her head whipped around. She was back in Grayson's office, with the messy desk and plush chairs.

Stunned and shaking, Kailani rested her hands on her knees and tried to catch her breath.

Tilly stood off to the side, her mouth hanging open. "Holy gods."

Kailani understood her surprise. Because somehow, some way, she'd just disintegrated all of Tilly's illusions.

CHAPTER NINETEEN

·····

*K*ailani woke late the next day.

She was up late into the night with shivers and
anxiety, a hangover from the Strange magic that her body still
wasn't used to. Her body was stiff, achy, and her head felt like it
was full of fluid.

She'd spent the past week training to fight illusion magic,
sleeping, or exploring Mirstone with Patrick, Lyla, and Nori.
People either treated her like a well about to burst or a celebrity.
At every opportunity she could find, she grilled Grayson about
her family's history, how Mirstone came to be, and what he knew
about the Staff of Darkness. But she hadn't found out much more
than after his alleged death, Mom had faked their family's deaths
and joined him. But the Far Lands were no place for a child, and
Grayson hadn't yet established Mirstone. So Mom and Dad
landed in Saxton, where they were sure the monarchy wouldn't
look. But the longer they stayed, the more they fell in love with a
quiet, simple life. It didn't take long for them to grow closer with
the people surrounding them.

Mom had started making her potions and Dad took any work

he could find, until they had enough to start the shop. By the time she'd started school and became best friends with Patrick, Mom and Dad had started recruiting people against a monarchy they were sure would be the end of Talisia.

They weren't wrong.

As Grayson said, the war left the kingdom scared and brittle, and Queen Stasorin was the hero that built it back up, conveniently leaving out the part she played in creating it.

But now, there was finally a chance for real change to be made.

And it was all riding on Kailani's shoulders.

Feeling stiff, she dragged herself out of bed and went to the vanity, fixing her loose braid. Despite everything, she smiled at herself in the mirror. Getting her matured magic wasn't the celebration she had dreamed of, but she was finally starting to control her magic. It was starting to blend with her will, like a third hand, instead of feeling like it was its own separate entity. Like her powers had ignited something inside of her, something that only she could see beneath the surface of her skin.

Grayson finally believed her to be ready for the Realm, and Briggs was prepping his team to escort her there the following day. Kailani felt confident for the first time in a long time.

Humming to herself, Kailani got dressed and strode out of the cabin, savoring the crisp air on her face. Lyla and Nori were having breakfast on the cliffside. As she approached, Lyla brushed her hair behind her ear and laughed at something Nori said. Kailani hovered a few paces behind them, grappling with a strange sort of reluctance to interrupt, then Nori glanced over her shoulder and smiled. Lyla followed her gaze.

"Kailani!" Lyla grabbed the books resting on the blanket and placed them in her bag, making room for Kailani to sit. "We were just talking about my aura therapy session this morning."

"Cool." Kailani smiled, dropping down beside them. "How'd it go?"

"It actually was great," Lyla pulled her hair into a low ponytail and smiled, looking off in the distance. "Seneca has made such a huge recovery since aligning his auras. And Roca is such a wonderful teacher. You could come with me sometime, if you wanted. Patrick comes too. We've actually started training together, because Vita and Charm overlap so much."

"Oh yeah?"

"Well, Charm's Aura manipulation and Vita's Empath abilities are actually quite similar, you know. Though, they do differ in one big way. Charm magic can manipulate an emotion, while Vita magic only takes emotions away. It's a subtle, but pretty important way of discerning the two," Lyla said.

Kailani nodded, wishing she was in class with her best friends, training normal powers for a normal life.

"It's crazy, you know." Lyla's voice was soft as she looked down at her shoes. "If we were home in Farrow, my parents wouldn't have let me take that apprenticeship. The one at Williamson Institute."

Kailani's stomach twisted. Lyla would have moved to Magnolia, gone to a fancy Charm school with a fancy apprenticeship. She'd have been guaranteed a job at the most prestigious hospital in Talisia as a healer. All in exchange for testifying against Kailani's parents.

"But when I'm in there, doing the aura therapy, there's something so incredible about it. There's such a connection between us and the patients." Lyla's eyes misted over. "It's just sad, you know, thinking about what I would have missed out on. Everything I did miss out on, because of them."

Nori turned over on her side, brushing her hand over Lyla's. A spark of jealousy spread through Kailani as they shared a smile that looked a lot like Kailani was missing something. Then Lyla cleared her throat and nodded before them.

"Patricks back."

Any jealousy left inside her dissipated at the sight of Patrick strolling toward them, the wind tossing his hair into his face. Kailani grinned, but it quickly turned into a frown the closer Patrick got.

He was rushing, his robe whipping in the wind behind him. Sweat dribbled from his forehead as if he'd been running. He was carrying a large crystal ball in one hand, his wand in the other, and a look of terror was painted on his face. Nearly tripping over herself in her haste to get up, Kailani rushed forward, followed by Nori and Lyla.

"What happened?" Kailani asked, as her heart dropped to her stomach.

"Kailani..."

His voice was raspy, like he was out of breath. Kailani rushed forward, grabbing the heavy ball from his hands and setting it gently on the ground.

"What is it?"

"I saw a vision... with Nyia..."

Kailani's eyebrows shot up. A vision. A real *vision*. Sure, they'd played with tarot cards and Patrick had pretended to see the future before, but he'd never actually seen anything real. It was like Mirstone made his abilities more powerful. Despite herself, she let the corners of her mouth curve upwards, momentarily forgetting everything but her pride in what Patrick had accomplished—

Then a vicious gust of wind roared past, flinging her hair in her face. Kailani wrinkled her nose and tried to push it back, against the wind.

Once she got her hair under control, the world settled back in by degrees. Overcast skies, static in the air. A distant gray cloud that heralded an impending storm. The others were silent.

A hollow pit sank into her stomach. Patrick had a vision, but he wasn't smiling. Nori's face was grave, and Lyla's lips were parted as she stared at Patrick, as if waiting for an explanation.

For a moment, heavy silence hung between them. Not one dared to shatter the spell, even though the question was on the tip of Kailani's tongue.

It was Lyla who found the courage to speak. "What was it?" Her voice was nearly lost in the wind.

Patrick took a deep breath, rubbing his sweaty palms on his pants. "Your parents." His voice was shaky, his movements jerky, as he twitched his head towards Kailani. "I saw them in a cell. There were red flashes, the Strange symbol, a lot of screaming. And Kailani…"

Kailani couldn't breathe. The ground threatened to slide out from under her as Patrick looked up and met her eyes.

"I could smell blood."

Darkness tunneled in Kailani's vision, her feet wobbly beneath her. "Blood?" she sputtered, body rigid.

Her parents slumped over in her mind's eye, particles of light floating from their bodies, Azarro collecting their blood. Only this time, it wasn't one of Tilly's illusions. This time it played in her head on repeat.

The sun was hotter than it was before, she threw off her robe and fanned herself with her hands. Patrick rushed her, so close… too close…

Lyla's hands were on her shoulders and Nori stood back, a look of horror plastered on her face.

Her head spun. She couldn't breathe.

"Kailani…"

Lyla's voice was in her ears. Patrick's hands steadied her.

Her hands shook and her heart pounded as Baylock's words came back to her.

The execution date has been set.

"I have to get to them."

She turned quickly, sprinting down the hill towards Mirstone proper. Wind blasted her face and leaves crunched beneath her feet. All she could focus on was the blood pounding in her ears as she took one step after the other, her thighs screaming as she sprinted faster. Faster.

The portal. She needed the portal. She had to find Grayson. "Kailani, no!"

Footsteps thundered after her, but she didn't slow down.

"Kailani, what if it's a trap?"

She stopped in her tracks and whipped around. Lyla was breathless, taking deep breaths in and out. She held up a finger indicating she needed a moment. Nori and Patrick caught up behind her. Kailani bit the inside of her cheek, a cool metallic taste filling her mouth.

"What if Stasorin is messing with you again?" Lyla panted. "She visited your dream. What if she implanted the vision in Patrick?"

Patrick shook his head, his eyes narrowing. "It seemed pretty real. They were in a cell…"

"Atonement," Kailani said instantly. Grim flashes of the dark fortress, one she'd only ever glimpsed in history books, whirled in her mind. "It has to be Atonement. Where else would they be keeping them?"

"Let's just wait," Nori said calmly, holding up her hands in a placating gesture. "Slow down, we can talk to Briggs."

No. She couldn't slow down, she couldn't wait, her parents needed her. Her eyes darted towards the portal. Ten steps and she could teleport to Atonement. She might get caught but at least she'd be with her parents. Their broken bodies flashed in her mind and she squeezed her eyes shut, trying to free her mind of the gruesome images. When she opened them, Lyla was fiddling with her talisman. Nori was biting her lip, and Patrick's eyebrows were almost touching. They had to understand…

She looked towards the portal again. It swirled to life and two soldiers arrived. They locked eyes and bumped fists before heading the opposite way. Soldiers. Briggs.

Maybe talking to him wasn't such a bad idea.

"His team! We can go to Atonement, rescue them!"

"Wait, what?" Lyla's eyes were wide.

Baylock said the execution date was set for the blood moon. But what if Azarro found a way to complete the ritual without the blood moon? He could have found another way to lock the gods away, he wouldn't need her parents anymore. They wouldn't be worth anything alive... What if they'd miscalculated and the ritual was tonight?

What if... what if...

"I have to go for them. I don't have time to go for the staff, and we don't even know if that plan will work. Please, Nori, do you know where Briggs is?"

Nori bit her bottom lip, waiting a moment before speaking. "I think so."

Kailani followed Nori on her heels as she typed in the coordinates to the portal. Her hands trembled and she looked around nervously as screams echoed in her ears. She flung her hands over her ears trying to drown them out, squeezing her eyes shut and mumbling numbers over and over again. It didn't help. Seconds seemed like hours as the portal swirled on, the orange hue swirling violently. She jumped through without caring where it took her, ending up right by the training arena and offices.

Nori checked her watch. "He's probably with the team now."

Nori creaked open a door into a dimly lit building, but Kailani barged past her. She didn't care who she interruipted. They needed to *move*.

A room full of holoscreens stared back at her and she looked around at the many doors surrounding the circular room.

"This way," Nori said, motioning towards a corridor in the back. Kailani rushed down the hallway but Nori held out a hand. "It might be better to wait until they're done—"

Kailani burst through the double doors, Patrick right on her heels and taking a place at her side. Multiple pairs of eyes landed on her. Lyla crereped in behind them, hiding out of direct view, followed by Nori who was staring directly at Briggs.

For a moment, everyone was still, but then Briggs shot to his feet. His face was a mask of concern as he stepped around the table towards them, crossing the room to Nori's side in three quick strides.

"Nori, is everything okay?"

Her cheeks flushed. "Yeah, uh—" she motioned towards Kailani.

"What is it?" Baylock stood too; her eyes narrowed.

"Please." Kailani's voice shook. "My parents are in Atonement. I know they are."

Briggs and Baylock shared a glance. Somebody moved behind them. Kailani's face burned as she looked from face to face. Tilly lounged behind the table, shaking her head, along with Josie and the two other Kairo mages in Briggs's squad—Leonard and Arun.

None of them really reacted. Their steady, impassive gazes made Kailani's pulse rise. They should be moving, making plans—anything. Mom and Dad had risked everything for this rebellion, and they were just... sitting there. Like Mom and Dad didn't matter, like they didn't believe her. "I know how it sounds. But Patrick had a vision—"

"He had a vision?" Baylock's eyebrows raised. "Explain."

His face flushed, but he stepped forward and cleared his throat. "I just had my session with Nyia, she was showing me how to see visions. At first I was seeing small things, like food and stuff. But then it was like something... something took over my mind, made me feel like I was there. And I saw her parents." Patrick's throat bobbed, and his voice became shakier, as if every word was a struggle. "They were in a cell, the Strange symbol appeared. I could smell blood and see flashes of spells. I couldn't tell what was going on, but the screams..."

Kailani shuddered, her mind flitting back to the gruesome

astral projection. How her grandmother looked as she crumpled, the murderer's sword stained in blood. And suddenly, seeing Pat so haunted, so emotional, she wanted to wrap him in a hug and never let him go.

But instead, she held her chin high and looked at each rebel in turn. They had to see. They had to. Yet, as she looked from face to face, *still* no one moved. Briggs tapped his fingers on the table, as if deep in thought. Tilly arched an eyebrow and Leonard and Arun shared a skeptical look. Only Josie looked somewhat concerned as she started to rise from her seat, but a quick glance at the others made her sit back down.

Kailani could only stare at them, blood pounding in her ears. Did they not hear him? Why was no one moving?

It was Baylock, whose arms were folded, who spoke first. "That's it?"

That's it? *That's it?*

Gaping, hardly able to believe what she was hearing, Kailani glanced at Patrick. Silently, she begged him to say something. Anything else, as long as it convinced them. Maybe if he lied, added more to the story...

Without meeting her gaze, he muttered, "yeah," and looked down at the floor.

"That could have been any cell," Baylock said briskly, turning back to Kailani with a stoic look on her face. "I'm sorry, but your parents are not in Atonement. We have sources—

It was like something in her snapped.

Suddenly, she didn't give a damn about their sources. She didn't give a damn about their authority, or their excuses. Roaring Brute magic surged within her, a murderous swell, making her heart thunder and heat burn her palms. Spots crowded into her vision as sweat beaded on her forehead, and all she could see was their indifference, their dismissal, for two people who had given up *everything* for them.

She couldn't take it.

"How do you know for sure?" she demanded, marching towards their table. "I could go-"

"Absolutely not." Baylock's voice was firm. "Your parents are not there. Your only focus should be on the Realm of Chaos. This is a distraction. A ruse, possibly planted by the Dark Queen herself."

Her muscles quivered. She wanted to scream at them, to make them see sense, but through the haze of Brute magic there was enough of Luminate's logic to soothe the temptation. Shouting would accomplish nothing.

Forcing her voice to steady, Kailani lifted her chin. "The Strange symbol was in the vision. It had to mean Atonement... and the blood moon is only a few days away!" Fia's words rang through her mind. "I'm running out of time."

"Kailani..."

"No!" she snapped. Tilly narrowed her eyes, but she was past the point of caring. She knew this was right. Like the gods implanted the vision in Patrick, to warn her so she could save her parents. "I can help them! Tilly, you said yourself my magic is strong."

Baylock shook her head. "You're not going anywhere. We need you to focus on the Realm—"

"The Realm of Chaos, yes, yes I know. But what if the staff isn't there? Or what if I can't obtain it? What if it's a freaking myth and Azarro guts my parents? They're going to be exected for gods sake!" Her voice cracked, and she hated how everyone in the room was looking at her. But nothing else mattered. Her lip quivered. "I have to go to them."

"Your parents aren't there, Kailani." Briggs' voice was full of pity, and she hated it. "We will be leaving for the Realm tomorrow. Your mind must be at its sharpest. This is the only way to save them."

Kailani bit her trembling lip, trying her hardest not to cry as gruesome images played like a reel in her head. They didn't understand. Her parents could be dying this very moment, and they wanted her to go back to her cabin and get a good night of sleep. She couldn't do it. She swallowed, glaring at the ground. She was the one with the unity symbol on her wand. She was the champion. She should be heard, at the very least. If they didn't want to take her seriously, then fine.

She'd just have to go herself.

———

KAILANI PUSHED OPEN the doors of the command building. Patrick rushed after her, Nori and Lyla following slowly behind. Kailani's eyes fixed on Lyla's fingers, pattering against her thumbs repeatedly. There was risk, sure. Major risk. But if Patrick's vision was correct, and she was certain it was, her parents were in Atonement. If she could get to them, then Azarro wouldn't be able to complete the ritual at all.

"Kailani, I don't know…"

"I know it's dangerous." Kailani looked around, her voice low. They were outside, but Briggs or one of his soldiers could come out any minute. "But if I don't try, I won't be able to live with myself if something happens to them."

She couldn't stop thinking about the dream since Patrick's vision. Stasorin's voice haunted her, telling her the only way to save her parents was to turn herself in.

Unless the Queen really was messing with her, attempting to lure her away from Mirstone or buy time until the blood moon. Her stomach lurched, but she shook the thought out of her head. Patrick wasn't dreaming or pretending. She felt it inside of her. Like her magic was telling her to go.

"We don't even know any defensive spells," Patrick pointed out.

Kailani frowned. "We?" She looked back and forth from Lyla

and Patrick, noting the resolute expressions on their faces. As her eyes widened, she shook her head. "No. *No.* You guys aren't coming."

Patrick scoffed. "Don't be ridiculous."

"Kailani, we're not letting you go alone," Lyla said.

She paced back and forth, still shaking her head. "You guys have already risked enough for me."

"And look where we're at!" Patrick exclaimed. "Without you, we would never have known this existed."

"Or what the monarchy was really up to."

Kailani's chest felt like it was twisting. If she was honest with herself, having Patrick and Lyla there would make her feel a lot better. But if something happened to them, she'd never forgive herself.

"No way." She folded her arms resolutely.

Patrick reached for her hand. "They're like my parents too. You aren't going alone."

Kailani winced. "I can't stop you, but really, you've already done enough for me."

"I could go too!" Nori said.

Kailani shook her head. "No way. I mean, I appreciate it, but I don't want Briggs to kill me himself."

Nori raised an eyebrow. "I don't think he's going to be happy regardless."

The image of Briggs' face when he found out they went against orders filled her mind and she winced. But come to think of it, maybe Nori could help. "Is there anything you can tell us about the prison?"

Nori's eyes lit up. "I think I have a map! Somewhere, in my lab…"

"You mentioned you designed tech for missions. Is there anything that might help?"

"Well, most of my stuff is in the prototype phase. I mean, it's not like it's dangerous… probably. But—" She raised a finger in the air. "Ahh, I do have one thing! Follow me!"

Nori took them back near Grayson's lab, and went to a smaller building down the way.

"My study." Nori dug through a large box, pulling out safety goggles, a long golden robe, and finally a large metal vest. She handed it to Kailani. "It's supposed to repel curses, but I only have one."

Kailani looked over the vest. "Repel curses?"

"Yeah…" Nori smirked, but she looked at the vest and frowned. "It hasn't been tested yet."

"That's amazing. Do these types of things exist in the kingdom?"

"The monarchy's Protectors have them. But there aren't many in circulation that I know of."

Kailani set the vest aside. "Thank you."

"I have the map here somewhere." She dug through more bins and threw stacks of paper behind her. "I've spent years eavesdropping on my brother and the rebels. It might not be an exact replica, but I think I was able to sketch the layout pretty well."

Lyla grabbed the map, her eyes roving over it. "You drew this yourself?"

Nori smiled. "I have many. I love drawing maps of the kingdom, the Far Lands, the outside world. I know there's more out there to see, and one day, I'm going to see it all. Then I'll be able to draw real maps."

Lyla set the map aside. Her eyes were glued to Nori, and Kailani took the opportunity to look over the map while they indulged in making them.

There were thirty-three floors. The first twenty-five were labeled with fifteen cells each. Murderers and thieves all had different floors. Rebels were in the middle. The hair on Kailani's arm stood up. Floors twenty-six through thirty were labeled execution floors, and thirty-one through thirty-three were labeled experiments.

"Change of watch is at six am. You should probably go right before that, that's when the Protectors will be sleepy. Chances are, they'll be goofing off and not paying attention. Nobody ever tries to break *into* Atonement after all."

Kailani nodded, trying very hard to ignore that last part, and Nori went on.

"There's this broken part of the fence here, one of the rebels' contacts from inside fixed it up so people can go in and out. But it's covered up so Protectors can't tell unless it's open. You'll have to go in there—" she moved her fingers over the map. "And through this door. From what I understand, it's a utility hallway, almost always empty. The portal will take you to our contact's house next to the prison. It's pretty... well, not the greatest location. But it's our only contact there at all. You'll have to wait for the guards to pass the broken fence. Then you'll have three minutes until they circle the prison. Three minutes to get inside."

Nori threw her arms around Kailani, squeezing her tight. "Good luck."

With the vest tucked in her pack, Kailani, Lyla and Patrick walked back to their cabin. Dragonflies and lightning bugs flew around them. Any other time Patrick would be holding his hands out, letting them land on his fingers. Kailani would be dancing in the moonlight and Lyla would be laughing at them both. But the only sounds were the grass crunching beneath their feet and their shallow breaths.

Kailani was sure Patrick and Lyla's minds were running wild, though, if her own was anything to go by.

Their room was dark, the moonlight lighting them up enough to see their scared faces. Kailani took the vest out of her pack and set it between them.

"Me and Patrick have elemental magic, Lyla, so you should wear the vest."

"No way," Lyla reached for the vest, running her fingers along the cool metal. "You should wear it, Kai. You're the champion. If this doesn't work out, you're the only one who can go on to still get the staff."

Kailani's stomach lurched. It had to work out... it had to.

"Kailani's right," Patrick argued. "We have our elements to protect us. You should wear the vest."

They went to bed without saying another word. Kailani tried closing her eyes, but she already knew sleep wouldn't come. She loved Patrick and Lyla for wanting to go with her. The trek sounded less scary with them along, but at what cost? She listened for the sound of their breathing, and sat up.

If she left now, maybe she'd be back by the time they woke up. She shook the idea off, because the idea that she'd make it back, going alone, was unlikely. But she couldn't let them risk their lives, again, for her. They'd be safe here in Mirstone. Standing up, she reached for her pack. Patrick stirred in bed and looked over at her. "Are you okay?"

Kailani swallowed. No. She wasn't. But what did that matter now?

"I'm fine."

He got out of bed, shuffling over towards her and sitting down. "I can't sleep either."

Kailani leaned into him. "I don't know if this is the right idea. I'm just so confused. I want to save my parents. But I'm afraid I won't be able to get the staff. It could drain me of all my powers and then they'd be dead anyway. There's no right answer. I'm failing at this quest."

Patrick pulled her closer to him, his hand rubbing her back. "Not even close."

"I'm messing everything up. What good is this symbol if I can't make the right decisions? Save my parents?"

Taking off his gloves, Patrick locked his hand around Kailani's wrist and the world came back into focus. The anxiety was gone.

He pulled her in, Kailani basking in his calming embrace. Tears stroked her cheeks and her chest heaved.

When he pulled away, she felt a little better.

Patrick tilted his head and rested it on top of Kailani's. She rested her hands in his, and he squeezed. A sense of peace seemed to flow through her. She didn't want him to take on her sadness, or stress, but it was too late to stop him now. And when he finally let go, she was much lighter than before. She hugged him and he put his gloves back on, trying to hide the pained look on his face.

A heavy feeling of guilt settled on her chest, as it always did after the rare instances she let him use his Power of Touch, and the incessant need to apologize nearly overwhelmed her. But he would only shrug it off, so instead, she murmured, "I appreciate when you do that, but Pat, you really shouldn't. You don't need any more stress in your life."

Patrick's lips turned upward, but the smile didn't reach his eyes. "I know, but you don't have to bare it on your own."

Kailani leaned into him. "What if I'm making a huge mistake?"

Patrick wrapped his arms around her. "You're still learning, Kai. You have all these new powers, and your parents are gone. After my mom died, I was really reckless. Remember? I was only a kid… but I never thought anything through. I'm just saying, you're handling this really well. Better than most people would. The gods chose you for a reason, and I don't think you'll let them down."

Kailani fiddled with a loose thread on the couch. "Thank you." She gave him a weak smile, looking up at him. "Thank you for coming with me."

Patrick took Kailani's hand. "I'd follow you anywhere."

Kailani smiled, a real smile, because no matter what happened, she'd always have Patrick. And as long as she had Patrick, she'd be okay.

"Do you think Grayson will forgive me?"

Patrick nodded. "He'll have to, when we succeed."

Kailani swallowed. She had to succeed, because if she didn't, she would ruin everything. She pulled the covers up over her and Patrick. It was going to be a long night.

CHAPTER TWENTY

*V*iolent shades of orange danced in Kailani's vision and the familiar feeling of swirling through a portal overtook her. The only thing she could comprehend was the sound of air or water speeding past her ears. A burning smell filled her nose and she started to cough. She suffocated in a tornado of wind and smoke—then her feet landed on the ground.

The dizziness didn't stay quite as long this time, but she doubled over coughing. When she could breathe again, she steadied herself, looking around the dark. She was in a cramped, small, musty place. She reached her hands out, trying to get her bearings, and felt a door. Sliding her hands down, she grasped the knob and opened it. The portal was in the closet of a dusty old home close to the prison. According to Nori, the house was the rebels' only base in Teulon territory—their only way to get in and out of the territory undetected.

So they couldn't mess this up.

The house was dimly lit, and a layer of fog brewed below as if the windows and doors had been left open and the house was just part of the environment. Kailani stifled more coughs as the musty air filled her lungs. She gripped her wand, waiting for the owner to appear, but no one came.

Lyla whizzed through the portal and Kailani helped her to her feet. She stepped out of the closet, her eyes darting around the room. Then her gaze met Kailani's, and the sheer depth of terror in her gaze made Kailani swallow hard.

Kailani grabbed her hands to steady her. "You can still go back. I'll understand."

Lyla took a deep breath, shaking her head. "No, I can do this."

"Are you sure?"

Patrick swirled through, cutting them off as he coughed in a layer of dust. They locked hands. Kailani squeezed his hands and took a deep breath.

Patrick's throat bobbed, but he nodded. "Let's go."

A long, narrow hallway led them to a run-down kitchen. A small stove that looked like it hadn't been used in years squatted in the corner, next to a fridge emitting such a wicked stench that Kailani held back a gag. The home was eerily quiet. If someone lived here, they weren't living in the best conditions, even by Saxton's standards. Kailani's eyebrows pinched together. Teulon was the territory of Strange mages. Given that Strange mages ran the monarchy, it didn't make any sense for their residents to live this way.

Patrick edged to the back door and slid it open slowly, wincing as the old hinges creaked. A thick fog obstructed Kailani's vision, blurring the sand path ahead of them. Red, broken rocks stuck out as far as she could see. She could just about make out a jagged line of ruined buildings scattered in the distance. The air was dry and cool, and the wind blew sand and debris in their faces. Kailani's skin bubbled with goosebumps. As she stepped out of the house, the fog lifted enough to reveal a uniform row of crumbling sandstone houses running alongside the house they were hiding in. They were all dark, so she couldn't see much through the fog and gloom, but they felt vacant. Like something terrible had happened here, turning this place into a ghost town. She shuddered.

In a way, she knew she should be glad that there was nobody around, but her skin crawled as she lingered just outside the doorway. It didn't make any sense. According to Nori, Strange mages were almost all in Stasorin's pocket, and in exchange for ravaging the kingdom with torture and murder for Stasorin, they typically lived pretty comfortable lives. But there must have been some Strange mages who wouldn't comply with Azarro's psychotic policies, and this had to be the result.

"Come on," Kailani whispered.

She led them around the corner of the house, keeping her body pressed up against the sandstone. As she peeked around the corner, a tall, concrete building loomed over the rest. Smoke rose from the top of the tower, and it stuck out in the middle of the red rocks surrounding it. Smaller houses rested between them and the prison, and Kailani was thankful for the cover. Their footsteps were silent as they crept towards the next building.

Kailani froze.

Voices drifted from an open window and she ducked, pulling Patrick and Lyla down with her. She pressed her finger to her lips, locking eyes with Lyla as if that would give them both strength. The voices inside were faint. She could barely make out what they were saying, but it sounded like a family.

Patrick waved them along and they kept moving, ducking further down as they passed each window, but they came up to a sign that had the green Strange symbol graffitied all over it.

ATONEMENT: KEEP OUT. DANGEROUS CRIMINALS. HIGH ALERT.

Kailani's shoulders tightened. She looked back to the house they'd come from, with the portal hidden inside. It was too late to go back, but a part of her wanted to. If her parents weren't here and it was a trap, Briggs might not ever forgive her. Squeezing her eyes shut, she took a deep breath. Mom and Dad's laughter echoed in her mind. She smelled Dad's famous risotto and sipped Mom's mint lemonade tea. They danced in her memory, and she smiled.

It didn't matter if it was a trap. She couldn't risk losing them.

Kailani opened her eyes and swallowed. She could do this.

After she was sure no one was coming, she turned back to Patrick and Lyla. Lyla was clutching the map, studying the drawing as if she hadn't looked over it one hundred times since yesterday.

Lyla swallowed hard, pointing to a circled spot on the map then to a spot in the chain link fence up above. "That's where Nori said the fence gives in. It takes three minutes for the guards to walk around the building. So once we see them pass, we only have three minutes to get inside."

Footsteps thudded up ahead and Kailani jolted towards the building, pressing her body against the cool stone. The others followed. The shadows of the tall rocks kept them hidden, but Kailani held her breath, hoping she wouldn't have to use her wand just yet. She squinted towards the prison. Two very large Protectors strolled around the fence, mid conversation. She bit her lip, squeezing her eyes shut, as the footsteps passed.

"Okay, come on," Lyla whispered.

And they sprinted towards the prison fence.

Kailani's chest burned, begging for her to stop, but she wouldn't let up. Couldn't let up. She counted in her head, seconds passing by, and urged herself to move faster. Sixty seconds gone. Patrick made it to the fence before her and he pushed it forwards, revealing a small hole that would be unnoticeable unless pressing on the fence. He held it open and she dove through, her robe catching on the metal and digging into her skin. She yelped, slapping her hands over her mouth. Pulling at her robe, her heart raced. Ninety seconds.

"I got it," Patrick whispered, pushing Kailani's flailing hand away and pulling the robe off the metal.

Lyla crawled through and Kailani held the fence up for Patrick, who crawled through and aligned the metal back where no one would notice the hole. Lyla's hands were squeezed into fists as she looked backwards towards the direction the Protectors would be coming from.

Sixty seconds left.

"Come on!" Kailani cried, rushing towards the door on the side of the building.

A rattling screech cut through the silence. Kailani froze, her skin crawling. She looked around, trying to determine where the noise was coming from, before looking up at the tall building. Whoever it was, they were close. And they were in pain.

Kailani looked at her friends. Her own terror was painted on their faces.

"Maybe we should go back," Lyla whispered.

"We have no time." Patrick's voice shook, but his tone was determined.

Their eyes darted to Kailani's like they were looking for her to lead, for her to make the call. She understood why, but her mind was a storm of doubt and fear. Patrick was right, though. In less than a minute those Protectors would be coming around the corner, and they needed to be inside by then.

"Just in and out," she said, her lip quivering. "Just to see if Mom and Dad are here."

Lyla nodded. Her fingers tapped her thumbs over and over again and Kailani wrenched her gaze away. She took a deep breath, trying not to think about whether she was making a mistake, leading her friends into a sure capture. After all they'd done for her, after how far they'd come. How could she be so stupid to think the three of them, untrained mages who hadn't even graduated, could break into Atonement?

Voices echoed from around the corner, smashing aside her

doubts, because they needed to *move*. Swearing inwardly, Kailani opened the door and shoved her friends through. The hallway was bright and empty just as Nori had promised, thank the gods. Lyla studied the map, shifting it so that it made sense, and motioned for them to follow her. As they turned the corner, a glass room full of buzzing holoscreens lit up. Kailani got one glimpse before throwing herself back against the wall.

Her heart slammed against her ribs. Protectors.

There had to be three dozen of them trailing the computer room, watching screens, pointing at different monitors. The low hum of chatter echoed through the hall, followed by a bellowing, deep laugh. There was no getting past them.

Patrick tugged on Kailani's sleeve and she glanced back, her pulse thudding in her ears. His calm expression helped her breathe as he waved for her to follow him the opposite direction. Kailani caught a glimpse of Lyla's face. She looked pale, clammy. Kailani grabbed her hand, startling her. Her eyes were wide.

"It's okay," Kailani whispered.

"I want to go back."

Kailani's breath caught in her throat. Her eyes darted to the door they'd come through and her chest tightened. They had no way of knowing where the patrolling guards were on their route. Even if they successfully found her parents, she hadn't thought about getting out of the prison. Lyla was right. This was a mistake. She had to get them out of there. She'd go out first, take the risk. Once she made it outside the fence, she'd call the others with their talismans, letting them know when the coast was clear.

Kailani nodded, grabbing Lyla's hand, and heading back towards the door.

"Up ahead," Patrick interrupted, his voice sharp.

Kailani's heart lurched as the door swung open.

Patrick pushed them into the nearest room. It was cramped, hot, with a ladder that seemed to stretch forever. Kailani jammed between Lyla and Patrick as footsteps got louder, and she froze.

"Did you hear something?"

A voice. A Protector's voice. Right outside the door.

Lyla's breathing was getting heavier. Kailani's heartbeat thrashed in her ears. If the Protectors heard, they were done for. She locked eyes with Patrick, who nodded. They smothered Lyla into a hug to try and quiet her breaths. The footsteps faded, but she sat in silence, only staggered heartbeats filling the space. Patrick grabbed Lyla's hand. Tears brimmed in Kailani's eyes at the sight of them. She wasn't sure what was worse, Lyla's fear or the way Patrick's expression seemed to harden with every passing moment.

"We can't go back," Patrick said. "We've made it this far. We'll be in and out."

Tipping her head back, Kailani tried to pick out the top of the ladder, but it seemed to go on forever. She was torn between getting out of there right that moment, and checking every floor for her parents.

"In and out." Lyla repeated Patrick's words back to him, holding her chin high and pulling out the map.

And that settled it.

"There are thirty-three floors." Lyla's voice was low and quiet as she moved her finger over the map. "It looks like we're—" She moved her finger over the map, before stopping in a small closet room. "Here. The map shows the stairs entering each one. The Protector stations are on every third floor."

Kailani nodded, going over the plan again in her head.

"Nori said the rebels are usually on fifteen through eighteen," Lyla added. "Let's start there."

Kailani's stomach churned as her mind taunted her with echoes of the screaming woman.

Patrick puffed out his cheeks. "Ready to climb?"

He started up the ladder first. Kailani went next, followed by Lyla. After only ten seconds, Kailani's arms were screaming for her to stop, but she kept climbing. She really needed to start working out if she made it back to Mirstone. By the time they got to level fifteen, her muscles shook with exhaustion. Patrick turned around to help pull them up. Kailani held her breath, balancing on the rickety ledge clinging to the walls. She didn't understand how Patrick could bear looking down. She was determined not to; she didn't want to see how high they were.

Screams engulfed the narrow passageway, chilling Kailani to her bone.

"What…" she stammered. "What's going on up there?" Lyla's face somehow paled further as Patrick pulled her up beside them. "We're near the execution chambers. And… the experiments…"

Words stuck in Kailani's throat as Nori's words from the beach came back to her. She wiped her forehead with her sleeve, swaying on the ledge, and gulped.

Patrick was the first to shake himself out of it. He pushed to his feet, cracking open the nearest door so he could peer out. "Let's search this floor and get out of here."

Kailani tiptoed, her body shaking as they moved through the door. Cells lined the walls. She shivered. It seemed so long ago that she was trapped in a tiny concrete prison, so long ago that she could've been sent here.

Chills raced along her spine.

The cells were grimy. Water leaked from tiny windows, and the walls were covered in green gunk. The stench of damp and mold flooded her senses. Kailani pressed her hand to cover her mouth and nose.

A couple prisoners cried out to them as they passed, reaching through the bars and grabbing at them, even though they weren't close enough to touch. But mostly they sat back in their cells, their deadly eyes trained on them, questioning them. Kailani's heart wrenched. These people were all scheduled to be executed, probably for the same crimes as her parents. Trying to break free of the monarchy.

Kailani kept her eyes focused on the tiled floor, trying to

ignore the cries of the prisoners on the floors above her, but their wailing echoed in her ears, growing louder and louder. What kind of person would she be if she stood by and let them suffer? She racked her brain, trying to think of any spell Briggs had taught her that she might be able to use...

"Kailani?"

Her head jolted up. Two prisoners were cowering in cells just ahead and Kailani raced towards them, her heart in her mouth. They sat pressed against the bars, their bruised and bloodied hands outstretched, holding one another. Just like in Patrick's vision. Tears filled Kailani's eyes. She was only paces away and...

Her stomach dropped, and she staggered to a halt. Her jaw fell open.

They weren't her parents.

Professor Linde and Professor Gorgan let go of each other's hands to push to their feet, but grabbed hold again instantly. Kailani stared at their dirty fingers as Patrick and Lyla caught up to her. Tears burned her eyes.

"Kailani?"

Kailani shook her head. Linde and Gorgan couldn't be the rebels in Patrick's vision... they couldn't be. It was her parents. It had to be her parents. Linde didn't even *like* Gorgan. No one liked Gorgan. It all had to be a mistake, because the man sitting behind the bars, whose face was streaked with dirt and blood and whose hand clutched Linde's like she was the most precious thing in the world... he looked nothing like the rude, contemptuous professor who'd made history class a living hell.

But the truth was right there in front of her.

It wasn't her parents.

Kailani's throat felt like it was going to close up as Lyla appeared by her side.

"Professors?" Lyla's jaw hung open.

Professor Gorgan shook his head wildly. "No, you shouldn't be here! What's going on?"

Kailani glanced at Linde. Her face was gaunt, her cheekbones shallow.

"Please." Kailani pressed in close, trying to focus. "I'm looking for my parents. You have to help me—I can get you out."

Linde reached out from behind the bars and grabbed her trembling hand. It was cold and damp and made Kailani's skin crawl. "Kailani... your parents aren't here. You have to get out of here." Her eyes darted towards the end of the hall. "If they catch you..."

Lyla pulled on Kailani's arm. "We should go. This was a mistake."

Footsteps sounded from the distance.

"You have to go back." Gorgan's voice cracked. "Get out of here, now!"

Patrick grabbed Kailani's arm and pulled her away from the cell, but she couldn't tear her eyes away. Her heart was pounding. Her chest hurt. Patrick's vision had been wrong, but her parents had to be here, otherwise she'd put her friends in danger for nothing. This *couldn't* be a wasted trip. She *wouldn't* return to Mirstone empty handed.

So, as she watched Gorgan grab Linde's hand through the bars once more, Kailani dug her heels in and wrenched her arm free.

"We have to help!" she hissed, keeping her voice low.

Lyla frantically brushed her hair behind her ears. "There's nothing we can do. We have to get out of here!"

"But my parents!"

"Your parents aren't here," Patrick said, shooting a fearful look towards the end of the hall. "They didn't see them."

"That doesn't mean they aren't!"

"We have to get out while we can!"

"But your vision..."

Patrick grabbed her shoulders, shaking her slightly as he pulled her close. His eyes were wide, as he reached up a hand to

245

cup her face. "I'm sorry, Kailani. But this was a mistake. We can't do anything for them right now."

Maybe a part of her knew Patrick was right, but her head was spinning and the world with it. And with every beat of her heart, she could feel her magic stirring, begging to fight, because that would be better than failing. That would be better than being a fool. She wouldn't give up on her parents. She wouldn't give up on her quest. Her parents could be in this very building, and if she left now, she may never get a chance to see them again. If only she could freeze time, stop the Protectors, do something.

"Come on," Patrick urged.

"Please!" Lyla cried.

The world seemed to slow as Kailani looked back down the hall, locking eyes with Linde. Beneath the grime, despite the shadows around her eyes, she looked just as she had when she broke the law for Kailani. More and more prisoners loomed at the bars of their cells now, peering out at the commotion. Sweat formed on Kailani's forehead. The musty, damp air of the prison suffocated her. She couldn't leave these people. Their crime was fighting for justice. She could use matter manipulation... and...

She took out her wand and pointed it at the cell.

"*Scindo!*"

As soon as she released the spell, bars rattled around them and a blaring alarm filled Kailani's ears. Her jaw tightened. She was frozen in place, body trembling, as free rebels stormed the floor and a wall of Protectors thundered down the hallway.

CHAPTER TWENTY-ONE

ands grabbed Kailani's shoulders, yanking her up. Her jaw dropped. She could cry, because in front of her stood Briggs and his team of rebels. They raced past Briggs, wands outstretched.

"Kailani!" Briggs roared. "What did you do?"

But Kailani couldn't answer him because she couldn't think. She could only stare as the alarm rattled her brain. The cells around her split open; the metal bars snapped in half. Linde ran through the opening, her robe catching on the broken metal, and Kailani's breath caught. But Linde ripped her robe free, dashing to pull Gorgan out of his cell. Around them, prisoners swarmed the floor, fleeing from their cells in all directions.

"Intruders—" a voice sounded overhead.

Kailani's mind was just starting to catch up, just starting to understand what she'd caused. The Protectors swarmed the floor. There weren't enough rebels to fight. Even if the prisoners helped, most of them were weak, starving. And they had no wands. What if Lyla and Patrick were injured? What if Nori's brother got hurt? Would freeing these prisoners be worth it?

That was, if Kailani had freed them at all.

For a shrieking whine drew all eyes upwards, and Linde screamed.

"*No!*"

Kailani watched in horror as thick sheets of glass shot down from the ceilings, closing over the bars and the cell doors, enclosing the prisoners who hadn't made it out in time.

Briggs' grip on Kailani tightened, as Linde sank to her knees, tears filling her eyes.

'What's going on?" Lyla cried.

Linde could only shake her head. "They're releasing the poison!"

Kailani's stomach dropped.

"W-what...?" she stammered.

"The Draught of Bane," hissed Briggs, through clenched teeth.

Head spinning, Kailani slumped in Briggs' arms. *No, no, no.*

The prisoners were all up now, their screams muffled by the glass, their fists thumping against it. But it didn't matter that Kailani couldn't hear them. It was bad enough that she could see them, their eyes wild with panic and their mouths stretched wide. A jolt swept through her, and she yanked herself away from Briggs, her eyes sweeping the hallway, desperate to find something to smash the glass.

"Help me!" she screamed.

But nobody did. Briggs only tried to grab her again, and she shoved him away with a cry, flinging herself at the closest cell. She slammed her fists against the glass, dragged her nails down it. Was that the prisoners screaming? Or was it her? Was that their blood streaking the glass, or was it hers as she tore off her fingernails in her desperation to break through?

"Help them," she shrieked, blood pounding in her ears.

Footsteps pounded the ceiling overhead and the doors at the end of the hall burst open. More Protectors swarmed in. Arms wrapped tight around Kailani's chest, dragging her backwards. Briggs, or somebody else, she didn't care. She kicked and screamed and writhed against whoever it was. She couldn't leave them. She had to save them.

She'd *killed* them.

"It's too late," a voice roared, over the screams and groans of the dying. Streaks of light flashed past them as the Protectors screamed curses. Rebels turned to make a wall in front of them, throwing spells back. Prisoners dove towards the Protectors, some gaining access to their wands, others being struck down. "Get to the portal!"

Kailani's vision was spotty. Her head throbbed. Everything sounded like it was underwater.

Lyla's voice wavered, somewhere close. "What about the hut?"

Green smoke seeped under the prison cells, threatening to overtake the hall.

"There's not enough time! Portal's three levels below."

Briggs took off towards the descending stairwell. Tilly grabbed Kailani's shoulders and dragged her along, and she needed to be dragged. Because her legs weren't working properly, and her mind was still caught on what she'd just done. She was tripping over herself as the screams became more and more distant and the hallway was overtaken by fog. Still, they rattled in her skull, even as she tried to focus. To help. To not be a burden.

Briggs burst through an open door and raced down the stairwell, Kailani clattering after him. Near the bottom, Briggs leapt over the banister, landing with his wand outstretched. Kailani stumbled forward as a spell smashed into the next door, blasting it open. Briggs stormed through with rebels behind him. Tilly all but shoved Kailani after him, and a sharp pain jolted up her spine as she landed badly. But then Patrick was beside her, grabbing one arm, and Lyla grabbed the other. They heaved her up and she spotted Linde and Gorgan cowering, wandless.

"We'll hold off the Protectors," Tilly shouted, ducking as a spell raced past her head and collided with the wall behind her, splitting the concrete. She turned to face the Protector and screamed, *"Ignitis!"*

A fireball roared from the tip of her wand, hurling at the Protectors. They flew backwards, slamming into the wall and slumping over.

"Run straight to the portal, okay? Don't stop for anything!"

Kailani's lips parted. She wanted to scream, wanted to argue. She couldn't go alone. She couldn't be trusted. But Briggs and Tilly were fighting off a dozen more Protectors that had turned the corner. For a moment, she froze again, terror rooting her to the spot. Her ears pulsed at the blaring alarm. She couldn't think. She'd already caused so much damage. She'd made a terrible mistake.

But she *had* saved Linde and Gorgan, along with countless others.

Kailani took a deep breath. She'd made her choice, and maybe it was the wrong one, but if they stayed where they were, they'd all die. They still had a chance.

Jaw clenched, she grabbed Linde's arm, meeting her eyes. "Let's go."

Kailani hid behind the wall of rebels as they sprinted towards the portal room. She veered to the left as Tilly and Briggs backed the Protectors up towards the right. The portal room was blocked by Protectors. Prisoners who had gained access to wands were fighting them from the opposite direction.

She held out her wand and screamed, *"Atro Dora!"*

The spell knocked a guard to the ground but four more turned to face them. Kailani's stomach lurched. She dove behind a wall as his spell whirled past her, but the curse collided with Gorgan's back and he fell to the floor.

Linde screamed.

Kailani looked back. Her mouth fixed in a silent scream.

Gorgan's eyes were fixed open, the ghost of determination still etched on his face.

She fought the urge to break down and sob. This couldn't be happening. Linde's wailing threatened to burst Kailani's eardrums. Then Tilly slammed into her, pulling her and Linde down as another curse flew at them, bringing her back to the present. The rebels were back with them, barricading the Protectors in on one side, the prisoners on the other.

Pieces of broken concrete flew down from the ceilings and walls. Curses collided with each other and flew in all directions. Kailani dodged debris, making her way towards the portal room.

Just as she was about to make a run for it, an orange light collided with Lyla's chest.

She collapsed.

Kailani's heart stopped.

No, *no!*

Jumping up, she dove towards Lyla, pulling her limp body behind a piece of broken concrete. Everything inside of her went cold. She could feel the pull of Brute, the push of Strange. Anger roared inside of her. Anger at herself, for getting them into this mess. Anger at the gods, for choosing her for an impossible quest. Anger at her parents, for leaving her in the dark.

She pulled out her wand, searched inside of her for the warmth of Charm magic—but Lyla stirred, gasping for breath.

Looking down at her chest, Kailani let out a sigh of relief as it moved up and down. Lyla groaned, and Kailani helped her to her feet, blinking back tears.

Up ahead, Tilly waved them forward as Briggs and his team held off a group of Protectors. Prisoners fled towards the portal, shoving each other out of the way to escape. Kailani's legs were weak. Hopefully it was only rebels like her parents she let free, and not serious criminals.

"Move!" Briggs yelled to Tilly, motioning her towards the portal, and they burst in the room as more Protectors sprinted down the hallway towards them.

Kailani lunged for the portal, desperately searching her mind for a way to work it. She fiddled with the coordinates, willing the directions to unfold in front of her. Her mind tunneled on the screams behind her. Patrick was holding Lyla up. They looked terrified.

But she could still save them, if she could just focus—

She was knocked aside. She stuck out her wand, ready to attack, but it was Briggs pushing her out of the way. Her shoulders slumped. Relief and shame coiled inside her. He held up a stone and muttered coordinates, willing the portal to life.

He grabbed Kailani's arm. "Go!"

Kailani lifted her wand behind Briggs and shot at a Protector. "*Atro Dora!*" She looked towards her friends. "You guys first!"

"Now!" Briggs screamed.

But it was too late.

The Protector rebounded Kailani's spell, sending it shooting towards them. Kailani dove to the floor as Lyla, Patrick, and Briggs dove in different directions. The portal sizzled, smoke rose from the machine, and a loud pop filled the room.

Briggs grunted, shooting to his feet and running at the Protector. He pointed his wand at the wall and yelled. "*Deducto!*"

The concrete crumbled down on top of the Protector, building a small barrier between them and the hallway.

Kailani's stomach turned to ice. "Where's the nearest portal?"

"The hut, but it's too far," Briggs said through gritted teeth. His face contorted. With a raging cry he sent another curse at the wall. "*Transmino!*"

A hole blasted through the wall in front of them, raining concrete on their heads. The building shook. Briggs used his wand to maneuver the rocks, creating a ladder of sorts for them to run down.

"Get off the prison grounds, then teleport them out!" Briggs yelled, glancing at Josie.

Kailani's heart pounded in her ears as she sprinted down the rocks. Patrick jumped before her and helped Lyla get to the ground. Kailani's foot slipped. She fell, but caught herself as she landed hard on the ground. Pain shot up her leg. She forced herself to her feet and ran with Briggs, dodging spells being thrown at them from behind. Kailani turned, just for a moment, and winced. The prison walls tumbled. Remnants of concrete crumbled to the ground from spells and curses. Prisoners scaled the building, leveraging themselves down from higher floors. Bile rose in Kailani's throat. The prisoners ran in different directions, clearly trying to escape before the Protectors called in reinforcements.

Sand spiraled around her and obscured her vision, but she sprinted forward, desperate to get off the prison grounds. Desperate to save her friends. Desperate.

A few feet ahead, Linde jolted backwards and crumbled to the ground. The entire front of her body was scorched by a spell. Kailani reeled, gasping for breath.

If Linde died, then all of this...

"Stop!" Briggs screamed, and everyone skidded to a halt. "Forcefield!"

Chest heaving, Kailani ran to Linde. She dropped to her knees, putting her fingers to her throat until she felt a faint pulse. Blood coated her hand. Linde's skin was smoking.

This time the bile didn't stay down. She retched.

"Up ahead," Briggs called, grabbing Kailani and dragging her up.

She cried out, unable to stop herself. She was exhausted, her leg hurt, and they were all going to die. She turned around. Protectors lined the prison, holding their wands in the air. A translucent hue shot from the tips, creating a barrier around them. They were stuck.

"We can't teleport out!" Lyla shrieked.

Kailani closed her eyes. That was their last chance at escaping. She had to do something. But what? She prayed to the gods of magic above. *Please, if you're up there. Please help me. You chose me, but why?* She willed her brain to stop spiraling. Willed herself to feel her magic, really listen to it. Anger and fear coursed through her in a flash of heat. That was Brute magic, telling her to fight. Her head pounded and chills raced through her body—Luminate magic, telling her to flee.

When she opened her eyes, it was like the world around her was in slow motion. Briggs and Tilly yelled, but she couldn't understand what they were saying. Sweat and dirt covered their faces. Lyla's robe was singed, burned by the shimmering force-field. Patrick shot spells above him with no real intent.

Her forearm burned and Kailani startled, grabbing her wrist. The place Queen Stasorin had touched ached, though there was nothing there but a faint scar. She took a deep breath. The unity symbol appeared, clear as day, right in her mind.

She pointed her wand towards the force field, imagined a crack running down the center, splitting it in two. Everything in her body ached, screamed at her, but she pushed the pain down.

Her arm jolted as a spell flung from her wand.

It bounced off the forcefield like nothing.

Tilly and Briggs were beside her now, circling her, defending her from any loose spells.

"Just like in the arena," Briggs said.

Kailani breathed, nodding her head.

She was the champion.

She was enough.

"Transmino!"

A crackling ball of light shot from the tip of her wand, and she thrust her hands forward. The magic pulsed inside her, growing, growing, then spinning out of control. Black specks floated in her vision. Her head spun. Electric energy flowed from her fingertips. The blast knocked her off balance, and sent Briggs and Tilly flying backwards.

The forcefield split in two.

All eyes were trained on her. Her knees trembled and she

gasped for air. She gripped her wand, and her hands shook. Small particles of light floated around her in a shower of energy and flames. Dazed, she sprinted towards Briggs. Buzzing filled her ears. The ground tipped beneath her feet.

"Hurry!" Briggs' voice echoed over the screams and explosions, snapping Kailani back to reality.

Josie, Leonard, and Arun sprinted forward, past the crumbling debris. Their only escape. Arun grabbed Linde's wrist and they vanished in a stream of light and smoke, whipping past the spot where they'd just stood.

Shaking herself, Kailani ran towards Leonard. She glanced back to check on Lyla and Patrick, and her world shifted again. She skidded to a stop.

The Protectors were dragging their unconscious bodies back towards the prison.

"No!" Kailani screamed.

Briggs grabbed her arm. "Let's go!"

"I'm not leaving them!" Kailani tried to rip her arm away, but Briggs pulled her forward. He was too strong. She dug her boots into the ground, fighting and clawing. "No!"

But then Leonard grabbed her arm and the world turned to flashes of light, whipping above their heads. Kailani's vision swirled, pain ripping through her body as she fought against the teleportation. Then her body smacked against unyielding cement.

Her breath gusted out of her. Her cheek pressed against the cold stone. For a moment, the abrupt silence shocked her into forgetting what had just happened.

In an instant, it flooded back.

With a horrified cry, Kailani forced herself upwards. Though her world was spinning around her, one thing was abundantly clear.

Lyla and Patrick were gone.

CHAPTER TWENTY-TWO

A scream tore from Kailani's lips, but it was foreign to her ears. It sounded distant, as if she was hearing herself on a recording from another room. She crumpled to her knees, grabbing a fistful of hair in her hands. Anger consumed her. Shrieking, she slammed her head against cement. Fog clouded her vision, but the pain cleared her head.

Gasping for breath, she trembled where she sat until the throbbing faded. Then, slowly, she looked around, trying to get a sense of where she was. She'd been dropped on a narrow ledge in some sort of tunnel. Light peeked through a hundred feet away, lighting up the tunnel just enough to see. A shallow stream of water rolled through the middle, and more droplets fell from the ceiling onto her hair.

Linde was slumped against the concrete. Rebels surrounded her, tending to her wounds. She scanned the rebels' faces, looking for an ounce of sympathy, even though she knew she didn't deserve it. Tilly crossed her arms, glaring at her from a few feet away. Arun and Leonard turned away from her gaze and walked down towards the other rebels.

Black smoke filled the space in front of her and two figures emerged. Briggs stomped towards her as Josie disappeared again.

"What the hell were you thinking?" Spit flew from his mouth when he spoke.

"You disobeyed an order and almost got us all killed. We barely made it out. Prisoners died, prisoners escaped. The portal's broken." He paced back and forth, his boots slushing through the dirty water. "Our only ally in Teulon is dead. We'll be lucky if we ever get past the boundaries of the territory again. Or any territory, for that matter. The portals were our way to get in and out undetected. And now they know about those, too!"

Kailani opened her mouth to speak, but no words came out. She buried her head against her knees, unable to look at any of them. Her heart was going to explode. All of that blood was on her hands. Gorgan's lifeless eyes flashed through her mind, and the memory of the horrific burns that covered Linde's limp body made her shudder.

The screams as the Draught of Bane spread through the cells rang in her ears.

She'd done that. She'd killed them.

Had she doomed Patrick and Lyla too? Patrick, who'd been there for her since they were kids, who had walked her home every day for years. And Lyla, who'd defied her parents to continue their friendship, who'd left her perfect life behind for her. They'd done so much for her, and she'd abandoned them. She hadn't even glimpsed her parents.

It was a trap. The rebels were right.

They were all dead, because of her.

"I just wanted to save them," she whispered, looking up.

Briggs opened his mouth, his eyes blazing. Kailani couldn't stop a sob bursting from her mouth. He spun away from her, cursing as he marched down the tunnel, and Kailani crumbled. Pressing her face into her knees again, she sobbed. She'd ruined everything—the quest, and any chance of finding her parents. They could have been in one of those cells…

"I just wanted to save them," she repeated, more to herself than anyone.

"We need to get back to Mirstone, now." Briggs peered out the tunnel, before stomping back towards her, sloshing water on her as he passed. He held out his wand and muttered something Kailani couldn't hear before looking back at Tilly. "We aren't being tracked. Yet. We need to go. Leonard, take her."

He gestured to Kailani before grabbing Arun and disappearing in a cloud of smoke.

Leonard held his hand out, looking almost as furious as Briggs. Keeping her eyes low, she grabbed his hand, pulling herself up. Her breath caught in her throat as she was whirled again. Her head continued to spin, then she landed flat on the ground. Wincing, she steadied herself. The training area loomed in one direction, the labs and meeting rooms in the other.

When she looked up, Baylock's angry eyes were directed right at her.

"What on earth were you thinking?" Baylock demanded.

"I—" Kailani stuttered, her eyes fixed on the ground. Heat flushed her face as the rebels teleported beside her, all eyes on her. How could she have messed up so badly?

Even Nori was there, her eyes wide from the door of the labs up ahead.

She must have told Briggs. Kailani couldn't blame her. If Nori hadn't told him, she'd probably be dead right now. The other soldiers turned to walk away, leaving her with Baylock, Briggs, and Tilly, who didn't seem so keen to let her off as easy as the silent treatment.

It got worse.

A crushing sensation filled her chest as Mr. Mahoney and Grayson walked out of the lab towards them. At first, Seneca's eyes were wide with hope, but Kailani didn't let herself look away as that changed. His eyes widened; his mouth trembled.

"Patrick?" His voice crumbled.

It felt like something pierced Kailani's heart. "I'm sorry..." she managed to squeak. "I'm sorry, I'll fix this... I'll—"

"You've already done enough," Tilly snapped.

Grayson watched her with a mix of sympathy and anger on his face, like he couldn't decide which to show first. Silent tears fell down Kailani's cheeks, and she choked back sobs. "I'm so sorry."

Baylock's jaw clenched. Her hands balled into fists as she took a deep breath, stepping back. "We told you this was a trap. And you didn't listen."

"Easy," Grayson chided. "She's only a child."

"We were all children when we came here." Tilly took a step towards Kailani, and Briggs grabbed her wrist, pulling her back. Tilly narrowed her eyes, her body shaking with anger. "But we had to grow up real quick, and we didn't have the powers of the gods behind us. You know that better than any of us, sir."

She said *sir* with such resentment, and Kailani turned to Grayson just in time to see him wince. Tilly opened her mouth to speak again, but seemed to think better of it and whirled around, stomping towards the training arena. Briggs followed her without a second glance at Kailani.

"You were a child, Kailani," Baylock said. "But that changed when you went through the mountain pass."

Baylock, too, followed Tilly towards the arena.

But Grayson, unlike the others, didn't leave. He strode towards her, his eyes filled with tears. He wrapped her in his arms and she let herself sink into him.

"I'm glad you are safe," he murmured.

Kailani fell into him, sobbing freely now. She let her great grandfather lead her. She didn't look at anyone else, keeping her face buried in his robe as they stepped through the portal and ended up near the cabins. She sucked in a deep breath, trying to control her sobs, and turned to Grayson.

"I'm so sorry... I just thought, I mean, I didn't think..." She faltered, and when he didn't speak, the silence between them grew heavy. She'd expected Grayson to yell. Or to at least lecture. But he was quiet and still until Kailani found the nerve to look back up at him. "It's just that Patrick had a vision and I thought for sure my parents would be there."

Grayson nodded, stroking his beard. "It was likely a vision implanted by the Queen, as Baylock said, to get you to the prison and stop you from getting the staff."

Another sob crept up Kailani's throat, but she pushed it down. "I know, but the blood moon... I thought if I could just get to my parents, we wouldn't need the staff."

"You could've been killed."

Kailani hung her head. Her body fought against standing. Her magic ebbed and flowed inside her, like it didn't know if she was safe and should calm. She kicked her shoe against the ground and bit her lip. She'd never forgive herself. For messing up the quest, for putting the rebels and prisoners in danger, for the deaths. All those people died because of her... Lyla and Patrick were captured *because of her*...

She swallowed hard. That blood was on her hands and she couldn't ever take that back, but there was one thing she could do to help.

"Please, I know I screwed up, but Patrick and Lyla..."

Grayson held up a hand. "I will talk to Baylock about them. In the meantime, I think it would be wise to steer clear of the training facilities for a few hours. Let the rest of the soldiers calm down."

Kailani winced. Everyone would be angry with her, surely. Not just the soldiers. She didn't even know the full extent of what she'd done, how royally she'd screwed up.

"The blood moon..."

Grayson sighed, his head hanging low. "I will have to consider the options we have left."

Her head pounded. She squeezed her eyes shut as Grayson left her standing on her cabin steps. Once the sound of his footsteps had faded away, she trudged inside and locked the door behind her. Lyla's bed was made just like she always did it at home, neat with her pillow propped up in the middle. Patrick's sheets and blankets were strewn over his bed. A stabbing pain twisted in Kailani's chest.

It was over.

A STORM RAGED in the distance, over the darkening sea. Kailani sat in the sand with her knees curled to her chest. The waves called to her, colossal and deafening.

Footsteps sounded behind her. She whipped around, heart racing.

Queen Stasorin strode towards her.

Kailani flushed with anger, jumping up and reaching for her wand. But her pockets were empty. Her hands balled into fists. She didn't care about Stasorin's past, what her uncle had made her do. She just wanted her to pay.

"You!" she cried. "You did this!"

The Queen laughed, the sound slapping the air. "Silly child."

The laughter hurt. It burned. Because the Queen had fooled her, Kailani had fallen for it, and now everything was ruined.

Trembling with rage, Kailani snarled, "You created the illusion in Patrick's vision. Made him see my parents instead of the professors."

Queen Stasorin smirked. Her eyes reflected the stormy gray skies, but then her green irises turned angry and her eyes grew dark. Slowly, she morphed into Azarro. Kailani stumbled backwards as his laugh drifted in the breeze. "Can't you see now that you are nothing compared to me and my magic?"

Kailani's chest heaved as she marched forward. She wanted to attack. She didn't care that Azarro couldn't be harmed, that her fists would simply sail through him. She needed to expel her rage and she was going to.

Azarro's smile widened. Like he was enjoying Kailani's anger, like it made him feel good.

Clenching her jaw, Kailani planted her feet in the sand.

"Your time is running out. Which will you choose? The kingdom or your friends?"

Kailani opened her mouth to shout her defiance, to roar it at the top of her lungs. Even if she didn't mean it, even if she crumbled after. She wanted to see a spark of fury in Azarro's eyes, the smallest fraction of what she was feeling.

But he disappeared.

"Kailani, help!"

Patrick and Lyla sat in front of her. Death binders curled around their wrists and ankles as they struggled to free themselves from the chairs they were tied to. Kailani screamed, running towards them. But the closer she got, the further they sat. Patrick raged in his chair, his back arched as sceams tore from his lungs. Lyla slumped over, crying, as if she'd already given up.

Kailani squeezed her eyes shut. She pictured Lyla, lying on a beanbag chair in her room and writing in her journal. She pictured Patrick, bobbing his head to music as Kailani sprawled out on her bed with her family's old book of stories. When she opened her eyes Patrick's face was a gruesome mix between his delicate features and Azarro's rageful leer. His eyes were dark. Blue veins twisted up his neck and across his face.

Kailani snarled. She reached for her Strange magic, clawed at the icy strings that rested deep within her, and slashed through Azarro's illusion. He stumbled backwards, for just a moment, his face full of shock. He was quick to recover and he glared at her, his lips turning upwards, before disappearing completely.

Kailani's anger vanished. She slumped to her knees, with the waves breaking behind her, and pressed her hands over her eyes.

Kailani jolted awake.

She shot up in bed, panting in the dark cabin. Howls of wind beat against the glass of the windows and she pulled her knees to her chest, wrapping her bedsheets around her shoulders. She was shaking so violently the bed creaked, and the first thing she did was look for her friends.

Her heart split in two.

Patrick's bed was still unmade, and Lyla wasn't rolling from side to side above her. She wanted to live in another dream, one where they'd simply woken up first and seen that the sun had risen. One where they'd decided to surprise her by fetching her breakfast in bed, because she *hadn't* failed. Because she'd saved her parents, and nobody had died.

Despite her tears, despite *knowing*, Kailani stared at the door and willed it to open.

It didn't.

After seconds or minutes, she wasn't sure, Kailani wrenched her gaze away from the light spilling into the cabin and took stock of her battered body. Every bone screamed in pain. Her magic was at war inside her, like it too was angry, like it too had wanted to lash out at the Queen and Azarro. She didn't move. She couldn't. She simply sat there until her tears dried and she heard a faint knock at the door.

For a moment, she considered ignoring it, but the knocking was insistent, and she didn't want to disappoint anyone else. She got up slowly, her body throbbing, and winced as she pulled the door open.

Nori waited outside, her shoulders slumped and her eyes wide with worry.

She must've thought Kailani would be angry with her, for telling Briggs. But she was only angry with herself.

And the monarchy.

"I'm so sorry," Nori cried.

A frigid breeze gusted past the open door and Kailani shivered.

"Don't be," Kailani choked out. "I'm sorry I ever involved you."

Nori looked down at her shoes. "Briggs is so mad. He hasn't spoken to me since I told him where you guys went. He knew something was up when none of you showed up to your training session."

"He'll forgive you."

Kailani was sure of it. But she couldn't say the same for herself.

Briggs would probably never speak to her again. The thought turned her stomach to stone. He was the best teacher she'd ever had. The first one to truly understand her magic. And that was all gone. She didn't think any of the rebels would want to train with her again after this. She didn't think she *should* train.

Drawing in a ragged breath, Kailani forced herself to ask, "Do you know if Linde is alright? The prisoner who was burned?"

A small smile crept to Nori's lips. "She's okay."

Kailani breathed a sigh of relief. "At least I saved one person." The moment didn't last long. "But there were so many others…"

Before her tears fell once more, Nori pulled her into a hug and Kailani sobbed. "I have to turn myself in. It's the only way to save Patrick and Lyla."

Nori jerked back abruptly, her grip tightening on Kailani's arms. Her eyes were wide. "No, you can't do that."

"Azarro visited me in my dream last night. He said if I turn myself in, he'd let Patrick and Lyla go. I should have done it a long time ago."

"No." Nori shook her head wildly, pulling Kailani inside. A gust of wind slammed the door shut behind them. "You don't understand. The monarchy isn't going to simply let Lyla and Patrick go, can't you see? You defied them in front of the entire kingdom. The rebellion is finally coming to light, people are starting to wake up and see the truth. She will use Lyla and Patrick as an example. She's just using them to get to you."

Kailani sunk deeper into despair. Into panic. If there was truly nothing she could do to save them, she'd doomed them to their deaths. There had to be a way.

"But what choice do I have? The blood moon is tomorrow. I've ruined our chances of getting the staff. It's the only way their lives might be spared…"

"You can still get the staff. There's still time."

"And who's to say I'll be worthy of it? I've betrayed the rebellion, betrayed my friends. I'm not worthy of the staff. It'll strip my powers, or worse, I'll be stuck in the Realm. What if I can't make it out? What if the others can't make it out?"

Nori bit her lip, seemingly deep in thought. But she was silent, because Kailani was right. There was no guarantee she would be worthy of the staff, no guarantee they'd make it out alive to stop the ritual.

"You don't see how special you are," Nori tried. "You broke through the barrier, led your friends to Mirstone—"

"I can't exactly claim credit for that, my outbursts…"

"You did it, Kailani, your magic. And you fought Tilly's illusions, broke the forcefield—"

Kailani's head snapped up.

"—yeah, I heard Briggs telling Baylock about it. Who knows what else you're capable of? But you'll never find out if you don't believe in yourself. Stop downplaying your successes and start owning them. Be proud of them."

Kailani pulled at a loose thread on her robe, rolling the string up into a little ball and rolling it around her palm.

"Kailani," Nori pleaded. "Please, talk to Briggs first. You can't just leave again."

Kailani shook her head. "He's not going to speak to me."

"Then talk to Grayson!"

Kailani pressed the heels of her hands to her eyes, desperate to stop crying, but it was hopeless. She could try the Realm of Chaos on her own. Go for the staff without endangering anyone else. But Nori was right, she couldn't just leave again. They'd only come after her, and more people would die. Besides, she wouldn't know where to turn herself in even if she wanted to. The thought of facing Briggs' anger made her squirm, but then she imagined what her friends were facing right now. Azarro's torture methods flashed in her mind and her breath hitched. She took a deep breath, raising her chin high.

If talking to Briggs was what it took, she'd do it. She'd do anything the rebels wanted her to.

If they'd just save Patrick and Lyla.

CHAPTER TWENTY-THREE

*K*ailani paced outside the training arena.

Her hands trembled, and she threw her hair in a bun at the base of her neck. The sun was high, beating down on her. Taking deep breaths, she wiped the sweat from her forehead. She kept waiting for Briggs to be alone, but his team was always with him, and the blood moon was one day away. If she was going to convince him going to the Realm was still an option, she didn't have time to waste.

She reached for the large black doors, pushing it open a fraction of an inch. Her heart sank as a long, drawn out creak echoed throughout the arena. The soldiers' heads whipped towards the noise. Kailani's heart faltered. Tilly and Leonard looked at each other, and Tilly mumbled something Kailani couldn't hear. She didn't think it was a warm welcome, though.

Her legs were unsteady, which worked in her favor. She was so focused on staying upright, she couldn't spare a thought for the whispers.

One... two... three...

She balled her sweaty hands into fists as she trudged across the arena. Briggs was the only one that kept his eyes on her, but a muscle twitched in his jaw. Any hope that he wasn't still angry evaporated.

"I—" Kailani faltered, unable to hold his hard stare. She had to force the words out. "Can I talk to you?"

Still, Briggs only stared and now Kailani heard them, the voices rising throughout the arena as the rest of the soldiers whispered to each other. Her face flushed red. She was about to give up, to run away, when Tilly pushed past her, knocking her shoulder into Kailani's, hard. Leonard gave Kailani a sympathetic look before following after Tilly. Only Briggs didn't move, so Kailani took that as a sign she could stay.

She left a lot of space between them, though.

"I'm really sorry."

Again, Briggs was silent and this time he stuck his wand in his pocket, his eyes moving to the door. Kailani forced herself to breathe evenly. She'd known this wouldn't be easy, but she had to see it through. For Patrick and Lyla.

She licked dry lips, leaning towards him to whisper. "I'm going to the Realm of Chaos."

Briggs' eyes snapped towards her. "*What* are you talking about?"

"Azarro visited me in my dream," she blurted, the words spilling out of her. "He seemed... off. Even more so than the last time I saw him." Kailani shuddered, thinking back to the horrible day that seemed so long ago now. "He wants my blood for his ritual. Stasorin said before that if I turn myself in, they'll spare Mom and Dad. He's desperate. And he's willing to keep my friends alive if I turn myself in. If I can just get to the staff..."

With an exasperated sigh, Briggs rubbed his eyes. "She's visited you before? Why didn't you say something?"

"Well..." Kailani looked down, shuffling her thumbs together. The other soldiers were on the other side of the arena now. Tilly and Leonard had joined them, and kept shooting glances her way.

Kailani tried to ignore them. "You guys were kind of keeping me out of the loop."

He didn't respond but fixed his eyes on a spot past her shoulder. Like he was deep in thought. *Or* like he was about to erupt again.

"I'm sorry—" Kailani started, "I…"

"It's too late." Briggs stuck his wand in his pocket, turning his back on Kailani to walk towards the rest of his team." The blood moon is tomorrow," he called over his shoulder. "There isn't enough time—"

"I have to try," Kailani cried, racing after him. "I'll go alone, just tell me where it is. If it doesn't work, I'll turn myself in. At least then I might be able to save Parick and Lyla."

Briggs whipped back around. "It's done. We're going to the castle. We'll try to stop him on our own."

"It won't work! He's too powerful, you know that. We need the staff."

Kailani swallowed as her eyes started to burn. Tilly turned around, shooting them a dirty look from across the arena. Then she turned her back towards them again.

Briggs stood still for a moment before speaking. "You are *not* going to the Realm of Chaos by yourself." He looked to his soldiers then back to Kailani. "What makes you think you can secure the staff now, when just a day ago, you were so willing to give it all up for Atonement?"

Kailani bit her lip. Her entire life she'd never felt good enough. Like she was always taking a second seat to her friends, her parents, her classmates. Even when she was granted the quest and found out she was a descendant, somehow, she didn't truly believe any of it. Afraid it would never work out. That she'd flounder, be mundane just as she'd always been. She rubbed her arm, looking down at her shoes. "I panicked." That was an understatement. She'd made a horrible decision that cost her best friends everything. "But I'm done running. I'm done hiding. This *is* my destiny, and I am powerful enough. Please, let me prove it."

Briggs looked up at her, one lip raising into a slight smirk. "That's the spirit I'm looking for."

Kailani let out a breath. "So, you'll go with me?"

"We're going to need a team."

Kailani looked over at the soldiers. They were practicing breaking through illusion magic. Tilly caught her eye as moved her wand, narrowed her eyes, then looked back at the other soldiers.

Kailani winced. "I don't think she'll agree to go."

Briggs frowned, staring after his team. Kailani couldn't read his expressions but his eyebrows furrowed together. "I'll talk to her. She wants Azarro gone as much as anyone."

KAILANI SAT AWKWARDLY on the chair outside the briefing room. She didn't dare speak as soldiers filed past her. Briggs had promised to secure a team of rebels—a feat, he promised, that would not be easy. Kailani's body went cold as Baylock entered the doors, walking through the hallway.

Kailani stood, fumbling with her thumbs. "I... uh-"

"General."

Kalani turned, thankful for the interruption. Grayson stood in the doorway behind her. She winced. His eyes were sunken, like he hadn't been sleeping, and his long beard was tangled.

He nodded to Baylock. "Briggs is waiting on you to start the meeting."

Baylock nodded, moving past Grayson and disappearing inside the doors. Kailani sat back down on the chair, resting her elbows on her knees and her chin in her hands. Grayson lowered himself onto the chair beside her. She looked up at him. The lines around his eyes seemed deeper than she remembered.

"You're not attending the meeting?"

Grayson shook his head, his lips thinning as he pressed them together. "They already know my input on the matter."

"And what's that?"

"The Realm is the only option. Azarro must be stopped tomorrow, or I'm afraid the magic of Talisia will be done for good."

Kailani's stomach turned. That didn't make her feel any better. "I can do it," she muttered, more to herself than to him. "I *will* secure the staff."

Grayson smiled down at her. "I know you will. You have the spirit of the Neptuna and Mistrahl women behind you."

Beyond the sparkling glass window, birds swooped towards the running stream. Grayson's eyes bore into her, but she couldn't look at him, not after what she'd done.

"Take out your wand."

Kailani turned to him, her eyes narrowing, but slowly pulled out her aquamarine wandstone. Grayson examined it.

"Your mother learned her first spells on this wand."

Mist filled his eyes and his face flushed as he looked at the engraved symbol. Kailani's stomach twisted. He'd lost both his daughters in the war. His wife. His sister. His granddaughter. Probably others too. The astral projection flashed in her minds eye, her family being slaughtered, the agony in Grayson's eyes at what he'd witnessed.

Kailani was so lost in the horrific memory, she almost didn't notice Grayson pull out a thin black box from his robe, but the sun's rays caught on the purple calligraphy. He held it out to her, but Kailani hesitated.

"Go on," he said, "open it."

Tentatively, Kailani accepted the box, turning it over in her hands before popping off the lid. She gasped, her eyes widening as a brilliant rose gold wand tipped into her lap.

Flowered golden filigree shone around a beautiful Sunstone. Kailani's breath caught. She'd never seen a Sunstone in real life, only in her history books. They were extremely rare, reserved for Vita royalty. The first Vita royals had used the stones to help build Mount Vita.

"Wow," Kailani breathed, cradling it like glass. A wand like this must've cost a fortune. "It's beautiful."

The goddess of Creation *herself* had one. Such a wandstone was pure, magical, strong, and it was said to clear and energize one's magic. She ran her fingers up and down the metal, examining the tip and craftwork. The Vita symbol was engraved on the top of the core.

"This belonged to my daughter, Kai Neptuna, the first royal in history to be born of two magical deities."

Kai Neptuna's image floated in Kailani's mind and she let the warmth wash over her. "With a wand like this, I bet she was very powerful."

"She was a powerful mage, a wonderful daughter, and an even better mother."

Kailani shifted awkwardly. There was nothing she could say to that. Reluctantly, she handed the wand back to Grayson.

But he didn't take it. Instead, he took her hand gently and curled her fingers over the stone. As her breath caught, Kailani jerked her head up. Grayson's eyes shimmered as he smiled at her, and a lump rose in her throat.

"It's yours now," he whispered.

Kailani's jaw dropped. "Mine?"

"Your grandmother loved you so much. Do you remember anything about her? She used to take you to the water every day."

Kailani's heart fluttered as a weight lifted from her chest. In truth, she didn't remember her grandmother. Mom never talked about her. But she *did* love the water, and knowing that love was a gift from her grandmother made her lips curl upward. She tried not to think of the massacre, instead holding the image of Kai Neptuna in her head from before everything had fallen apart.

"I do remember the water. I always thought my parents were

born in Magnolia, near the house I was born in." Her smile faded. "But I guess that was just a part of the lie."

Grayson squinted, looking into the distance as birds landed on the open windowsill. Finally, he sighed. "Take out your wand."

Kailani held it out. Grayson took it, putting the tip of her old wand to the tip of the sunstone wand to transfer ownership to herself. She had only done so once before, when she started school and Mom gave her the aquamarine wand. A stream of light formed between the two. Kailani stared in awe as the Vita symbol transitioned into her own, unique, symbol of unity.

"My dear, you don't know what you're capable of yet."

Her vision swam and she wiped her eyes, looking away.

Grayson cupped a wrinkled hand over hers. "Tears don't make you weak, Kailani. They are proof of how strong you are, how strong you've had to be. You will do great things. Impossible things. You are strong, and before this ends, you'll be even stronger."

Kailani met his eyes. "What if I can't secure the staff?"

Grayson let out a long breath. "You've seen some great cruelty in your short time since the ceremony. And no doubt the Realm will twist those memories into unimaginable horrors. But your parents are the strongest people I've known. Not only because they've had to be, but because they choose to be. You're just like them. And I know the staff will see that too."

The door opened behind them. Kailani's heart raced as she jumped from her seat.

Briggs stood in the doorway, Tilly behind him. "We're ready."

CHAPTER TWENTY-FOUR

Kailani trudged forward, her boots scraping against the salty earth.

They were two hundred miles south of Talisia, outside the forest of the Far Lands. The warm sun beat on her face, yet a shiver ran down her spine. The closer they got to the Realm, the eerier the air felt. Like a heavy weight was placed on Kailani's chest, and just kept pressing harder with each step. The Kairo soldiers had teleported them as close to the Realm as they could get, but there wasn't one person in Talisia who knew exactly where the Realm met the salt flat. She'd never seen a salt flat before now, but she'd heard about people getting lost out here—going insane.

She prayed to the gods that this wouldn't be a waste of time. That they hadn't chosen wrong.

Rebel soldiers flanked her on all sides, and though they tried to be discreet, Kailani could see the way that their eyes darted towards her. As if they feared her. As if they hated her. It was strange—only days ago, she would've felt so excited to be surrounded by them. Now, she felt like a stupid kid. She bit her lip, trying to shake the thoughts out of her head.

I'm doing this for Lyla and Patrick.

The call of the staff pulled her forwards, her feet growing heavier with each step. The sun was setting fast, the air growing colder with each passing minute. Only a few hours were left until the blood moon started. Kailani wrapped her fingers tight around her new wand, closing her eyes and letting herself feel the Sunstone's warmth spreading Vita magic through her. But the closer they got, the less she could feel the warmth. It was slowly replaced by a feeling of foreboding that cast dread inside of her.

A quick glance at the other soldiers confirmed they felt it too. Kailani squared her shoulders. They were near.

Kailani...

A sharp pain pierced her mind, and she cried out, jerking to a halt. The pain passed as quickly as it came and she turned her panicked eyes to Briggs.

Lines formed between his eyebrows. "Are you okay?"

Breathing heavily, Kailani was aware that all eyes were on her, but she was too shaken to feel embarrassed. "Did you call me?"

Briggs' frown deepened. "No."

Skin crawling, Kailani shook her head, feeling like her brain was frozen. That voice...it had to be something to do with the staff, and it would only get worse as they got closer to it. Her stomach flipped at the thought, but she couldn't waver. She just had to focus...

Briggs raised his eyebrows as he stepped closer to her. "Remember, stay by me. The Realm could start anywhere, and it doesn't give a warning. The last thing we need is to get separated."

Kailani nodded, taking a deep breath and fixing her eyes on the cracks in the earth, which created clusters of crusted salt formations throughout the land. Crystals of salt oozed between the cracks, the wind scattering loose pieces into strange images on the ground. Kailani bit her lip, counting the crystals in her head. She was with the rebels. She would be safe.

Kailani...

Kailani's head jerked up again. Large bat-like creatures swooped overhead, their elastic wings creating a breeze as they ducked down in the distance, picking at the earth. Kailani gulped, glancing over her shoulder. The distant trees of the forest were no longer visible, just miles of flat earth. They were hundreds of miles from civilization, hundreds of miles from safety. She glanced around at the soldiers. Not one of them was looking her way.

"Prepare yourselves."

Kailani tensed at Briggs' words. The other rebels spread out, and Kailani spun on the spot, her heart pounding as she sought whatever it was they were seeing. Instead, her throat constricted as two faces loomed in the deepest part of her mind.

Kailani...

Patrick's face, warped with agony, flashed in front of her. Kailani gasped, and she saw Briggs move towards her from the corner of her eye. She blinked Patrick's face away and tried to focus on the back of the soldier directly in front of her. Tried to focus on putting one foot in front of the other. Ignoring the illusions. That was all they were. Just illusions.

It's all your fault, Kailani...

Another flash—but this time, it was Lyla.

"I know." Kailani cried before she could catch herself. "I know it's my fault. But I'm going to make it better. I—"

Suddenly, Kailani was weightless. She tried to focus on her breathing. The only stable thing in the world was the way her chest heaved in and out with each aching wheeze. When she looked up, she seemed to be in slow motion, the world smearing into stripes of color around her. Kailani had the faintest memory of painting with watercolors. She remembered knocking over a glass of water nearby, and watching the paint run off the canvas. That was what the world looked like right now—just colors and abstractions.

"Kailani."

She blinked hard, shaking away the thumping in her head and the rush of color. She was on the cold ground, the heat from the day having been stripped away as soon as the sun set. Briggs hovered over her, his face a mask of concern.

"I'm fine," Kailani rasped, pushing herself up.

But her trembling hands gave her away, and she bit the inside of her cheek until she tasted blood. Her mind tortured her with memories of Azarro and his methods of getting information, and her stomach turned queasy thinking about Lyla and Patrick.

Briggs reached out a hand and helped her to her feet. "I'm not sure you are."

It was the first gentle thing Briggs had said to her since the incident at the prison. It was far from forgiveness—but Kailani's chest tightened, and she managed a watery smile. She had to be okay. She had to succeed this time.

"I'm sure. I'm just…" She shook her head. "The visions are starting."

He released her slowly, and Kailani dusted herself down, hoping nobody could tell the world was still spinning.

"Thanks," she added.

He didn't seem to believe her. On one hand, she was thankful Briggs cared enough to see through her lies. On the other, she didn't want him to force her to turn around and abandon the plan. She needed this to work if she ever wanted the rebels to trust her again. And more than that, she needed this to work for Patrick and Lyla's sake. Drawing a wide smile onto her face, Kailani lifted her chin, opening her mouth to insist she could handle this.

You couldn't save us, Kailani.

She winced. Lyla's cry seared into her brain.

A hand came to rest on Kailani's shoulder, making her jump, but when she whipped round, she was relieved to find Tilly at her side. Her head was still ringing with Lyla's voice, but Kailani let

Tilly pull her close, so the other soldiers couldn't hear. "Stranges learn early on to have power over their own minds. It helps sometimes when nerves set in."

Nerves? Was that all that was happening?

Licking dry lips, Kailani whispered, "What do I do?"

Briggs and Tilly shared a look, and Kailani squirmed under the weight of all the eyes upon her.

With a deep sigh, Briggs said, "Do you remember the first session we ever had together? Manipulating mass? It's a bit like that, except you must do the extra work of conceptualizing a physical form for your thoughts."

You failed.

Kailani flinched, but she closed her eyes and focused on Briggs' words, the real ones. She imagined the thoughts invading her head like they were arrows piercing through her brain.

You don't deserve us. You don't deserve them.

"Stop," Kailani said, not knowing whether she'd spoken aloud.

You're a failure. A monster.

"Stop!"

She could almost feel Lyla's lips touching her ears. The ghastly form of her best friend made her shiver. *You'd be better off dea—*

"STOP!"

She imagined a ring of light circling her brain, forcing the intrusive thoughts away. The world around her, which moments before had been spinning like a nauseating top, was once again stable.

She took a deep, shaky breath. Then, she exhaled, and opened her eyes. The other soldier's eyes darted away from her and her cheeks burned.

"Thank you," Kailani breathed, her voice hardly a whisper.

"Of course." Briggs turned forward. "I wouldn't want anything to go wrong with this plan."

Kailani nodded, her exhilaration fracturing, though only slightly. That was one thing they could both agree upon. Perhaps he would never truly forgive her—but as long as Briggs could find a way to trust her again, Kailani could learn to live with that.

There was a noise overhead, but when she glanced up to inspect it, she found nothing but the giant bat, swooping away. Briggs did a quick glance over the land before motioning the team to keep moving. The soldiers' boots crunched against the salty earth like leaves in a forest. She felt lighter now that the voices weren't plaguing her mind, but the sky was growing dark and the clouds rolled like a storm was coming. Chills ran up Kailani's spine as a void crawled through her. She squinted, a shimmering wall seemingly right in front of her, but when she held out her hands there was nothing there.

Kailani ducked, a bat swooping overhead sending a gust of wind in her face. She gasped. The creature seemingly flew sideways, before disappearing mid air.

"Hang on," Kailani said, holding her hand up. "Something's happening, I can feel it."

"Over there!" one of the rebels yelled, pointing a few yards away.

Kailani squinted, she couldn't see anything. But then her breath caught as the soldier flung his arms over his head, screaming curses at nothing. Their ranks froze and Kailani froze with them, ice trickling down her spine. Only Tilly was unaffected. She raced to the screaming soldier's side, grabbing his face between her hands and whispering something Kailani couldn't hear over the pounding of her heart. Slowly, Tilly pulled him out of whatever horrible illusion he was seeing.

Kailani had just heaved a sigh of relief when a dark shadow fell over the salt flat and her body went cold. It was as if the stars and moon had shut off, leaving them in an abyss of darkness, and she couldn't tell if her eyes were open or closed.

They were in the Realm.

Lights sparkled from the ends of the rebels' wands and Kailani rushed towards Briggs, grabbing for his arm in an effort to keep calm. She took deep breaths, counting in her head, but she could hear jeers deep in her mind, trickles of images that she tried to bury. She walked slowly. Briggs and Tilly's faces lit up on either side of her in the dim light of their wands. She tried to close her eyes, to feel for the staff, but all she could hear was her heart beat rising.

Then, in the forefront of her mind, a string lit up and guided her. Magic tugged her towards three tombs encircling each other a few yards away. The staff had to be there.

"This way!" she called to Briggs and Tilly.

"Are you sure?" Briggs asked, already motioning for his soldiers to follow her lead.

Kailani nodded, but she didn't spare him another look. Her pulse pounded with certainty, with a confidence that was exhilarating. Trying to imagine which tomb was real, she pressed her hands to the ground and tried to feel for the staff's presence. It was like the magic of the staff called to her, like Fia was guiding her hand, and finally, she located a small alcove deep within the tomb. Judging by the powerful magic calling to her, it had to house the staff.

She held up her wand and sliced the air, as though she was attempting to do a breaststroke through the water, and her path lit up in front of her. Her muscles burned with effort as she pushed her magic to split the rocky tomb. She *knew* the staff was here. She couldn't see, but she could feel where she was going.

The air was cool inside the tomb. Goosebumps formed on her skin.

"We're so close," Kailani cried, breathless. She could practically feel the smooth surface of the metal staff in her palms. The rebels yelled behind her. They were fighting with their own illusions.

She could only hope Tilly had given them lessons on fighting them.

Finally, Kailani found herself at a dead end. But it was steel. She stepped back, examining the wall. Trying to feel for a way around it.

"The tomb could collapse," Tilly warned. "Briggs, break the wall."

Briggs gave Kailani a small smile. "It's only fair you do the honors."

Kailani swallowed hard, pressing her hand to the cool stone. Brute magic was a storm inside her, and she reached for it, letting the force release itself as she imagined bursting through the wall.

"Industria!"

The stone cracked, but it hadn't broken yet.

With a deep breath, she pulled for her magic again.

"Industria!"

This time, the storm released and she fell through the wall as it gave way. Above her, the ceiling began to crumble under the weight of the collapsing tomb. As rocks rained down, Kailani stood, and her mouth dropped. Before her stood the Staff of Darkness. It glowed brilliantly, long cool metal wrapped with spikes around a shining Bloodstone.

"Grab it!" Briggs yelled, the alcove lighting up as he casted spells at the crumbling ceiling to hold it in place.

Kailani took a deep breath, counting to three. This was it. The staff would either accept her or deem her unworthy and drain her of her powers. She'd be lost in the Realm, forever.

Squaring her shoulders, Kailani fixed her eyes on the Bloodstone. She thought of her parents, her friends, the goddess. She *had* to trust in her own powers.

With the tomb collapsing around her, and the screams of the other rebels echoing in her ears, Kailani lunged forward and grabbed the staff.

Her body froze.

As soon as she touched the cool metal, the tomb was washed in an inky sea of impenetrable blackness.

She was alone.

Kailani sank into darkness, deeper, deeper…

The shadows ripped at her limbs, pulling the magic out of her. She tried to release the staff, but she couldn't unclench her fingers. With each tug and pull she felt more numb, like life was being sucked from her. She tried to fight it, but the darkness clawed at every inch of her, ripping her apart.

Everything about her had always been mundane, but she didn't understand the magic inside of her until now. Until it was being ripped from her. Until she was nothing but a shell of her real self.

Empty.

As the fight faded from her, she looked through the dark, desperately searching for a spark. For a light. For anything to pull her out of the unimaginable, incomprehensible dark. Her ears rang in the silence, and it was as if a blanket had been laid on top of her. She tried to push it off, but it only got heavier with each fighting movement. And she was so tired. Wasn't it easier to just lay there, numb? Empty. Safe.

Safe from the pressure of her quest. From the crumbling kingdom and heavy weight of expectations. From the rules, society, history.

Safe from her own magic.

It was so safe, Kailani smiled. Deeper and deeper she sank until she was floating in the sea of nothingness.

Then she felt something. A morsel of fire, barely an ember. But it was there, deep in her gut. For a moment, she wanted to ignore it. She wanted only to sleep, to rest and be safe forever. But the ember burned brighter, until it was more than an itch. Until she had no choice but to reach for the growing flame, to grasp at it.

And with it burning against her palm, she remembered. She still had a fight to finish. For her parents. For her friends. For herself and the life she'd never known, but desperately wanted now.

Kailani grasped the emptiness, clawed at the void. The first magic she felt was Kairo, and she let it fill her with confidence, ambition. Then came Luminate, reminding her of all the nights spent with Dad in the shop, filling her with determination and curiosity. Vita sparked deep inside her and she pulled at Mom's magic, basking in compassion and creativity. Then Charm magic rose, and she smiled as she brimmed with selflessness and pride. Brute was next, and she harnessed it, pulled at the power. And finally, she felt her Strange magic, the darkness deep inside her. But instead of letting it overtake her, she welcomed the darkness. Invited it in. At last, she saw the beauty in it.

With power surging inside her, Kailani laughed. There was nothing to fear in the dark, and she had the power to illuminate it anyway.

With a single thought, a burst of light lit up the darkness, and she emerged with her feet on the ground, and the staff in her hand.

Blood pounding, she held it high in the air, the bloodstone spreading light through the tunnel and guiding Kailani out of the tomb. The light spread through the Realm, in different directions, striking through the illusions deep in her mind. She charged forward. She didn't know what she'd see out there, or who she'd find, but she could only hope Briggs and Tilly and the rest of the team found their way out of the tombs.

She stepped outside. The moon lit the salt flats now, a tiny sliver of red creating a hue and her stomach lurched at the sight. She had to get to the castle, to stop Azarro before it was too late.

"Kailani!" She looked around and let out a breath of relief. Briggs rushed towards her. "You did it!"

Tilly and the rest of the rebels flanked her and Kailani let herself breathe. They still had a chance.

The ground rumbled and Kailani froze, throwing out an arm

for balance. She shot a look towards Briggs as the sound reached deep into her chest. His eyes were wide, and he took a step towards her.

Then a jagged shard of salt rock speared the ground between them.

"Kailani," Briggs roared.

Clutching the staff, Kailani made to dart around the rock, to launch herself towards the others, but another salt shard burst from the ground. And then another. Every way Kailani turned, the salt earth blocked her path with a splintering crack. She could hear the rebels shouting, struggling.

"Briggs," she cried, spinning on the spot.

One path lay open to her, but Kailani hesitated. If only one path was left open, she wasn't sure she wanted to find what waited at the end of it. But the rock formations surrounded her, circling her like sharks, closing in.

Kailani!

Patrick's voice screamed her name and Kailani cried out, flinging her free hand to her ears. *No. No. No.* She tried desperately to follow Tilly's advice to block out the voices, but with the chaos unfolding before her, her thoughts scattered. Magic spurred, causing shocking sensations to burst through her body. She squeezed her eyes shut, but nothing would drown out their voices.

Kailani! Why can't you save us?

Why can't you move?

What are you even good for?

Still, Kailani would not move. Not even when the rocks pressed against her. She ground her teeth together and forced herself to breathe. Strange mages controlled their minds. They didn't let their minds control them. Kailani shakily rose to her feet, despite the world shifting around her. She could vaguely hear someone yelling in the distance. Briggs? No, Tilly.

It didn't matter.

Because right in front of her, she could see Queen Stasorin.

Kailani's entire body went cold. Anger boiled in the pit of her stomach, and she reached deep inside of her to grab her magic.

Seeming to sense the confrontation brewing, the salt formations shifted to surround them both, encircling them, as the two circled each other. Queen Stasorin wore a detached expression, as if she had no doubt she would win.

"You're doing this!" Kailani cried, staggering forward as she drew the staff.

Queen Stasorin didn't seem fazed. "Oh, I don't deserve all the credit. The magic may be mine, but the thoughts are all yours."

Kailani's head pulsed. "What are you talking about?"

"Metaphysical magic—magic that affects the psyche. I can coax it along, but I can't choose how it manifests. Whatever it is you're seeing, or hearing, is simply a projection of your own worst thoughts. Your guilt, your self-hatred, your pain." Stasorin didn't smile. Rather, she narrowed her eyes—as if Kailani was an experiment she was having great fun with. "So, tell me. What is it you're seeing?"

Stasorin raised her wand.

Lyla and Patrick appeared in front of her, their eyes soulless. Patrick reached out to her, his lips drawn into a persistent plea.

"This is all your fault," Patrick said, his voice hoarse.

Kailani whimpered, falling back. "You're not real."

"How long until they abandon you?" Lyla crooned. *"How long until they realize that behind your wasted magical potential, you're nothing but a scared little girl?"*

"Please stop," Kailani begged, trying her best to ignore their accusations. They were just figments of her imagination. They weren't real. They didn't have power over her.

"You've done me a great service, you know," Stasorin drawled. "You made it so easy for me to reach out to you with my magic. It would've been a much greater task for my Protectors to find you otherwise…"

Kailani froze, painstakingly tearing her eyes from Stasorin to scan her surroundings. But there were no Protectors in sight. She gripped the staff until her knuckles whitened and then she launched forward with a roar, bursting through her illusions of Patrick and Lyla. They exploded around her like dust, and their voices drifted to nothing. She pointed the staff at Stasorin, but she stumbled on her feet, throwing her hands up for balance.

The ground rumbled as a row of salted formations slid in front of her, blocking her path to Stasorin, only Kailani didn't stop running. She lifted her wand and tried to move the formations with her magic, but they didn't so much as budge. Summoning all her courage, all her energy, she closed her eyes and barreled headfirst for the closest rock.

The impact never came. When Kailani opened her eyes again, the formations were behind her, and she was still running. Protectors surrounded her, but she didn't know what was real and what wasn't. The faster Kailani ran towards Queen Stasorin, the farther away she seemed to be.

"Kailani!" Tilly screamed. "Come back! It's just another trick!"

Kailani skidded to a halt, and her eyes darted between Tilly and Stasorin. Around them, rebels clashed with Protectors. But it was still impossible to tell what was real.

Stasorin narrowed her eyes. "Do I look like an illusion to you?"

Kailani took in a shaky breath, trying to clear her mind. If only she could have a moment to think!

"Kailani, please!" Tilly shouted again.

Stasorin laughed. "Can't you make a choice, Kailani?"

She clenched her jaw, a scream bubbling in her throat. Prison alarms blared in her ears, mingled with the screams of prisoners. The smell of the rusting iron bars of the cells drifted up her nose. The taste of blood filled her mouth.

She fell to the ground, her confidence wavering.

Save us, Kailani.

Patrick's voice. Lyla's voice.

In the end, she couldn't save anyone. In the end, all she was good for was destroying.

Destroying.

But even if all she could do was destroy, she'd destroy Stasorin —even if it was the last thing she did. Shakily, she rose to her feet.

She looked back. A Protector had Briggs locked in a fight. Only a few yards behind her, Josie lay collapsed on the ground.

As her pulse thundered, Kailani made up her mind. "I'm sorry, Tilly," she yelled, "but I can't risk losing this chance."

Then, Kailani ran. This time, Queen Stasorin didn't move. Blood pounded in Kailani's ears as she raised her staff and commanded the blast of magic.

Her feet fell from under her as Queen Stasorin's form evaporated.

"No!" Tilly screamed. "Briggs! Josie!"

Kailani jerked her head around, just in time to see Briggs and Josie racing towards Tilly. But wait—that meant...

As her stomach sank, Kailani's eyes darted to Josie's crumpled form on the ground behind her. The illusion smiled at her before disappearing. The salt flats materialized. The edge of the Far Lands loomed in the distance.

Kailani's shoulders slumped and she swayed on her feet, the shimmering hue of the Realm behind her now.

She gripped the staff, turning on the spot, and her heart sank into her stomach. She pushed the staff forward but it was ripped from her hands as four Protectors' wands pointed directly at her, all screaming *"Levare!"* The staff flew forwards in the air and hovered in the middle of the Protectors, their wands trained on it.

Protectors swarmed her, securing her arms and her wand. Kailani couldn't think. She couldn't breathe. All she could focus on was the rage swirling inside of her.

Then, Azarro materialized into the night, a snarling smirk on his raging face. He bent so his face breath was on her cheeks. "I've finally got you."

CHAPTER TWENTY-FIVE

*K*ailani's body screamed in agony as a tight cloth was fastened around her eyes and death binders were wrapped around her wrists.

Then the ground was ripped from her feet as she swirled in air, landing hard on uneven ground. Her hands trembled, sending a burning sensation up her arms. But this time, she knew not to struggle. She wasn't the same person she'd been after the Choosing Ceremony. She wouldn't make the same mistakes.

Her magic brewed, just beneath the surface, waiting to be called forward.

Kailani let it simmer.

Hands gripped her arms as she was led forward. She stumbled along a path, up a flight of stairs. Her boots caught on each step. Her captors didn't slow so she could regain her footing. They simply dragged her along, so her shins knocked into stone and the death binders burned against her wrists. She clamped her mouth shut against her grunts of pain, trying to mask the anger and fear swirling inside her. She needed to be in full control if she wanted her magic to work. She wouldn't be tricked by the Queen's illusions this time.

The blindfold was ripped off.

Kailani gasped.

The air was crisp on her face and her head pulsed as the world spun away below her. She was standing on rocky ground. Mount Vita loomed in front of her. Whimpering filled her ears and she turned, squinting as she was led closer and closer to the mouth of the mountain.

Her heart dropped.

Lyla and Patrick were bound with death binders locked around their wrists and arms. Burn marks glared beneath the rope.

"No..."

Forgetting herself, Kailani jerked towards them, but her own ropes tightened, and she cried out. Their heads shot up at the sound. Tears filled Kailani's eyes as she stared at them. They struggled against the binders and Kailani winced. Their muffled cries echoed through the mountain pass.

The Protectors pushed her closer and Kailani stumbled, noticing another figure tied further up the mountain pass. The rebels. They couldn't all have been captured... but she could barely make out the face in the dense fog that hovered above the ground. Pain split up her arm as the Protectors yanked her forward towards the figure. It couldn't be...

One... two... three...

Then, Kailani's heart all but stopped. She tried to cry out, to run, but her body was cemented in place and her voice caught in her throat.

Mom!

Their eyes met, and Mom held her chin high, not breaking gaze. Blood dripped from a gash on her forehead, and she had a rope in her mouth, keeping her from speaking. She sat in rageful silence, not moving an inch. Heart pounding, Kailani looked around desperately as her stomach twisted into knots. Mom was alone. And if Mom was alone, that meant Dad...

Kailani shuddered. She couldn't think the worst. He was here, or in the dungeons. He was anywhere but dead.

As Kailani returned her tear filled gaze to her mom, Mom's own eyes narrowed.

Heart in her mouth, Kailani turned. The hair on her arms stood up.

Azarro loomed over her, flanked by Protectors on each side. Queen Stasorin stood a few paces behind. Kailani's stomach jolted. The Staff of Darkness hovered beside her, a ring of light shining around the glowing bloodstone as the four Protectors levitated the staff with their wands. It seemed that neither Azarro nor Stasorin had dared to touch the staff yet. They must've understood the dangers.

But Kailani felt a strange pull to the staff, like it was already hers.

Azarro took a step towards Kailani and she flinched, stumbling backwards. His skin was ghastly, pale with dark veins running along his face and neck. His eyes were dark, just as they had been the day of the Choosing, but now blue veins spindled the whites of his eyes and the skin around them was red and bulgy.

"Stupid child," he spat.

His voice was more of a hiss.

Hatred boiled her insides, and she lifted her chin.

His smile only grew more manic. "Your pride, your ignorance of your own power has led you here."

"Let them go." Kailani balled her hands into fists, trying to sound braver than she felt, but her voice was heavy with guilt, like the weight on her conscience. Lyla yelped a few feet from her. Kailani bit the inside of her cheek, forcing herself to stay calm. "They haven't done anything. I'm the one you want."

"Oh, we will use you." Azarro's face twitched, his words screeching like nails on a chalkboard.

Kailani's skin crawled. He was inhuman, and she was certain his misuse of Strange magic had driven him to this point.

"Your potent, powerful blood," Azarro continued. "The blood of all six gods. As well as your mom's blend of Luminate and Vita—"

Kailani swallowed. Her eyes flitted to Mom. She was trying to fight the Protectors, but her efforts were futile, and her screams of rage echoed along the path.

Azarro laughed. "Of course, I could've completed it without you. The gods wouldn't have been sealed for good, the curse would have eventually weakened, like it did when you went through the ritual. But it would have bought me more time. However, your blood, the blood of the champion—" malice flickered in Azarro's eyes— "your blood will lock the gods away for good. I will be eternal."

Kailani's chest tightened. Her blood for theirs. Her eyes flickered to the staff. If she could just get her hands on it, she could end it all.

Azarro lunged towards her and she hated herself for flinching, for squeezing her eyes shut, for the whimper that still escaped her.

But no pain, no blow came.

Chest heaving, she peeked an eye open to find Azarro inches away. Up close, she could see the bulging of veins running across his skin like spiderwebs—his corrupted magic, trapping him in the hate-filled depths of his own mind. His teeth were stark white and razor sharp, like he'd taken a saw and filed them to be weapons. Kailani swallowed, resisting the urge to back away but when Azarro moved closer still, sniffing her, it was too much. She jerked back, then cried out as the death binders burned her skin.

"I can smell it, you know," he whispered. "Smell the power that festers inside of you. You're too weak for it. Too soft. Just like the very gods who bestow us such powers. Pathetic. That's why they don't need to interfere with the kingdom any longer."

Unable to bear looking at him, Kailani turned away only for her gaze to fall on Stasorin, standing still as a statue and expressionless. With a flash of boiling anger, Kailani snapped her eyes to the staff hovering beside the Queen, willing it to come to her, to obey. She didn't know how to summon it, or if she even could, but she could *feel* its power within her, and she had no other plan. When she looked up, the moon peeked out from the clouds and her stomach lurched. It was half red now, and she didn't know how much longer she had until the peak of the blood moon.

She *needed* that staff, but without her sunstone, she didn't know if she was powerful enough. She turned back to Azarro. She had to keep him talking, keep him distracted, so she could concentrate on getting the staff.

"You already have control of the kingdom. Why do you need to lock them away?"

Azarro looked to the sky and smiled greedily. "Since I have to wait for my crowning achievement to begin, I might as well indulge you. The gods of magic are too giving with their blessings. With your blood, I alone will have the power to decide. The fate of all mages will be in my hands. The gods care about unity, about respecting magical boundaries. But look where that got them. I want to push the magical boundaries further than they've ever been pushed. I want to see what magic can do when it has no limits. Strange has been shut away because people are afraid. I'm just getting started discovering what power we're capable of."

Kailani shuddered. If Azarro took all the powers of the gods, he alone would have the power to choose who had what magic, how much magic.

Lyla whimpered. Kailani's gaze shot to her. Her friends had stopped struggling, but Lyla trembled as tears streamed down her face. Patrick's head hung low, and his body shook.

Kailani's hands clenched into fists. There had to be *something* she could do, but what? She was alone, bound, without her sunstone. She was surrounded by Protectors, captive of a monster. She was supposed to be a champion, but tears burned her eyes before magic came to her. She was useless, she'd always been useless.

She tipped her head back to the sky, her chest tight. *Please, gods, I am here. Tell me what to do.*

But they were silent, and when she tried again to summon the staff, no magic came.

Shoulders slumping, she could only shake her head. Her voice was small as she said, "You'll only destroy yourself. Like you destroyed the kingdom."

"Big words for such a defenseless child." Azarro smirked. "I did what I had to do for my kind. No one ever took Strange mages seriously. We were shut up, locked away in Teulon. Offered meaningless work as bounty hunters and criminals for the monarchy. And because of that, the number of Strange mages dwindled. The magic became rare, and people feared our power."

Anger thrummed in Kailani's chest. "For good reason—look what you did! You killed so many people, and for what? Power?"

Azarro laughed and Kailani clenched her jaw.

"You think your precious great grandfather was so innocent? That life was peaches before my niece took over, do you? He committed his own crimes, every good ruler does."

Kailani bit her tongue, her pulse pounding. Grayson united the branches, celebrated magic. He would never do something as vile as Azarro.

"You're lying—"

Azarro chuckled. "My brother and I had a lot of plans for this Kingdom. And Mistrahl didn't even give him the time of day." He shook his head, his lips curling. "When those disgusting magicless murdered my family, I knew it was time to set our plan into motion. And my niece here played her part well. She won over the council, a sad teenager whose family was murdered in front of her. Those weak descendants couldn't help but take her under their wing. Kai Neptuna was the dumbest of all, even offering

Nina a wing in her very own palace. It was so easy to play her like a fiddle..."

Anger roared inside Kailani like a volcano ready to erupt. How *dare* he insult her family when he was the one who orchestrated their deaths?

"Your grandparents were almost as naive as your great grandfather. You were never supposed to be born, you know. Royal bloodlines were never supposed to mix. But Grayson Mistrahl fell in love. He couldn't live another day without Neptuna. So, he changed the law in his favor. Not for the first time, either."

Kailani almost laughed. So, he changed the law for love? That was nothing compared to what Azarro had done. "You *murdered* them."

"I murdered them so I could accomplish what truly mattered! The gods were interfering too much. Your family was becoming too powerful. Our ritual locked the gods away in the mountain pass, and everything would have gone splendidly had it not been for you. But this time will be different. This time, your blood will give *me* their eternal and full power."

Azarro grabbed her jaw and she bared her teeth. His breath reeked of rot.

He pointed at the moon. "Your time is almost up."

The red hue covered most of the moon now, and Kailani's heart sank as realization dawned on her. She willed the staff, begged the gods, but she couldn't bend her magic to bring the staff to her. She was powerless against Azarro, and the rebels weren't coming to save her.

They were out of time.

"Take her to the mountain!" Azarro yelled, and the Protectors dragged her backwards, to the very top of the steps at the mouth of the mountain. Whatever warmth was left in her rushed away, leaving her cold and hollow. He was going to kill her, like he killed her grandmother, like he was going to kill Mom. Their souls wouldn't go to the Wonder Grounds. They'd be stuck in an eternal place of mourning, in agony of what could have been.

She screamed, kicking at the Protectors, but it was futile. The death binders shot burning pain up her arm and she grinded her teeth.

They thought they'd won, but she wasn't done fighting. Her magic was stronger, she had the power of the gods. Letting loose a scream, she urged her magic forward, but nothing came.

She was at the top of the mountain pass. It was over.

"Mom!" she cried, as the Protectors threw her on the ground.

Through her blurred vision, she saw Mom thrash against her restraints, despite the agony it must have been. But there was no point. Tears rolled down Kailani's cheeks as she slumped to the earth, holding her Mom's stare.

Azarro stood in front of them. His wand pointed at Mom's face. Greed shone on his face as he looked up at the full moon, waiting.

Mom grunted something through the rope in her mouth. Kailani wanted nothing more than to reach out and squeeze her, to go look for Dad, to find out what happened. She didn't look like the same Mom Kailani had known before the Choosing, and that broke her heart. Her hair was tangled and knotted, her delicate face bruised, and the sight made stomach churn.

Her mother, descendant of the goddess of creation. Her mother, who'd risked her entire life for Kailani. For the people she loved. Her mother, whose blood was full of knowledge and creation, who showed her every single day how magic was revered, a gift.

Her blood, which ran through Kailani.

Her blood was a gift. Blessed by the gods.

And as Kailani lay in the dirt beneath the red glow of the blood moon, cool relief washed over her. Because if she was going to die, she was going to die fighting to save Mom.

She willed her magic back to the surface and fought to release it, and it surged, but fell back down. Her body shook. Nausea swirled inside her and sweat beaded on her forehead. She reached deep down, but her magic was like water slipping through her fingers. She felt it, but it was impossible to grip. Without her wand, without the sunstone, it was much harder to command. Her pulse thundered as panic tightened around her lungs.

Azarro cackled, motioning for the Protectors to bring Lyla and Patrick forward.

Kailani yelled, attempting to rip herself out of the Protector's grip. Pain shot through her body.

"Please, you don't need them! They don't have royal blood— you don't have to kill them!"

Her voice broke, only for a moment. She didn't care about the ropes or the staff. She couldn't let this happen.

"No, I don't have to," Azarro leered. "Maybe I'll send them back to the Realm. How was that for you?"

Kailani snarled. Electricity shot through her veins and her magic was a wave inside her, but she couldn't bring it to the surface. She *needed* the sunstone.

The moon was fully red now.

She was out of time. As Mom struggled beside her, Kailani hung her head.

After everything—Mirstone, fighting the illusions, wielding the staff—it hadn't been enough. She *still* wasn't enough. Kailani's eyes dimmed, her vision narrowing as Azarro reached out his wand and held it in her face.

Then, a bright light filled the mountain pass. Kailani closed her eyes, looked up, and let the light wash over her.

She felt no pain. She let herself fall into the depths of space. Felt herself floating, traveling.

She heard movement. Her eyes cracked open, and she gasped.

The six gods of magic floated in front of her.

Fia Azarro's shining essence filled the darkness. Kailani looked around, but it was as if time had stopped. Mom, Lyla and Patrick,

Azarro and Stasorin—they were all frozen. As her chest heaved, Kailani turned to Gaia Mistrahl with wide eyes. The goddess of knowledge—her legacy on Grayson's side—held her hands out in front of her. Golden strings danced from her fingertips and ensnared the mountain. The strings coiled around a coin, and she stabilized it as her hands shook.

"I can't go on for long, sister," Gaia grunted, her long red hair floating as she bobbed up and down. She shot a strained look at Fia. "My power is growing weaker by the moment."

Kailani's jaw hung open. Her entire body was warmed by the essence of the gods. She felt nothing, but not like when she was in the Realm. Her magic was bliss.

She looked at each of the gods in turn. The gods of power and strength bowed to her. The goddess of healing floated towards Gaia. A blue wisp flowed from her hands and wrapped around the Gaia in some sort of healing charm. Then Kailani's eyes caught on the goddess of Creation. She could see Mom in the delicate way Leila carried herself, even as a celestial being.

Fia nodded at Gaia, then floated towards Kailani.

"You're nearly there, Kailani. The tether is so close to being broken."

Kailani shook her head. "I can't stop him. He's too powerful!"

"That is untrue. Azarro is at his weakest. He needs this ritual and is desperate for it. A desperate man is easy to overcome."

But Kailani could barely breathe, let alone fight. "It's too late." Her lip trembled as tears swam in her eyes. "I've failed you. My time is up. The blood moon is here. My magic isn't powerful enough without my wand."

"While your journey is far from over, Kailani, you have succeeded in this quest. You are here now, on the night of the blood moon. All is not lost. You must dig deep inside, find the control that my magic demands. You have your ancestors' power behind you. Inside of you."

Another flash of light, and time moved.

Kailani's breath rasped, and her vision went spotty. Azarro's wand was at her throat. Protectors pinned her down. Sweat dripped from his forehead, his face. His hand shook as he stood, raging, watching the moon for the perfect moment. Then his eyes darted towards her.

"It's time."

He lunged towards her, grabbing her arm, and running his wand down her arm. Kailani couldn't help but scream as he sliced open her skin.

Kailani.

Her heart all but stopped. *Grayson?*

As her body shook, Kailani tried to lift her head, but her vision blurred as blood pooled around her. She'd imagined the voice. No one was there. She was going cra—

Kailani, I can help you.

Grayson's voice was in her head, cool and drawn out just as he'd been the last time she'd seen him. Hope surged in her heart.

"Help!" Kailani shrieked, hoping he could hear her, too.

"No one is coming to save you," Azarro mocked, as his dark laugh echoed up the mountain.

You are a powerful mage, Kailani. You have the lifeforce of those before you. The gods chose you. You are their champion. You don't need your wand to call on your powers. Your magic has been inside of you all along. You've always been special, Lani. Prove it.

Kailani cried out. She screamed until her throat was raw.

She pictured her grandmother's face from the projection. Kailani had inherited her wild and curly hair, but her grandmother had Mom's sweet smile. Kailani focused on Grayson's eyes next. She squeezed her eyes shut and pictured every face of the Neptunas and Mistrahls she could remember from her textbooks. Then she pictured Mom. Fighting beside her, her spirit to never give up encompassing her. Then Dad.

Smart and funny and kind. Rage burned inside of her at the

thought of Azarro torturing him, at not knowing where he was, at the worst possible thought. Bile burned her throat.

Your magic has been inside of you all along.

Kailani closed her eyes and conjured her magic, letting it build and swirl inside of her until she could feel it at the tip of her fingers. When it was on the brink of exploding, she grabbed it, twisting the energy in her hands as the death binders seared into her.

She released her power in its full form. Chaotic tranquility. Blissful sorrow.

The mountain pass exploded with light.

CHAPTER TWENTY-SIX

Wrapping the magic around her wrist like a rope, Kailani let it flow from her fingertips, holding the ends tight. The death binders blasted off her wrists. She flung the air at Azarro and the Protectors flew backwards. Kailani lunged, grabbing the closest Protector's wand. She pointed it towards Lyla and Patrick and yelled.

"*Laso Laxo!*"

Their ropes fell to the ground. Kailani stunned the Protector next to them. Lyla snatched the Protector's wand and pulled Patrick behind a jagged rock. Pain shot through Kailani's body, but her magic sizzled beneath her skin. She only hoped her adrenaline would keep her going. For now.

She turned to Mom and allowed herself half a breath of relief. She'd been knocked back by the force of the spell, too, but she was struggling with the ropes around her, still alive. Rushing forward, Kailani used her magic to untie the ropes.

"Mom!"

She didn't recognize the sound coming out of her throat, raspy and far away. But steady. Brave. Mom rushed towards her, bloodied and bruised, but racing across the rocky earth at full speed. Kailani ran too, barely breathing.

"Baby!"

She flung herself into Mom's arms. For the first time in weeks, a feeling of warmth and safety enveloped her.

"Mom." Kailani squeezed her tight, drinking in the familiar smell, the familiar feel of her. She wanted to stay in that moment forever, but the Protectors were already starting to stir. So Kailani sucked in a deep breath. "Where's Dad?"

Mom pulled away, her eyes widening, and a lump formed in Kailani's throat. But before Mom could speak her horrible truth, she tensed. Grabbing Kailani, she pulled her to the ground. A curse flew over their heads. A Protector was rushing towards them and Kailani squared her shoulders.

Mom grabbed the wand from Kailani and stood. "*Atro Dora!*"

The Protector froze, crumbling to the ground. But a dozen more replaced them, raising their wands. Kailani stood tall, locked eyes with Mom, and nodded. Mom directed her full power towards the Protectors. Her hands moved in a circle as if she was gathering air, then she sent a whirling wind spiraling towards them. They flew backwards. She raced towards them, grabbed a wand. Mom gripped her robe, pulling her behind a boulder.

"I need to get to the staff," she cried, looking around the mountain pass.

Her heart sank.

Dozens of Protectors surrounded the staff, all their wands trained on levitating it midair. Azarro stood underneath the staff with Stasorin. Kailani squinted, it looked as if they were arguing.

Mom yelped, and Kailani's head whipped around. She threw her arms up to cover her head. A blast of energy had split the rock in two, sending the rocks flying up at their faces. Kailani ducked as another curse shot in her direction. There were too many. Particles of light floated through the air, remnants of the curses being thrown around. Black spots crowded her vision. She lunged behind another jagged rock. Her knees trembled, threatening to collapse.

Mom flung spells over the boulder and Kailani trained her eyes on Azarro. He pointed to the sky, then to the staff. Stasorin was shaking her head wildly.

She had to get to the staff. It was the only way. But more Protectors raced up the mountain pass.

Then, three loud pops snapped through the silence. For a moment, Kailani thought somebody had cast a spell on her ears. Frowning, she reached up a hand.

One of the Protectors fell face first to the ground.

Kailani's jaw hung open because there, behind the wall of Protectors, stood hope.

Briggs towered at the base of Mount Vita, an army of rebels with him ready to fight.

The scene was chaos. Rebels and Protectors fought in a vicious display of light. Pellets of dirt and small rocks rained down on them. Kailani's gaze fell to Patrick, who fought one on one with a large Protector. She sprinted towards him. The Protector turned to her and narrowed his eyes, snarling. Blood dripped from his mouth as he locked eyes with Kailani and lunged. She raised her wand, but Patrick's voice cut through the air. Kailani gasped.

Patrick's wand was pointing not at the Protector, but the earth.

"*Mut Nexis Radix!*" he yelled, and the ground started to rumble.

Kailani stopped in her tracks. Her mouth hung open. Roots emerged from the shaking ground and wrapped around the Protector, entangling him against the earth.

Kailani rushed towards him. "Patrick, nice!"

Patrick looked up at her with a smile, but his face was bathed in red. Kailani's heart raced as she looked up at the moon. It was a cloudy red, encompassed by earth's shadow. The blood moon was almost over. Then Azarro couldn't complete the ritual.

She looked around, and her heart dropped to her throat.

It was as if she was seeing it in slow motion. Azarro wasn't far away. Lyla's back was to him, and a wicked grin crossed his face.

Kailani lunged, barely knocking Lyla to the ground as an orange stream of light singed the top of her head. Her wand fell to the ground, and she desperately reached for it, but Azarro cackled, pointing his wand directly at her and Lyla. Kailani ducked, ready for impact.

"No!"

Mom dove in front of them. Kailani's mouth fell open in a silent scream.

She watched in wonder as Mom threw out her hands, catching Azarro's spell and thrusting it aside. Kailani blinked, hardly able to believe her eyes.

Mom conjured air from her fingertips and threw a whirlwind towards Azarro. He slammed backwards, but recovered quickly, screaming as he snapped to his feet. And Mom, still fragile from the death binders and captivity, was weakening. Kailani staggered to her feet—with Lyla and Patrick at her heels—and threw herself forwards.

But it was too late.

Kailani's chest tightened.

Azarro screamed, pointing his wand at Mom. *"Agorra Voce Morre!"*

Heart shattering, Kailani staggered backwards. Her mouth fell open, but she made no sound as the curse collided with Mom's chest and she slammed to the earth.

Kailani tried to run to her, but her legs gave way beneath her. So, she crawled. And her arms slipped in the dirt, but she didn't stop, and she didn't look away. She wished she could. She wished she could stop seeing. If she blinked, this nightmare would end. She just needed to blink, and Mom would be on her feet, rejoining the fight.

So, then she blinked, and she blinked until she was close

enough to touch her limp body, but she never woke up. Not as she pulled Mom onto her lap. Not as the Protectors surrounded her, grabbed her. She didn't even try to fight as Azarro's laughter came back into focus.

He lunged towards Mom's body. Speckles of blue incandescent light floated above her form, and Kailani screamed, jerked, ripped away from the Protectors. Behind Azarro, four Protectors walked the staff down the mountain. Kailani eyed the staff, then Mom. As if in slow motion, Azarro collected Mom's life force into the jar, letting it fill to the top. Protectors' wands raised slowly. She turned and yelled. *"Transmino!"* They were blasted out of her way.

The staff was right there. Ten feet away, and Azarro turned to Stasorin.

"Take the staff."

Stasorin gasped. "I can't—"

Azarro's skin was translucent, his eyes pitch dark. "Take it!"

Kailani ran, tripping over stone and rocks, a horrible numbness overtaking her body. She felt nothing except rage. A desire to kill Kiran Azarro and the Queen even if she died in the process. She held out her trembling hands and felt vibrations lingering at her fingertips. Then she called forth the Staff of Darkness. She felt its presence, its connection to her. And she could feel the power getting closer, summoning her. But it was going to be too late. Azarro scrambled in his pocket for the lid, the lid that would trap the gods. The lid that would trap Mom's soul.

"Grab the staff!" Azarro screamed to Stasorin. "Kill her!"

Kailani's legs burned. She had to get to the staff before Stasorin did. Stasorin's eyes flickered from her to the staff and back to her.

Then Stasorin knocked the jar out of Azarro's hands.

Kailani froze. The particles of light sped out of the glass jar, floating around the sky and dissipating. A flood of emotions overcame Kailani and her knees buckled beneath her. Mom's soul would go to the Wonder Grounds after all. She wouldn't be trapped like her grandmother. Queen Stasorin had given her that much.

"You stupid child!"

Azarro's voice snapped her back to reality. He dove for Stasorin, wrapping one hand around her neck. With his other hand, he reached for his wand.

"Kailani, come on!"

Leonard was calling her towards him as rocks and rubble rained down, piling into a barricade between them. But she had to finish what she started. She had to break the tether.

She held out her hand, one last call.

I am Kailani Slate. I have the power of the gods behind me. I am the controller of darkness.

The staff whirled through the air. Metal clanged in Kailani's hand, and electricity shot through her arm, lighting up her entire body. The bloodstone glowed brilliantly. Azarro faltered, his face falling. He shouted a curse at her, but Kailani aimed the staff as Queen Stasorin dove away from him. Azarro's curse hovered in the air, as if frozen in time. Then she summoned the power and sent the curse flying back towards him. He stood to face her, snarling, and launched himself forward.

Kailani imagined the gods of magic in her mind's eye. She imagined them refilling the mountain with magic as Azarro released their power.

You are not worthy.

Azarro fell backwards, his body convulsing.

Streams of blue, purple, green, red, orange, and gold shot out of him, up into the air. They swirled, interlocking with each other, before ripping through the air and colliding with the shrines of the gods of magic. The shrines glowed, rumbled.

The essence of the six gods shot into the air and encircled the mountain. The entire mountain shook. Kailani steadied herself as thunder echoed overhead. Then the gods essence lit up the pass, sending lightning bursting into the sky, before disappearing.

The streams of light had completely drained from Azarro and he laid there, motionless and pale, his eyes still open in shock. Kailani spun, wild, untamed, and broken. Protectors stopped in their tracks, looking from her to the staff to Azarro's crumpled body in horror, then they turned and ran. She smiled, enjoying watching them flee after everything they'd done. She reached inside of her, pulled on her Strange magic and slammed her fist into the ground. A vibration hurtled towards them, lifting the ground beneath their feet and sending them flying.

Rebels were shouting to her, battling the Protectors who hadn't fled. Leonard waved frantically, trying to catch her attention, but she had one more mission.

One more fight.

A Protector lunged, but she held her palm up and flicked him to the side as if he was weightless.

"Kailani, come on!" Briggs roared.

She turned. Yards away, Kairo soldiers were grabbing rebels and fleeing. Josie and Arun disappeared with Lyla and Patrick, but Kailani turned and cornered Stasorin.

They locked eyes. Fury burned inside of her. It didn't matter that Azarro had been behind everything, she needed to take her pain out on somebody. She let go of the staff—it didn't matter whether she was holding it, she was still in full command. She yelled as all the pain since the Choosing Ceremony engulfed her like flames. Yet there she stood, amongst the rubble, a small ember.

Broken. But not defeated.

Flames erupted from Kailani's palms. The heat only tickled her fingertips as she threw her hands back, ready to cause pain. Ready to destroy. She sent the fireball flying towards Stasorin, but the Queen blocked the curse, her expression wild. Roaring, Kailani sent another, and another. Stasorin blocked each one, but she didn't send anything back. She stood there, her chin high, blocking spell after spell.

Kailani screamed again. "You did this!"

She hunched over, calling on every single ounce of magic inside of her, and flung it at Queen Stasorin.

Stasorin slammed backwards, colliding with the rock. Kailani rushed towards her. Stasorin's face was pale. Her eyes were wide; her body trembled as her wand fell from limp fingers. Kailani seized her anger once more, wearing it like armor, and reached for the staff. She *needed* this.

But then, Kailani stumbled.

In her mind's eye, nineteen-year-old Stasorin entered the room of the royal council. It all played out, just as it had that day: the way her grandmother smiled at Stasorin. The look of agony on her face as she watched the door. The sword, almost slipping into her own skin, before her uncle awoke.

Tears welled in Stasorin's eyes and Kailani squeezed her own shut. Pain and sorrow washed over her like a wave. Her heart pounded. She didn't want to see this. She wanted to hurt somebody, like she was hurting.

Stasorin's face was pale. Her lips trembled, but she didn't fight back. She just stared at Kailani, accepting her fate.

Kailani stumbled back as more images flashed through her mind.

"*This is all your fault," Azarro snarled, pushing Stasorin up against the wall. "Your sister is dead because of you.*"

With a jolt, she was back at Mount Vita, face to face with Stasorin. The flashes were coming faster now. Kailani's head was spinning. She grabbed the staff, clenching her jaw.

Stasorin looked between Kailani and the carnage on the mountain, then held her hands in the air.

The terrified teenage girl from the projection flashed in Kailani's head once more.

"*My—my uncle," Stasorin stuttered. "He wants war. He wants revenge.*"

More flashes, of Stasorin rushing around the room, gathering blood, gathering life forces. She wasn't innocent. Her life was tragic, but that didn't excuse what she'd done. Kailani had lost everything. *Mom* had lost everything.

But she'd spared Grayson. She'd spared Mom's soul.

Letting out a shuddering breath, Kailani released the staff, forcing her magic to subside. She locked eyes with Stasorin, and Stasorin stared back. Around them, rocks tumbled from the cliff, thunder roared, and Protectors and rebels yells echoed. But only silence lingered between them. Kailani could only focus on Stasorin trembling, gripping her necklace in her shaky hand. Then she turned, sprinting towards Leonard. He caught her, and before she could even blink, they were spinning through the air, leaving the battle far behind.

They landed hard, and Kailani collapsed.

CHAPTER TWENTY-SEVEN

*E*very part of Kailani's body ached.

She hadn't gotten out of bed for three days. Lyla slipped in and out of the cabin, dropping off food but giving her space. She'd let Kailani know she was there when she was ready.

How could she ever truly be ready, though? Sure, Azarro didn't complete the blood ritual. Sure, she broke his tether between him and the gods. But Mom was dead anyway. And she had no answers to what happened to Dad. And like always, the mere thought made her chest cleave in two.

Rolling over, she buried her face in her pillow.

What she wouldn't give to hear Mom's laugh one last time. She'd never spend another day in the shop, joking with Dad and going over lessons. She'd never have another family dinner around the kitchen table or curl up and listen to them tell stories about how they'd met, about how Dad was such an insufferable know it all they'd almost disintegrated their potions classroom.

The only thing left was numbness.

Many people came to her door, but Kailani ignored them. She couldn't stand the looks of pity plastered on their faces. She desperately wanted to go back to the looks of fear and anticipation that people had given her before the blood moon. At least then, her parents were alive. At least then, there was hope.

The door creaked open, but Kailani didn't roll over. The curtains were drawn so the sliver of light illuminated her cot, but she didn't see Lyla's short figure and long hair in the shadow. She turned around as Patrick opened the door further. He opened the curtains and windows. Kailani squinted at the light. The fresh air felt wrong on her face, like it was too crisp for what was going on inside of her. She wrapped herself back up in her heavy blanket as he walked over and sat on the edge of the bed.

They sat in silence for a moment. She knew she'd have to talk to them eventually. She hadn't spoken to anyone since she'd gotten back. Patrick shifted next to her and she squeezed the blanket tighter around her.

"I'm proud of you, Kailani. I know your parents would've been too."

The pressure of his hand rested on her shoulder, and it was as if something released inside of her. She turned around, leaning into him, and let a silent sob escape her lips. Her mind fluttered back to the day of the Ceremony. Her parents had told her how proud they were of her, and that no matter what happened during the Choosing, they'd be together. Mom had said they were going on vacation. She must've been planning to bring her to Mirstone. Mom was supposed to show her around, Dad was supposed to teach her.

A tear dropped onto her arm, but it wasn't her own. Jerking her head up, she locked eyes with Patrick. He wiped his own tears and offered a watery smile.

"I hate that you're going through this," he whispered, "but... it gets easier, with time."

Kailani sniffed. Patrick was speaking from experience.

Not only did he have to mourn his mother, but his father too. Seneca couldn't recover from losing his wife, and he'd been doomed to eternal misery.

What if she never recovered, either?

But it was different, now. They had more tools, more resources. Seneca was doing much better since getting to Mirstone, and she'd have to get through it too.

Patrick sniffled, trying to hold back a fresh wave of tears. "I'm sorry," he mumbled. "I should be strong for you."

Kailani grabbed his arm. "You have every right to be upset. I'm sorry I didn't check on you sooner."

"They were your parents."

"Yeah." Kailani nodded, her chest aching. "But they were like yours, too."

Kailani thought about the late nights spent cooking and dancing, reading and telling stories around a fire. There were so many things left she wanted to do. Needed Mom for.

"You know, if it weren't for your parents, I'd probably be dead. Or in an orphanage somewhere."

Kailani nodded. There was nothing she could say. Nothing to say.

"Your parents always made sure we had enough to eat. And if it weren't for the potions they made for Dad, he—" Patrick stuttered. "He would have been gone a long time ago. Your parents were amazing people. And they raised you to follow in their footsteps."

He pulled Kailani closer. "I love you, Kai. And I'll do whatever it takes to avenge her death."

Kailani squeezed her eyes shut, but tears still streamed silently down her face. She couldn't think about what came next, because that would mean admitting Mom was really gone, and Dad was likely gone, too. She swallowed a sob, burying her head into Patrick's chest.

"I love you too, Pat. You'll always be my family. No matter what happens."

Kailani sank into the silence, her face buried in Patrick's chest.

He held her tight, until someone walked by the window, and he sighed.

"We should go down to the Ceremony."

Kailani's stomach lurched. She'd been trying to avoid it, but it was inevitable. She nodded, wiping at her cheek and rubbing her eyes. Patrick guided her up as she slowly rose from the bed. "I'll wait outside."

Patrick waited on the steps, sending Lyla in to help her get ready. She sat Kailani down, running her fingers through her hair and braiding it down the back. Tears welled up in Kailani's eyes. She couldn't look in the mirror. It was too painful, thinking about how Mom would never do her hair again. But she slipped on some jeans and a shirt, threw a robe over her ensemble, and let Lyla put on powder to try and hide the dark circles under her eyes.

It was no use.

They walked in silence to Mirstone proper. A ceremony was being held in Mom's honor. Chairs were set up in a field where wildflowers sprung in all different directions, colorful, free, and wild. Briggs, Nori, and Tilly were up in the front row. The entire rebellion had come out to show their support. Kailani sank into a seat in the back row, pulling the hood of her robe up over her head. She'd promised to come, but she never said anything about talking to anyone.

Mages jumped at the chance to get on stage and reminisce, talking about how much of an impact Mom and Dad had on them. It was like a dream, like Kailani was watching them speak from overhead. Their words filtered in and out of her mind. She couldn't focus, and just when she thought she might vomit, the guest would stop speaking and she'd let herself breathe again. She wanted no part in speaking in front of the crowd, and she told Lyla and Patrick she was going to leave before anyone asked her to. She didn't have anything to say. And while their stories spoke of a side of her parents she'd never really known, she wanted to keep her precious memories to herself for now.

"Hey, Kailani." Kailani jumped. She hadn't realized that Nori, Tilly, and Briggs had gotten up and moved towards her. Nori had a huge bouquet of lavender in her hands. Her lips trembled. "I'm sorry for your loss."

Kailani accepted the flowers with a wavering smile, sniffing the sweet scent and holding the bouquet to her chest. Little seeds fell from the flower. "Thank you."

Tilly patted Kailani on the shoulder and Briggs smiled, steering Nori away and giving Kailani her space. Once it started, the train was endless, people she'd never met letting her know how much of a loss this was and apologizing for something they had no control over.

Linde came up to her, and Kailani's stomach lurched. Bandages covered most of her face and arms. Her hair was still singed. As they stared at one another, Gorgan's cries echoed in Kailani's ears.

"Kailani…"

Tears swam in Kailani's vision and Linde pulled her into a hug. "I didn't get a chance to thank you."

Kailani pulled away, looking up at her. "For what?"

"For rescuing me."

No, she couldn't accept that. Couldn't have this conversation. She turned to flee, to run down to the beach where nobody else would follow, but Linde gripped Kailani's chin, gently lifting it. "You are your parents' daughter. They would have done the same thing, saved the innocent, if the roles had been reversed."

They stood in silence, a moment to honor her parents and Gorgan, before Linde walked on.

Footsteps approached her and Kailani turned. Seneca stood a few paces away. He shuffled his feet awkwardly. Kailani saved him the trouble of walking all the way to her and drifted closer to him.

Seneca frowned, clearing his throat. "I am deeply sorry for your loss."

"Thank you." Kailani's chest tightened. She hadn't spoken to Seneca much growing up, he was either working or sleeping or hiding in the shadows. But with every day in Mirstone, his eyes seemed to sparkle a little bit more.

Now, his eyes were fixed on the ground and he shuffled his shoes. "I never got to thank your parents," he stuttered, "for being there for me. For Patrick. It's a debt I'll never be able to repay, but if you ever need anything…"

He trailed off, but Kailani's heart warmed. The energy therapy was working, and she couldn't imagine what that meant to Patrick. "Thank you, Mr. Mahoney. It means a lot."

Seneca nodded, then turned to leave.

There was a long line behind him, but Kailani couldn't take it anymore. Desperate to get away from the crowd, she locked eyes with Lyla, who wrapped her arm through Kailani's and slipped her away.

She fiddled with the lavender bouquet, picking even more seeds off and dropping them on the earth. She didn't care where she was going, just that she was getting her away from the noise.

"Come here," Lyla said, guiding her down the cliffside.

Grayson was kneeling over a patch of dirt that had been dug up, with a small headstone protruding from the ground. Her throat caught at the sight, and she bit her lip to stop tears from falling. Patrick and Lyla held back while Kailani walked towards Grayson, kneeling next to him. With shaking hands, she placed the flower over the dirt. Grayson put an arm around her, and she leaned into him.

For a long moment, they sat still, overlooking the waves. They were still today, water caressing the shore in a gentle kiss. She'd give up ever hearing the waves again if it meant she could be back home, with her parents and her charmed walls and her ordinary magic. But she'd never see that room again.

315

She'd never be able to hear Mom's stories about growing up as a descendant. Never know how Dad felt when he found out about Mom's family, or how afraid they were when they gave up everything and moved to Saxton. How brave they were. Mom had given up her right as a descendant to keep Kailani safe, and she'd spent every moment, until her dying breath, defending her.

Her sacrifice wouldn't go to waste. She knew that for certain. The gods hadn't chosen wrong when they'd picked her to be their champion. She might have stopped the ritual. She might have released the gods.

But her quest was far from over.

ACKNOWLEDGMENTS

ABOUT THE AUTHOR

Kelsey Brownlee writes young adult novels inspired by magic and nature. The Champion's Quest is her debut novel.

Kelsey has a deep love of animals and spends most of her time with her horses and dogs. She finds inspiration in every season- from the crisp air and orange colors of fall. To the freshness and new blooms of spring. To the salty air and waves of summers at the beach. To the chilly (very lightly cold) sweater weather of winter.

Kelsey graduated from University of Missouri - Columbia with a Bachelor of Science in Health Sciences. She's worked in ElectroNeurodiagnostics since 2015. When she isn't writing, you can find her traveling with her husband and friends, curled up watching movies, and drinking copious amounts of coffee.

Kelsey is the owner of Moontrek Press. You can find her on Instagram and Tiktok @authorkelseybrownlee.

Printed in Great Britain
by Amazon

79338825R00189